Shadow

Christi J. Whitney is a former high school theatre director with a love for the arts. She lives just outside Atlanta with her husband and two sons. When not spending time with them or taking a ridiculous number of trips to Disney World, she can be found directing plays, making costumes for sci-fi/fantasy conventions, obsessing over Doctor Who, watching superhero movies, or pretending she's just a tad bit British. You can visit her online at www.christijwhitney.com or connect on Twitter (@ChristiWhitney).

Also by Christi J. Whitney

The Romany Outcasts
Grey

Shadow

CHRISTI J. WHITNEY

Book Two of the Romany Outcasts Series

Harper*Voyager*
An imprint of HarperCollins*Publishers* Ltd
1 London Bridge Street
London SE1 9GF

www.harpervoyagerbooks.co.uk

This Paperback Original 2016

First published in Great Britain in ebook format by Harper*Voyager* 2016

A catalogue record for this book
is available from the British Library

ISBN: 978-0-00-816024-1

Typeset in Sabon by Palimpsest Book Production Limited,
Falkirk, Stirlingshire

Printed and bound in Great Britain

To my family

1. Silent Cries

Monsters don't attend graduation parties. Not even when their best friends send invitations decorated with enough glitter to nauseate a fairy. I held the card between my clawed fingers and sprawled across the bed as I read it for the tenth time.

You're invited to a
Graduation Party
In honor of
Katie Noele Lewis
Friday at 8:00 pm

Katie didn't know what I'd become. How could she? I hadn't set foot inside the school since the night my life had changed. The only people who knew were a clan of Outcast Gypsies, and their secrets were now mine.

A familiar lump of emotion wedged between my lungs, and I held my breath until the ache eased. After five months, I'd learned to live with the sensation. Some days were easier than others, but I'd known graduation day was going to suck.

There was a sharp rap at the door. 'Sebastian?'

I hid the invitation under my pillow. 'Come in.'

My foster brother stepped into the room then jerked to a halt. He squinted. 'Sebastian, you know you freak me out when you do that.'

'Do what?'

'Sit here in the dark,' Hugo replied.

'Oh.' I glanced at the window. The shade was pulled and the curtains drawn, as usual. Lighting wasn't something I thought about these days, since I could see as easily in pitch-black as I could the middle of the day. 'Sorry.'

Hugo leaned against the doorframe. 'Hey, it's your room. Besides, who am I to complain about saving some electricity around here? Money's tight enough as it is. I'd just like to see more than two silver dots when I talk to you.'

I blinked at the dim glow filtering in from the hallway outside my room. My brother often compared my eyes to the way a wild animal's mirrored light.

'Well, what do want me to do?' I leaned over and switched on the desk lamp. 'Wear bike reflectors?'

'I was thinking more like those glow strips little kids wear on Halloween.'

'Perfect. I'll run out and pick some up tonight.' My stomach rumbled, and I pressed a hand against my torso. 'And while I'm at it, maybe I'll head into town, terrify the locals and eat some livestock.'

'Hungry again?' he asked, sounding curious. 'You ate just an hour ago.'

I uncurled myself from the bed and stretched. 'When am I *not* hungry? I know you guys said I needed additional sustenance and all, but this is ridiculous. I have the appetite of a sumo wrestler.'

'Maybe your body's still adjusting, Sebastian.'

'Adjusting,' I repeated. 'You make it sound like I'm suffering from jet lag.'

Ignoring my complaining stomach, I walked to the window and peeled aside the curtain. The remains of the evening sun glistened against the newly green trees. I felt Hugo studying me – or trying to, anyway. The way my body blended with shadows made me difficult to pinpoint in dim light. I knew I was more intimidating than I used to be – back when I'd just been Hugo Corsi's kid brother.

'So, how *are* you doing?' he asked suddenly.

I studied him in return. My brother owned the *Gypsy Ink Tattoo Parlor*, and he looked every bit like a tattoo artist. His brown hair had grown out over the winter, and he'd trimmed his goatee, but his grungy T-shirt didn't hide the myriad of designs he sported over most of his skin. Hugo Corsi was also the head of a clan of Outcast Gypsies, which made him even more secretive and mysterious. Talking emotions with him never came easy – for either of us.

'I'm fine,' I replied.

He wasn't convinced. 'I know graduation was this morning—'

'I told you, I'm fine.' A growl welled up inside my throat, and I paused to swallow it down. 'It's not like I didn't know this was coming, Hugo.'

'Yeah,' he replied with a shrug. 'I just thought you might want to talk about it.'

'Why?'

Hugo and I had patched things up, but neither of us could totally forget the past. He'd kept the truth of what I was hidden from me. I understood why he'd done it, and I'd forgiven him, but it was still hard not to get suspicious. I could read unspoken things in my brother's eyes every now and then. Secrets seemed to be Hugo's specialty, and that made trusting my brother an ongoing challenge. But I kept trying.

And so did he.

'I want to know how you're feeling, Sebastian.'

Processing my emotional state was like taking a swim in the middle of a swamp. Everything was murky. There was something inside me – a cloudy part I didn't like dwelling on – that had been feeling all kinds of strange things lately, things that didn't feel very human. I couldn't explain them to Hugo because I didn't understand them myself.

'I don't know how I'm feeling,' I said finally. 'It's not like I really have something to base all this on. How am I supposed to know what's normal for a—'

'Gargoyle,' Hugo finished the sentence for me.

Hearing the word still made me flinch. Gargoyles were mythical creatures, pieces of Gothic architecture. They weren't supposed to be real. 'Yeah.'

Hugo rubbed his chin. 'Well, you said you've been feeling better, right?'

My lips tightened into a smile. He made it sound as though I were recovering from a cold. 'I guess so.'

'And all the weirdness stopped after—'

My brother cut himself off, but I knew exactly what he'd been about to say.

After the Romanys left town.

I reached under the collar of my shirt and touched the dandelion pendant. Its glass surface was warm, as always. My wrist throbbed in response. The dandelion tattoo inked into my skin was like an open wound: never scabbing over, never healing.

Pretty much like my heart.

'I'm okay, really,' I said with as much conviction as I could. 'After all, missing a few graduation parties isn't the worst thing that can happen to a guy, right?' I smiled and lifted my eyes to meet his, knowing my silver irises would reflect the light from the hall.

'All right,' Hugo replied. 'Just checking.'

My smile widened. 'You're such a big brother.'

'Well, I don't have a manual to go by, but maybe I'll earn an Eagle Scout badge or something for effort.' He backed out of the room. 'The guys are on their way, and they're bringing food. Didn't think you'd want to miss that.'

'Sure. I'll be there in a minute.'

Hugo shut the door behind him. I heard the thud of his steel-toe boots as he left the apartment. My stomach rumbled again. I crossed the room and dug Katie's invitation out of hiding. She was having the party in her parents' enormous backyard. There were a lot of trees. And it would be pretty dark by the time the festivities really got started. Maybe I couldn't attend a graduation party, but I could definitely observe one from a distance.

Anything was better than staying cooped up in the apartment.

I stuffed the card in my pocket and scrounged for a clean shirt. Finding clothes for people who had wings wasn't as easy as the superhero movies made it out to be, but Genella, James' wife, figured out a way to alter my shirts to fit around them using a combination of zippers and buttons up the back, enabling me to wear regular clothes.

I discarded my old shirt and struggled into the new one

– fastening it from behind without too much effort, thanks to many weeks of practice. Then I turned my attention to the heavy nylon straps I wore, even around the apartment. They crisscrossed my chest, held together by Velcro, passed over my shoulders and under my arms – effectively pinning my enormous leathery wings against my back.

As I checked the closures, I caught my reflection in the fractured mirror over the dresser. Hugo wanted to replace the glass like he'd done with the other mirrors I'd smashed months ago, but I'd gotten used to seeing my shadowy features through the spiderweb cracks. Or maybe I just preferred it that way. I'd accepted my new body, I supposed, but I was nowhere near being okay with it. The sight of my pewter hair, the conspicuous shape of my harshly pointed ears, and my weird gray skin – always made me jump.

It was like seeing a face in the background of a horror film.

I curled my upper lip, exposing two rows of sharp, jagged teeth; then forced my attention away from the mirror. I retrieved my jacket from the closet and worked it over my protruding back, feeling a bit like Quasimodo. The jacket had been a present from Hugo: long, and roomy enough to accommodate my strapped-down wings, and with a deep hood to hide my face.

The jacket was also Hugo's answer to my being confined to the apartment – a way for me to get outside without being noticed. I couldn't exactly walk into McDonald's and order a value meal, but I could take a somewhat guarded stroll in the park.

I made sure the other essentials of my disguise – leather gloves and extra dark sunglasses – were stashed in the pockets before I exited the apartment and headed down the hall to the *Gypsy Ink*. My gaze swept over the red walls and eclectic furniture. The lights of the waiting room had been dimmed, mainly for my benefit. Outside the shop window I could see the silhouette of the town of Sixes just beyond the parking lot. Inside, Hugo lounged on one of the two purple sofas, sipping a mug of coffee and reading a magazine.

'Hey, I'm just going to step out for a few,' I said.

Before he could respond, the shop's doorbells jangled. James, Kris, and Vincent – my brother's best friends and fellow shop owners – barged in. Behind them came James' wife, Genella, and Kris' girlfriend, Dali, each carrying several large bags. The smell of food smacked me in the face, awakening my overactive gargoyle senses. I had to stifle a groan. My body was seriously craving some protein.

'It's the graduate!' Vincent declared.

'Happy Pomp and Circumstance and all that crap,' added Kris.

James handed me a large envelope. 'This was in the mail.'

I glanced at the return address. It was from the high school. I slashed open the envelope with one claw and pulled out an important looking document.

My diploma.

'I told you all that work you did with Ms Lucian would pay off,' said Hugo.

The paper in my hand should've meant something to me. It represented the culmination of my high school achievements. 'Thanks, guys. But I don't see the point. It's not like I really need one in my line of work.'

'But you earned it,' said Hugo. 'That makes it worth something.'

The others nodded while staring and not staring at me

at the same time. I'd grown accustomed to their occasional awkward pauses when dealing with me. After everything we'd gone through and despite the support they'd offered, a real live gargoyle standing in the middle of the tattoo shop was still unnerving.

'So, anyway,' said Genella quickly. 'Congratulations.' She dropped her bags on the counter, engulfed me in a tight hug, and then pulled back with a frown. 'Why do you always keep your wings strapped down, Sebastian? It's got to be uncomfortable.'

Kris grunted. 'I'll tell you why. It's because he's broken two lamps, our best coffee pot, and half of Vincent's pirate ship collection.'

My shoulder and wing muscles cramped under the constrictive bindings, but I only smiled. 'Guilty as charged.' I glanced at the members of the Corsi clan, watching their faces shift into expressions of oddly placed excitement. 'Okay, what's going on? You guys look like someone just bought you a puppy.'

Genella shrugged. 'Well, we thought since you couldn't go to graduation, we'd have our own celebration here.'

'A party?'

'Who needs all that boring commencement stuff anyway,' said Dali, as she slid a box of pizza from her bag. 'This is way better. Now, come on Sebastian, use those knives you've got on your fingers and help us dig into this food. I bet you're starving. I had Frankie load these babies up with sausage and ground beef, just for you.'

I wiped my sleeve across my mouth, already beginning to drool. Meat sounded perfect, and the smell alone was causing me to waver. But it was nearly eight o'clock. If I was going to Katie's, I had to go now. 'Thanks, guys. I really appreciate it. And I promise I'll eat as soon as I return.' I backed away from the pizza, trying not to breathe through my nose. 'I've got to step out for just a few minutes, but I promise I'll be back before you've opened the second box.'

Hugo's brows knotted over his eyes. 'Where exactly are you going?'

'Just a walk,' I replied. 'I need some air.'

'This is about Katie Lewis' party, isn't it?'

I couldn't get anything past Hugo Corsi. 'Yeah.'

He leaned forward and crossed his arms. 'I'm not going to stop you, Sebastian. But if you're looking for some kind of closure by seeing your old friends, I think you're going to be in for some disappointment.'

'Don't worry,' I said as I slipped my hood over my head. 'I'll keep to the woods.'

Katie lived in a nice subdivision near the school. Thankfully, the stretch of undeveloped land between the tattoo parlor and that section of Sixes provided easy concealed access for me to travel. Various paths ran through the woods connecting with the city park's bike trail and a nature walk. I chose one of the less worn paths and started off at a brisk pace.

I'd made it halfway to Katie's house when I noticed my eyes and nose were stinging. I brushed my sleeve across my face, wondering if someone was burning leaves – though it wasn't really the season for it. I sneezed twice and cleared my throat. The air smelled like sewage. Then, I shivered.

Cold.

The temperature dropped around me. It seeped through the pores of my skin and settled in my midsection. It had been months since my warning sense had fired like this. So long I'd almost forgotten what it felt like.

Almost.

I glanced over my shoulder as I walked. The trail appeared empty, but the sensation of eyes watching me increased with every step. I eased slowly off the path and passed behind a clump of azalea bushes.

The putrid smell lingered, but nothing else happened. I was far from trusting any of the abilities I'd gained, but I couldn't shake the ominous prickle of danger either. I waited, muscles tight and body impossibly still. I didn't like this feeling at all.

Gradually the scent weakened and the air turned warm again. My stomach unclenched, and I ventured out onto the path. The sensation of being watched had vanished, along with the smell, but I knew I hadn't imagined it. At least, I didn't think I had. I decided to jog the rest of the way through the woods, just in case.

By the time I arrived at Katie's, the party was in full swing. It was nearly dark, and the evening sky was the color of blood and gold; shadows were growing long in the tall oaks on the edge of the Lewis' property. I really didn't know why I'd come. Maybe I *was* looking for closure, like Hugo said.

Through the cracks in the wooden slats of the fence, I had a decent view of the party. Several guests milled around the food – which I could smell with uncanny distinction – while others congregated in the enormous pool. I spotted Katie immediately. She wore a bright pink dress, her blonde hair piled high on her head.

I pulled out my phone and dialed her number.

'Hey, Katie,' I said as she answered. 'Nice party.'

I heard a choking gasp on the other end of the line. 'Sebastian! You're here? Avery said you weren't coming, but

I didn't believe him. There's no way you'd miss something this important.'

'Absolutely not,' I replied, smiling as I watched her through the slats. 'I couldn't pass up the chance to see my favorite girl.'

'Careful now,' Katie replied brightly. 'I *do* have a boyfriend, you know.'

'So you and Mitchell are an official couple now?'

'Yup, he's totally off the market, thanks to me,' she replied as she scoured the food line. 'Now, about you . . .'

'Nope,' I replied, my smile widening. It felt good to have a normal conversation again. 'I'm still off-limits.'

'Some things never change,' she said with a laugh. 'Now, tell me where you are. Mom invited way too many people to this party.' She weaved through tables and lawn chairs, searching for me. 'She thinks all my friends are going to scare off my family.' She craned her neck. 'I don't see you, Sebastian.'

I hesitated. 'That's because I'm behind the fence.'

'Seriously? I didn't think it was locked. Hang on a sec, and I'll let you in.'

I whirled around, pressing my back against the wood. 'No, I can't stay. I just stopped by to say hello.'

Katie laughed. 'Yeah, I don't think so, Sebastian. I haven't seen you in forever, and you think you're getting off with a stalker phone call? Not going to happen.'

The latch rattled, and I flung my hand across the gate. 'No, Katie. I don't want you to see me like this.'

'See you like what?' she said, pushing the door I'd wedged closed with my foot. 'It's not like I haven't seen you since the accident. You can't possibly look worse now than you did then.'

The accident.

I hated the story Hugo and Ms Lucian had concocted to explain my absence from school – the car accident I'd supposedly suffered the night of the Circe de Romany's opening performance at the Fairgrounds. Serious injuries, long recovery times, and homebound studies had worked to get me through the last semester of my senior year, but it had also meant lying to my best friend.

'I know,' I replied with a heavy sigh. 'It's not that.'

Katie and the others tried to visit me, but Hugo kept everyone at bay – allowing them in only twice, and both times my brother made sure the lights were low and I was bandaged up enough in bed to effectively hide the truth. But my excuses were wearing thin.

'So what's the deal then?' Katie pressed.

'It's just . . . it's not that simple.'

I felt Katie hesitate on the other side of the fence, and the pressure on the gate went lax. I heard her slow intake of breath. 'Do you have scars?'

'Yeah.' There was more truth in my answer than Katie would ever know. I shook myself off and changed the subject before she could start digging for details. 'Hey, I got my diploma in the mail today, so I guess that makes me official.'

'Please come in, Sebastian. At least get something to eat.'

My mouth watered at the mention of food, but I gritted my teeth and ignored my gnawing insides. 'No, I'm fine, really.'

'Then let me come out.'

'No.'

'Sebastian, let me out right this minute, or I swear I'll punch you in the face.'

For some reason, my hand dropped from the handle. She

opened the gate. I averted my gaze and kept my head low, grateful for the increasing shadows. 'Thanks for the invite,' I managed, not sure of what else to say. Making contact like this with Katie had not been one of my smarter decisions. My wrist throbbed, and I rubbed at it with my glove.

'You're one of my best friends, Sebastian,' she said, sounding offended. 'Why wouldn't I invite you?'

'Maybe because I've basically dropped off the face of the planet?'

Katie gave a small huff. 'Yeah, there's *that*.'

'Can you forgive me?'

She placed a hand on my arm, and I flinched at her touch. 'Sebastian, why are you avoiding me?'

I fixed my eyes on the ground, pinned under the crushing weight of Katie's stare. She wanted eye contact, but I couldn't give it to her. I shrank further into my hood. 'I told you, I'm not healed up yet.'

'You think I care about a few scars?'

I gritted my teeth. 'No.'

'But you're still not ready to tell me what's been going on, are you?'

'No.'

Katie was silent for a moment, waiting for me to say something more. My chest hurt. I wanted to fix this – to fix what had crumbled between us – but it just wasn't possible. Not tonight.

'Okay,' she said finally. 'If that's what you want.' Her gaze moved to my back and she examined the lumps of my jacket. I shifted self-consciously, pressing my body into the fence. 'Speaking of healing up, how long did the doctor say you had to wear that back brace thing?'

'I'm not sure,' I replied vaguely.

The attention was making me uncomfortable. Crazy uncomfortable. Katie peered hard into my hood, shifting closer. I felt something awaken inside me – a survival instinct. A rush of heat spiked into my skull, and my fingers curled into my fists. I jolted as Katie's hand touched my back. Warning prickles skittered down my spine.

'It feels really weird for a back brace,' she said.

'Ah, well . . . it's a new kind,' I stammered, trying to twist my body out of her grasp.

Katie moved before I could stop her.

'Let me see.'

She yanked up the side of my jacket. There was a rush of air, and I felt – rather than saw – the bottom corner of one wing exposed.

'Katie!'

I pushed away, my lip curling defensively. Katie's eyes went wide.

'Did you just . . . snarl at me?'

Don't panic, Sebastian.

My breathing was shallow. My wings quivered dangerously against their straps.

I had to leave.

Now.

'I'm sorry, Katie.'

I backed away from her, into the shadows of the woods.

'What's wrong with you?' she demanded.

'I never should have come,' I said, clutching my wrist to my chest. 'I'm really sorry.'

Then I turned and fled.

I ran for all I was worth, and I didn't stop until I was well away from Katie's cultivated suburbia and deep into the woods. I skidded to a halt in front of a rippling stream. I yanked off my gloves and sunglasses and hurled them into the water. Pressure built to unbearable levels inside my chest. I dropped to my knees, threw my head back, and let out a roar of frustrated rage. The sound echoed eerily through the trees.

But the feeling didn't pass. I gasped for breath between snarls I couldn't choke down, and I dug my claws into the rocks along the bank like I was holding on for dear life. The tattoo on my wrist burned in a way it hadn't in months, and the pain only made me think of one thing.

Of one person.

Josephine.

Each beat of my racing heart carried her name with it. Time had done nothing, except to deepen the hurt. I'd made my choice. I'd accepted my life with the Corsis, and I didn't regret what I'd done. But no diploma, no party, and no forced attempts at closure would ever cure what was really eating away at me.

I surged to my feet, stripping off my jacket and clawing with a madman's frenzy at the straps around my torso. They snapped, and the lumps on my back expanded like an accordion. I filled my lungs with air. Then I flexed my shoulders and spread my wings.

I hated them. I hated everything about them. But at that moment, it was the most glorious feeling in the world – like taking a long hot shower after a really hard day. My cramped shoulders relaxed as sixteen feet of wingspan unfurled around me. I stood there, gingerly flexing muscles that were still too new and disconcerting. The leathery membranes rippled in response as I exercised the bony joints and framework.

A desire to take to the air suddenly flooded my system – so much so that my wings shuddered and ached. But I stubbornly resisted. I had flown only once, and I would never fly again. I refused to give in to this thing I'd become – not when the entire reason I'd done it was to protect someone who no longer existed in my life.

'Whoa!' yelled a voice out of nowhere. '*What are you*!'

I stumbled, wings flailing, and landed in the middle of the stream. Two young boys stood on the opposite bank, fishing poles in hand, gawking at me. My wings snapped flat against my back, and I scrambled out of the water. The twilight shadows weren't enough to hide me from their wide eyes.

'I'm, ah, nothing,' I stammered. I grabbed my jacket, pulling it on as fast as I could. 'Just, um, trying out a new costume. For a . . . upcoming . . . gaming convention I'm attending. Next week. In the city.'

The first boy stared at his buddy. 'Dude, he looks just like Azgog the Demon King from my video game, remember?' The boy turned to me, bouncing excitedly. 'Is that who you are?'

I threw on my hood; but the action was really to hide the dark flush creeping over my face rather than to disguise my already observed appearance. 'Oh, yeah,' I said quickly. 'That's totally who I am.'

'Freaking awesome!' said the other boy.

'Thanks.'

'Man, it looks so *real*,' said the first boy.

I backed away slowly. 'Oh, believe me, sometimes it feels pretty real, too.' I stuffed my hands in my pockets and smiled. 'Well, I've gotta get going. Finishing touches to put on the costume and all that. It was, ah, nice meeting you.'

The second boy grinned. 'Yeah!'

I turned and hurried away before my fan club decided to follow. How stupid could I be? I shook my head in disbelief. First, I stalk a graduation party, then I snarl at my best friend, and now I was gallivanting in the woods in all my gray glory.

'I have *got* to get home,' I said aloud.

I glanced at my surroundings, trying to determine exactly where I was. I knew the strip mall was nearby. I saw the hint of buildings through the tree line. I picked up my pace, eager to be back in the safety of the *Gypsy Ink*. It may have been stifling there, but at least I didn't have to hide what I was.

My jacket fell from one shoulder, and I forced it back. Ripping off the wing straps hadn't been very smart. Without the thick nylon to rein in my wings the jacket wouldn't button. I considered going back to retrieve them. A wisp of breeze rustled the leaves above me, and with it came the slow realization that I wasn't alone.

A twig snapped behind me, and I stopped with a sigh. 'Look, guys,' I said, not bothering to turn around. 'It's not that big a deal. A little grease paint, some cheap prosthetics, and you've got yourself a costume.'

No answer.

I spun quickly on my heel, another excuse forming on my lips, but no one was there. I could hear the rippling of the stream and, just beyond that, the faint voices of the boys as they moved farther away. The air wasn't cold, but I shuddered anyway.

Someone was following me.

My heart kicked up a notch, and I felt the tingles of adrenaline along the back of my neck. Something dropped to the ground beside me. I yelped and fell back, catching myself against a tree trunk. Esmeralda Lucian rose from her crouched position and looked me over.

'Just a costume, huh?'

'Ms Lucian!' I panted, struggling to recover my wits and my dignity at the same time. 'I mean, Esmeralda . . . Ezzie . . . sorry. There were some kids back there and I . . . they thought . . . well, it's not important.' I took a steadying breath and stared at my former teacher. 'I thought for a second you were something else.'

'Something else?'

I stared past her into the woods, though I didn't have a clue what I was looking for. 'It's nothing. Well, I mean, I don't know if it was nothing, but thought I was being followed earlier. Was it you?'

'I only just arrived,' she replied.

'What are you doing out here?'

Esmeralda put her hands on her hips. She wore jeans and a T-shirt, and her red-streaked black hair was pulled back against her neck. She was still smiling, but there was a silver glint in her eyes – a subtle reminder that she'd once been a gargoyle like me. 'I knew you were in the woods, though it took a few minutes to determine your exact location.'

'You were tracking me?'

'Of course.' She brushed her hands over her jeans. 'We can do that sort of thing, you know.'

'I guess I never really thought about it,' I replied. In truth, it was more like I refused to think about it, or any of the other inhumanly freakish abilities I'd inherited. Then I tilted my head, suddenly curious. 'How exactly, if you don't mind me asking?'

She smiled slyly. 'I can smell you.'

'Hey, don't believe Hugo. I do take regular showers.'

'You try it. Go on. Take a good sniff of the air.'

My eye twitched. 'Okay, that's just weird.'

'You've experienced the sensation before,' said Esmeralda with a knowing look.

I colored. 'Yeah, but I didn't *try* to smell her. I mean, I just . . . she just . . .'

'Has a signature scent?'

My face felt hot. 'Yeah.'

'By now, you've discovered you can pick up on quite a number of things using your nose, but it goes far beyond simply being able to determine what the people across the street are cooking for dinner. Gargoyles were specifically designed to detect others of our kind – as well as those of Roma blood – by using a mixture of scent and internal sensation. It's your own special radar. Now, just close your eyes and sniff the air.'

'You make me sound like Lassie.'

'Just do it.'

I obeyed, closing my eyes and taking a deep whiff. Esmeralda's scent was strong, but it wasn't like the other gargoyles I'd encountered all those months ago. Anya and her gang had smelled like rotting fish and made my stomach turn. Ezzie smelled cool and crisp – like a summer's night.

'Not what I was expecting,' I said, opening my eyes.

'It takes some practice, discerning signatures. But it's something you'll get better at doing. You've been too confined since your awakening. No doubt you can't even differentiate any of the Corsis at this point.'

'Well, they do all have a certain smell. I just assumed it was a hygiene problem.'

'That could be the case, too,' she said. Then her expression grew serious. 'But I must ask, what are you doing out here? I thought you were going to look in on Katie Lewis' party.'

I grimaced. 'Hugo told you?'

'Yes, but unless I'm mistaken, she doesn't live in the middle of the woods.'

'I was there, but I had to leave.' My gaze drifted to a growth of wild shrubs as I pondered what to say next. Discussing things with Ms Lucian was still uncharted territory. I worked the words around my tongue before continuing. 'I'm starting to feel weird again.'

Esmeralda leaned against a tree. 'Care to clarify?'

'I was trying to keep out of sight, but Katie found me, and then she almost saw my wings, and my emotions just all of a sudden went haywire. I was afraid I was about to lose it, so I ran away.' My clawed fingers closed around the dandelion tattoo. 'I came out here to cool down, I guess.'

'And that's it?'

I swallowed hard. 'I've also been thinking about her again.'

Esmeralda's gaze shifted to my wrist. She knew exactly who I meant. She pursed her lips together for a moment, her eyes narrowing. 'Sebastian, what you're experiencing isn't your fault. A great deal has happened to you. Managing such raw emotions would be difficult for anyone, let alone a fledgling gargoyle.'

'No, it's more than that,' I said quickly, rubbing my wrist. 'I didn't tell Hugo earlier, but I think something's wrong with me. I mean, besides the obvious. My appetite's crazier than usual. I get headaches even when I'm not out in the sun, and there's something . . . something I can't define . . . constantly churning in my chest.' I shoved my hands into my pockets, my claws picking the denim. 'It's like my control is slipping again.'

'And you haven't mentioned this to Hugo because . . . ?'

I almost laughed. 'Have you seen the way the Corsis look at me? There's enough walking on eggshells around the *Gypsy Ink* as it is.'

Esmeralda nodded slowly. 'I see.'

'But why now? I thought I was done with the flirting with insanity stuff.'

'Actually, that brings me to why I was looking for you, Sebastian. Your brother sent me to fetch you back to the shop.'

'Hugo?' I frowned. 'Why?'

'It's not my place to say,' she replied. 'Now, come on. They're waiting for you.'

'Can I change first?' I asked Esmeralda as I pushed open the back door of Hugo's apartment. My feet sloshed inside my shoes, and my jeans were plastered to my legs.

She glanced at my wet clothes. 'Don't be long.'

I hurried to my room and pulled on a fresh pair of jeans, socks, and Converse. I didn't want to keep Hugo waiting. He was probably ticked about my bailing out of their dinner party. But my stomach cramped as I walked down the hall, and there was a weird chill in the air – a sensation I hadn't felt in a while.

The waiting room of the *Gypsy Ink* was full, but not with customers: Hugo and the rest of the clan stood quietly around the counter. Esmeralda hovered in the corner. But it wasn't the Corsi clan or Ms Lucian who held my attention. I stopped dead in my tracks. Nicolas Romany was sitting on the couch, staring right at me.

The Circe de Romany left town months ago.

So why was the head of their clan in our shop?

The front door banged open, jangling the bells, and two men stomped in. They wore dark clothes. Thinly concealed weapons glinted at their hips. My stomach exploded with warning ice; the sensation nearly knocking me off my feet. I clutched my torso and breathed hard through my teeth as a third man entered the shop.

Quentin Marks regarded me, and a deep scowl crossed his face. My lip curled from my teeth. I snarled. Quentin's hand dropped to his belt and his fingers closed around the hilt of a glimmering knife. I crouched defensively. My wings shuddered underneath my jacket.

Nicolas Romany rose from the couch. 'Sebastian Grey,' he said gravely, 'we need your help.'

2. *Unexpected Fate*

My brain registered Nicolas' words, but I couldn't rip my focus from Quentin Marks. Not only was he the leader of the Marksmen – the official bodyguards for the Romany clan – but he was also Josephine's boyfriend. And he despised me. I heard myself growling, but I couldn't stop. The sound rumbled from my chest with each breath I took.

'Control your pet, Corsi,' said Quentin coldly. 'Or I'll tame him for you.'

Hugo glared. 'That's enough from you, Marks.'

'Quentin,' admonished Nicolas. 'Let's be reasonable.'

'Of course,' the tall Gypsy replied, his voice like syrup. His hand slid casually from his knife. 'I'm always reasonable. After all, *I'm* not the animal in the room.'

The other men sneered, and I choked down another growl. Though I'd only had a brief encounter with the Marksmen, as it had included a volley of arrows aimed at my gargoyle hide, I'd developed an extreme distaste for them.

'All right,' said Hugo. 'You wanted to see him. Now you have.'

Nicolas started towards me then seemed to change his mind. He observed me from the edge of the couch. His expression reminded me of a scientist scrutinizing the details of an experiment. 'And you awakened him yourself?'

'I told you, he belongs to the Corsi clan.'

'I'm afraid I must disagree with you,' said Nicolas.

My hand went to my wrist, my claws curling around the dandelion tattoo. It throbbed against my fingers. 'I don't belong to anyone,' I said, looking pointedly at Hugo before turning my eyes on the Romany leader. 'But I've chosen to stay with my brother.'

Nicolas appeared taken aback, as if he hadn't expected me to speak. 'Guardians don't have a choice in such matters.' His gaze fixed on my wrist. 'It took me some time to discover exactly what happened between you and my daughter last autumn. But I've done my research. I know about the *sclav*, Sebastian. I know the truth.'

I glanced sideways at Esmeralda. She'd been the first to tell me about the *sclav* – an object owned by a guardian's intended charge. Once physical contact was made between a gargoyle's brand and the Gypsy's *sclav*, the two became sealed in a guardian-charge bond. Even Hugo, whose clan prided itself on branding gargoyles through the centuries, hadn't known how to complete the process. If he had, then I might truly have belonged to the Corsis.

Josephine's pendant pulsed with heat under my shirt. The necklace was her *sclav*. But she'd given it to me when her family left town. Hugo thought the separation would be enough to break the seal. But I knew it hadn't been. And neither had anything else my brother had tried. I may have chosen to stay with the Corsis, but my decision didn't change the truth.

I *was* Josephine Romany's guardian.

'Sebastian's my brother,' said Hugo. 'You have no claim to him.'

'He's a *gargoyle*. He's not related to you or any of your clan. You may have branded the creature, but you can't keep what's clearly been chosen for us.'

'Nicolas,' said Quentin, using that low, controlling tone of his that set my nerves on edge. 'The Corsi clan doesn't want to give up their pet. It's exactly like I told you it would be. We've wasted our time coming here.'

'You've had your say,' Nicolas said to the Marksman, a warning edge to his voice.

Quentin bristled. 'And I've told you, my men are more than adequate to—'

'The discussion is over!' Nicolas snapped.

'Why do you need this gargoyle?' asked James. 'You've got so many protectors of your own.' He jerked his chin derisively at the Marksmen. 'Aren't they enough?'

'The Romanys are one of the head families in the *kumpania*,' replied Nicolas. 'You know that having such a prominent position among our allegiance of clans doesn't come without risk. Surely you've heard of the unrest among our people up north over the past few months. Rumors of power struggles among the *bandoleers*. Members of the head families are concerned for their safety.'

My heart leapt up my throat. Was Josephine in danger? Why hadn't I felt anything? I clutched my throbbing wrist as the pendant burned against my chest. Maybe I *had* been feeling something, after all. I just hadn't realized what it was until now. My wings shuddered under my jacket. 'How can I help?'

Hugo stepped forward. 'Sebastian—'

I cut him off with a wave of my hand.

'Our troupe will be arriving from Maryland tomorrow,' continued Nicolas, shifting his gaze to me. 'We'll reside in Sixes through the summer until we determine our next course of action. Sebastian, I want you to come and stay with us at the Fairgrounds.'

The possibility of being near Josephine again sent a rush through my system and, for the first time in weeks, hope fluttered with fragile wings inside my chest.

Vincent scowled. 'I don't think that's a good idea.'

Nicolas ignored him. 'You've been branded for us, Sebastian. Their clan has no say in the matter.'

Hugo glowered. 'He was branded for *one* of you.'

'And your clan left,' added James. '*She* left . . .'

Everyone from the Corsi clan looked solemnly at me, and I braced myself against the counter. Instincts flooded my head with conflicting messages. I felt incredibly protective of Hugo and the others – they *were* my family – but it was nothing compared to what I felt towards Josephine Romany. In the pit of my stomach, the war rekindled with a vengeance. Going against my brother's wishes was like swimming upstream, but fighting against this never-ending pull was even worse.

'Hugo,' I said lowly, my inward struggle causing my voice to thicken with a growl. 'Maybe there is—'

'No,' he said sharply. He pointed at Nicolas. 'I don't believe sending him with you is in the best interest of either clan, and I won't let you take him by force, no matter how many Marksmen you've brought along.'

The Corsis moved closer to me. The other Gypsies shifted in response. Their close proximity set my emotions on fire. I was hemmed in – trapped like a cornered animal. My vision blurred red and my head clouded. On whose side did I fall? I couldn't think straight. I pressed my hands to my temples as a guttural sound wrenched from my throat. 'Stop,' I snarled fiercely. 'Just stop it.'

Weapons flashed in the Marksmen's hands, but no one moved. A tense silence fell over the room, broken only by the inhuman growls coming from my own mouth. Before I could bring myself back to my senses, a voice spoke from the corner.

'Have you considered what you're doing to the boy, Hugo?' Esmeralda pulled herself from the shadows with an expression of glassy calm.

'What are you talking about?' he demanded.

'He's confined to limbo here,' she continued, her voice as pointed as her gaze. 'The process that began with his being sealed to the Romany girl isn't complete. As long as he remains with you he's incapable of fully changing into what he's meant to be.' Her silvery eyes flicked to mine. 'Sebastian's fighting a battle that will only grow worse if he's prevented from fulfilling his duty. He'll never be able to win unless he's given the chance. Is that in his best interest, Hugo? Is that what's best for him?'

Hugo stared at Esmeralda, and a muscle jumped in his jaw. He didn't speak for several moments. The other Corsis looked at each other uneasily. Finally, Hugo leaned against the wall, crossed his arms, and turned his gaze on me. 'Sebastian, it's your decision.'

My instincts instantly cooled like water thrown on a blaze. I'd made my choice to stay with the Corsis. Life with Hugo hadn't always been easy, but he was my brother, and he cared about me. It was only recently that I realized how much.

But the pull to go with the Romanys – to go to Josephine – strained violently inside my chest. I stared hard at the floor until I was able to push past the ache in my ribs. I wouldn't turn my back on my brother now. Not after everything we'd gone through.

Suddenly, I felt an odd buzzing in my head like a burst of static.

A voice pulsed through my thoughts.

Don't worry about them, Sebastian. I'll look after your brother and his clan.

I blinked, confused. The voice belonged to Ms Lucian, though her lips hadn't moved. She looked at me, her face expressionless, but it felt as though she'd practically shouted inside my head. Just as I started to dismiss the voice as part of my imagination, the sensation hit again like bees swarming inside my brain.

You already know your answer. Let the Corsi clan go. They will be safe.

'Well, Sebastian?' asked Hugo.

I jerked from my thoughts to meet his gaze. There was no indication from him that he'd heard anything. Everyone had grown deeply quiet. They were waiting for my answer.

The voice in my head – Ms Lucian's voice – was right. I knew, deep down, that I was only fooling myself. As much as I wanted to make this work I couldn't stay here anymore. My life meant nothing the way it was now. But how could I just abandon the only family I knew? I searched Esmeralda's face with the glimmer of silver in her hazel eyes, and I saw written in them the promise of Hugo's safety.

It was the reassurance I hadn't realized I'd needed until that moment.

'I'll go with the Romanys.'

My brother's face went rigid. Guilt squeezed at me, but I set my shoulders. I wasn't changing my mind. Not this time.

'You have your answer,' Hugo said to Nicolas.

'Good,' Nicolas replied, satisfied. 'We'll see you tomorrow at the Fairgrounds, Sebastian.'

As Quentin fell into step behind Nicolas the Marksman shot me a threatening look. The hair on the back of my neck prickled, and it took a good deal of effort not to snarl at him in response. He and the rest of his darkly clad posse followed Nicolas out of the shop, and the *Gypsy Ink* was quiet.

'Sebastian made the right decision,' said Esmeralda, breaking the silence.

A scowl darkened Hugo's features. 'Yeah, and how do you know that?'

'Because it's what he's *supposed* to do,' she replied. 'You, of all people, should know that, Hugo Corsi. Your ancestors helped infuse those powerful traits within the guardian psyche. Sebastian chose to stay with your clan – an action more difficult than you will ever know – but keeping him here has only postponed his true calling.' Esmeralda's eyes narrowed. 'Sebastian deserves the chance to find himself. You owe him that.'

It was eerily heavy in the waiting room as my brother and Esmeralda regarded each other. The rest of the clan watched the exchange – some with interest and others with wary caution. But before I could ponder either her words or the intensity of the standoff between them, Esmeralda broke the wordless deadlock by heading for the front door.

'You're leaving?' I asked, shocked. 'Just like that?'

She smiled that weird, mysterious smile of hers. 'It's not

as though I'm needed here, Sebastian,' she said. 'Besides, I have some things to take care of.'

'Like what?' I pressed.

The smile remained on her lips as she placed her hand on my arm, leaned up, and kissed me gently on the cheek. When Esmeralda's gaze met mine, the silver spark was visible within her hazel eyes once more. My head buzzed with electricity.

I want you to be careful, Sebastian. Change is coming, and there is something dark on the horizon. I'm afraid that many of the Outcast clans will soon become involved in a very old strife.

I jerked back, disturbed and uneasy. Once again I'd heard Ezzie's voice, but she hadn't spoken aloud, and no one in the room reacted to her words. I took a deep breath, feeling weirdly vulnerable. She blinked at me with her silvery hazel eyes, encouraging me to respond. Instinctively, I replied with a question in my head.

Is Hugo in danger?

Esmeralda's lips quirked upward, and I got the feeling she was pleased with my communication. My head buzzed again.

Don't worry. I've already told you. I'll watch over them while you're gone.

I started to reply, but Esmeralda squeezed my arm.

'Goodnight, everyone,' she said aloud with a casual flair.

Her gaze fell hard on me.

You need to guard yourself, even as you guard the Romany girl. This new life of yours isn't going to be easy, Sebastian. But I have faith in you.

Esmeralda opened the door, and then she was gone.

The tingling in my head dissipated – leaving me stunned

and a bit disoriented. She'd done most of the talking in my mind, but I'd somehow talked back, and she'd heard me as perfectly as if we were having a normal conversation. Was it some special talent of hers, or was it a gargoyle thing?

'Well.'

Genella's voice broke my reverie. She ducked behind the counter and pulled out a cardboard box.

'What are you doing?' James asked.

'It's Sebastian's graduation day,' she replied. 'I made a cake, and I'm not about to let it go to waste.' She flipped open the box, daring us to disagree with her. 'Come on, Sebastian. You get the first slice.'

The weight of the Corsis' stares added to the enormity of the decision I'd just made. I swallowed hard and leaned forward to examine the contents of the box. Written on the top of the cake in bright yellow icing were the words: CONGRATULATIONS SEBASTIAN.

I wanted to laugh and cry at the same time.

It rained that night.

Storms in the South are unpredictable, exploding out of nowhere with thunder and wind. I lay awake, listening to the hail pelting against the roof. Lightning lit the room in intermittent flashes, casting ominous shadows on the wall.

I slid my phone off the nightstand and scrolled through messages to the best of my clawed-fingered ability. Most were from Katie. Though we'd talked weekly during the course of my 'recovery', it was largely a shameful collection of lies on my end – most recently, how I was going to spend the summer out of town, visiting Hugo's family. Until I could tell her the truth – *if* that day would even ever be possible – Katie was a part of my life I'd have to learn to live without. I squeezed my eyes shut, desperately missing our friendship, and I waited for my stomach to unclench.

Thunder crackled, followed by a rush of howling wind. I tossed the phone aside and walked to the small window above my desk. The blinds and curtains were closed. I yanked back the fabric and pulled at the cord.

There was a face in the window.

I snarled in fright and flung myself backwards. My wings snapped free from their restraints and shot out wildly – knocking everything off my dresser and desk. Lightning flashed, illuminating a hideous head. Darkness again. Then another bright streak. The face disappeared. I gaped at the window, shuddering all over.

The face hadn't been human.

Hugo burst through the door wielding a baseball bat. 'Sebastian!'

I stared at the window, panting like an animal, my teeth bared. Outside, everything was dark and stormy. I squinted, straining for some visible proof of what I'd just seen – the gray and monstrous head pressed against the glass – but there was nothing there. Just water-streaked panes.

'It's okay, Hugo.'

'Man, Sebastian . . .'

I looked over my shoulder, suddenly aware of the picture I'd created – crouched in the middle of the room, enormous wings unfurled, and debris scattered everywhere.

'I thought I saw something in the window.'

Hugo looked past me. 'I don't see anything.'

Memories of the time before my transformation came back to me in a jolt. I'd spent weeks thinking I was going insane. I didn't need to revisit those days. 'I guess I just imagined it,' I said, rubbing my eyes.

I wasn't sure if I believed my own words. The sense of being followed earlier and now a beastly face at the window? It was beginning to seem less like my imagination and more like the gnawing fear I'd been stubbornly ignoring all night: that Augustine or his gargoyles might have returned.

My brother cleared his throat. 'Want to put those things away?'

He was looking at my impressive wingspan. I tightened my back and shoulder muscles, and the wings retracted with a snap. I grabbed my jacket off the desk chair and worked it clumsily over the leathery membranes. 'Sorry about that.'

Hugo dropped the blinds and closed the curtains. 'Nasty storm,' he commented as he crossed back to the door. He tapped the baseball bat gently against the doorframe. 'Well, try and get back to sleep. You've got a big day tomorrow.'

'Hugo?'

'Yeah?'

I sat on the edge of the bed, lumps of folded wings draping on either side. 'Thanks. For letting me go, I mean. I know it's a big deal, going against your parents like this, especially after everything you've done to keep their rules.'

'Right,' said Hugo with a huff. ''Cause you see how well that's worked out for me.'

'Pretty much blew up in your face, huh?'

'Like a hand grenade.'

I allowed myself to smile for a moment before pressing on. 'Hugo, I told you I would stay with your clan, and a big part of me still wants to, but we both know I don't belong here. I'm not really your brother, anyway.' I ran the pad of my thumb hesitantly along the tip of one thick claw, repulsed by the sight. 'I mean, I'm not even . . . human.' The confession was difficult to swallow – like downing a bottle of medicine. 'But I want you to know how much I appreciate the way you took me in and cared for me. I don't remember much about my past, but I'll always remember that.'

I closed my eyes, waiting for Hugo's response. But instead of words, I found myself crushed in a tight embrace. I tensed, startled by the display. This wasn't like Hugo. Protective, yes. Mushy? Hardly ever. But slowly, the awkwardness melted away, as did the last of my negative emotions.

'I'm really sorry, Hugo.'

'God, you have nothing to be sorry for, Sebastian,' he replied, pulling away and running a hand through his hair. 'I'm the one who's sorry for all of this.' Hugo leaned forward, and I thought the conversation was coming to an end, but then he sighed heavily. 'Sebastian, before you leave, there are some things I need to tell you – things I probably should've told you sooner.'

I felt wary again. 'More Gypsy secrets?'

'I didn't *want* to keep you in the dark about your heritage, but I don't have the authority to make every decision. I've had to keep secrets, and there are others I still keep.' His brown eyes narrowed. 'The Roma are a tight-lipped people, and we don't share things with *gadje*.' I nodded at his term for non-Gypsies. He'd told me as much before. 'Our law is powerful, and we're all bound to it – even the Outcasts.'

'No offense,' I said, my brows lifting. 'But I've never really thought of you as the model of an upright citizen.'

'I'm not talking about running red lights or shirking the cops, Sebastian. This is more than some simple *gadje* code of conduct. You obey Gypsy law or you suffer the consequences. And when the leaders of our *kumpania* speak, you listen. End of story.'

'What's a *kumpania*?'

Hugo twirled the bat in his hands. 'It's an allegiance of Outcast clans. Some are small, others are large. Our *kumpania* stretches across the Southeast.'

'Okay,' I said, rubbing my temples. 'You've told me the Outcast clans broke away from the Old Clans in Europe a long time ago and you settled here. I get that. But I don't understand what any of it has to do with me.'

Hugo regarded me closely, and the muscle working in his jaw told me he was debating something. 'My parents brought you to us a little over three years ago,' he replied at last. 'They showed up in Sixes after being gone for nearly a month in Europe. It was All Saints' Day.'

'November first,' I said quietly. 'That's my—'

'Birthday,' Hugo finished for me. 'Yeah, that's the date we gave you, and now you know why. It's the day you arrived.'

'Arrived from where?'

'They wouldn't say. But I do know that my parents went to great lengths to get you here.'

I bit my lip, instantly tasting blood as my sharp teeth pierced flesh. Everything felt surreal, like listening to some sort of bedtime story. 'And your parents didn't tell you anything else? You didn't want to know what was going on?'

'Of course I did,' he replied stiffly. 'But Zindelo and Nadya Corsi move in guarded circles, Sebastian. I don't question them.' As I studied his expression, I realized the Gypsy world of secrets extended far beyond my limited knowledge. It had to, if Hugo's parents kept things from their own son. 'But they told us what you were,' he continued. 'Or rather, what you were *supposed* to be.'

Without warning, my past opened in front of me, and I wasn't sure I was ready for it. I covered my eyes, probing the darkness, reaching for something I could remember before the Corsis, but there was nothing. 'Go on,' I said, pushing past my trepidation.

'Well, you were – for all intents and purposes – a 15-year-old kid. I mean, that's where we placed you, physically.' Hugo paused. 'But you didn't speak, didn't interact. You didn't eat, sleep, or even move, really – like some kind of statue. We were instructed to keep you in complete darkness until you began showing signs of life.' His eyes clouded in memory. 'It happened slowly, over the course of a few weeks, and then, one day, you began speaking and relating to us – growing up like a regular kid – as though you'd been here all along.'

My mouth went dry, making it difficult to speak. 'How is that even *possible*?'

'Zindelo and Nadya have abilities that I don't totally understand,' he replied in a heavy tone. 'My parents dedicated years of their lives learning ancient crafts that most Outcasts left behind decades ago.' Hugo stood abruptly, jostling the bed. 'I'll be right back.'

He exited the room with swift steps. I leaned forward, feeling the unnatural weight of my wings against my back. But they weren't as heavy as my brother's words, which had plummeted like rocks into the pit of my stomach.

Hugo returned in less than a minute, baseball bat still in one hand, but a crinkled envelope in the other. He held the paper out to me as he sat.

'Open it,' he said.

I stared at the envelope, recognizing it immediately as the one my brother had kept in his jacket pocket. The letter from his parents. My hand shook slightly as I took it from him, staring at the flowing script on the outside. My claws got in the way as I attempted to pull the letter free, and I felt embarrassed heat on my neck, knowing Hugo was watching. I unfolded the letter, took a deep breath, and began to read:

> Hugo,
> We trust this letter finds you well. In our current situation, it is neither safe nor wise to use other communication. Our quest to find Keveco's urn has remained unfruitful, and we remain in Europe for now.
>
> Watch the creature carefully. The memories we have implanted in his mind will allow him to sustain a normal human existence while we are gone. But if the creature shows signs of awakening too early, you are commanded to seal him to our clan as quickly as possible.
>
> Sebastian must remain with you during our absence. Do not disobey me in this. To do so will mean disaster for us all. Do nothing more until you hear from me again.

'Well?' Hugo asked, searching my face.

I rubbed my eyes, feeling exhausted. 'What exactly is this thing your parents are looking for?'

Hugo took the letter from my limp hands and stuffed it in his back pocket. 'I don't know. It's important, and it has something to do with you.' Bitterness crept into his voice. 'It's their quest. I'm just the one—'

'Who got stuck babysitting the gargoyle,' I finished.

The edges of Hugo's mouth quirked – almost a smile.

'Yeah, pretty much. But it wasn't too bad. I kind of got used to having him around.' His lips tightened, and he grew serious once more. 'But you're sealed to a Romany now,' he continued, voice heavy with resignation. 'And I guess I'm just going to have to accept it whether I like it or not.' Hugo placed his hand on my shoulder. 'But I still have major reservations, and not just because of Zindelo and Nadya. Leaders in our *kumpania* have been growing uneasy these past few months, and power struggles are becoming more common. Prominent clans like the Romanys tend to attract conflict. Joining them won't exactly keep you hidden.'

'I hadn't really thought of it like that,' I replied.

Hugo nodded. 'Gargoyles are rare among the Outcasts, and my parents wanted to keep you off the radar until you were effectively awakened and sealed to us. Unfortunately, you caught more than just Nicolas's attention.'

'Augustine,' I said, feeling a growl wedge in my chest as I thought about the renegade Gypsy who'd tried to prevent me from being sealed to Josephine. 'What's the latest word on him, anyway?'

Hugo glanced sideways at me. 'There isn't any word. Wherever he ran off to after that fight on the bridge – he hasn't been seen or heard from since. Neither in Sixes nor around any of the other Havens we have contact with.'

'I never understood why you just let him go.'

'I didn't,' said Hugo with the familiar edge to his voice that still made me stop short. 'Believe me, I'd love a chance to deal with that *marimé* scum. But we're not allowed.'

'Says who?'

'The High Council,' he grunted. 'When Augustine was banished from Gypsy society years ago, he was declared the responsibility of the Romany clan. No other Outcast is permitted to interfere – with him, or with those three gargoyles of his. That's why I didn't want you having any contact with him, but I couldn't do a whole lot about it.'

'So that's why you told Quentin Marks to handle him,' I said, remembering the tense exchange between the two at the Fairgrounds. 'And what about his gargoyles?' I cast a brief look at the darkened window. 'What happened to them?'

'If Marks had his way, they'd be dead,' Hugo replied, 'But, since they fall under the same protection as Augustine, you can be sure that wherever the Romanys sent him off to, his wretched beasts went with him.'

'But how did Augustine get them in the first place?'

'Look Sebastian,' said Hugo, sounding suddenly weary. 'I see all the questions brimming in those weird eyes of yours, and I get it. You deserve more answers than I can give, and as much as I hate to admit it you'll find them with the Romany clan. But you've read my parents' letter. I don't know what's going to happen if you leave. You're still so young and, like Ezzie said, you're still growing. If you stay with us a little longer before you—'

'I can't,' I said quickly, holding up my arm. The tattoo glared at me: red and inflamed – an unhealed wound. 'The seal isn't the only reason I'm doing this, Hugo. I still love Josephine. That hasn't changed. If I can help her family, I want to do it.'

'Even if she doesn't feel the same way towards you?'

I sucked in a breath and let it out slowly between my teeth. 'This isn't about me,' I replied. 'It's about doing the right thing.'

We held each other's gaze for a long time.

'I understand,' he said finally.

And I knew that he truly did. I felt the weight lift somewhat. 'Thanks, Hugo.'

I stood and walked to the door of my bedroom.

'Where are you going?' he asked, brow raised.

I pressed a hand against my muttering stomach. 'To the kitchen. I'm starving.'

Hugo smirked. 'I hope the Romanys plan on giving you a large food allowance.'

'Yeah, or I'm going to be ordering a whole lot of Mongolian Beef and sending the bill to you.' I smiled at my brother; the vice of guilt finally releasing inside me. 'So, I guess I'll see you in the morning.'

'Yeah, in the morning,' he agreed. 'But try to get a little sleep, okay? You make me nervous wandering around in the dark all night.'

'Okay, but only if you put the baseball bat away. You make *me* nervous.'

Hugo grinned. 'Deal.'

3. Fearful Hope

The morning sun streaked through the blinds, waking me from a fitful sleep. I groaned and grabbed for the covers to shield my eyes. Then, I remembered. *Today was the day*. I was going to see Josephine again.

I leapt out of bed, instantly awake, and rushed to the bathroom. I struggled through a quick shower, cramming my wings into a space the size of a telephone booth, then got dressed. I fastened the Velcro straps around my torso, binding the leathery monstrosities as tightly as I could to my back. Then I shrugged on my jacket, grabbed my bags, and headed eagerly for the kitchen.

The tantalizing smell of eggs, sausage, and pancakes hit me full in the face. James and Genella were in the kitchen, busy over the stove. Hugo sat at the kitchen table with Kris and Vincent, while Dali perched on the kitchen counter poking fun at James as he cooked.

'I didn't think it was legal for you guys to be up so early,' I said as I dropped my bags by the door.

Kris looked up from his coffee. 'We're here to say goodbye,

but believe me, we'll go back to bed when the caffeine wears off.'

'Take a seat,' Vincent said, motioning to a metal folding chair at the table.

I readily complied, spinning it around and straddling the chair backwards to accommodate my bulky, wing-laden back. I wiped my mouth with my sleeve as the smell of breakfast taunted me. My stomach threatened to eat itself if I didn't put something into it soon. James plodded over with a huge skillet full of scrambled eggs and dumped the contents onto the empty plate in front of me.

'Growing gargoyles need their grub,' he said.

'Don't the rest of us get to eat?' Hugo asked, glancing over his coffee mug.

'It's James' first attempt at making a proper breakfast,' said Dali. 'But we've figured Sebastian would eat anything, so he gets to try them first.'

'Hey,' I said around a huge mouthful of eggs. 'I don't eat *everything*.'

'Tell that to my pantry,' said Hugo.

I grinned at James around another bite. 'These are good.'

He pointed his finger accusingly at Dali. 'Ha, take that!' He dug his hand into the pancake batter and flung it.

She screeched as a glob of white ran down her face. 'Oh, you are so going to pay for that!'

Dali lunged across the counter, grabbed the sink hose, and soaked the front of James' T-shirt. He laughed, using the skillet to defend himself. My smile faded as I felt a twinge of somber nostalgia. I knew it was time to leave – to join the Romanys and to finally step forward into my uncertain future. But I was going to miss the Corsis.

After breakfast, we hung around Hugo's apartment for

a while, talking about nothing. I knew they were delaying their goodbyes as much as I was. My head spun with thoughts of seeing Josephine at the Circe, but I lingered as long as I could. Finally, Hugo seemed to sense my anxiousness. He stood and clapped his hands once.

'Okay, time for everybody to get out of here,' he said. 'I've got a shop to open, and Sebastian's gotta go and be a carnie for a while.'

I nodded gratefully and proceeded to endure a round of fierce hugs and slaps on the back. Then Hugo pulled me aside and shoved a wad of cash into my hand.

'What's this for?' I asked.

'In case you need it.'

'For popcorn at the movies?' I grinned and shoved the money in my backpack.

Hugo smiled, but it didn't quite reach his eyes. 'Listen, I contacted Karl and told him you're coming. Make sure and find him as soon as you get settled in. He's a Corsi, and you can trust him. But more importantly, he knows more about the shadowen world than any member of our clan, apart from my parents.'

My grin dropped into a frown. 'Shadowen?'

'Shadowen . . . shadow creatures . . . names the Roma gave to creatures brought to life from stone. To most Gypsies, your world is just fairy tale stuff. But to Outcasts, it's an inescapable part of our history.'

'Got it.'

Hugo sighed heavily, looking me square in the eyes. 'And I'm going to say this one more time. Be careful. Gargoyles aren't the only shadowen out there. And not every Gypsy is as accepting as we are.'

Before I could reply, Hugo yanked me into a hesitant

embrace. He pulled back and clasped my shoulders tightly. 'Take care, Sebastian. And don't forget, we're here, if you need us.'

'Thanks, Hugo,' I replied, deciding to leave the rest of my questions for Karl when I got to the Circe. 'For everything.'

I slipped out of the apartment and through the waiting room of the *Gypsy Ink*. I paused, taking in the checkered linoleum floor and red walls of the place I called home. The Gypsy painting above the counter caught my eye.

Hugo reframed it after my battle with one of the gray figures. That had been the night I'd thought Hugo was dead. I shivered and rubbed my arm, remembering the feel of broken glass cutting into my flesh; and for an instant, I felt a pinch of doubt about leaving. But Hugo was one of the toughest guys I'd ever known. He knew how to take care of people. And Esmeralda had promised to keep an eye on the clan. They didn't need me.

I left the *Gypsy Ink* and stepped outside. The midday air remained sticky with the remains of last night's storm. A few clouds, still heavy with rain, hovered low in the sky. I broke into a jog, leaving my van behind. Hugo would probably get more use out of it than I would.

I flipped up the hood of my jacket as I ran. I hadn't packed the rest of my disguise since the Romanys already knew I was a gargoyle. Still, I felt more comfortable hiding my face in the shadows. The strip mall was deserted, but I checked for cars before crossing the street towards the railroad tracks that ran through town.

It felt strange leaving the confines of my small world. Most of Sixes had been deemed off-limits for me since I'd turned into a creature from a monster movie, but now I was on my own, and the feeling was exhilarating. I placed my foot on the metal track. My heart beat faster. It had been so long since I'd used any of my new abilities, apart from my heightened senses.

My balance was perfect as I raced down the railroad tracks, and my muscles seemed to coax me on, demanding to be used. I made my way swiftly through the outskirts of town, but as I entered the historic district, I slowed my pace. My eyes drifted to the bell tower of the *Cathédrale de Gargouilles*. It seemed like an eternity since I'd walked into the cathedral and confronted Augustine and his gargoyles. I stared at the outlines of the statues along the roof. Like Hugo and Nicolas, the renegade Gypsy also believed something was lurking on the horizon.

I just wished I knew what it was.

After leaving the railroad tracks, I entered the stretch of woods that bordered the Fairgrounds. A soft peal of thunder echoed above me. It smelled like rain, and I wondered if I would make it to the Circe before I got caught in the downpour.

I heard the rushing waters of the Sutallee River just ahead, and a breeze rustled the leaves. Something twitched in my stomach. I lifted my head – remembering Esmeralda's instructions – and tentatively sniffed the air. Instantly, I caught a scent. My nostrils wrinkled under the smell – spicy and hot, tinged with sulfur. It burned my nose. I took another whiff and, suddenly, my insides turned icy. Though I didn't recognize the smell, I certainly recognized *that* sensation.

I ducked behind a tree, dropping to a crouch as I concentrated on pinpointing the scent. It was close, perhaps only a few dozen feet ahead. I scanned the heavy underbrush. Thunder rumbled again from the sky, and then I heard a low growl. The sound prickled the hair on the back of my neck.

Something black leapt from the brush, hitting me hard in the chest. My instincts flared. I rolled back, throwing the thing off. I came up on my hands and knees, a snarl on my lips. A massive black dog crouched before me. It leapt, and I ducked. The dog spun and lunged for my face. I grabbed its body, digging my claws into the thick fur. The animal snarled in fury and bit down on my arm. I hissed at the pain.

A voice yelled from the trees.

'Down, Caliban!'

I snarled wildly and gripped the muzzle of the dog. I pried its teeth from my arm and hurled the beast into the nearest tree. It hit with a thud and a whimper, landing on its back. But it immediately sprang up, teeth bared. I crouched, ready for another attack, but the voice yelled again, harsher this time.

'Caliban! Down!'

The dog's matted hair stood out along its hackled haunches. But it didn't make another move towards me. Another burst of spicy sulfur flooded my nose as two cloaked men appeared through the trees.

'Down!' the first man commanded the dog.

Caliban – the ferocious Rottweiler that had just attacked me – retreated, growling fiercely until it had reached the man's side. Its enormous body quivered with rage as it stared me down with fiery black eyes. My lip curled in response as I fought against my surging instincts – instincts I'd thought I'd conquered while confined with the Corsi clan. Here, out in the open, they were harder to manage. My wings strained against their straps, and I shook uncontrollably, muscles flexing.

'My apologies if Caliban hurt you,' said the man. 'It's what he's trained to do.'

The men lowered their hoods. It was Phillipe and Stephan – two of Quentin's Marksmen. They watched me with disgusted expressions as I forced myself to stand. My muscles felt like iron cords.

'You've trained him to attack innocent people?' I snarled, brushing myself off.

'Of course not,' Phillipe sneered. 'He's trained to attack your kind.'

My kind.

I really hated that phrase.

I examined my arm. The sleeve of my jacket was ripped, but there wasn't a mark on my gray skin. My eyes widened. Not even a scratch. But it still hurt like crazy, and I rubbed my arm gingerly.

'It's fortunate we weren't out with the rest of the dogs,' said Stephan with a cold smile. 'Caliban here is relatively mild-tempered.'

As if on cue, the dog's muzzle flashed with sharp teeth.

'Nicolas asked me to come,' I said evenly.

Stephan tilted his chin. 'Yes, we know.'

I was about to get an escort, I realized.

'Come with us,' Phillipe ordered.

Stephan slid his bow from his shoulder and fitted an arrow to the string. 'Caliban and I will follow behind. Just as a precaution, of course – in case you start getting any ideas in that ugly gray head of yours.'

Quentin Marks' welcoming committee was not something I'd anticipated. I gathered my bags, and Phillipe led our unpleasant little party across the Sutallee Bridge. I unconsciously slowed as we passed over the abandoned mine shaft where Josephine and I had taken refuge so long ago. There was a sharp poke in the middle of my back, right between my pent wings.

'Move it,' Stephan said, jabbing me again. 'We're already late for lunch.'

I fought the insanely strong desire to whirl around and shove the arrow down his throat. Instead, I bit my lip, tasting coppery blood, and picked up my pace. We reached the iron fence that surrounded the Fairgrounds. Phillipe pulled out a ring of keys and opened the gate.

I'd assumed everything would look as it had the last time I'd been within the walls of the Circe de Romany. But there were no tents or pavilions. No rides or decorations, either. Only trailers – along with several RVs, trucks, and buses – arranged in a tight circle right in the middle of the property.

Their configuration created a large open space in the center of the caravan. Tarps were arranged over tables and chairs. A fire pit had been built, and laundry hung from clotheslines spread between trailers. People bustled around the clearing, preparing for the approaching storm. Another peal of thunder echoed overhead. The clouds had thickened and the sky looked ready to split apart at any moment.

'Hurry it up,' said Stephan with another jab to my back. 'I don't intend to get wet.'

Lightning flashed. Women scurried to get the clothes off the lines while men anchored the tarps more securely in the ground. Phillipe led me to a small trailer and flung open the door.

'Get inside.'

The howling wind was motivation enough – even without Stephan's sharp arrow in my back – and I scampered up the steps. My nose instantly wrinkled at the unpleasant smell. Phillipe caught my look.

'The dog trailer,' he said.

'Just be glad they're out on patrol,' said Stephan with a malicious laugh. 'They're quite territorial.'

The Marksmen backed me into the stinky enclosure, weapons drawn.

'We'll come for you when Nicolas returns,' said Phillipe. 'Until then, welcome home.'

With that, he slammed the door, locking me inside.

I snarled in frustration and backed against the wall, prepared to throw myself against the door. Heat built in the pit of my stomach, churning like lava. I hated being confined, but I hated feeling this way even more – like I was on the verge of losing it. Dark emotions beat on the back of my skull. My shoulders curved, and I flexed my clawed fingers, taking shallow breaths through clenched teeth.

'Calm down,' I growled, trying to focus on something other than escape. Such an action wasn't going to get me anywhere. The Marksmen were probably waiting outside, daring me to try. 'It's just a dog trailer. It could be worse.' I took a deeper breath and gagged on the scent of old food and wet dog. 'Or not.'

The rain beat against the roof of the trailer, but even over the noise I could hear the fierce complaining of my stomach. Breakfast had long gone and it didn't look like I'd be getting any of the late lunch the Marksmen had been grumbling about. Missing a meal didn't make my gargoyle body very happy. I felt grumpy, weak, and my hands trembled. I paced the length of the small space, finding it difficult to think clearly the hungrier I got.

I retrieved my phone from my backpack and checked the time. It was already after two. I considered calling Hugo, but stopped short of dialing.

'I can handle this,' I muttered. My stomach rumbled loudly. 'I think.'

I sat down and leaned – as much as my wings would permit – against the wall opposite the door. The smell of rain permeated the trailer, helping ease the stench. To pass the time, I let my mind drift back to Josephine. Did she know I was here? Would she be with Nicolas when he came? I cringed at the idea of our first meeting being inside the trailer. My insides felt more twisted than a pretzel, but I couldn't separate nerves from hunger anymore.

I really regretted not packing snacks in my backpack.

At some point, the rain dulled to a soft patter, then stopped altogether. Not long after, I heard voices, just outside the trailer door.

'How dare you put our guest in here!'

I peered through a hole in the rotting wall. Nicolas Romany stood near the door, scowling at Phillipe. Stephan leaned against the side of the trailer, arms crossed, and Quentin Marks watched calmly from a few feet away.

'My apologies, Nicolas,' Phillipe said. 'But where else were we to take him while you were gone?'

'We couldn't let him roam the camp,' added Stephan.

Nicolas jabbed his finger at the Marksman. 'You were out of line.'

'Nicolas, be reasonable,' said Quentin in his syrupy voice. 'They were only acting in the best interest of the clan. After all, we don't know anything about the creature.'

My lip curled and I dug my claws into the wall, leaving gouges in the wood.

'What are you implying?' Nicolas demanded.

Quentin jutted his chin toward the trailer. 'Who knows how long the Corsis hid this gargoyle from us? They've obviously been keeping him for their own purposes – probably seeking a shift in power within the *kumpania*. It's foolish to give the beast free rein in our camp.'

Nicolas' green eyes sparked. 'I've known the Corsis longer than you, Quentin. They are loyal to our alliance.'

'You knew the loyalties of the past, Nicolas,' he replied. 'We live in different times. There are new rules and new balances of powers. I say this gargoyle is a threat.'

Stephan snorted. 'He's just a fledgling: more boy than beast. How much of a threat could he be?'

Quentin turned his piercing gaze on Stephan. 'You told me Caliban attacked him in the woods.'

'Yes.'

'And what happened?'

The Gypsy guard shifted uneasily. I looked at my arm. The pain had long since stopped, and there was no evidence that the canine had clamped his teeth into my flesh. My gray skin was completely unblemished.

'Caliban is one of our best dogs,' Quentin continued. 'He could rip the throat out of a man with one bite. And yet this *boy* came away without a scratch?' Quentin's gaze slid to Nicolas. 'I'd say he poses *quite* a threat.'

Nicolas frowned. 'We may not share the same beliefs, Quentin, but that doesn't excuse your behavior. I asked him to stay with us, and he came of his own free will. Sebastian Grey is our guest, not our prisoner.'

'You know how I feel about having that abomination here.'

'Your opinions have been noted,' said Nicolas steadily.

'But I'm not changing my mind. My ancestors created the shadow creatures to protect our people, but it's been nearly a century since we've had a gargoyle in our possession. I won't waste this opportunity. Your Marksmen can't be everywhere, Quentin. If things continue to escalate we're going to need the creature's help.'

'If that's what you want, Nicolas,' said Quentin with equal steadiness, though I could see the hard set of his jaw. 'But I insist that he not be left alone with anyone from the Romany family until we determine not only his abilities, but also his intentions. That includes your daughter.'

At the mention of Josephine, my body tensed with a mixture of emotions: disappointment that she hadn't come, yet relief that she wasn't here to witness any of this.

'Yes,' Nicolas said softly. 'I am aware of the connection Josephine seems to share with him.'

Share?

I touched my shirt where the pendant rested beneath, warming my skin.

Quentin glowered. 'I don't buy this nonsense about *sclavs* and brands, Nicolas. If you think the clan has a claim on the creature, that's fine, but it's not the result of some connection between them. Of course, that doesn't mean the demon won't try and establish one. We must take precautions.'

Phillipe smirked. 'Sounds like Quentin's jealous of the gray freak.'

My jaw clenched, but I continued to watch in silence.

For a moment, it didn't seem that Quentin had even heard the comment. Then, slowly, his lips twisted into a thin smile, revealing his perfect teeth. 'You should learn to censor yourself before making such asinine remarks, Phillipe.'

The Marksman cowered under the dangerous glint in Quentin's black eyes. I leaned against the wall, working to keep my breathing even. Did Josephine still feel something towards me? I knew it wasn't love, but if even the tiniest connection existed on her end, then it was proof that I did have a purpose in joining the Romanys.

'Perhaps your relationship with my daughter has made you a little sensitive,' Nicolas said. 'While I do appreciate your protection – especially with regard to Josephine, let's not jump to conclusions about this gargoyle until we know more about him.'

'I'll be civilized to the creature,' said Quentin stiffly. 'But don't expect any more from me, Nicolas.'

'I'm glad to hear it. Now, it's time to get better acquainted with our guest.'

I dropped into a crouch, filled with a sudden urge to leap at Quentin's throat the moment the door swung open. The insults were bad enough, even if I couldn't really disagree with them, but the hatred I felt rolling off the Marksman like hot steam made it difficult to keep rationally calm.

I heard the clink of a key being slid into the outside lock. I flexed my fingers and stared hard at the ceiling to clear my head. It was obvious that my arrival at the Circe de Romany was under conflicting circumstances. If I wanted to see Josephine, I was going to have to play my cards right.

I rose to my feet as the door creaked open and Nicolas Romany's face appeared. 'Welcome to our camp, Sebastian Grey,' he said, then glanced around the trailer with a frown. 'I apologize for your crude accommodations. The Marksmen can be overzealous in their duties.' From outside, Phillipe shrugged and Stephan glared murderously at me. Nicolas moved away from the door, giving me room to exit. 'I hope you'll forgive the misunderstanding.'

'No problem,' I said, grabbing my bags. 'They say you haven't really seen the Circe until you've toured the dog trailers.' I stepped into the damp air. It was later than I'd first thought, judging by the darkened sky and the lights around the caravan.

'Good to see you again, Sebastian,' said Quentin, smiling pleasantly.

Heat seared the pit of my stomach, and my eyes burned. I knew the Marksman wanted to rile me up, but I wasn't going to give him the satisfaction. I took a slow breath in through my nose. 'You too, Quentin,' I replied, flashing a smile of my own – considerably toothier than his. 'I trust you're well?'

His lips tightened across his face. 'I've been better.'

Nicolas stepped between us. 'We've prepared a place for you in one of our extra trailers. It's not much, but it's certainly better than sleeping with the other animals.'

As soon as the words left his mouth, Nicolas seemed to regret them. Out of the corner of my eye I saw Phillipe grinning wickedly.

I nodded politely at Nicolas. 'Sounds great. Thanks.'

'I'll show you the way,' he replied.

The Marksmen stayed close behind me. I tried to ignore their presence – not an easy feat with their scent in my nose and their weapons glittering in my peripheral. I concentrated on studying the Romany camp instead. The circle of vehicles was actually two: an outer circle formed by semi-trucks and a smaller inner circle comprising the living quarters of the troupe. The vehicles were modern enough, but the atmosphere of the caravan was something out of another time.

My prickling excitement at seeing Josephine slowly ebbed with each step I took through the camp. She hadn't come to welcome me – which, honestly, I hadn't totally expected after everything that had happened. Even so, I found myself hoping she'd appear around each corner we took.

Nicolas stopped in front of a small trailer wedged between two RVs. 'Well, here we are,' he said, producing a ring of keys. 'We've used this trailer for storage, though it was my brother's living quarters when he traveled with us.' He swung the door back on rusty hinges. I glanced inside warily. Nicolas picked up on my uneasiness. 'Dog free, I promise,' he said, going in ahead of me.

I could see the room with perfect clarity well before he flicked on the lights. On one side of the trailer was a cot – complete with sheets, pillows, and blankets. Thick Asian rugs decorated the floor. A tiny sink and toilet were situated in one corner, and an old icebox was in the other. The remaining furniture consisted of a green leather chair and a small bookcase. It was larger than my bedroom at Hugo's, and cozier than I'd expected.

'It's perfect,' I said, setting my bags on the cot.

Nicolas glanced over his shoulder with a frown. 'Quentin insisted that a guard be posted at your door – not so much as a precaution, but as a means of reassurance. I'm ashamed to admit this, but your kind is a subject of controversy among our clan.'

My gaze strayed to the Marksmen outside. 'Yeah, I kind of picked up on that.'

'I'm adhering to his request, but only for the sake of those in our troupe that do not yet trust you. My hope is that, in time, opinions will change.'

'I understand.' I'd agreed to come here, and now I was

going to have to live by their rules – or Quentin's rules, it seemed.

'We'll be serving dinner outside in about an hour, now that the rain has stopped. You'll come and join us.'

My stomach growled at me and I pressed a hand against my shirt to silence it. 'Maybe it would be better if I ate here in the trailer, Nicolas. I don't want to cause any problems, especially if people aren't all that happy with my being here.'

'Nonsense,' he replied with a dismissive wave. 'You're a part of our troupe now. Besides, the others will want to meet you – regardless of opinions.'

'Well . . .'

'You're our guest, Sebastian Grey. The clan is honored by your presence. Eat dinner with us tonight.'

'Sure,' I said, allowing myself to smile. What did I have to lose? 'I'd love to.'

'Good. Then we'll see you there.'

Nicolas closed the door behind him, leaving me alone. I peered out the window. Where there had been nothing in the clearing just minutes ago, now there were people. *Gypsies*. Lots of Gypsies. This wasn't like the small band of Corsis. There had to be at least 150 in the Circe de Romany troupe. Hugo had warned me before I left that not everyone would be accepting of what I was. And now, I was about to find out for myself. I gulped nervously and closed the curtains.

People didn't trust me, Nicolas said. Definitely fair enough. I pushed aside the rising trepidation that Josephine might be included in that group. I'd replayed our meeting dozens of times in my head since we'd parted ways, and the majority of my scenarios ended in disaster. To take my mind off the impending meal – and my withering confidence – I unzipped my bags and unpacked.

After I'd made myself as at home as possible in my new accommodations, I plopped down on the cot and rubbed my stiff shoulders. My wings were aching, so I slipped off my jacket and peeled back the Velcro closures. I leaned forward and unfurled my wings as far as they were able to expand in the small trailer. I groaned, enjoying the sensation. Suddenly, there was a knock at the door, and I jerked, snapping my wings against my back.

'Yes?'

Stephan's voice was muffled from the other side. 'You coming to dinner or not, freak?'

I snarled quietly. The Marksmen certainly had their share of nicknames picked out for me. I wondered if they'd sat around coming up with a list of insults before I'd arrived. 'I'll be right there.'

'Hurry up!' he demanded. 'I'm hungry.'

I strapped my wings and concealed them with my jacket. Then I paused at the sink to splash water on my face, my hands shaking with hunger and nerves. I gave my reflection a critical glare in the mirror before reaching for my hood. I yanked it forward, and my gray gargoyled features were obscured in shadows.

Stephan shot me an indignant look as I opened the door. 'Let's go,' he said.

He turned on his heel and stomped off, his bow and quiver of arrows thudding against his back. I glanced past the Marksman's retreating form to the clearing beyond. The sound of music and lively conversation echoed through the camp. I raised my chin, setting my jaw determinedly. 'Well, I said aloud, with more confidence than I felt. 'Here we go.'

And I stepped out into the Gypsy evening.

4. *Stepping Backwards*

A large pavilion dominated the middle of the clearing, framed with kerosene lamps and colored party lights. Underneath the tent, members of the circus troupe had gathered for dinner. The large fire pit was ablaze, grills were smoking, and people hovered around tables, laughing and enjoying one another's company. The scene reminded me of a modern version of the Gypsy painting in Hugo's tattoo parlor.

Stephan pushed through the crowd, leaving me without as much as a backwards glance. He joined a table of dark-clothed Marksmen who stood out like a disease against the rest of the eclectically dressed troupe. They glowered at me, faces ripe with disdain. I hovered on the outskirts of the pavilion area, searching for a familiar face.

Quentin wasn't present – which put me more at ease – but then I realized, neither was Josephine. I bit back another surge of disappointment. She had to know I was here. A heavy sensation pressed into my chest. Was she avoiding me? I looked for Karl, the old circus trainer who'd helped me during the turbulent days after my transformation, but

I didn't see him either. I contemplated returning to my trailer, despite my hunger, when Nicolas suddenly appeared and motioned me over.

'Sebastian,' he said as I approached, 'so glad to see you've joined us.'

I chose to ignore the fact that I couldn't have refused, even if I'd wanted to — not with Marksmen beating on my door. 'Well, it smelled way too good out here.'

'And it should,' he replied. 'We've got barbeque on the menu tonight.'

I almost drooled. 'I hope you've got enough.'

Nicolas chuckled and ushered me under the pavilion. 'But before you settle in to eat, I want to introduce you to the rest of the troupe.'

I stopped dead in my tracks. 'Right now?'

'Of course.'

My heart lodged in my esophagus. Everything was happening way too fast. 'Nicolas, I really don—'

Nicolas clapped his hands, and someone whistled sharply. The music stopped. The clatter of utensils against plates silenced. Everyone went quiet. I recoiled, looking for escape. But there was none.

'Good friends and family,' Nicolas addressed the gathering. 'I must take a moment to interrupt your festivities . . .'

There was a general lighthearted groan from the group. Had circumstances been different, I would have laughed.

'I want you all to meet Sebastian Grey.' All attention was suddenly riveted on me, like a display unveiled at a museum. 'He just arrived this evening. I hope you'll make him feel welcome as he'll be staying with us for a while.'

It was so quiet I could hear my blood rushing in my ears.

I felt every stare, but I also sensed every emotion – the hatred, the mistrust, the uncertainty – each one so powerful that my head swam with them. My tongue sealed itself to the roof of my mouth. I tried to nod, but produced nothing more than a swaying of my hood. I was grateful, at least, for the minimum protection my jacket provided.

'*This* is the gargoyle?' someone muttered, breaking the tense silence.

A soft murmuring rippled through the crowd. Heads lowered across tables, and I could pick out snatches of conversation, none of them favorable. The Marksmen's gloating satisfaction was like a punch in the jaw. My breathing went shallow as a tendril of anger wrapped itself around the base of my skull. My hands closed into fists, and the prick of claws jerked me from my emotions. I instantly refocused my energy towards the task of staying calm. The last thing I needed right now was to lose it.

'This is *not* up for discussion,' Nicolas said in a booming voice. The air of his authority rushed through the pavilion, and the murmurs ceased. His face hardened. 'Sebastian Grey is here at my request, and you will give him the respect demanded by our traditions as my guest. Is that understood?'

Heads bobbed up and down, and the Gypsies slowly returned to their meals. Conversations gradually started up again. Shaded glances continued in my direction, and my overly sensitive hearing caught a few snide comments from the table of Marksmen, but the general mood of the pavilion gradually lightened.

Nicolas clasped his hands behind his back as if nothing had happened at all. 'Well, now that we've taken care of business, are you ready to eat?'

As uncomfortable as I felt, I couldn't resist the offer of

food. It had been too long since I'd eaten, and being hungry made it harder to focus. 'Way past ready,' I replied.

'Then take a seat,' said Nicolas, 'and I'll have a plate sent to you.'

There was an empty table in one corner of the pavilion, away from the rest of the troupe. I tugged at the hood of my jacket as I sat down. I could feel eyes boring into the back of my skull, staring at the large lumps protruding from under my jacket, straining to see my monstrous face through the shadows of my hood. I was reminded of the inhuman appearance of my hands as I clasped them together on the table, but I resisted the urge hide them in my pockets.

'Hey, Sebastian.' I glanced up to see Francis Romany – Josephine's twin brother – standing over me with a plate in his hands. 'Dad told me you needed some food,' he said matter-of-factly.

Francis shared the same green eyes and brown hair as his sister, but nothing else made it obvious they were twins. He was stocky and much darker skinned with thick arms and a broad face.

He set the plate in front of me, grinning. The savory smell of barbequed ribs was so strong that my teeth ached against my gums. I pressed a hand against my jaw. The disturbing sensation in my mouth was growing more pronounced as time went on. 'Thanks.'

Francis glanced at my vacant table. 'Mind if I sit down?'

I found it difficult to take my eyes off the food. 'If you can find room.'

The Gypsy chuckled and slid onto the bench across from me. I pulled the plate close, inhaling once more. I stifled a whimpering growl, and swallowed hard. Then I dug in, devouring the food. I could feel Francis staring at my ravenous display – probably with the same look Hugo used to give me when I'd polish off an entire pizza by myself.

'You know, I didn't think you'd actually go through with it,' he remarked.

'Go through with what?' I asked around a mouthful of meat.

'With coming here,' he said. 'I expected you to back out of my father's invitation to stay with us.'

'I didn't have any reason to refuse,' I said carefully. I picked up a rib and gnawed at it. The pressure felt wonderful against my teeth, easing the ache.

'I guess so.' Francis' gaze drifted to my arm, and he leaned forward. 'So,' he said casually, 'can I see your tat? The brand, I mean.'

I set the bone down and wiped my hands. 'You know about that?'

He cocked his head to one side. 'Everybody knows about that, man.'

I pulled up the sleeve of my jacket and held out my arm. The dandelion tattoo was as red and inflamed as ever.

Francis made a face. 'Man, that looks pretty bad. Has it always been like that?'

'No,' I replied, shoving my sleeve back down. Francis studied me carefully, but I didn't offer any more details. I returned to my food, and soon the plate was clean, save for the mound of bones that I was – strangely enough – half tempted to eat. I pushed the plate aside before I followed through with the whim. 'You know,' I continued, turning my attention to the Gypsy, 'I'm surprised you're talking to me. Aren't I off-limits or something?' I glanced meaningfully towards the Marksmen.

'Quentin may have a lot of people riled up, but you don't scare me.'

'Oh, really?' I tilted my head into the lantern light and allowed my upper lip to curl just enough to reveal my sharp teeth.

He nodded appreciatively. 'Nice grill.'

I sat back, stunned. 'So you really aren't bothered by me?'

'Hey, don't get me wrong. You're a total freak show. I'm just saying that *I'm* not freaked out, that's all.'

'I think that's the nicest thing anyone's said to me since I arrived.'

'You're welcome.' Francis tapped his chin curiously. 'So, now that we've established things between us, let's see the rest of it, then.' He pointed at my hood.

'I don't really feel comfortable with—'

'Oh, come on,' he pressed. 'It's not like we don't know what you are.' But as soon as I shifted my hood enough for Francis to view my face, his eyes went wide. 'Dude! You really *are* a gargoyle!'

'I thought we'd just covered that.'

'Yeah, well I knew, I just didn't realize how much . . . I mean, the last time I saw you it was just the gray hair and—' He caught my expression and cut himself off. He recovered quickly, then offered me a broad grin. 'Sorry. Shock factor contained. My bad. Won't say another word about it.'

'It's okay,' I said, adjusting my hood again. I appreciated his honesty. 'I've gotten used to the reactions.'

'Really?'

I shrugged. The look in Francis' eyes was one of friendly understanding. It made him easy to like – a complete opposite of Quentin.

'Well then,' he continued, 'changing subjects. How's everyone from school?' He propped his elbows on the table. 'I hated that Jo and I had to bail before graduation. I was really looking forward to wearing the pointy cap and doing the whole walking thing. All I have to show for my education is a certificate from some home schooling company in Indiana.'

'Everyone's fine,' I replied, suddenly distracted. He'd mentioned Josephine, and now I knew I was going to have to ask. The question had been weighing on me all evening. I cleared my throat awkwardly. 'So where *is* Josephine?'

'Probably in our trailer with Quentin.' He shrugged and rolled his eyes. 'They've been pretty antisocial lately.' The Romany twin caught the expression on my shadowed face before I could go stoical again. 'You've still got a thing for my sister, haven't you?' he asked, a smirk tugging on his lips.

'What?' I said, taken aback. 'No, I . . . of course not . . . I mean, no.'

'Whoa,' said Francis lowly. 'I didn't think that your kind was supposed to, you know, get feelings like that.'

I straightened slowly. 'How do you know about that?'

'I've heard my share of bedtime stories,' Francis replied, 'about how guardians were created by my people to protect us, but they weren't given the capacity to love or have any emotions except service and duty, blah, blah, blah. But I remember how you used to look at Josie in school.' The wooden bench creaked as he leaned closer. 'So, is it true?'

'I didn't say I had any feelings *like that*, Francis.' My voice was starting to sound like I was eating gravel: a reminder to keep my inexplicable emotions carefully in check. I forced a smile into my words. 'I was just asking about her.'

'But it's because of the brand and *sclav* thing, isn't it?' The Gypsy's tone was suspiciously curious. 'It connects you two somehow, right? That's what my dad said, but I've gotta admit, I really don't know how any of that works.'

'That makes two of us,' I replied. He narrowed his eyes, and I waited for some brotherly remark from him – telling me to stay away from his sister – but when he didn't say anything, I frowned. 'What is it?'

'Now, don't take this the wrong way, Sebastian,' he said slowly. 'I don't mind you being here, and I definitely don't have a problem with what you are – not like some people around the Circe – but I just don't think we need you.'

'Pardon me?'

'For protection,' the Gypsy continued. 'I get what you're supposed to be doing, but we can handle ourselves just fine.'

'I'm sure that's true.'

Francis cocked an eyebrow and crossed his arms over his wide chest. 'You don't believe the stuff my father talks about either, do you?'

'I'm not sure what to believe,' I replied, glancing far away into the darkness, where the caravan's lights couldn't penetrate. 'Everything's happened so fast. But when your father invited me to stay here, it was the first time in months that I've actually felt there was a *reason* for me being what I am. I had to come.'

'And what about my sister?'

I didn't blink. 'If I can help your family in any way, that's why I'm here.'

Francis propped his elbows on the table. 'Fair enough.'

'Do you mind if I join you?' asked a pleasant feminine voice from behind me.

I peered over my shoulder, keeping my head bent low

and my features concealed inside the hood. A young woman hovered at the corner of our table looking on warily. She had warm brown eyes and impossibly curly brown hair. Francis broke into a grin.

'Sure thing,' he said, making room for her on his side of the table.

She slid in next to him, trying hard not to gawk at me.

'Hello,' I said, attempting to sound as gentle and non-threatening as possible. I took a tentative whiff of the air. My nose twitched at her scent, like a mix of summer flowers. 'I'm Sebastian.'

'I know,' she replied. 'I was here for the introduction.'

'Oh, right,' I said, shaking my head. 'It was a great first impression, I'm sure.'

'I'm Phoebe Marks.'

Seeing my surprised reaction, Francis nodded. 'Yup. Quentin's her brother.'

I waited for the uncomfortable block of ice to form in the pit of my stomach the way it did when Quentin or the other Marksmen were near. But I didn't feel cold at all. I took it as a good sign. 'Pleased to meet you, Phoebe.'

'You see what I mean?' said Francis, putting his arm around the girl. 'There's nothing to be scared of. It's not like Sebastian bites.' He shot me a look. 'Do you?'

'I try not to make a habit of it.'

Francis laughed, and I nearly grinned but, given the circumstances, I didn't think flashing my teeth was the best idea. Phoebe crunched a few brown curls nervously in her hand, watching my shadowed features under my hood, and I allowed her to stare. The expression on her face slowly relaxed.

'So, are you really what they claim you are?' she asked suddenly.

'I suppose it depends on what they say I am.'

Phoebe cast a shaded glance around the pavilion before replying. She lowered her voice. 'Well, some say you're one of the ancient guardians that's been awakened to protect the clan from something bad that's going to happen.'

'And the rest believe you're a horrible abomination from our dark past, and you pose a threat to the entire clan by simply being here,' Francis added.

'What do you believe?' I asked, glancing at him.

His green eyes met mine. 'I haven't decided yet. But I'll let you know.'

'So, what made you come here, Sebastian?' Phoebe asked. 'I don't mean to pry, but Quentin's absolutely furious with this whole thing, and he has most of the clan worked up over it, too. This is the last place I would've come, if I were in your shoes.'

'I'm a glutton for punishment,' I replied. 'So I couldn't possibly stay away.'

Phoebe looked amused. 'Well, I guess I'd better be going before word gets back to my brother that I was consorting with the enemy.' She turned an annoyed gaze towards the Marksmen. 'It was good to meet you, Sebastian.'

I dipped my head. 'You too, Phoebe.'

She stared at me for a moment, then whirled and darted through the tables.

Francis watched her go, his tanned face beaming. 'I bet she'll be dancing tonight.'

'Dancing?'

'We have sort of an evening ritual around here after dinner. It's a little stereotypical, but hey, it's tradition.'

I shifted my gaze around the pavilion. Dinner was being cleared around us. Several groups were actively trying to avoid me as they went about their chores, while others were watching me with apprehension.

'Is the entire circus troupe made up of Gypsies?' I asked.

Francis seemed surprised at my question. 'Yeah, it is. We don't trust outsiders. We maintain everything ourselves.'

'So, how are you all . . . ah . . . connected?'

'We're not all related by blood, if that's what you mean. There are lots of families in our clan: the Marks, the Stoakas, the Costas, the Jansens, the Bailles—'

'And the Romanys.'

Francis rolled his shoulders proudly. 'We're the head family, and my father's the *bandoleer*. His word is pretty much law around here, if you haven't noticed.'

I opened my mouth to ask another question, but the sound of fiddle music prevented me. It was only then that I became aware that Francis and I were the only two left under the pavilion. He stood and motioned for me to follow.

It appeared as though the entire clan had crowded around the fire pit. A group of men were playing fiddles and drums, and several women danced around the fire, flipping tambourines against their hips. Ankle bracelets jangled under their long skirts. The scene reminded me of the Native American festivals I'd seen in Hickory Springs: a blending of old and new, traditional and contemporary. Only this world I stepped into – this Roma world – was all strange to me.

'Like I said,' Francis remarked with a shrug, 'it's tradition. Well, that and a lack of a decent internet connection out here.'

The women swirled around the crowd, and I saw Phoebe, her curly hair flying around her face. Then I felt a chill. It started in the center of my belly and worked its frigid fingers into my spine. It didn't take long to spot Quentin Marks sitting nearby, watching the entertainment. Sleek, polished charm oozed off him, and everyone seemed to feed off his presence. I felt the muscles along my neck stiffen.

'A piece of advice, Sebastian,' said Francis at my shoulder, his gaze following mine. 'I'd keep out of his way, if I were you. The Marks take their job seriously. And after the stink you're causing, trust me, he's not the guy you want to mess with.'

'I haven't done anything to him.'

'Yeah, I know. But you might.'

I shot him an inquisitive look, but Francis merely clapped me on the shoulder and bounded into the crowd. He was quickly swallowed up by the colorful explosion of festivities. I remained in the shadows of the tent, contemplating my next course of action. I didn't feel comfortable joining the group, but I didn't want to be alone, either. Before I could make a decision, another scent wafted across my nose.

My knees almost buckled. Esmeralda was right. Even amid all the tangy smells of the Gypsy camp, I could pick out that one particular scent with undeniable clarity. *Her* scent. My mouth went dry as I scanned the crowd with a sudden sense of desperation. I didn't see Josephine Romany at first. Then the strange radar I seemed to possess when I was near the Gypsy girl activated once more.

Somehow – though I was hidden in shadows and she was buried in the crowd – our eyes met. My tattoo flared to life under my sleeve. Electricity sparked, and the pull towards her was so strong that I gripped the pavilion's support pole to keep from launching forward.

Her eyes darted to a grouping of trailers just beyond. She passed through the crowd looking back at me, beckoning me to follow. There was no time to think about my actions.

I immediately stole out of the pavilion – keeping to the shadows – and made my way along the edge of the caravan, my eyes fixed on Josephine.

No one seemed to notice her departure – not even Quentin, who was busy talking. I trailed after her, feeling like I was about to leap out of my skin. It was dark away from the campfire, but my gargoyle eyes had no trouble finding her. Josephine stopped in the middle of a grassy lane between the vehicles. Her back was to me, her head down. Her hair was loose and poured over her shoulders like a waterfall. I froze in my tracks, heart pounding, as she slowly turned.

'Hey, Sebastian.'

Every feeling I'd ever had for the Gypsy girl punched me hard in the chest. All those months feeling like my insides had been scraped out, aching with her loss, so incomplete and hollow. And in one moment, it all changed. I struggled to keep my emotions in check. 'Hello, Josephine.' Goosebumps skittered up my arms as I said her name.

She clasped her hands in front of her – a casual enough gesture – but I could see the knuckles turning white. 'So I hear you're joining us.'

'Your father asked for my help,' I replied carefully. Guardedly. 'And I couldn't refuse. I've been trying to make it work with my brother's clan, but nothing's felt right. I was supposed to be here.'

'That's what my father's been trying to convince Quentin for weeks.'

'I have to admit, I'm a little clueless, but I really want to try and be of some use around here, if I can.' I glanced over the caravan of trailers, remembering the last conversation we'd had and feeling the hard lump of emotion that wrapped like scar tissue around my heart. 'But please, don't worry. I promise I'll keep my distance.'

'No,' Josephine said quickly, shaking her head. 'I don't want you to stay away.' Her bright eyes peered into the darkness of my hood as she continued in a hushed, rapid voice. 'Look, I don't understand any of this, Sebastian. And I've tried. Believe me, I've tried. You're not supposed to be here, and yet, you are. I don't know what to think anymore.'

'I understand,' I said as steadily as I could. Nothing seemed to be going right since I'd arrived. I'd wanted so desperately to see Josephine again, and now it all felt so conflicted. It was too much, too soon. I took a few hesitant steps backwards. 'Maybe I should just—'

'Can I . . . see you?' she asked softly.

It was the one thing I'd been dreading — having Josephine see me like this again. Her expression of horror after I'd transformed on the Sutallee Bridge was seared into my memory. But I'd never been able to refuse a request from Josephine. And, it wasn't as if I was going to find a cure for my condition in the next thirty seconds anyway, so I grit my teeth and let my hood fall to my shoulders. Josephine's widened eyes registered my face only briefly before she turned away.

'I'd forgotten how much you'd . . .' she whispered.

Though her words trailed off, I knew exactly what she meant. *Changed*. She focused her eyes on a spot near the roof of one of the trailers, and my chest tightened painfully.

Was I so grotesque that she couldn't even look at me?

'I'm sorry,' I said, hiding my face again with my hood. I didn't know what else to say. Impulsively, I yanked the pendant from my neck and held it out to her. The glass was warm against my gray palm and the dandelion in the center shimmered brightly. 'This is yours, by the way. It's about time I returned it.'

Her gaze went to my hand. 'No,' she said; her face was composed once more, and the fear was gone from her eyes. 'I gave it to you.'

'I have no right to keep it.' I studied the sparkling pendant I'd treasured since the Circe had left town. It gleamed with a life of its own. 'But thanks for letting me look after it for a while.'

At first, I thought Josephine was going to refuse. But then, her fingers reached out and curled around the necklace. Her fingertips brushed against my skin and electricity crackled in the air. I felt the jolt of it along my spine. I could see that Josephine felt it too, and I held my breath as we both froze in the strange current.

Suddenly, there was a loud shout from the campfire, and the music screeched to a halt. Josephine clutched the pendant in her hand, and the electricity fizzled. She stared at me in surprise, then hiked up her skirt and ran to the bonfire. I followed close at her heels.

A man was on his knees in the center of the crowd. Marksmen surrounded him, their weapons drawn. The rest of the troupe hovered nearby, looking confused and wary. Nicolas stood near the fire, his face tight as he glared down at the stranger.

'What's the meaning of this?' he demanded.

The man's scraggly hair framed a face that was splattered with dirt and blood. His eyes were wild. 'Sanctuary, please,' he gasped hoarsely. 'I beg you . . . sanctuary!'

'You have it,' Nicolas replied. With a motion of his hand, he ordered the Marksmen to lower their weapons. 'Now, tell us who you are.'

'Peter Boswell,' he sputtered.

'Of the Carolina Boswells?'

The stranger nodded, and the crowd murmured uneasily.

Quentin stepped forward, his eyes narrow. 'Why do you need sanctuary?'

The man stared at him. 'Because they're trying to kill me.'

5. A Sure Uncertainty

'Who's trying to kill you?' Nicolas was deadly calm.

'There's no time for this!' Peter rasped. 'I need sanctuary now!'

Sweat dripped from his nose, and there was a strange gleam in his bloodshot eyes: a crazy look that iced my blood. I clenched my fists, stifling a growl that was working its way up my throat. My wings strained uncomfortably against their straps underneath my jacket. I felt Josephine tense beside me.

'Sanctuary from whom?' demanded Nicolas.

'Please,' the man begged. 'Protect me!'

Quentin lunged forward and grabbed Peter by the shirt, yanking him to his feet. 'You will answer the *bandoleer*.'

'So many . . .' The stranger sniveled, his eyes rolling back. 'Came for us in the night . . . killed my brother. They want to kill us all!'

An ominous, sickening feeling permeated my body. Something smelled foul in the air, and I wrinkled my nose against the scent.

'What is it, Sebastian?' whispered Josephine.

'I don't know.' I could hear my voice thickening, tinged with a growl, as adrenaline seeped through my gargoyle blood. Josephine stared up at me, and I knew she'd heard the change as well. I glanced at her then back to the stranger. 'Something's wrong.'

Peter squirmed in Quentin's grasp. 'Don't you see?' he wailed. 'I need protection!'

A biting wind whipped through the camp. It fluttered the pavilion and aggravated the flames of the fire. Old women huddled in their shawls, and a few children whimpered. Then a foreboding silence fell. Quentin released the man and shrugged off his bow, notching an arrow. Its tip sparkled in the firelight. The Marksmen copied his movements, bows at the ready as they spread themselves with slow precision out along the circle. The air was smothered with hushed anticipation and fear.

I ground my teeth together. Adrenaline pumped hotly through my blood now, awakening my protective instincts. I immediately positioned myself in front of Josephine, breathing rapidly, struggling to maintain control of myself. My shoulders flexed, stretching the fabric of my jacket, as the disgusting smell around me grew stronger.

Nicolas glared at Peter. 'What have you done?'

Suddenly, something buzzed inside my head, followed by a voice – a voice that was nothing like Esmeralda's in my mind. It was cold and dark, barely intelligible.

Gargoyle . . .

I sucked in a sharp breath and turned my eyes to the sky. Nothing but stars and rolling clouds. But I could feel the presence of something wild in the night, something filled with hate and fire. I planted my feet and shot back an answer in my thoughts.

Who are you?

My head rang with harsh, static laughter.

There was no time to think about how my presence in the circle would be taken. I had to warn the *bandoleer*. 'Nicolas,' I called out. My voice sounded eerily close to a growl. Heads snapped in my direction. I hesitated only a moment before pressing forward. I felt Josephine at my heels as the crowd parted to let us pass. Nicolas stepped to meet me. 'Whatever's after this man,' I said, pointing at Peter, 'I believe it's very close.'

Nicolas' eyes found mine under the shadows of my hood. 'How do you know this?'

I paused before answering. 'I heard its voice in my head.'

The crowd shifted uneasily. Quentin moved towards me, his mouth open to protest, with a furious expression on his face, but Nicolas held up his hand, commanding silence. Peter Boswell stared at me, transfixed and suspicious as he tried to peer through the long shadows cast by the bonfire.

Nicolas kept his gaze on me. 'How many are out there?'

I concentrated on the scent, really concentrated, like Ezzie had instructed, filtering through the various scents of the circus troupe. 'It's hard to pinpoint,' I replied. Ignoring the wary glares from the Gypsies, I yanked off my hood and turned my face to the sky, drawing a deeper breath. A putrid, rotting smell hit me, worse than anything I'd experienced. 'I think there's only one.'

Quentin whirled on Nicolas. 'You're seriously going to trust this demon?'

Before the Romany leader could reply, the stranger jolted towards me, his bloodshot eyes wide and wild as he stared me down. 'What is this?' he demanded.

He pulled a knife from his belt. I'd seen that kind of

weapon before – the same glittering, diamond-encrusted blade – the same material that coated the Marksmen's weapons. My instincts fired a warning in my gut.

'I'm here to help,' I said, holding my hands up disarmingly.

'Shadowen scum,' the man spat. 'You want us all dead!'

My head prickled. The dark voice resounded in my brain.

Mine . . . mine . . . mine . . .

I hissed. 'It's here!'

An inhuman shriek filled the air. Several people screamed. Something dark swooped through the camp, knocking people off their feet. The Marksmen unloaded several arrows as the thing ascended into the night and disappeared. There was another shriek. Then silence.

The men trained their weapons upward, waiting. Gypsies crowded together, huddling under the pavilion. Marksmen surrounded Nicolas and Josephine like bodyguards. All eyes were on the sky. Everything went still.

I shut my eyes and took a breath, preparing to focus on the scent again. Then something hit me from behind. I cried out as pain ricocheted between my shoulders, and I went down on one knee. Peter Boswell loomed over me, the knife poised over his head. It was coated with dark liquid.

'I'll kill you first,' he cried.

My hold over myself finally snapped. I surged to my feet with a roar. My jacket strained, then ripped away as my enormous wings unfurled behind me. Peter yelped in horrified surprise. His shoes skidded in the dirt as he launched forward for another attack. But this time I was ready. I knocked the knife from his hand and grabbed him by the scruff of his neck.

'I don't want to hurt you!' I panted between growls,

trying to piece myself back together. Instincts burned through me like lava, narrowing my vision. I shook him firmly. 'Do you understand?'

'Let him go, gargoyle!'

Quentin stepped in front of me, his arrow aimed at my chest. I snarled at the Marksman through a film of hazy red, and bared my teeth at the Gypsy in my grasp. Peter's bloodshot eyes bugged from their sockets. The look of insane fear on his face scared me back to my senses.

What was I *doing*?

I fought back my instincts and released my grip. Peter scrambled away from me. Two Marksmen yanked the Gypsy to his feet and restrained him. I dropped to a crouch, shaking all over. My right side – no, my right wing; it was difficult to place the sensation – was burning with pain.

'Stand down,' ordered Quentin, pulling his bowstring to his cheek.

I rolled my shoulders, folding my wings to my back. Every eye was on me. I could hear Peter Boswell shouting curses. But my attention was on the sky. My stomach turned to ice as wind rushed through the camp. I spun and sniffed the air, concentrating on the terrible scent on the breeze. And then, suddenly, I knew.

'Quentin!' I yelled, pointing behind him. 'There!'

He didn't hesitate. He whirled on his heel and aimed towards the sky. His arrow left the bow. A loud, gurgling scream split the air. The other Marksmen targeted the sound and fired. A black form dropped out of the night sky. It landed with a sickening thud in front of the fire, six arrows protruding from its misshapen body. The thing convulsed and writhed on the ground, and then, without warning, it turned to stone.

I stared in revulsion at the lifeless form. Its winged body – jointed limbs, talons, and a snake-like tail – resembled something between a large feral cat and a reptile. The hideously deformed face was drawn tight with death, and black blood continued to ooze from the stone corpse.

For several moments, no one moved. I heard Josephine's shallow breathing and felt her fear. My instincts flickered on again, and I felt compelled to move closer, but was prevented by the Marksmen's protective circle. Quentin approached the stone creature and knelt, examining the granite body.

He glared over his shoulder at me, then stood and waved at the Marksmen. 'Phillipe, take your men and patrol the woods. The rest of you, ready yourself for another attack.'

Nicolas snapped his fingers, and the Marksmen that surrounded him backed away. He pointed at me. 'Are there any more?'

I blinked, feeling lightheaded. 'I don't th—'

'I need you to be sure.'

I steadied myself and took a deep, discerning whiff of air. Beyond the stench of the corpse, I could only smell Gypsies. I nodded stiffly, still finding it difficult to sort through the haze of adrenaline. I felt tighter than an overwound clock. 'I'm sure,' I replied, 'there was just that one. And it wanted him.' I jerked my head in Peter's direction, my lips rippling into another snarl.

'How do we know you're not protecting your own,' snapped Quentin, thrusting his bow at me. 'There could be others nearby, waiting for the opportunity to swoop in while our defenses are down. In fact, how do we know you didn't call them here yourself, *gargoyle*?'

'Enough,' shouted Nicolas, his eyes full of indignation.

'Quentin, take care of the camp as you see fit. Post whatever guards you deem necessary, and send out your patrols. The rest of you will return to your trailers for the remainder of the night.'

'You're going to let that demon loose in your camp?' exclaimed Peter, his murderous eyes on me. He wrenched in the grasp of the Marksmen who held him. 'He'll have a host of shadowen on your doorstep, Nicolas. Mark my words.'

'You're the one who brought danger to my doorstep,' said Nicolas coldly. He retrieved the glittering knife I'd knocked from Peter's hand. 'And we have much to discuss with you as to the reasons why. Henrik, Ami . . . take our guest to my trailer.' He looked at Quentin. 'I'm calling a *divano* immediately. Gather the leaders and meet me there in ten minutes' time.'

Peter was hauled through the crowd, but it didn't stop him from shouting obscenities at me as they carted him away. Attention was still on me: a sea of Gypsy faces with dark expressions. The mixture of emotions I felt was like a heavy weight pressing in from all sides. I stood slowly, longing for the shadows of my hood, but my shredded jacket lay in a heap at my feet.

'Father, he's hurt,' Josephine said suddenly.

I realized my right wing was jutting awkwardly from my body, and it was bleeding. The blood wasn't red, but rather a dark, purplish-black. It dribbled down the membrane of my wing and puddled on the ground.

'I'll take him back to his trailer and tend the wound,' said a voice from behind. It was Karl Corsi, the Romany's trainer. 'Josephine, will you go and fetch my bag? It's just inside my door. I'm going to need some help.'

'Yes, of course,' she replied and hurried away.

Quentin's face went taut as a bowstring. It was wrong, I knew, but I couldn't help feeling a tiny sense of smug pleasure. Gaining a few extra minutes with Josephine was definitely worth getting my wing sliced by a crazy Gypsy.

Nicolas pulled Karl aside. 'After you've treated him,' he said in a low voice – but one that my pointed gargoyle ears could easily hear – 'make sure he stays in his trailer. I'll have Quentin place a guard at his door. Emotions are running high tonight, and I don't want his presence adding to the chaos.'

'Of course,' Karl replied.

'Come, Quentin,' said Nicolas in a louder voice as he left.

The Marksman shot me a look that was sharper than the arrow he'd just pointed at my chest. Then he followed Nicolas across the clearing, his bow clutched tightly in his hands.

'Are you in pain?' asked Karl as he mopped my weirdly colored blood away from my wing. It was the first time I'd bled since fully becoming a gargoyle and the sight was a little disconcerting.

'Not really. Just stings a bit.'

'I'm sorry I wasn't here when you arrived today, Sebastian, but I wasn't expecting you to leave Hugo's so soon. I was in town, stocking up on medical supplies.' The old man wrung out the bloodied cloth and set it aside. 'Although, I heard the Marksmen gave you quite the reception while I was gone.'

'Ah well, you know,' I said, giving a half shrug. 'Deep down, I think they really like me. In fact, I'm sure we'll all be great friends.'

Karl chuckled. 'I'm sure you're right.'

With the purple-black blood gone from my wing, I could see the extent of the wound: a long jagged rip that had separated the bottom section of one of the leathery flaps. 'So how bad is the damage?'

'Thankfully, it's mostly superficial,' he said. 'The knife missed the bone structure. As soon as Josephine arrives with my bag, we'll get you stitched up. You'll be good as new.'

I held out the tattered remains of my jacket and Velcro straps that I'd brought back with me. 'Can't say the same for these.'

Karl set the straps aside, then studied the jacket. 'Don't worry, I'll take this to the costume ladies tonight.' He tossed it near the door. 'They'll have it mended in no time.'

'Thanks.' I sat back on the cot and pulled my wings in as tight as they would go, feeling exposed on multiple levels. I hated that I'd lost control with Peter Boswell in front of the whole troupe, even if he *had* tried to stab me. But the crazed Gypsy wasn't the only thing bothering me. My body trembled with leftover sparks of adrenaline, and my nose still burned with the stench of the creature the Marksmen had killed. 'Karl, what was that thing?'

'One of your more brutal cousins,' he replied.

I flinched. 'You can't possibly think I'm related to *that*. It was some kind of demonic monster . . .' The words fizzled on my lips as I studied the edge of my wing. 'Okay, so maybe we do share a *few* traits, but it felt and smelled totally different from anything I've ever experienced. It was like an animal . . . like something straight out of one of Hugo's art books.'

'It was a grotesque,' replied Karl.

I scratched my head. 'Are you referring to its looks, or is that a name?'

'It's a type.'

'I've never heard of them,' I said, feeling suspicious again. 'Hugo told me right before I left that there were other . . . shadowen . . . the Outcasts dealt with, but that was news to me. He's never been big on talking about this stuff.'

'Because Hugo figured you had enough to handle with your own transformation.' Karl's shaggy brows furrowed in thought. 'I think he always knew you'd end up with the Romanys, despite his parents' plans. That's why he instructed me to stay with the Circe – so you'd have an ally here. But Hugo didn't believe there was any point in introducing you to more shadowen knowledge until you'd first come to terms with being a gargoyle.'

'Okay, so what *are* grotesques, exactly?'

'There are three types of shadowen,' Karl said. 'Grotesques, chimeras, and gargoyles.' He studied me for a long moment. 'Surely you're at least aware of that? You mentioned seeing similar images in Hugo's books.'

'Yeah, I did.' I rubbed my eyes, feeling suddenly overwhelmed. 'My brother has this one book. He was really touchy about it and only let me look at it once – the night he explained what I was. Everything was written in French and some other languages I couldn't understand, and all the pictures were just drawings: statues on cathedrals, mainly.'

'We've got a lot of history to cover, then.'

'I guess so,' I said, propping my elbows on my knees. The room was warm, and my head throbbed. 'But could we maybe just do the CliffsNotes version right now? I don't think my brain can handle too much more.'

The circus trainer nodded. 'Well, the carving of shadow

creatures goes back many centuries. The original designs were called grotesques, and the Old Clans believed God ordained them to protect holy places from evil. They were simple creatures, at best, fashioned after images of animals and beasts from the ancient world.'

'But why so hideous?' I asked, glancing at my claws. 'If God told them they were supposed to protect holy places, why didn't the Old Clans make some kind of, I don't know, angelic statues?'

Karl smiled. 'Grotesques were created to frighten away evil spirits, Sebastian. The Roma chose to fight fire with fire, so to speak. But shadowen weren't just protectors of cathedrals. They looked after those of Roma blood as well: a gift to my people for all the persecution we'd suffered over the years.'

I turned my attention to the window. Most of the Gypsies had retreated to their trailers, but I could see the dark forms of Marksmen patrolling the grounds. 'So what happened, Karl? If your people created them, then why are they attacking you?'

'Because our ancestors became greedy,' replied Karl with a scowl. 'They sought to use this gift for their own personal gain, for conquest and dominance. Soon, blood feuds divided our clans. More shadowen, like the cunning and vicious chimeras, were created. Rather than protectors, shadowen became weapons. But the creatures became too beastly – impossible to manage. War followed and led to the Sundering of the Clans. Though the Outcasts fled Europe, we couldn't fully escape our past. We continue to endure the consequences of delving into powers beyond our control.'

I frowned. 'So how do gargoyles fit into all this?'

'Gargoyles were our ancestors' saving grace,' he replied.

He leaned forward and placed his hand on my shoulder. 'They battled the chimeras and grotesques that turned on our people. They became our true guardians. But that was long ago, and much has changed. Not everyone shares the same beliefs regarding shadowen these days.'

'Really? I hadn't noticed.'

Karl searched my face. 'You're taking all this remarkably well, Sebastian. I'm impressed. You do realize that it's not going to be easy for you, living here?'

'Hey, it can't be any harder than picking steak out of my teeth. You should see what these babies can do to a spool of floss.'

Karl laughed and scratched his beard. His expression turned thoughtful. 'Speaking of food, how *is* your appetite these days?'

'Hungry,' I answered. 'A lot.'

'Hmm.'

My brows lifted. 'Hmm?'

Karl waved his hand. 'But back to what I was saying, about living here—'

'I've made my decision,' I said firmly. 'But honestly, I don't see how I'm going to do much good. Quentin and his men seem to have everything under control, and they know more about this shadow world than I do. Not to mention the fact that they're keeping guards posted at my door.'

'Give it time, Sebastian. You've only been here a few hours, you know.'

I paused for a moment. 'Karl, what do you know about my . . . I mean, where I came from? Hugo said his parents wouldn't tell him. Or he was keeping something from me. It's impossible to tell with him.'

'Your origins *are* a mystery, Sebastian.' Karl regarded me

carefully. 'Hugo was telling the truth about that. Shortly after his parents arrived, Hugo contacted me, wanting as much information as I could glean about shadowen. So I began researching – collecting books, speaking with other clans as the Circe traveled, rereading everything my grandfather left to me – but it hasn't been easy. After the Outcast clans split from the Old Clans most of the information was either destroyed or hidden away.'

'Why?'

'Someone with the ability to not only awaken but also control shadow creatures could easily rule the Outcast realms,' he replied. 'Only a select few from each clan are entrusted with pieces of our old lore. I believe Hugo's parents went into hiding to guard that knowledge, like my own grandfather did when I was a boy. Knowledge is a potent thing, just as willing to be used for evil as for good. But until Zindelo and Nadya return, I'm afraid the truth of your origins will remain with them.'

'Well, Nicolas seems to know things,' I said. Karl surprised me by laughing, and I frowned. 'He's the *bandoleer*, right? He's the one who asked me to come here, and he knew about the brand and *sclav* and everything.'

'The leadership doesn't know as much as they would like the clan to believe. You see, all official records of the shadowen as well as our written histories are kept by the High Council.'

'But you just said—'

'Yes,' Karl said, cutting me off. 'I have my own limited collection of shadowen knowledge. Why else do you think the Romanys allow me to stay here? I'm an asset to them, just like you are.'

I pondered this in silence. Outside, I could hear voices

as people hurried through the caravan. 'So what is this *divano* thing, exactly?' I asked as I watched a few Gypsies duck into the Romany trailer. 'And why's it all so secretive?'

'It's a meeting of our ruling body,' said Karl with a shrug. 'Every clan has a *bandoleer*, but there are leaders and elders that assist him. If matters can't be resolved in the *divano*, or if the issue is severe enough, a *kris* may be called.'

'*Kris*?'

Karl moved to the sink and washed his hands. 'Think of it as a kind of Gypsy court.'

I frowned. 'Are you a part of it?'

'Membership is rather selected, and I'm Corsi, remember?'

'So I shouldn't be expecting an invitation in the mail anytime soon.'

'I wouldn't count on it.'

I allowed my gaze to return to my wounded wing. I didn't like looking at the leathery things with their strange framework of bones and joints, but I couldn't exactly ignore them either. I expanded them slightly, feeling the power of the muscles I'd acquired when I'd transformed. I cleared my throat awkwardly. 'Karl?'

'Yes?'

'Do you know what happens to a gargoyle *after* he's been sealed to a Gypsy?'

The old circus trainer settled into the chair. 'How do you mean?'

I gathered myself and plunged ahead. 'Hugo pretty much kept me confined to the shop since all this happened. He said it was to give me time to adjust, but Esmeralda thinks being cooped up hasn't been good for me, that it's kept me in some kind of limbo.'

Karl leaned forward, his wrinkled face alert and curious. 'Go on.'

'The last few weeks, something's been going on with me.' I puffed out my cheeks and released the air in one quick breath. 'And it's a lot more than just my appetite. I've been feeling more . . . well, just . . . different. Do you think it's because the Romanys are back in Sixes?'

'It's very likely,' mused Karl, stroking his beard. 'A guardian and his charge were never meant to be so far apart. And you were separated immediately after the sealing took place. It could have affected your development. Now that you've found yourself near Josephine again, perhaps—'

The door opened suddenly and Josephine stepped inside. She was carrying a large black bag, the kind classic movie doctors used when making house calls. My pulse quickened at her presence. I'd spent months conditioning myself to her absence. Now she was here, flesh and blood – and back in my life. I took shallow breaths to reduce that mixture of flowers and spices that I now knew I'd recognize anywhere, but the temperature in the room kicked up several degrees, despite my efforts.

'Just bring it over here,' Karl said as he rolled up his sleeves.

Josephine placed the bag beside the chair and sat next to me on the cot. I kept my eyes on the old trainer, focusing on his actions. Karl popped open the bag and pulled out a silver case lined with intricate designs. Inside the case was a small sewing kit. But the needle looked odd, and the spool of thread was silver in color. With an expert's hand, Karl measured a length of line and cut it with a pair of glittering scissors. He threaded the needle.

'Are you ready?' he asked.

I'd never been to the doctor before, but I'd seen enough television. 'Don't you have to sterilize the equipment first?' I was feeling uneasy at the sight of the sparkling needle and thread. 'Or my skin?'

'You don't require any of those human precautions, Sebastian.' He held the needle out, turning it to catch the light. 'There's only one thing that can pierce a gargoyle's skin.'

'Diamonds,' breathed Josephine, staring at the needle in wonder.

My stomach did a weird flip. 'The needle and thread are made out of *diamonds*?'

'Coated with the substance, to be more accurate,' Karl replied. 'The Outcast clans perfected the process over the centuries, but it's very difficult.'

My eyes widened. 'So the Marksmen's weapons—'

'Are made the same way,' Karl finished. 'After all, diamonds are harder than stone, are they not?' He gestured pointedly at my gray skin.

'So I've heard.'

'Now, Josephine,' said the old trainer, 'if you'll hold Sebastian's wing steady, I'll get him fixed up.'

Apart from Karl, I'd never allowed anyone to examine my wings since my transformation, let alone touch them. I felt strangely embarrassed as Josephine's hands gripped the edges of the leathery membrane. My arms sprouted goosebumps. I didn't dare risk a glance at the Gypsy girl, so I watched Karl carefully as he stitched up my wound.

With each stinging pass of the needle, I felt more uncomfortable, but it didn't take Karl long to repair the rip. With a quick snip of the scissors and a knotting of the thread, he was finished. He wiped the needle clean and replaced everything in the silver case. Then he handed it to Josephine to put away.

Karl rolled his sleeves back down. 'The diamond thread in your wing may be a little annoying, but based on my knowledge of gargoyle physiology, you should be completely healed in a matter of hours. We'll take it out, then.'

I looked up, a question forming on my lips that had been plaguing me for the last few minutes. 'Karl, what does it take to . . . to kill me?'

'Well, you know you can be wounded. And you feel pain.' His gaze drifted to the door, and he lowered his voice. 'Shadowen can kill other shadowen. But diamonds are the only human weapons that can do *permanent* damage to your kind. They can pierce your flesh and, once a diamond blade gets through your gargoyle skin, you're as vulnerable internally as any other living creature.' He put a hand on my shoulder. 'Fortunately for you, weapons fashioned in this way are hard to come by and generally entrusted only to those of Marks' blood. That's why this clan has been so well protected for so long.'

'What about Peter Boswell?' I asked, remembering his glittering knife.

'Stolen, most likely.' The circus trainer's eyes narrowed. 'Fear of the unknown can make people do irrational things, Sebastian. You have the approval of Nicolas and many of the council, but things are unstable. Give it time, and I believe the others will come to accept you. But until then, play things safe.'

Karl filled a glass of water from the sink and handed me two red pills. I eyed them suspiciously. 'What are these?'

'You can trust me, Sebastian,' Karl said. 'They contain a very low dosage of vitamin D.' I recoiled, remembering the nasty shots Hugo had used to sedate me. Karl read my expression and shook his head. 'No, not like you received before. These will take the edge off the pain and help you sleep. Nothing more.'

I closed my fingers around the pills. 'All right.'

'Well, my work here is done,' he said with a satisfied smile. 'I'll come by in the morning to check on you.' He retrieved my tattered jacket from the floor. 'And I'll have this mended.' He opened the door and was gone.

I placed the pills and water on the small nightstand. Josephine shifted beside me, and I jerked, startled, as I realized we were alone. I bit my lower lip between my sharp teeth, too afraid to move, scared that she would stand and follow Karl out. But she didn't. She didn't say anything either. We both stared at the wall. I slid my thumb over my wrist, and I saw Josephine watching the movement out of the corner of her eye.

'So,' I said, 'how've you been?'

The question hung absurdly in the air. Josephine made a noise that was almost a laugh, followed by a heavy sigh.

'Sebastian, I'm sorry,' she said, clenching her hands in her lap, 'about how I reacted to you earlier, when I asked you to take off your hood. It was rude, and cruel. Please believe me, I didn't mean to—'

'It's okay, Josephine, really. It took weeks for Hugo and the guys to get used to all the . . . well, you know.' I shrugged and my wings lifted. 'Changes.'

Her face softened a little. 'You know, for the record, you still look like you,' she continued with some hesitation. She grimaced with apology. 'What I mean is, you're still Sebastian.'

Was I?

My own silent question bothered me, but I shook it off. 'Thanks.'

'And your wings are really incredible,' she said after a moment's pause.

'I bet you say that to all the gargoyles.'

Josephine smiled, and I watched her study my wound. She reached out timidly, and then she touched the membrane that stretched between the joints. Her touch sparked a current through my body, eradicating what was left of the pain. Josephine pushed a strand of chestnut hair from her face and glanced quizzically at me, asking my permission. I managed a nod. Her fingertips brushed along my wing up to the joint. I sucked in a breath and shut my eyes.

'Does that hurt?' she whispered, her fingers pausing at the clawed tip.

'No.'

Her cheeks turned pink. 'Oh.'

Neither of us moved. My stomach was wrenched in so many knots that I was certain I was going to puke at any moment.

It felt amazing.

Josephine's fingers left my wing, and she clasped her hands in her lap. I looked away, my face hot with the embarrassed pleasure I'd felt from her touch.

'Sebastian, I'm so sorry about all of this,' she said. 'Everything's my fault.'

'No, Josephine, it's not.'

'I was so confused,' she pressed on. 'At school I was one person, and at home I was someone else. I didn't know who to be, especially around you.' Josephine's hand went to her throat, and I saw that she was wearing her pendant once again. 'You were so nice to me, and I felt . . . I feel

. . . this attachment to you. Things have been stressful enough, and Quentin—' Josephine broke off and took a sharp breath. 'Quentin's always been our protector, and this has been hard on him. The Marks think all shadow creatures are our enemies. And for a long time, I believed the same thing.'

'What changed your mind?'

'You did.' Josephine lowered her gaze, her green eyes hidden from me. 'When we were kids, my father used to tell us stories about the guardians of the Roma. The guardians of his tales were noble and heroic.' The Gypsy girl's face hardened in a way I hadn't seen before. 'The shadowen we deal with are horrible things, always stalking us. There've been rumors of bad things happening to the clans in Europe, and everyone's afraid it's spreading here. It's becoming harder for us to hide.' Josephine grasped my hand, and the room filled with heat. 'But you're different, Sebastian. You're like the old stories.'

I stared at her shapely hand wrapped around my gray one. The dandelion tattoo along my wrist was no longer red and inflamed. It looked as sleek and pristine as the day Hugo had inked me. 'You haven't talked to Quentin about this.'

'Not exactly,' Josephine replied. 'He's dedicated his life to keeping us safe, and now he feels like my father has betrayed him by asking you to stay with us.' She let go of my hand. 'That's why I tried to keep you from coming here, Sebastian. I don't want anything to happen to you.'

I couldn't take my eyes from hers. So many emotions flickered behind their green depths. 'You don't have to worry about me, Josephine. And there's no reason for you to feel guilty. You didn't do this to me. I . . . I've always been this way. A gargoyle, I mean. I just didn't know it before I met you.'

Josephine blinked: a beautiful flutter of thick lashes. She no longer looked uncertain, as she had when she'd first seen me, and I dared to hope that I wasn't as offensive to her as I'd first thought. My body tingled with a new form of electricity. Josephine leaned in, and I found myself leaning closer in response. Her gaze took in my gargoyle features slowly, intently.

Our faces were merely inches apart, and the smell of flowery spices filled my senses, clouded my head. Sight and sound went into overload. I was almost certain I could hear the Gypsy girl's heart beating. My wings quivered, and my gaze lingered on her lips. They were parted slightly, and her breath fell warm on my face.

The door swung open with a bang. We both jumped.

Phillipe pounded up the steps. 'Closing time at the zoo,' he said mockingly. 'Time to lock the animal up for the night.' He looked pointedly at Josephine. 'And your presence is requested at the *divano*.'

'I'll be right there,' she replied, her voice stiff.

Phillipe grunted and clomped back down the stairs. As soon as the Marksman was gone, Josephine placed her hand on the clawed tip of my wing. My cheeks grew warm again, and I swallowed hard. Her fingers drifted down the edge for a brief moment before she pulled away. I noted the shallow intake of her breath as she clutched her pendant against her neck.

'For what it's worth, Sebastian, I'm really glad you decided to come to the Circe, especially after everything that happened the last time my family was in Sixes.' She stood up, seeming reluctant as she did so. 'If you don't mind, I'd like to stop by tomorrow, to check on your wing and see how you're doing.'

My heart jounced in my chest. 'I'd like that, Josephine.'

She smiled. 'So would I.'

6. *Going Nowhere*

I sat in silent stillness, enjoying the lingering trace of Josephine's presence in my trailer. When her scent grew weak and the air cooled, I shook free from my trance and tested my wing. Karl had done a nice job sewing it back together. I spread my palm against the leathery flap. The weird, shimmery skin was warm and smooth to the touch, and I remembered the feel of Josephine's fingers.

I didn't care if I was locked in a trailer with guards at the door. I was happier than I'd been in an agonizingly long time. The torture of the last few months faded, and hope vibrated behind my sternum. Whatever the next stage of my life held, I was sure of one thing: Josephine *had* looked at me differently tonight.

I swallowed Karl's pills before I could change my mind. Then I sprawled face first onto the cot, letting my hurt wing drape over the side. As I lay there, I wondered what was going on in the *divano*. Was I on their discussion list? To the Gypsies, I was some sort of glorified pet to be ordered about and controlled – and that was by the ones who *did* want me around. And then there was Quentin Marks.

Much as he got under my skin, I couldn't fault him for his abhorrence of gargoyles. Based on the evidence so far, there wasn't much going in favor of shadowen, myself included. But the Marksman didn't just have a problem with gargoyles. He had a problem with *me*.

My head started to pound as the dose of vitamin D kicked in. I groaned and buried my face in the pillow, feeling groggy and heavy. They were sensations I didn't often experience unless I was out in broad sunlight. And I was sleepy – something else that had grown foreign to me since I'd gone gargoyle.

I yawned loudly and my eyelids drooped. Karl's pills really packed a wallop. My body grew heavier and heavier until I heard the sound of my limp wings thudding against the floor. Then sweet oblivion overtook me.

I wasn't sure when I woke. The curtains were shut and the trailer was dark. I blinked several times, studying the grayscale forms of the objects in the room. The night vision thing was crazy, but it sure came in handy.

My wings were still unfurled. I reined them in with some effort. I couldn't remember the last time I'd slept without my nylon and Velcro straps. I changed into a fresh hooded shirt and retrieved a new pair of bindings from my duffel bag. My shoulders ached and the wound was stiff, but it didn't stop me from my daily ritual. A few minutes later, sixteen feet of gargoyle wings flattened against my back.

I splashed water on my face at the small sink. I was going to have to figure out how to get a shower soon. Gargoyle or not, I didn't want to stink. My stomach cramped with hunger, and I reached for my jacket before remembering that Karl had taken it with him. I studied my reflection dubiously in the mirror. The straps pressed tight against my T-shirt, confining most of the bulk behind me, but the tips of my wings with their bony talons protruded visibly over my shoulders.

I wondered if I could sneak some food back to the trailer – that is, if I could actually leave. To my surprise, the door was unlocked. I peered outside. By the looks of things, it was early morning, still way before dawn. There wasn't a Marksman in sight. The center of the caravan was deserted. I leapt off the stairs and landed softly in the gravel on all fours.

Finally, a little freedom.

I slunk along the outskirts of the circle, tugging repeatedly on the flimsy hood of my shirt, which didn't cover as much of the real me as I would've liked. I felt naked without my long jacket, but at least the gray of the fading night hung in the air, providing shadows to blend into, if needed. I was in a good mood, even though I felt like I'd been run over by a semi-truck. I memorized the vehicles and made mental notes of living quarters as I explored the Circe.

'Morning, Sebastian.'

Francis leaned against a large RV, talking to Phoebe. I raised a brow, surprised to find two teenagers up so early on a summer morning. Then again, they weren't your average, run-of-the-mill teens. They studied me with thinly veiled curiosity.

'Hey, guys,' I replied.

Francis grinned. 'So they let you out, huh?'

'Yeah, I guess so. Time off for good behavior, maybe?'

'See you at breakfast?' he asked.

'Oh, yeah,' I replied, patting my stomach. 'Definitely.'

I hurried past the Gypsies, not wanting to miss the opportunity to take a self-guided tour of the camp before it was time to eat. As I rounded the corner of the RV, I heard Phoebe's whispered voice.

'Wow. I've never seen anything like him before.'

'Hey,' Francis returned, sounding a little hurt. 'I'm standing right here!'

I was too far out of range to hear Phoebe's reply, but I couldn't help smiling at the strange sort of compliment. It certainly felt better than being shunned out of fear. My gaze drifted over the vehicles. The outline of a tent loomed against the violet sky. It wasn't as large as the Circe's performance tent, but still impressive.

Music drifted quietly from the tent, and I paused in front of the entrance. My senses told me instantly who was inside. I planted my feet, determined to changed directions, but couldn't resist the pull. It was like being caught in a spaceship's tractor beam. I slipped through the canvas opening and ducked behind a collection of heavy crates stacked near the tent wall.

Josephine Romany danced alone in the middle of a small circus ring. I clung to the edge of one box, suddenly weak at the knees. She seemed otherworldly, and I visualized generations of Roma blood flowing through her as she moved. I felt awkward and insignificant as I lurked in the shadows – a beast watching his beauty from afar.

God, she was so beautiful.

I squeezed my eyes shut. This was stupid. Pointless and ridiculous. I had to stop torturing myself this way. Either I had to come to grips with my feelings and my place in this Gypsy camp, or I was going to be useless. I pushed myself away with newfound resolve.

A hand clamped around my neck. I tried to gasp, but no air came. My body was slammed against a thick crate. A shockwave exploded through my wings and down my spine.

'You demon freak!' Quentin squeezed tighter. 'How dare you come in here!'

The edges of my vision grew black with startling speed. I clutched desperately at his wrists, suffocating under the impressive chokehold.

'Stay away from Josephine.' His face pressed close to mine with fury blazing in his eyes. 'You hear me, demon? You may have Nicolas' blessing, but you aren't worth the price of one of my dogs. I've killed dozens of your kind. You're nothing special.' His fingers constricted like an iron vise, and my head swam. 'Only the *bandoleer's* command is keeping you alive.' He released his grip. I slid to the floor. 'Watch yourself, gargoyle,' he said, stepping away. 'It's only a matter of time before I find a way around Nicolas Romany. He's blind to what you are, but I'm not. Remember that.'

Quentin stormed out of the tent. I clutched my throat, gulping oxygen like a starving man. Suddenly, there was a hand on my shoulder. I recoiled, expecting the Marksman had returned for some additional gloating. But instead, I found myself looking into Karl Corsi's concerned face.

'Sebastian, are you all right?'

'I'm . . . fine.' I coughed a few times. 'Help . . . me . . . up.'

He pulled me to my feet, and I leaned against the tall stack of crates, still breathing hard. Out of the corner of my eye, I saw Josephine leaving out of the opposite opening of the tent; oblivious, thankfully, to what had just happened.

'What aren't you in your trailer?' asked Karl.

'Got bored,' I panted. 'And hungry.'

Karl frowned. 'You're supposed to be asleep. I certainly didn't expect to find you up before dawn and getting into confrontations with the likes of Quentin Marks. Vitamin D makes you weak, in case you haven't noticed.'

I rubbed my throat tenderly. 'You might have warned me *before* I took the pills.'

'And you should have waited until *after* I came and checked on you before gallivanting around the circus.'

I grimaced sheepishly. 'Touché.'

'Now let's get you back to your trailer before the sun comes up and really gives you some problems.'

'I go out in the sun all the time,' I said, staggering forward. 'I can handle it.'

Karl looped an arm under me. 'Not when you've already got an extra shot of vitamin D in your bloodstream.'

'What, are you telling me I can overdose on the stuff?'

'In a manner of speaking,' he answered. 'While a small amount can induce sleep and allow a gargoyle time to heal, you have to be careful.' The circus trailer raised his brow. 'Diamonds can kill you, Sebastian, but too much vitamin D can do so much more.'

Now it was my turn to raise a brow. 'Like what?'

'It will turn you to stone,' he replied, looking steadily at me. '*Living* stone.'

I didn't like the sound of that at all.

I sighed impatiently while Karl examined the stitches in my wing. I *really* wanted breakfast. But I played the good patient while he replaced the nylon straps with a satisfied grunt. I pulled on the freshly mended jacket that he'd brought; glad to hide my massive deformities from view once more.

'So, how's it look, doc?'

'Excellent,' he replied. 'I'll take the stitches out after you've eaten.'

'That's pretty fast.'

'A benefit of your gargoyle heritage, my boy.'

I studied the edge of my wing where it jutted out underneath the jacket. 'So, why don't the diamond needle and thread hurt me?'

'They do, to an extent,' he replied. 'But it's the difference between getting a flu shot and getting stabbed through the chest with a switchblade.' Karl's bushy eyebrows lifted. 'Both are wounds, correct?'

'Got it,' I replied, chagrinned.

The more I learned, the more I felt I didn't know.

'Your wing would have healed on its own,' Karl continued. 'Just not nearly as well.'

I nodded absently, my thoughts drifting away from my injury. A nagging fear had been lurking in the back of my mind since Quentin threatened me in the tent. Why hadn't I felt him coming? His presence usually made me want to puke chunks of ice, yet I'd felt no warning at all. But I *had* been focused on Josephine.

Perhaps that's what Esmeralda meant when she told me that falling in love with my charge made me weak. Maybe it did more than cloud my judgement. Maybe it also made me blind to danger around me – and that would inevitably put Josephine at risk. I gritted my teeth. This wasn't just about managing my feelings anymore. This was about protecting the person I'd been assigned to watch over.

Karl switched off the lamp and tossed a blanket over the curtain rod, dousing what little light remained in the trailer.

'Care to fill me in on what you're doing?' I asked. 'Last I checked I was a gargoyle, not a vampire.'

Karl shrugged in the darkness. 'You need to sit in the shadows for a while, Sebastian, build up your melatonin levels to counteract what's left of the vitamin D in your blood.'

'Say that again?'

'Your melatonin levels,' he repeated. 'The body produces it best while in darkness, and gargoyles seem to need much higher levels than humans. It's all linked to your special abilities.' Karl stepped to the door and looked back in my direction with a smile. 'In other words, consider yourself a creature of the night, Sebastian Grey.'

'Ah, fantastic.'

'Doctor's orders,' he replied. 'It'll help, you'll see.'

'So, how are you so good with all this shadow creature medical stuff, Karl? I didn't realize the Romanys were such gargoyle experts.'

'I'm a Corsi, remember?' He chuckled. 'I just work for the Romanys.'

'So how, then?'

Karl leaned against the door. 'My grandfather was fascinated by shadowen physiology. And he had a very curious grandson.'

'What about the Marksmen?' I asked. 'They know a lot about shadow creatures.'

Karl's smile dropped. 'The Marks know how to fight and kill your kind. That's the extent of their knowledge.'

'So noted.'

'Breakfast should be ready soon, Sebastian. Until then, try to stay in the trailer and rest, okay?' Karl closed the door heavily after him.

I sprawled on the bed, unsure of what to do, or even if I was really supposed to *do* anything. I couldn't lie on my back with my wings strapped, so I rolled onto my stomach, trying to imagine I was in a tanning booth, only absorbing dark instead of light. At some point, I must have dozed off, because a knock at my trailer door sent me bolting out of the bed with a startled snarl.

'Let's eat, Sebastian,' yelled Francis from the outside. 'Alcie's cooking bacon this morning!'

'Bacon sounds great,' I said as I yanked open the door.

'Dude!' Francis flailed backwards, nearly careening off the steps. 'Don't do that!'

I jerked in surprise. 'What? What did I do?'

'Jumping at a guy like that, with the teeth and the eyes and all that.' He shook his head, and then he laughed. 'My bad, man. I'm just not used to the . . . you know . . .' He gestured at me. 'The new Sebastian.'

'Oh, sorry about that.'

'Now come on,' he continued, 'we gotta hurry or we're going to miss out on the good stuff.'

I glanced past him warily and worked my hood over my head to conceal my features. 'Are you sure it's okay for me to be out? After last night—'

'You're good,' said Francis. 'Believe it or not, you're the least of the worries around here at the moment.'

We sprinted across the circle towards the pavilion. The smell of cooking meat nearly knocked me off my feet. I paused and ran my tongue over the jagged points of my teeth, which were suddenly aching in anticipation. A small growl escaped my lips. Francis cast me a sideways glance, but he didn't say anything.

The atmosphere under the crowded pavilion felt different. Conversations were hushed, and the jovial noise of last night's dinner had disappeared.

'That bad, huh?' I asked quietly.

Francis kicked at a rock. 'A lot went on during the *divano* last night.'

'You were there?' Francis looked offended, and I suddenly remembered who I was talking to. Of course he was there. 'So what happened?'

Conflict flickered across his features. 'I'll tell you later. Let's eat first.'

Circus folk congregated at a long table, helping themselves to an arrangement of biscuits, bacon, eggs, and coffee: sort of a Gypsy version of a continental breakfast. My mouth watered, and I wiped at it with the back of my sleeve. Francis grabbed two plates and tossed one to me. I caught it and filed in behind him.

I split a biscuit and doused it with thick gravy, adding a few more servings than was probably good for my arteries. Then I piled my plate to overflowing with everything else on the table. It wasn't until I had to set it down to pour a cup of very black coffee that I noticed an old, wrinkled woman on the other side of the table – Alcie, I assumed.

'Thank you for breakfast,' I said, careful to smile with closed lips.

The gray haired woman narrowed her eyes and raised her heavily bejeweled hands. For a moment, I was afraid she was going to speak some sort of ancient curse on me. 'Take some more bacon,' she said, much to my surprise. 'After all, you're a growing . . . boy.' Her old eyes sparkled and she dumped more bacon onto my plate.

Francis was waiting on me, trying to hide his grin. 'Come on,' he said, maneuvering around the tables. 'I found a spot.'

It was impossible to ignore the shaded looks from the other diners as I moved through the pavilion. I huddled into my hood, trying to avoid their stares. Francis plopped down at a table, but I hesitated as I realized it was already occupied. Eating with the Romany twin was one thing. Eating with a group of Gypsies I didn't know was another.

'This is Brishen,' said Francis, pointing to the first of three sitting on the opposite side of the table: a tall Gypsy, probably in his early twenties. 'He's one of our stunt performers.' Brishen gave me a look that was neither friendly nor hostile and went back to eating his breakfast. Francis turned my attention to the person in the middle – a thin girl with cropped auburn hair. 'This is Claire. She's a dancer and an acrobat.'

'And I'm Zara.'

The low voice belonged to a girl with black hair and wide electric blue eyes. Though I guessed she was probably close to my age, the way Zara smiled made her seem a whole lot older. She tilted her head, and winked.

'Zara's our public relations face,' said Francis sarcastically. Suddenly, he jerked and grunted. 'Hey, no need to kick!'

Zara kept her eyes on me. '*Gadje* still want to see the stereotypical fortune teller with a crystal ball bit, and, believe me, they pay good money for it, too.' She flipped her hair elegantly behind her shoulders. 'I just make sure the customer walks away satisfied.'

Brishen snorted softly, but quickly buried his head in his cup of coffee before Zara turned her glare on him.

'It's a pleasure to meet you,' I said as I sat down.

'Wow, you really *are* gray,' Claire remarked, leaning forward to get a closer look inside my hood.

Francis stabbed a lump of eggs with his fork. 'Nice, Claire. That was *real* subtle.'

The acrobat shrugged innocently. 'What? It was so dark last night I couldn't see him very well.'

Zara laughed and twirled a strand of hair around her finger. 'It's kind of sexy, if you ask me.'

I chomped down on a strip of bacon, my face flushing.

'Oh, leave him alone, Zara,' said Phoebe as she approached the table and slid onto the bench next to Francis. 'As if he doesn't have enough attention on him already.' Phoebe pushed a clump of dark curls from her face. 'Hey, Sebastian.'

I gave her a grateful nod. 'Good morning.'

'So why are you trying to hide?' asked Brishen, pointing at my hood with his fork. He scrutinized my shadowed face. There was something in his demeanor that reminded me of a Marksman, even without the black clothes and the cold, calculating expression. 'We all know what you are.'

'I'm going for the dark and mysterious look,' I replied.

To my surprise, a hint of a smile tugged at one corner of his mouth. 'You're different than I pictured you.'

'How so?'

'The Marks are painting you to be a brutal killer, sent to infiltrate the clan and destroy us from the inside.'

'Well, as impressive as that sounds, the Marks have it all wrong.' I shrugged and shook my head. 'And honestly, don't let all the gargoyle stuff fool you. I assure you, I'm perfectly harmless.'

'You didn't look so harmless last night,' said Zara in a sly tone.

I polished off another piece of bacon and stared at my plate.

'You had more than a few Marksmen ruffled,' said Francis, sounding pleased. 'It's a good thing you're on our side.'

'I didn't really *do* anything. Your boys in black took care of business.'

'But you sniffed the beast out,' said Brishen between bites.

'Or whatever it is you shadowen do. Heightened senses, right?'

I was growing uncomfortable with the attention. 'Yeah, I guess so.'

'How intriguing,' said Zara.

'Well, you can't blame people for being freaked out,' said Claire. 'It's like nobody knows who to trust these days. Tension between the clans is getting worse, and that Peter Boswell guy just set everybody off last night.' She glanced at me. 'He totally went after you. Good thing you scared him half to death.'

'Were you all at the *divano* last night?' I asked, eager to shift the focus.

Zara laughed. 'Oh, please. You think they'd let the simple folk invade their top-secret meeting?'

'I take offense at that,' said Brishen.

Francis smirked at me. 'Brishen was there as one of the reps from the Stoakas family, and I was there, of course. But Zara's right. it's a select group of members from all the families within the Romany clan. No one else is allowed unless the *bandoleer* calls for a clan-wide *kris*, and that doesn't happen too often.'

'So what happened last night?' asked Claire, her voice hushed.

Everyone grew quiet around the table. Francis moved inward and lowered his voice. 'Apparently, several members of the Boswell family up in North Carolina went missing. A few days ago, they showed up. Or, their bodies did, anyway. Peter claims the Boswells are being targeted by some sort of mercenary who's determined to kill them off.'

My blood went cold. 'Why would someone want to do that?'

'A few years ago, their *bandoleer* started claiming that he was King of the Gypsies. People didn't like that. We Outcasts only answer to one authority, and it's not him. Ever since then, things have been pretty tense with the clans up north. We've stayed out of it. Our family's never really cared for the Boswells. They're troublemakers, always involved in petty power disputes.' Francis' eyes narrowed. 'But this Peter guy was pretty shook up last night. He says their clan members were killed by a pack of shadow creatures.'

Brishen stared at me, his eyes hard. 'Do you know anything about that?'

I met his gaze. 'A few months ago, I didn't know any of this stuff *existed*.'

'How can you not know about your own kind?' he demanded.

A growl rumbled in my chest, and I inhaled deeply to cover the sound. 'Trust me, it's a long story, and I won't bore you with the details right now.' I shifted my gaze to Francis. 'I was under the impression shadowen were rare.'

'Well, your type definitely is,' agreed Francis. 'Most gargoyles were either wiped out or turned back into stone centuries ago. Same goes for chimeras. At least, that's what we've been taught. But groties are another story.'

I stopped in mid-bite. 'Huh?'

'Groties,' he repeated. 'You know, grotesques. Nasty dumb critters, slinking around the outskirts of our lives, attacking when they get a chance, then scurrying back to wherever they come from.'

'I'd never seen one before last night,' I replied.

Brishen hadn't taken his eyes off me. 'You're telling us you've never encountered them?'

My eyes flicked back to meet his. 'That's exactly what I'm telling you.' I did my best to smile, blinking my eyes several times against the burning sensation behind my pupils. 'I'm still new to all this.'

Brishen turned his attention to his coffee as he continued. 'A centuries-old nuisance is what they are. Groties are the cockroaches of the Gypsy world. You can't wipe them out, but they're easy enough to keep in check.'

'Thanks to the Marks family,' added Phoebe. She glanced towards one of the tables of black-clad Gypsies – all of whom were keeping a guarded eye on me, I noticed. 'We've got mad beastie extermination skills. Most of the larger clans in our *kumpania* have a contingent of Marksmen in their camps.'

'Then how were the Boswells killed?' I asked carefully.

Francis propped himself on his elbows. 'That's what everyone in the *divano* wanted to know. Boswell claims it was a pack of chimeras and groties working together – which, of course, is unheard of – and he escaped, only to have one track him here to our camp.'

'Why is it unheard of?'

Francis puffed out his cheeks and released the air with a whistle. 'Man, you really *are* new to this.' Phoebe jabbed him in the ribs. He grimaced and grinned. 'I just mean, we assumed you would know all this, coming from the Corsi clan and all that.'

I sighed, but this time without frustration. 'Karl's been giving me a crash course, but anything else you can tell me would be helpful. I'm still trying to wrap my mind around it all, to be honest.'

Claire stared at me in open surprise. 'Really?'

'Groties are what the Marksmen deal with most,' explained

Phoebe, offering a sympathetic smile in my direction. 'They basically look like mutated animals and they're completely disgusting. Some fly. Some don't. But they're purely instinct driven and way too stupid to work in big groups. They fight in pairs at most: one to distract and one to attack.'

'But they'd just as soon kill each other,' said Francis. 'As they would one of us.'

'Chimeras are completely different,' Phoebe continued. 'Which is why it's a good thing they're not so common. They're intelligent, cunning, and they have a basic humanoid shape, which makes them a lot more dangerous.'

'In other words,' said Brishen, fixing his eyes on me. 'Just like you.'

His words stung like a slap, and I sensed he was testing my reaction.

I didn't give him one.

Phoebe ignored him. 'I've never seen a chimera up close, but I've heard plenty of stories. My brother says they're a tough kill, but there's definitely no way a single creature could invade an Outcast clan and murder that many people.'

'Right,' replied Francis, rubbing his side. 'So basically, the Marksmen don't believe Boswell. They're convinced he's trying to cover-up some internal family feud.'

'But just to be sure,' said Brishen with a solemn expression. 'The council voted to send an escort back with Peter Boswell to North Carolina. They want to investigate, see if his claims are true.'

'And how's this for a bit of secretive information?' Francis leaned forward with a dramatic flair. 'Guess who Nicolas appointed to head up the little posse?'

A tingle ran down my spine. 'Who?'

'Quentin Marks.'

7. *Healing Wound*

I kept my face carefully blank. 'Oh, really?'

'Oh yeah,' Francis replied, looking smug. 'You can imagine that didn't go over very well with him. He argued with my father for at least an hour last night.'

No, I imagined Quentin Marks wasn't too happy about the situation at all: leaving a gargoyle whose guts he hated right in the middle of his Gypsy camp. I glanced around the pavilion. Phillipe and Stephan were nearby, as usual, keeping a shaded eye on me over their cups of coffee. 'Is anyone else going?' I asked, looking back to Francis.

Phoebe answered. 'My cousins Bruno and Daniel. But since Nicolas didn't want anything to seem out of the ordinary, my aunt and uncle are going, too. My aunt has a cousin who lives with the Boswell clan.'

Brishen shot Phoebe a warning glance. 'I don't really think everyone needs to know the Marks' business.'

By 'everyone,' I knew he meant me. But it didn't seem to make any difference to Phoebe, who kept talking as though she hadn't heard him.

'I wanted to go too, but Quentin said the group needed to stay small. He thinks I'm still too young for stuff like this.'

I studied her guardedly. 'So you're a Marksman, too.'

'Well, technically, that would be a Marks-*woman*, but no, I'm not. At least, not yet. There's a lot of training left to do. But I will be one day.' She smiled brightly. 'It's sort of in my family's job description.'

Francis tugged on one of Phoebe's curls. 'Ah, come on, you know you're really staying here just to hang out with me.'

The Gypsy girl slapped his hand away. 'Yeah, right.'

'Oh, just ask her out already, Francis,' sighed Zara. 'You know she'd say yes.'

Phoebe tossed a wadded up napkin at her. 'Stay out of it, Zara.'

'I *am* the fortune teller, remember. I know these things.'

Zara arched her brow meaningfully, and the others laughed. Even Brishen gave a smirk. But as the Gypsies around me fell back into conversation with each other, I looked away, my thoughts focused elsewhere.

If Nicolas was sending his head Marksman to North Carolina, he must be expecting trouble. I pictured the grotesque in my head. Was I ready to deal with more of those things if another incident occurred? Quentin didn't trust me, and I didn't know how much I trusted myself. I'd felt anything but stable since I'd arrived at the Circe de Romany. Sprouting a pair of massive wings didn't mean I'd turned into some kind of superhero.

'Hey, Sebastian, didn't you hear me?' Francis' voice snapped me from my thoughts.

'Hear what?'

'I asked you if you were coming with us tonight,' he said.

'And where would that be?'

Claire grinned at me from across the table. 'To town. We're all going to hang out tonight. You know, have a bit of fun before it gets really crazy around here.'

Zara leaned back and rolled her eyes. 'And by crazy, she means long hours and lots of work.'

'Hey, life of a traveling carnival,' said Francis. 'What can you do?'

'Enjoy one last evening of freedom,' Brishen replied.

Francis punched the other Gypsy firmly in the shoulder. 'That's exactly right. So you coming or not, Sebastian?'

'I don't think that's going to happen,' I chuckled, jutting my chin in the direction of the Marksmen across the pavilion. 'Quentin's guys watch my every move. It's as if they're just waiting to take me out if I breathe wrong.'

Phoebe grinned. 'Oh, don't worry about those two. I'll take care of them.'

'How?'

'I just need to have a word with my big brother,' she said. The curly-haired Gypsy stood from the table. 'Besides, it's not like you're capable of getting into too much trouble, not with all of us keeping an eye on you, right?'

A small smile tugged at the corner of my mouth. 'Still think I'm dangerous, huh?'

Zara leaned forward and cupped her chin daintily in her hand. 'Oh, I'm counting on it.'

My cheeks went hot, but my thoughts went to Josephine. Tonight – of all nights – Quentin would be sticking to her like glue. 'Well . . .'

As if reading my thoughts, Francis said in a pointed tone, 'With Quentin leaving in the morning, you know where he's going to be this evening. Here's your chance to get your mind off things, Sebastian. Remember what it's like to have fun.'

'I don't know,' I said warily. 'The whole going out in public thing isn't really possible for me.' I tugged on my hood. 'I tend to stand out.'

Zara stood up and walked behind my chair. She smelled of incense – rich and spicy. My nose twitched favorably. She placed her hands on my shoulders, and I couldn't stop the pleasant shiver than ran along my body. Her lips hovered close to my ear.

'You'll be with a group of Gypsies. We all tend to stand out.'

'It's not like we're going to parade you down Main Street or anything,' said Francis. 'Just a little drive, view the sights, maybe pull through a fast food place for a milkshake. You don't have to worry about anything, Sebastian. We'll keep you good and hidden, I promise.'

Claire shrugged. 'So, what do you say?'

A twinge of excitement pricked my nerves. 'Okay, I'm in.'

Phoebe clapped her hands. 'Great! I've gotta go help my family get packed and have a talk with brother-dearest. I'll see you guys tonight!'

'Around eight?' asked Francis. 'Right after dinner?'

'That's fine with me,' said Claire as she stood from the table. Brishen followed her lead. She smiled at me. 'It was good to meet you, Sebastian.'

'You, too.'

Brishen tipped his head at me, and the two left together. Phoebe waved and darted off in the direction of the trailers. As I started to wave back, Zara ran her hands down my shoulders to the lumps on my back. I tensed and bit my lip. But she only laughed and ruffled my hood playfully.

'Well, this should be fun,' she said in a cooing voice. 'I'll see you boys tonight.'

I watched her walk away, swaying her hips more than necessary, but definitely quite effectively.

'She likes you,' Francis chuckled.

I kept my eyes on her retreating figure. 'And why does that make me nervous?'

His chuckle turned into a full-blown laugh. 'Well, I've got load-in duty today, and we're behind. Lots of deadlines to meet. But I'll see you at dinner, okay?'

'Anything I can do?' I asked.

'Maybe later, Sebastian.'

'Sure, okay.'

The burly Gypsy walked off in the opposite direction, heading towards the larger tractor-trailer trucks on the outskirts of the caravan. I sat alone, feeling suddenly useless. Here I was in the Circe de Romany, eating their food and sleeping in their trailer, and I hadn't done anything to earn my keep.

A few women remained under the pavilion, cleaning up the mess. I gathered the leftover dinnerware and approached. I flashed what I hoped was a disarming smile underneath my hood –managing to keep most of my teeth hidden behind my lips – and held the dishes out. The Gypsy women stared at me for several seconds, caught somewhere between suspicion and fright. Finally, one took my offering.

'Thank you,' she murmured softly.

'Is there anything I can help you with?'

The woman's face softened. 'Well, actually, if you wouldn't mind taking the garbage out to the containers out behind the trucks . . .'

'Absolutely.'

She pointed to a couple of large bins, and then she suddenly blushed. She turned on her heel and quickly joined the other women who were piling the dishes into buckets. I shook my head – unsure if what had just happened was bad or good – but at least I had a task.

'Now *this* feels like home,' I said to myself as I tilted the bins onto their wheels and pulled them behind me.

The wheels bumped noisily over the gravel and dirt, attracting more than one glance from troupe members. I passed by a coop of chickens, and they squawked noisily at me, feathers scattering around their cage. It only took a couple of minutes to locate the containers and empty the bins. I was heading back to the pavilion when the grinding blender of ice switched on inside my stomach. Instinctively, I slipped behind a flatbed truck. From underneath the rig, I spotted two pairs of boots.

'Thank you, Karl,' I heard Quentin say. 'Your information will be useful.'

I hadn't planned to eavesdrop, but curiosity rooted me to the spot.

'Just be careful, Quentin,' Karl replied. 'If there are chimeras working together with grotesques to murder clan members, well, this could be a very serious problem. Chimeras are shrewd, and you know from experience their capacity for brutality. They're not like gargoyles. Gargoyles are protective creatures. They have souls.'

The Marksman gave a derisive snort. 'I don't care if they attend services on holy days and pray to every saint in the book. They're all the same to me.'

'Quentin, listen to—'

'Karl, I appreciate what you've told me, and your grandfather's knowledge will be an asset to us. But don't expect me to treat your fabled gargoyles any different from the rest of these shadow monsters. And that includes Nicolas' little pet, Sebastian Grey. One wrong move on his part, and I promise you, he'll end up just like the rest of them. A pile of rubble.'

Quentin stormed off, and I leaned against the side of the trailer, breathing heavily through my nose. Anger sparked up my spine. My vision hazed. I heard Karl's footsteps, and I grabbed him as he rounded the corner.

'Sebastian,' he choked. 'What are yo—'

'I'm tired of this, Karl,' I said between clenched teeth. The ice in my stomach turned to lava. 'I'm tired of Quentin's threats to end my existence every chance he gets!'

'And you're planning to do something about it, I take it?'

His remark caught me off guard. The haze cleared, and I realized I'd pinned him to the side of the trailer. 'I'm sorry, Karl,' I gasped, releasing him quickly. 'I don't know why I did that.' I took a cleansing breath and leaned against the metal, curling my claws into my palms. 'And no, I don't intend to try anything with Quentin. In case you've forgotten, I got my butt handed to me on a plate this morning.'

'That's only because you were weak with vitamin D, in case *you've* forgotten. If he'd confronted you on another occasion, things would've been different.' I stared at Karl in surprise, and he put his hand on my shoulder. 'You're stronger than you think you are, Sebastian, and Quentin knows that. That's part of why he feels so threatened. You'd be a match for him.'

I took several more deep breaths, forcing back the dark emotions swirling in my brain. 'I don't want to fight him, Karl. I just want him to leave me alone.'

'I'm not saying you should fight him,' Karl replied evenly. 'You both want the same thing, and that's to keep this clan safe. But you're going to have to find a way to channel this fierce energy of yours.'

I shook my head until my instincts finally released their grip and the weight lifted from my chest. 'How am I supposed to do that?'

'You need to hone your skills.' He regarded me intently. 'If you spent even half the time developing your abilities as you do fighting against them I think you'd be surprised at what you could accomplish. For example, how often do you fly?'

'Never.'

'And why not?'

'Because I don't want to.' I raked my hands through my hair as months of pent-up feelings seeped past my defenses. 'And the reason I fight it is because I'm scared I can't control it. Like what I did just now. Like it's going to take me over if I give in. I want to be normal, Karl. I don't want to be this . . . this *thing*.'

Karl folded his arms over his chest. There was something suddenly ancient about him. Much like there'd been something timeless about Josephine as I'd watched her dance. 'Fate doesn't ask our permission, Sebastian. You have a duty to fulfill now.'

'You sound like Ezzie.'

'Esmeralda Lucian is very wise.'

I had to agree. Though I knew only sketchy details of her past, there was wisdom within her that came from a lifetime of painful experiences – experiences she wanted me to steer away from.

'So now what?' I asked. 'Is this like the part in the superhero movies where you give me advice and show me how to develop my powers?'

'This isn't fantasy, Sebastian. This is your life.' His dark eyes grew serious. 'But if you're asking for my advice, I think you need to fully explore who you are. But you can't do that as long as you continue to hide from it.' He gestured to my hooded jacket. 'You're capable of more than you even realize.'

Fear clawed up my throat, choking my voice to a whisper. 'What if I don't want to know what I'm capable of?'

'Trying to suppress what makes you unique will only hurt you, not help you.' Karl gripped my shoulder. 'If you want to protect the Romanys, you're going to have to do more than just accept what you are. You're going to have to *embrace* it.'

I stared at my hands, the gray skin that still felt foreign to me, and the dark claws that used to be my fingernails. 'I know.'

'Come on, Sebastian,' said Karl, with kindness in his voice. 'Let's get those stitches out of your wing.'

My injury had healed nicely, and once Karl removed the diamond-encrusted thread from my wing, I felt even better. He left me with instructions to rest and to keep clear of activities around the camp. The troupe would be busy preparing for the opening of the Circe de Romany next week, and I would be – according to Karl – 'in the way'.

After waiting five minutes or so to make sure the old circus trainer left me to my own devices, I slipped out of my trailer. I appreciated Karl's concern, but any more resting was going to drive me insane. So I gave myself a task: finding out where to get a shower.

I located Francis, who was carrying a large packing crate across the center of the caravan. He laughed at my predicament and explained that none of the smaller trailers were equipped with bathrooms, but there was a communal trailer with a few showers and toilets on the other end of the camp.

'But all the riggers are fighting over the showers right now,' he said, shifting the weight of the crate to his other shoulder. 'Why don't you use ours?'

'I don't want to intrude.'

'No one's home right now,' Francis insisted. 'You'd have the place to yourself.'

I had to admit, the thought was much more pleasant than fighting with a bunch of irritated roadies over a shower stall. 'Okay, thanks.'

'No problem. The door's unlocked. Help yourself to everything.' He patted the crate. 'I've got to get these tent stakes over to Damien before he has a coronary.'

I rushed back to my trailer for my bag. Then I headed for the luxury recreational vehicle that the Romanys called home. I hesitated as I cracked open the front door. There was something almost forbidden about entering the living quarters of the Romany family. I'd only been inside their home once, back when Josephine had invited me to rehearse our parts for *A Midsummer Night's Dream*.

But this was different. I was about to leave watermarks on their rugs and dirty towels in the shower. It was an odd feeling. Finally, the need for decent personal hygiene won out, and I pulled open the door. Francis had been correct. The place was deserted.

I navigated through the space, noting once again the exotic decor and furniture. Something caught my eye, and I stopped abruptly. Sitting on a shelf behind one of the chairs was a small porcelain figurine in the shape of a dancing Gypsy woman. Her long hair, delicate arms, and bright skirt were frozen in a silent, graceful twirl.

It was the figurine I'd given Josephine for her birthday last autumn. She'd kept it, even after everything that had happened. I dropped my backpack on the rug and took the figurine in my hands, stroking the porcelain hair with my thumb. My chest tightened unexpectedly, and I returned the Gypsy to the shelf.

I found the bathroom and located a stack of neatly folded towels. I stripped down and unfastened the straps around my torso before cramming into the narrow shower. I barely fit, with my wings curled around my body like a cocoon, but the water managed to find my skin. I breathed a contented sigh and closed my eyes, letting warmth rush over me, feeling muscles in my back and wings finally relax.

The now-familiar gnawing in my stomach brought me back to reality. Time for food. Again. I quickly scrubbed myself clean and stepped out. The steam had left a filmy layer over the mirror. I used my hand to smear away the condensation on the glass so I could see my reflection. Charcoaled contours emphasized every flex of muscle under my gray skin as I leaned closer to the mirror.

There was nothing I could do to hide my slanted ears, which poked severely through layers of shaggy hair – hair the color of polished lead. Eerie silver eyes blinked back at me, and multiple points of jagged teeth protruded over my slate-stained lips as I frowned.

Karl's words returned to me, loud and clear.

You're going to have to do more than just accept who you are. You're going to have to embrace it.

'All right, I get it,' I murmured. 'I get it.'

Wrapping a thick burgundy towel around my waist, I turned to retrieve my clothes from my backpack. It was then I realized I'd left it on the floor of the living room. I folded my wings, making them as small as possible, and padded quietly down the hall. My bag was right where I'd left it. As I leaned down to pick it up, a sudden stirring – like a pleasant breeze – filled my senses. I snapped upright.

'No, please,' I whispered frantically. 'Not now.'

The front door swung open. I backpedaled, wings unfurling out of my control, but there was nowhere to go. Josephine's wide green eyes met mine.

'Sebastian!'

There was nothing I could do but stare back at her. Josephine looked me up and down. Her eyes swept across my wings and then to my chest. My heart threatened to break free from my rib cage, but I didn't move as her eyes continued to slowly pass over me. A sensation – strange and new – tingled along the back of my head.

Was she checking me out?

'I'm sorry,' I said, heat surging through my face. 'Francis gave me permission to shower here. I wasn't expecting anyone . . .'

'Yes, he told me,' she replied, and then she closed her mouth abruptly. Josephine's cheeks tinged pink. She cleared her throat. 'So, ah . . . how's your . . . injury?'

'Injury,' I repeated like a dumb parrot, my brain all fuzzy.

Josephine smiled and tentatively pointed toward my right wing. 'Yeah.'

'Oh.' I grinned sheepishly and ran a hand through my wet hair. 'It's fine.'

Her gaze searched my wing. 'You're right,' she said, sounding awed. She took a few steps closer. Her hand stretched out towards the section of membrane where the stitches had been. 'Do you mind if I . . . ?'

Everything had gone still. My wing expanded slightly, expectantly. I wanted Josephine's touch; wanted it more than anything. But in the space of one painful heartbeat, I knew I couldn't. To allow myself even that would be too much. I was a gargoyle – a gargoyle in love, maybe, but a gargoyle still. I wasn't meant for this. I wouldn't allow my feelings to get in the way of my duty. Karl was right. It was time I embraced what I was.

My wing snapped in before Josephine reached it.

Her face clouded. 'What is it, Sebastian?'

'I need to go.'

'I don't understand.'

I yanked up my backpack, and retreated behind the couch, slipping my jeans on quickly under the towel. My body quivered with embarrassment, and I couldn't look at her. 'I should leave before Quentin arrives. He'd think even less of me than he already does, and I can't afford that.' I couldn't throw my shirt on as easily, so I slung my backpack over my bare shoulder and hung the towel over the sofa. 'Thanks for letting me use your shower.'

I stepped past Josephine, leaving the door hanging open as I rushed out.

8. *Chained Freedom*

By the time I reached my trailer, I was shaky and starving. I ransacked my supplies until I located a bag of beef jerky. I sliced open the foil wrapper with my claw, trying to take my mind off Josephine and the way she'd looked at me. I felt like an idiot, and my nerves were fried. I chewed through several strips of beef, grinding them hard between my teeth. But neither my appetite nor my whirling head was completely satisfied. I glanced around the room, searching for a distraction. My cell phone blinked back at me from the bookshelf.

I curled up on the narrow cot and managed to scroll through voicemails and messages while I ate. They were all from Hugo and Katie. I responded to my brother's first. It was obvious by his short texts that he was trying to leave me alone but, at the same time, I could tell he was concerned. It took several frustrating minutes to tap out a short reply – using the side of my finger instead of my claw – letting him know things were fine at the Circe, and Karl was keeping an eye on me.

I listened to Katie's messages next. She was going to New

York to visit her dad for a couple of weeks. I braced myself and called her back, but only got her voicemail, so I left a lighthearted message complaining about my boring summer out of town with Hugo's family. I wished her a good trip, told her that I had sketchy cell service, and promised we'd talk when I got home. Then I switched off my phone, feeling heavy with guilt.

The next few hours crawled by. I skipped lunch, my embarrassment over what had happened with Josephine winning out over my uncomfortable hunger, but I polished off the rest of the jerky to appease my throbbing teeth and growling stomach. Suddenly, there was a knock at the door.

'Hey, Sebastian, let's go!' called Francis from outside.

I wiped the last of my snack from my lips and this time remembered to pull my hood low over my head before answering the door. 'Where are we going?'

'Into town, remember?' said Francis, staring into the shadows of my face and grinning broadly. 'I hope you don't mind skipping dinner here. Alcie's making borscht.' He made a gagging motion with his hand. 'Not my thing.'

Though I'd never had the Russian stew, I decided it wasn't my thing either. 'Oh, yeah, I'd forgotten about going out.'

'You're still coming, right? I know Zara would be very disappointed if you didn't.'

He took off before I could comment. I closed the door behind me. An evening out was probably what I needed – a distraction to level my rocking emotions and occupy my attention for a while. I squared my shoulders, determined to make the most of Francis' invitation.

I caught sight of Phillipe leaning against the trailer next to mine. The Marksmen made no attempt to stop me – which I attributed to Phoebe – but he shot me a nasty look as I passed. I flashed my teeth in reply. Judging by his reaction, my expression was fiercer than I'd intended. My snarl melted into a smile. I was feeling better and better about this outing.

We met Francis' friends near the front gate, gathered around an old blue pickup truck that reminded me of the one Hugo liked to drive. Brishen nodded curtly at me and climbed in behind the wheel.

'Come on, guys,' said Phoebe, waving us over. 'We don't have all night.'

'Thanks,' I said as we reached the truck. 'You know, for springing me from the coop.'

Phoebe looked pleased. 'Anytime.'

Zara opened the passenger door. 'I'm calling shotgun. The wind does a number on my hair.'

'Scoot over,' said Claire, piling in beside her.

I glanced at Francis. 'So, banished to the back, eh?'

He helped Phoebe into the bed of the truck. 'Well, somebody's got to keep an eye on the gargoyle, right?'

I chuckled and leapt over the side, landing in the middle of the bed. Francis' eyes widened appreciatively at my jump. 'I'll try and behave.'

Phoebe slid a hair tie from her wrist and piled her curls atop her head. 'Well, no offense Sebastian, but I totally get dibs on the front on the way home.'

I settled into a comfortable position in the corner as Brishen cranked the truck and sped through the iron gates. The summer evening breeze was cool against my skin, and I closed my eyes, enjoying being outside the walls of the Circe de Romany. Scents filtered through my nostrils – stronger and with more clarity. I inhaled deeply, concentrating on each one, trying to replace Josephine's ever-lingering signature.

But as we crossed the Sutallee Bridge, memories of my fight with Anya and the other gargoyles awakened. My eyes snapped open, and I stared past the churning water, reliving those horrific moments: the pain tearing through me; the agonizing shock of my transformation. Muscles tensed along my shoulders. My wings quivered against the straps as I remembered flying – the only time I'd done it. I felt the sickening fear when I thought I wouldn't be able to save Josephine.

'You all right, Sebastian?' asked Phoebe.

I clutched the side of the truck and jerked my focus from the bridge. The memories skittered back into the dark of my mind. I nodded. 'It's been a while since I've had this much freedom. Just taking it all in, I guess.'

Francis leaned forward and rubbed his hands together. 'Well then, I say that calls for some fast food. We'd better feed that bottomless pit of a stomach of yours. And I've been craving a good hamburger for weeks!'

It was crazy how just the mention of food made my mouth water. Images of grilled meat flashed before my eyes, and I licked my lips. 'If you're not a fan of Alcie's cooking, why don't you eat in town more?'

Francis' eyebrows shot up. 'And taint our reputation? No way. An occasional evening out among the *gadje* is enough.'

I studied him carefully. 'You don't care much for the non-Roma, do you?'

'It's not that,' he replied, waving his hand dismissively. 'We get along fine with outsiders. We just don't like them in our business.'

'But you and Josephine went to public school.'

'It's a generational thing. Most of the younger Gypsies tend to be a little more lenient with our interactions. Plus, me and my sister hated homeschooling. It was boring.'

I glanced at Phoebe. 'Why didn't you attend school when the Circe was here before?'

'I don't like getting involved with anything outside the Circe,' she replied, making a face. 'It's much easier that way. But an evening out every now and then isn't a bad thing, either!'

My lips twitched into a smirk. 'And how do your parents feel about you hanging around with *gadje*?'

Phoebe shrugged. 'About the same as they feel about us hanging out with gargoyles.'

Francis convinced Brishen to make a quick stop at the Burger Shack. I didn't like being so close to normal civilization, but my teeth were aching for food – like needles stuck in my gums – and my stomach wouldn't shut up. I huddled in the corner of the truck, my head low and my lumpy back pressed against the metal side. At least the sun had finally set, so I knew my face was lost in the shadows of my hood.

Zara passed us bags of food through the sliding window of the truck, and I set to work devouring my triple order of hamburgers. 'I like a man with a healthy appetite,' she said, smiling at me through the opening. I was too hungry to be embarrassed.

As we passed through town, my two worlds came into sharp focus. Like the fence that separated me from the graduation party, my new life separated me from the people and places I'd known before. Last year, I could've walked down the streets, eaten in the diner, met Avery at the bookstore or grabbed a coffee with Katie. I swallowed hard. The last bite of hamburger didn't go down so well.

Sixes was like a foreign country to me now.

I caught Phoebe peering at me over her milkshake. She

averted her gaze quickly. I crumpled the food wrappers and brushed my hands against my jeans. When I scooted closer, she looked up in surprise.

'I wanted to say thanks,' I said.

She regarded me curiously. 'I told you, convincing my brother to let you come was no big deal. I think the Marksmen were glad to be rid of you for a while.'

I laughed. 'I wasn't talking about that, but you're right. I'm sure their lives are way easier without me around.' I pressed my lumpy back against the side of the truck and pulled my knees to my chest. 'I actually meant thanks for accepting me. I know how most of your troupe feels about me, so it means a lot. Really.' The downtown shops whizzed by: shops I'd frequented in the past. 'I've missed hanging out with people since all this happened.'

Phoebe's eyes darkened with understanding, and she shifted her body, looking suddenly awkward. She twirled a curl of hair that had come loose from her bun. 'Oh, that's right. I forgot. You weren't always . . . I mean, you didn't used to be like this.'

'No,' I replied, breathing through the lump of emotion in my chest until it eased. 'Granted, my friends used to say I was a little weird, but I definitely didn't look like I was on my way to a Halloween party.'

'And this was because of Josephine,' began Phoebe, but Francis grabbed her elbow with a sharp shake of his head.

'No,' I said, my voice harsher than I'd intended. Phoebe shrank back. I cleared my throat before speaking again, softer this time. 'I mean, in a way, yes. But she didn't cause it.' I tugged at the collar of my shirt. What had happened to the breeze? The air was hot, stifling. It was giving me a headache. 'It wasn't her fault.'

'But you guys are, like, connected somehow, aren't you?' asked Francis with a skeptical expression on his tanned face.

I blinked hard, several times. Francis and Phoebe seemed to be drifting away, growing more distant, like I was staring through a funnel and they were on the small end. 'Yeah,' I replied absently. The hamburgers felt unsettled in my stomach. A trickle of sweat ran down the side of my face, and I brushed it away. 'I think so, anyway. It's hard to explain.'

'But the whole tattoo thing set stuff in motion, right?'

'Yeah, I guess.' I pressed the edge of my palm against my temple and winced. It hurt like someone was drilling on the inside of my skull. I scrunched my face and tried to shrug off the pain. 'I . . . I don't know.'

'Hey man,' I heard Francis say. 'You don't look so good.'

My skin buzzed. Adrenaline pounded – my heart, my veins exploded with it. A rush of instincts tidal waved through me. And suddenly, I knew.

'Stop the truck,' I growled.

'Wha—'

'Something's happened to Josephine!'

'Calm down, Sebastian.' Francis frowned at me across the bed of the truck. 'I'm sure Josie's fine.'

'No,' I shot back, my voice gravelly. I dug my claws into the metal with a harsh screech. 'I have to get to the Circe. Right now.'

'Someone would've called me if something was wrong,' he replied. 'I'm her brother.'

Somewhere in my hazy mind, I knew his answer was logical.

But it didn't matter.

My actions were no longer my own. Red coated my

vision. I sprang from the moving truck and hit the pavement, rolling on my side to take the impact, and came up on all fours. What I'd just done was stuntman impressive, but there wasn't time to dwell on it. I raced across the road, dodging an oncoming car. Its horn blared after me.

Francis yelled my name, but I didn't look back. I leapt up the curb and away from the traffic of the street.

Josephine!

My instincts screamed her name. My senses wailed like warning sirens. I had to get to her. I bolted through a yard and hurtled the hedge of shrubbery in my path. Scenery blazed by me, but it wasn't fast enough. My jacket slowed me down. I stripped it off and flung it aside. My wings fought against their straps, demanding freedom.

I hit the woods and ran until the gates of the Fairgrounds loomed above me. Once, I'd needed a tree to help me over the fence. Not anymore. I pushed off the ground with all my strength and surged towards the bars. I scaled the iron, catapulting myself over the top. I landed lightly on the other side.

My blood pumped stronger, crystalizing everything around me. Lights flickered inside trailers. Gypsies milled outside. I felt the icy presence of Marksmen nearby, making their rounds. All seemed ordinary. But there was a foul smell on the air, one that prickled the hair along the back of my neck. A fierce growl rumbled in my chest.

Instincts screeched at me again. My gargoyle radar honed in on Josephine immediately, and I shot through the camp like lightning. I snarled in frustration and fury as I closed the distance between us.

Why had I left the Circe?

Why had I left her?

My senses led me away from the Romany trailer, through a narrow alley of campers. Gypsies lurched out of my way as I thundered by. I didn't care. In moments, I found myself outside Karl Corsi's motor home. She was inside. I burst through the door.

And I immediately skidded to a halt.

Josephine wasn't the only one in the trailer. Nicolas whirled around at my entrance, and Sabina gasped. A muscular man near the door stepped menacingly in my direction. I clung to the doorframe, fighting the pounding inside my skull. I blinked several times, struggling to reconcile what I felt with what I saw.

Josephine sat on a small cot. Karl knelt in front of her, holding an icepack on her knee while Quentin held her hand. I felt suddenly like an intruder in the small room, with all eyes on me, except hers.

'Josephine,' I said, gulping down the wild emotions still trying to claw their way up my throat. 'Are you all right?'

Quentin's face went instantly dark. 'She's fine,' he replied lowly. 'And you can go back to whatever you were doing. This isn't a guardian matter.'

He used my apparent title like he was flinging a curse. I smothered a growl. My body was on fire. I couldn't make sense of things. 'She was in danger,' I said, hearing my own uncertainty under the thickness of my voice. I gripped the doorframe so hard I felt my claws sink into the wood.

'She was practicing her act for the show,' said Quentin in a threatening tone. 'She was never in any danger. I always make sure of that.'

'It's just a strain,' said Karl, finishing his work. 'She needs to keep off it for the rest of the night and apply some ice for the swelling.'

'Thank God,' Sabina breathed, seating herself next to her daughter. 'You scared me half to death, Josephine.'

'You weren't the only one,' said the muscular man – Josephine's partner, Andre, I assumed. He shot a disgusted look in my direction.

Sabina stroked Josephine's hair. 'The next time you want to attempt a new routine, please inform your partner, at least.'

Josephine had neither spoken to me nor met my gaze since I'd stormed in. Something wasn't right. My heart thrummed unevenly against my ribs. I shoved my hands against my pounding temples. What was going on? What was happening to me?

Karl patted Josephine's shoulder. 'Take something for the pain if you need to, Josie, but you should be on your feet in a day or two.'

Quentin helped her stand. She gripped his shoulder, her hair falling over her face, hiding her expression from me. She winced as her foot touched the floor, and I started forward automatically.

Quentin halted me with a glare. 'Like I said, *Sebastian*, she doesn't require your assistance.'

My stomach clenched. If Josephine was okay – and she certainly seemed to be – then why was I still feeling like this? Just when I was starting to trust my freakish instincts, they turned out to be unreliable. Quentin's eyes were hard on me, and I backed away, embarrassed by my explosive intrusion. I turned quickly and left without a word.

9. *Blinding Darkness*

Francis and the others were waiting outside. He caught my shoulder as I passed. 'What's going on, Sebastian? Is everything okay?'

I shrugged out of his grasp. 'Your sister strained her knee. She's fine. Everything's fine.' I pushed past the Gypsies, ignoring their gaping stares. I ground my teeth, breathing hard. The lights from Brishen's still-running truck blinded me as I passed. Francis jogged to my side.

'What hap—'

'I said everything's fine!' I snarled, cutting him off. Francis pulled up short, his face going tense. The other Gypsies hovered behind him with wary expressions. I clenched my hands into fists, choking down a bite of bitter emotion. 'I'm sorry. I didn't mean to snap like that. I just . . . I don't know what's wrong with me.'

I whirled on my heel and stomped off.

A warm breeze whipped my hair across my eyes. I reached for my hood before remembering I'd discarded my jacket in the woods on my wild run to the Fairgrounds. I shoved my hair back and kept walking, glaring helplessly into the night sky. My chest tightened with guilt and anger.

I'd come to the Circe to help the Romany family, not go traipsing around town. Instead, I'd given in to the selfish, helpless desperation steadily building inside me since I'd arrived. Questions poisoned every thought. What good was I doing here, and what was the point?

What was the point of *me*?

I couldn't prevent my charge from a knee injury; what made me think I could protect her from a real threat? I couldn't even rely on my instincts. I'd been so convinced that there was some terrifying danger in the Romany camp that I'd nearly killed myself getting back to the Fairgrounds.

I clawed at my chest, striving to quench the wild churning within. I didn't know what to do with the fury raging through me. I was angry that I'd left the Circe. I was angry for trusting my gargoyle warning radar, only to have it steer me wrong. And I was angry for having this stupid pity fest in my head. What kind of guardian was I?

I cleared a narrow alley formed by two rows of campers. The grounds were devoid of people, but lights shone in all the windows of the caravan. Stars peaked through the canvas of heavy trees populating the Fairgrounds. As I ducked under a string of laundry; a putrid stench burned my nostrils.

Not a gargoyle.

I fought through my gag reflex to take another whiff.

Not a grotesque, either. That scent was burned into my brain since the attack on Peter Boswell. But I'd smelled this stench before. I was sure of it now. My pace slowed. I'd smelled it on the way to the graduation party.

I heard flapping in the darkness above me: a weird, sickening sound. My stomach clogged with ice. A shadow passed across my face, and without warning, a large mass landed in front of me, and dust and gravel littered the air. Gigantic leathery wings obscured the sky. I recoiled in horror. My warning radar hadn't malfunctioned after all.

A hideous, deformed creature lumbered toward me. Muscles rippled beneath skin as gray and cracked as old pavement. Bones protruded like weapons. It walked upright, and its basic features were like a man's, but the head was lined with deep fissures harboring a face that was more animal than human – with wicked teeth, spiked horns, and a bulging forehead. Eyes without pupils or irises gleamed solid silver as they fixed on me.

It was the face I'd seen in my bedroom window.

The hairs on the back of my neck stood at attention as our eyes met. As animalistic as the figure appeared, the expression on its face was wickedly intelligent. My head buzzed with static, and a voice seared my brain like acid.

You . . .

Somewhere in a distant corner of my brain, facts began drawing themselves together. I'd encountered this creature before, but as more than a face outside a rain-splattered window or a nasty scent on the forest trail. I studied the square jaw and the crook of the smirk running over its blackened lips.

Clarity clicked into place.

'Thaddeus?'

The creature cracked a smile that turned my stomach sour. Thaddeus had been one of the gargoyles under Augustine's command. I'd fought him and Matthias on the scaffolding of the Big Tent during Josephine's performance. I could still feel the sting of the diamond knife as it sliced my palm. But the monster advancing slowly towards me wasn't the Thaddeus I remembered. His appearance – like the other two gargoyles – had once matched what I stared at in the mirror every morning. But not anymore.

He'd changed.

The thing that used to be Thaddeus screeched. I dropped into a crouch, and the hair rose along my scalp. My brain crackled with static.

Miss me . . .

The voice was harsh, and the words felt forced, as if it took the entire creature's energy to communicate them to me. To communicate.

I'd heard the same voice last night at the bonfire. That's why I'd had difficulty pinpointing the scent. It wasn't the grotesque that had spoken. It was Thaddeus. He'd been there, too; at least, at the beginning of it all. Sweat dripped down my back as I looked into the terrifying face, saw the cunning in the solid eyes and the brutal coldness in the expression.

Adrenaline raced through my blood, and my body tightened in response. I snarled, baring my teeth. 'What do you want?'

A wicked smile lit its nasty face.

Hungry . . .

The creature licked his lips with a sickening, sloshing sound. My stomach threated a revolt. Thaddeus didn't have to say more. I knew he wasn't talking about grilled hamburgers.

'Kitchen's closed tonight,' I hissed. 'But I'm sure you can find some nice rats to feed on in the woods.'

He threw his head back, exposing hideous fangs as he laughed. The teeth oozed with an oily substance that ran over his lips and dripped from his chin. He sniffed the air; eyes without pupils gleamed with primal intensity.

Want . . . Gypsy . . . flesh . . .

My wings strained harder, pulling the nylon straps taut against my chest, making it difficult to breathe. I planted my feet and met his glare. 'Leave.' I panted against the surge of instincts flooding my head. 'Now.'

His inhuman eyes flicked to my wrist. Then, with a movement too fast for me to counter, he grabbed my arm. His massive talons scraped over the skin of my dandelion tattoo. His foul smile widened.

How . . . will . . . she . . . taste . . .

We were in each other's faces like rabid dogs: circling, snarling. My vision blurred the more I tried to focus. My insides felt like they were ripping apart. Thaddeus made the first move. With a speed that stole my breath, he hurled me to the ground. The force rattled my skull as the creature's weight crushed air from my lungs.

Talons struck my face. The pain released fury, which detonated in my veins. I slammed my forehead against the bridge of his nose. The creature screeched. It jerked me to my feet, tearing my shirt, and flung me through the air like a rag doll.

I nailed the corner of a trailer. The metal crumpled. I ricocheted to the ground, tasting dirt. I heard another shriek, and I rolled violently to the side, dodging the massive talons. My fist cracked across his jaw. The creature skittered over the ground with more force than I expected. Its body left a deep groove in the gravel. I lunged, but its wing smashed into me like a wall of iron. Blackness and stars swirled my vision. Another hit knocked me into orbit. I saw the glass of the trailer window. I threw my hands up protectively. Glass shattered. My body crashed to the ground.

Everything hurt. I curled into myself, head in the dirt,

my body shaking. I clutched at gravel, crushing it in my hands in an attempt to hold myself together. My lips pulled away from my teeth. I had to focus, to think, but I couldn't. I was losing it.

'No,' I pleaded. 'Please . . . no . . .'

I gasped for air, suddenly drowning in the instincts that clawed up my throat, ripping me apart. I was slipping away, and there was no holding on – not this time. My teeth ached. My eyes burned. I heard a wild roar, felt it reverberate through my bones. It was mine. My wings snapped their nylon straps.

My vision went red.

Instinct consumed me. Drove me. Infected me like poison. I was helpless to stop it, and unwilling to try. I was free. All that remained was motion, borne of pure adrenaline. I felt every movement, every blow and excruciating pain. But my world was only a swirl of red and black, a rush of senses. Primal rage and animal fury.

At some point, I became aware of men shouting. The haze around me cleared. I returned to myself. My mouth tasted like gravel, and something warm and sticky trickled down my chin. Fierce growls echoed in my ears. With a sudden jolt, I realized the sounds were coming from me. My world snapped into focus.

I was on the ground, crouched over the stone corpse of the creature. Its grotesque face was frozen in an expression of gut-wrenching pain, and its stretched neck looked mutilated, as though someone had taken a pick and cut chunks from the stone. Around the body, purplish-black blood pooled and coagulated. I wiped my mouth. My hand came back covered with the same blood. It ran down my neck and under my shirt. My throat stung with nausea.

What had I done?

Dark shadows moved over the ground. Nicolas stood over me, Phillipe and Stephan at his side. 'Dear God,' he whispered.

I staggered to my feet, swaying under the effects of adrenaline and instinct. The Marksmen trained their bows on me. I raised my hands defensively. 'Came out of nowhere.' My voice remained thick and growly. Not quite my own. 'He attacked.'

My legs buckled, threatening to give way as Nicolas waved the Marksmen back and knelt beside the stone corpse. Its blood had dried and turned to black dust. Nicolas looked steadily at me. 'I know, Sebastian,' he said. 'We saw you kill it.'

I wiped at my lips again, brushing off the now powdered blood. I could still taste gravel in my mouth. I turned away from the body, feeling sick. 'No,' I whispered, my voice cracking. 'I . . . I didn't mean to. It . . . attacked me, and then I . . . I don't know what happened.'

Nicolas continued on as though I hadn't spoken at all. 'I knew my faith in you had not been misplaced. Well done.'

'But I—'

The sentence died in my mouth. I didn't know what to say. What I'd done to Thaddeus – or *how* I'd done it – was sketchy in my mind, like fragments of a nightmare. Aftershocks of adrenaline rumbled through my body, making me lightheaded. I clenched my fists against my high-strung impulses and tried to breathe.

Nicolas pointed to Phillipe. 'Clean this up.'

The Marksman pulled a pouch from his pocket, and sprinkled a sparkling powder over the corpse. The stone figure cracked and crumbled, then turned to dust. The wind caught the remnants, and soon, nothing remained of the shadow creature. I stared at the empty ground, a heavy weight pressing on my chest. Would my death look like this? Would my ashes disappear with the wind as though I'd never existed at all?

'I'll inform Quentin,' said the Marksman as he slipped the pouch into his pocket.

Nicolas' expression turned stern. 'No. You will tell him nothing of this.'

'But sir,' Phillipe protested. 'A chimera infiltrated our camp.'

My breath caught like jagged glass in my throat. I stared at the spot where Thaddeus' body had been just moments before. A chimera? How was that possible? It was Thaddeus. I tried to speak, but my mouth felt full of sand.

'The chimera is dead, thanks to our gargoyle,' said Nicolas. 'I will speak to Quentin myself about this incident.'

Phillipe nodded. 'I'll round up the dogs, and we'll do a perimeter sweep of the camp. Make sure no more of the beasts are lurking about.'

Nicolas turned to me, and I saw the question on his face. I sighed and closed my eyes, sniffing the air, letting my instincts give the answer he sought. The putrid stench was gone. I shook my head.

'Good,' said Nicolas.

But the Marksmen didn't put their weapons away.

'If you don't mind,' said Stephan. 'I'd rather use our own resources.'

Nicolas waved his hand. 'Yes, of course. Go ahead.'

The Marksmen dipped their heads and sprinted across the caravan. As soon as they were gone, I sank to my knees. My head felt like it was splitting open, and I reached up to rub my temples. My hands encountered something hard, protruding from my skull. I sucked in a sharp breath. Nicolas' eyes drifted to my forehead.

'Karl,' he commanded.

I glanced up, unaware that Karl had been standing a few yards away, watching the scene. The circus trainer approached and smiled with a doctor's disarming demeanor. 'May I?' he asked. I nodded. Karl took my chin in his hand, tilting my head from side to side. 'The scratches shouldn't take long to heal,' he said. I winced, remembering the way the creature had sliced at my face. 'That was some impressive fight, Sebastian.'

'I don't remember much of it.'

'Probably for the best,' he replied, glancing over his shoulder briefly to where Thaddeus' body had been. 'As you develop your skills, you'll learn better control. But your protective nature will ultimately always take charge.' Karl's gaze shifted to my temples. 'As to these, well, I imagine tonight's events must have brought them on.'

I stared at him, confused. 'Brought what on?'

Karl reached up, his fingers wrapping around something just over my right temple. 'This,' he said simply, and he gave a small tug. My head snapped forward in tandem.

I swallowed hard. 'It's what I think it is, isn't it?'

Karl's expression said it all. I rose and stepped past him to the trailer window – the only one I *hadn't* smashed with my durable gargoyle hide. I peered at my reflection in the moonlight. Two horns protruded from my skull, just above my temples. Each was roughly the length of my thumb but twice as thick, twisted with black spirals, and curling into my hair.

'Well,' I said. 'It looks like my modeling career for *Gargoyle Weekly* is really going to take off now.'

The circus trainer suppressed a gentle laugh.

Nicolas approached, his green eyes glinting with firm determination. 'I'm going to speak with Quentin,' he said. 'Sebastian, I'd like you to meet me in my trailer in half an hour.' Nicolas looked past me. 'And Karl, I want you there as well.'

'Of course,' he replied.

Nicolas disappeared behind the trailer.

Karl put a comforting hand on my shoulder. 'Well, Sebastian,' he said, looking me over. My jeans were filthy, my shirt bloodstained. The remains of my nylon straps hung limply from my shoulders. 'Let's get you back to your trailer. I think you're going to need a change of clothes.'

Twenty minutes later – after I'd cleaned up and Karl treated the scratches on my face – he and I were on our way to the Romany's trailer. I'd left the nylon straps behind, and my gargantuan wings were hanging freely behind me. I ran my fingers absently across my shirt. It felt strange to be without my bindings. But there was no point in trying to hide from the Gypsies anymore.

Or from myself.

We strolled in silence for a while. I flexed my wings hesitantly, getting used to the new freedom. They seemed larger than they were before the fight. I curled and uncurled them, like flexing my arms with weights. The muscles felt more developed, and my mastery over them was better. I sensed Karl watching me, his presence calming, unthreatening.

'So, how are you feeling, Sebastian?' he asked after a few moments.

'Karl, I *killed* someone tonight.'

He pulled up abruptly, staring hard into my face. 'No, Sebastian. *That* was not a person. It was a chimera, an evil abomination.'

I'd washed away the taste of gravel from my mouth, but my stomach remained nauseous, and guilt and dread churned together like a bad meal. I glanced back to the clearing where we'd fought. 'He didn't used to be.'

'What do you mean?'

I shuddered, feeling suddenly cold. 'He was at the bonfire last night. I never saw him, but I heard his voice in my head. At first, I thought it was the grotesque talking, but all I felt from it were primal emotions – no logical thoughts. The voice was different, and I recognized it. I just didn't know from where until tonight.'

'So the legends are true,' said Karl. 'Shadowen do communicate telepathically.'

'Yeah, I guess so,' I replied, my throat tight. 'But the point is . . . I *knew* him, Karl. He was with Augustine, when they first tried to recruit me. This wasn't some mindless killer. His name was Thaddeus, and he was a gargoyle once.'

'One of Augustine's gargoyles?' questioned Karl, his wrinkled face darkening. 'No, that's impossible. As I told you before, gargoyles and chimeras are two completely different kinds of shadowen. You share no more in common with them than you do those vermin grotesques.'

'Yeah? Then how do you explain him? The last time I saw Thaddeus he looked like me. How do you know we're different?'

'Sebastian . . .'

'I just sprouted horns, Karl,' I continued, shaking my head fiercely. 'Not to mention the fact that I'm trying to break the world record for longest wingspan. The list of differences is getting pretty short.' I stared at the ground. 'You said yourself that shadowen knowledge is sketchy. What if you're wrong? What if we're all the same?'

'Listen to me.' Karl grasped my shoulder. His grip was strong, as though he was determined to hold me together, to make me understand. 'A few physical changes don't mean you have anything in common with that thing. Chimeras were created as weapons, used during the dark times when our people sought power, even at the price of their own blood. They are savage brutes – killers bent on revenge. Gargoyles fought against them. They saved us from ourselves.' He placed his other hand on my opposite shoulder and turned me to face him. 'The chimera is an animal. Its instincts are driven by primal desires. Yours are borne out of protection and duty. There's humanity within the gargoyle. And that makes you different.'

'But I can't focus my instincts half the time!' I growled, pulling free from his grasp. 'I feel like I'm all over the place. My emotions are on a constant roller coaster. My senses are all screwed up. When does it end, Karl?'

He studied my features carefully. 'When you embrace your changes, Sebastian.'

'You don't understand, Karl,' I countered, my voice desperate. 'Tonight, something inside me snapped. I couldn't control it and . . . and a part of me didn't *want* to control it.' I buried my face in my hands. 'I don't know what happened to Thaddeus, how he changed into that thing. But he *was* a gargoyle once. If he wasn't a person, then what does that make me?'

The circus trainer fell silent. The quiet spoke volumes.

The Romany trailer loomed against the night sky, its painted dandelion logo dull in the dim light. Karl entered first, and I followed, my shoulders hunched under more than just the weight of my wings.

The Romany family was waiting on us. Nicolas and Sabina sat on the couch while Francis lounged on the floor flipping through television channels. Josephine reclined in a chair, her leg propped and a pack of ice on her knee. My head tingled with pleasure and pain at the sight of her.

'Please, have a seat,' said Nicolas as we walked in.

Two high backed chairs had been brought in from the kitchen. Karl sat in one, but I looked doubtfully at the other. Unless I straddled it backwards, there was no way I could fit with my bulky wings. I glanced sideways at Josephine, but she still refused to meet my gaze.

'I'll just stand, if that's all right,' I said.

Nicolas frowned a moment, then understood my predicament. 'Yes, yes. Of course.'

Sabina poured a cup of hot tea from a pot and handed it to Karl. 'Would you care for some?' she asked me. Her eyes roamed my face, but to her credit, her reaction was no more than a slight widening of her eyes.

It was like I was a stray they'd picked up on the side of the road, and they were feeling me out, trying to see how tame I was. 'Yes, please,' I answered, trying my best to look *un*dangerous.

Sabina poured another cup and handed it to me. I took her offering with a grateful nod and set it on the table beside me. Francis switched off the television. His face was uncharacteristically somber. I shifted closer to the wall, maintaining as much distance as I could without leaving the room. I was grateful for the soft glow of a single lamp. The shadows were comforting.

Nicolas clasped his hands together and focused on Karl.

'Quentin is leaving tonight with several of our Marksmen. They will be escorting Peter Boswell back to his clan in North Carolina.'

Karl sipped his tea. 'Is there some reason for the change in plans? I thought the party was scheduled to leave first thing in the morning.'

'They were,' Nicolas replied, 'but because of the incident tonight, I think it's wise to send them early. I won't allow Peter Boswell's presence to put our troupe in any additional danger. But I promised him sanctuary, so we will ensure his safe return home.'

'So you informed Quentin of the chimera,' said Karl.

The *bandoleer* shook his head. 'No. I've told him nothing. I need my most experienced Marksman focused on his task. If Quentin were aware of this incident, he would insist on staying behind, and he'd put the Marksmen on high alert. That's not what I want right now.'

My face remained blank, but my head buzzed at Nicolas' declaration.

Francis stretched his legs under the coffee table. 'Isn't that what the Marksmen are supposed to do? After all, protecting the clan is their family occupation.'

Nicolas walked to the window and pushed aside the curtain. He glanced outside then drew it closed again. 'That's exactly what Quentin is doing. Escorting Peter under my orders *is* protecting the clan. I need to know exactly what's happening with the others in our *kumpania* up north.'

'I can tell you that,' huffed Francis. 'It's called the Boswells running their mouths off and making enemies.'

'It's more than that,' Nicolas said ominously. 'You know we've been hearing rumors, son. Unexplained murders.

Mercenaries running loose. Combined shadowen attacks. There are several Outcast clans dealing with the same thing.'

'Yeah, and look at us,' Francis shot back. 'The proud Romanys just keep running. We're the head clan, and we're running from freaking rumors, dad. Moving from town to town, avoiding everybody. I don't get it. Why don't we just take a stand?'

Nicolas' face tightened, his eyes glinting in a way that made my wings shudder against the wall. 'We haven't had the resources in the past, Francis. But things are changing.' His gaze fell meaningfully on me. 'After what I witnessed tonight, I'm convinced that my decision to bring the gargoyle here was the right one.'

Josephine took a shallow breath. To me, it sounded as loud as a gasp. My eyes flicked to her, but she turned away.

'I don't understand,' I said, keeping my voice deliberately soft. My words brought the instant unwanted attention of multiple stares, but I forced myself to continue. 'If the Marksmen's job is to protect the clan, and I'm here for the same reason, shouldn't we be working together?'

'You *are* working together,' Nicolas replied.

'How is that, exactly?'

The *bandoleer* poured a cup of tea. He dumped a spoonful of sugar into his cup and stirred as he talked. 'The Marks family has pledged themselves to the safety of all the Outcast clans. Quite a daunting task, but one in which they've excelled over the decades. Quentin has put Phillipe and Stephan in charge while he is gone, and the Marksmen will continue to look after the Circe.'

'And as for me?'

Nicolas took a long drink. 'You have another duty.'

'Which is?' I asked with some caution.

Nicolas crossed the living room, this time to Josephine's chair. 'The Romanys haven't had a guardian living among us since the time of my great-grandfather and, with the exception of Karl, most of what we know comes from old tales and legends. But there is one thing I'm certain of,' his hand moved to his daughter's shoulder, and I followed the movement, feeling a strange stirring inside me, 'you were branded, and Josephine's *scalv* sealed you together. I'm not expecting you to single-handedly protect this clan, or even my family. But I do expect you to protect my daughter. Josephine is your charge.'

My heart crashed so hard against my ribs that I was sure one was going to break. 'Protect her from what?'

My question seemed to spark something inside the Romany leader. He pointed at me, his eyes hard as concrete. 'That's not your concern, gargoyle.'

Sabina stood quickly. 'You've heard the rumors, Sebastian. The Boswells are a head family; so are we. Which means these threats could be aimed at us as well.' She stole a sideways glance at her husband with an expression I didn't understand. 'There must be a reason that our daughter was set apart to have a guardian. We can't ignore that.'

Nicolas' demeanor was calm once more, but his eyes held their fire as they remained on me. 'I'm ordering you to stay with Josephine at all times. She is your top priority, and I'm entrusting you with her life.'

I found it difficult to take a breath. 'And Quentin?'

Josephine's luminous eyes met mine for the first time.

'Would not understand,' she finished quietly.

10. *Alone Together*

My gaze locked with hers, electricity singeing my skin. It was only a second, but felt like decades. Then Nicolas was speaking, and Josephine dropped her chin, hiding her beautiful eyes behind thick lashes.

'Karl, you will find out everything you can about these chimera attacks we've heard about. Contact as many clans in the Southeast as you're able. I don't believe their sudden presence and the mercenary rumors are coincidental.'

The old trainer scratched his beard. 'While I agree there's some link between them, I don't understand why someone would go after your daughter, Nicolas. Wouldn't the *bandoleer* be the obvious target?'

'One would think.' The tone Nicolas used shut the topic for further discussion. 'But I'm not a fool, nor will I take any chances. I've assigned Phillipe and Stephan to watch over myself and my wife. And Jacque will look after my son.'

'Oh, joy,' muttered Francis.

Karl set his empty cup on the table. 'It just doesn't make

any sense. Chimeras following orders from a Roma? Those beasts have been out of our control since the Sundering of the Clans, centuries ago.'

Nicolas' eyes narrowed into green daggers. 'What are you saying?'

'I don't know,' Karl replied. 'We could be dealing with something new here, Nicolas. These renegade Gypsies, whoever they are, may have uncovered some form of shadowen knowledge that has been lost to us. Perhaps even found a way to harness the chimeras.'

Sabina made a sign with her hand, and Francis muttered a curse under his breath.

The *bandoleer* scowled. 'That defies the laws of the Court.'

'The desire for power often blurs the lines of law,' Karl replied.

'If such is the case, then we have to find the puppetmaster who's pulling the strings,' said Nicolas.

Karl cast a sideways glance at me. The image of Thaddeus' vicious animal face flashed in my mind, and I shut my eyes to block it out. As soon as I did, another face sparked across my memory – long and dark, with piercing eyes and a white scar winding along the cheek.

'I believe you already have,' I said.

Nicolas frowned at me, as though he'd forgotten I was standing there. 'Explain.'

I looked around the room, my heightened senses prickling under the touch of adrenaline caused by their stares. 'The creature that I kil — that I fought tonight . . . I knew him. His name was Thaddeus, and he was a gargoyle.'

'You're mistaken,' said Nicolas with a fierce shake of his head. 'I saw that monster with my own eyes. It was a chimera.'

I squelched the growl rising in my chest. I had to maintain my calm, especially here. I paused, ensuring my voice was level and steady before continuing. 'Last autumn, when I first began . . . changing . . . three gargoyles showed up at my brother's shop. One of them was Thaddeus. They tried to convince me to join them. They said the Gypsies had enslaved them, but they'd found a way to free themselves.' I heard Josephine's intake of breath like a rush in my ears. But I didn't look at her. 'That's when they introduced me to Augustine.'

Nicolas' face went fiercely dark. 'You think the creature was one of Augustine's demons?'

The word stung, and I felt my claws curling into my palms. Karl's eyes bore down heavy on me, and I wondered what territory I was treading into. I raised my chin. 'I do.'

Nicolas rose slowly. His eyes narrowed to slits. The emotion radiating from him was deadly. 'How can you know that? Have you had contact with him?'

'No,' I replied. 'And I haven't seen his gargoyles since the fight on the bridge, when Quentin's guys chased them off and Hugo took me home.' My wings shuddered against my back. 'Not until tonight, when that thing that used to be Thaddeus attacked me.'

'I thought Augustine was taken care of,' Karl interjected. 'Your sister promised to—'

'I *know* what she promised,' Nicolas snapped in reply, his tone almost vicious. He turned away from me to face the others. 'But if what this gargoyle says is true, then we have another problem on our hands.'

'What's that?' I asked.

Nicolas ignored my question and paced the narrow length of the living room. 'Karl, I must consult with the council.

You will join me. Sabina, you and the children stay here. The gargoyle will watch over you until I return.'

I opened my mouth, but caught Karl's eye. He shook his head, with a look that told me the rest of my end of the conversation would have to wait. The old trainer followed Nicolas out, and the door banged shut behind them.

'This is crap,' Francis said, storming into the kitchen. 'I *was* in a good mood at the thought of your boyfriend leaving for a while,' he called back to Josephine. 'Now, we're going to have his lap boys in our business 24/7 while he's gone.'

I heard him rummaging in the cabinets. A part of me wanted to smile, knowing at least one person felt the same way about Quentin as I did, but I kept my face void of expression. Sabina collected the teacups from around the room.

'Would you like something to eat, Sebastian?' she asked in a kind voice.

It was obvious that my presence unnerved her, like she was offering food to a crocodile, but I was grateful for the hospitality. I was starving, but the last thing I wanted to concentrate on was food. I shook my head and attempted a smile. 'No, thank you. I'm fine.'

'Okay,' she said. 'Let me know if you change your mind.' Sabina returned my smile, then called over her shoulder into the kitchen. 'Francis, would you help me fold down the canopy outside?'

Francis muttered a reply and followed Sabina out the trailer door.

Just like that, I was alone with Josephine. Electric currents pulsed in my veins, and I inched closer to the wall, folding my wings in as far as they would go. How had everything changed so suddenly?

I'd sworn to keep my distance; I'd find a way to help the Romanys without interfering in her life. But now, the *bandoleer* had ordered me to stay with his daughter. My head pounded at the thought. I rubbed my forehead, my fingers brushing against my new, spiraled horns. I flinched, wondering what Josephine thought of me. It seemed that each time I saw her, I was less of a man and more of a—

'How's your knee?' I asked quickly.

Josephine took the ice pack from her leg and dumped it on the floor. 'It's fine,' she replied with a nonchalant wave of her hand. She didn't look at me, but her eyes were wet with unshed tears. The sight made my heart thump harder and hurt deeper.

'What happened?'

'I don't want to talk about it.'

It would've been easier to let it drop, turn away and concentrate on something else – like not breaking anything in the small room. But, before I could stop myself, I was kneeling beside her chair.

'Josephine.' Saying her name gave me goosebumps. 'Please tell me what's wrong.'

She stared past me, her jaw working. Then she sighed. 'It was my fault.'

'What was?'

She clenched her hands tightly in her lap. I looked at her fingers, which were long and shapely, but with short nails that bore the evidence of nervous biting. It was a minor human detail. Flawed. Real. *Comforting*.

'The chimera.' Josephine said the word as though she were convinced speaking it aloud would make one appear. 'It's my fault it attacked you.'

'Why would you say that?'

'Because I saw it earlier tonight, while I was at rehearsal. It was lurking in the rafters of the tent.' She squeezed her eyes shut, like she was trying to block out the image. 'I can't explain it, but I knew it was after me.'

A flame of hot fire shot up my spine. 'But—'

'Yeah, I know,' she said, cutting me off. 'Quentin was right outside the tent with his men. They could've handled it. *Should've* handled it. That's what Marksmen do.' Josephine rolled her bottom lip under and chewed on it for a moment. 'But I wanted you here.'

I put a hand on the floor to brace myself. 'Me?' My voice sounded raspy in my ears.

'We're supposed to have this connection, right?'

I nodded slowly, unsure of where Josephine was going. 'Yes.'

'Well, I thought you might . . . I don't know . . . sense it or something, and you'd come find me.' Josephine fixed her gaze on the wall, and her expression grew narrow, almost angry. 'It was a stupid thing to do, really. I don't know what I was thinking. But then you actually showed up in Karl's trailer. I couldn't look at you without giving something away, and I couldn't risk Quentin suspecting anything because . . .' She trailed off for a moment. 'If Quentin thought I was in danger . . .'

'He wouldn't leave,' I finished softly.

'You've seen the tension between my father and Quentin,' she replied. 'If he defied the *bandoleer's* orders to escort Peter Boswell home, it would only make things worse between them.'

The lump of emotion I harbored in my chest grew spikes and wedged deeper. 'I don't know what to do, Josephine. I don't want my presence causing more friction than it already has, but I don't see how I can ignore your father's command either.'

At last, Josephine looked at me.

I immediately wished she hadn't. Her luminous eyes focused on my forehead, and I felt her recoil, even though she tried to hide the movement. I rocked back on my heels, creating more space between us.

'No, Sebastian,' she said firmly, grabbing my arm. Our eyes met again. 'I don't want you to ignore it because I'm the one who convinced my father about you. I'm the one who believes you're my guardian.'

Josephine's confession hung between us. Then suddenly, she let out a frustrated cry and pushed herself from the chair. I leapt up, catching her under the arm as she stumbled. She clutched my shoulder for balance, and her hand lingered there. The warmth of her palm radiated into my skin.

'Well, it worked, didn't it?' I said, smiling with closed lips. 'I came back because I knew something was wrong. I can't explain things either. but I knew.' I remembered the look on Francis' face when I leapt from the truck. 'Of course, your brother probably thinks I'm insane now.'

A brief spark returned to her eyes. 'But what about the fight?' Her gaze roamed to my cheek. 'You had to face that chimera alone.'

'I'm a gargoyle, remember? Apparently, I can take care of myself,' I smiled again, but this time, I felt sick inside. If Josephine had seen what had happened, the way I'd totally lost it, I doubted she'd be standing this close to me.

She leaned closer. Creases appeared between her brows. 'What are you thinking?'

I blinked away images of the dead chimera and the sight of its body turning to ash and floating away on the wind.

My stomach cramped. 'I don't understand why you wouldn't tell all this to Quentin. He wants keep you safe.'

Josephine bowed her head. Her hair brushed against my cheek. I tried to avoid her scent, but it was impossible. My head buzzed with it. My mind conjured images of my lips against hers, and I had to force them away.

'How do you tell the man you love that you don't think he can protect you?' Her voice trembled. 'How can I do that to him? I don't want to hurt him.'

'You shouldn't have to,' I replied. I felt suddenly heavy, and I realized my wings were sagging. 'I'll talk to Nicolas when he gets back. There has to be a way I can watch over things from a distance and still keep your father's orders.'

'Sebastian, it's more than that.' Josephine gripped my bicep with surprising strength. She took a deep breath, letting it out slowly, like she was preparing for a stunt. When she spoke again, her voice was just above a whisper. 'I've always known something bad was going to happen to me. It's hung over me my whole life, and no matter how many Marksmen we have, no matter how many places we've traveled to, I've never felt really safe.' She blinked slowly. 'Until I met you.'

The blood pounded in my ears. 'Josephine—'

'I didn't understand what I felt, so I tried to play it off.' She looked suddenly pained. 'I tried to be your friend, thinking it would go away. But there was this connection, and it made me feel scared. Guilty. Like I was betraying Quentin. I couldn't explain things in a way that he'd understand.' Her fingers went white as they pressed into my arm. 'I thought things would be okay after we left Sixes. But they weren't. And it's because you were meant to be here the whole time. I'd been letting my fears control me, but the second I saw you at the bonfire, all hooded and cloaked and . . . alone . . .' she tilted her chin to look at me, 'that's when I knew.'

'I'll do whatever it takes to protect you, Josephine.' My wings quivered against my back. 'But I'm not this guardian warrior from your people's stories.' I glanced away, shame flooding my cheeks. 'Honestly, I don't know what I am anymore.'

She placed her hand against my jaw, coaxing me back to her. She studied my features, this time with a steady, determined gaze. 'You're Sebastian,' she said gently. 'Even before I knew you were a guardian, from the first time we talked at my birthday party, I knew you were special. You have a good heart.'

Joy mingled with pain as I leaned hesitantly into her hand. Josephine smiled, her fingers tender over the healing scratches on my cheek. My skin tingled with electricity under her touch. Then she seemed to realize what she was doing and abruptly withdrew her hand.

'Thanks,' I said, feeling the heat of her touch melt into embarrassment.

'We'll figure this out, okay?'

I nodded. 'Okay.'

Sabina appeared in the doorway, and I retreated, increasing the distance between myself and Josephine. Her mother didn't say anything, but she glanced at us as she disappeared down the narrow hall of bedrooms. My head continued to spin, but gradually the air cooled around me, and I cleared my throat.

'Well, I guess I'm stuck here until your father returns,' I said. 'He was pretty direct in his orders.'

Josephine eased herself into the chair. 'He's used to being in charge.' She took the ice pack, positioning it on her knee once more. 'Quentin doesn't see eye to eye with him, but he respects him.'

Quentin's threat reverberated in my memory.

It's only a matter of time before I find a way around Nicolas Romany. He's blind to what you are, but I'm not. Remember that.

As many secrets as Josephine kept from Quentin, I wondered if he kept as many from her. Fierce ambition simmered under the Marksman's calm control. But I wouldn't taint Josephine's opinion of me by demeaning her boyfriend. I studied the wall decor instead.

One oil painting caught my eye: an ancient cathedral, with spires and ornate Gothic architecture, loomed against a midnight sky. On the front steps, a Gypsy woman stood with outstretched arms. Along the parapets of the cathedral, statue upon statue clung to the stone – elegantly carved monsters of all shapes and forms, their faces cold.

One gargoyle stood apart from the others. It was suspended in midair, wings unfurled against the starry sky. At first glance, it seemed the monster was preparing to attack the Gypsy woman. But there was a soft expression on its hideous face – a sadness that was completely at odds with its beastly form.

'The painting belonged to my grandmother,' said Josephine. 'Some evenings, I just sit here and look at it. It makes me feel better, I guess.'

I reached out to touch the painting then caught sight of my thick claws. I curled my hand into a fist, hiding them from view. My hand dropped to my side. 'Josephine, if I'm going to be watching over you, I'd like to know something.'

I heard Josephine shift in the chair. 'What's that?'

My eyes lingered on the girl in the painting. 'Why do

you think I was sealed to you? Like Karl said, your father's the *bandoleer*. Wouldn't he be the one in danger? Why haven't a host of gargoyles appeared to protect your family? Why just me?' I pulled my gaze from the artwork and glanced over my shoulder. 'Why do you believe I'm meant to protect you?'

The color drained from Josephine's cheeks, replaced almost immediately with a strange, faraway look in her eyes. Her mouth opened then shut again. She looked at her hands, wringing them together in a way that almost made me regret my questions.

'I can't tell you,' she whispered.

Her words were like little shocks up my arms. 'Why not?'

She didn't look up. 'Please, Sebastian. I'm not allowed to say more.'

'But there *is* a reason,' I said carefully. 'And you know what it is.'

Josephine's head lifted, and the expression on her face was the look of one who'd carried a burden too long. 'Yes. Or, rather, I know what my father believes is the reason. But he won't talk about it, and I'm sworn to silence until he decides otherwise.'

'Do you believe his reason?'

Josephine rubbed her forehead wearily. 'I don't know. Maybe. But that doesn't change my own feelings. You're supposed to be my guardian, even if I don't have all the answers. Sebastian,' she breathed, 'I know it's a lot to ask of you, especially after everything you've been through, but can you trust me on this? At least, for now?'

I blinked back at her, choking off the rest of my questions. My instincts demanded I keep her safe. My heart beat faster with each thought of Josephine that passed through my head. Everything inside me knew that she was my charge – just like Josephine was convinced I was her guardian.

Did it really matter why?

'Of course, Josephine,' I replied. 'I trust you.'

The trailer door opened, and Nicolas entered the room. I moved against the wall. Josephine turned her attention to her knee. Francis entered behind his father and headed straight for the couch.

'So, what's going on?' Francis asked, plopping down.

Nicolas looked at me, ignoring his son's question. 'Thank you for staying here, Sebastian. You may return to your trailer now.' He shifted his glance to his daughter. 'Josephine, Quentin and the others will be leaving in a few minutes. He's on his way to say goodbye.'

Josephine nodded. 'All right, Father.'

Nicolas looked at me again. In his eyes was the look of a man who saw danger in front of him but was confident that he was master over it. 'Tomorrow, we'll relocate your trailer next to ours.'

He didn't wait for my reply. The Romany leader disappeared down the hall, and I heard a door closing.

'Well.' Francis shrugged at me. 'Guess we're going to be neighbors.'

Once inside my trailer, I washed my face and shrugged off my T-shirt. My numerous wing straps were scattered on the floor – right where I'd left them when I'd changed clothes after the fight. I picked them up and studied the thick, constrictive nylon. They'd become so familiar to me: part of a daily routine I trapped myself in for months. I'd convinced myself that I needed them.

That I couldn't function without them.

I crushed the straps into my fists, crossed the room, and dumped them in the trash. As soon as the bindings left my hands it was as if I could breathe. Really breathe. The endless weeks I'd spent confined and shut away at Hugo's lifted from my shoulders with each influx of oxygen to my lungs.

I sprawled on my bed, taking in deep gulps of air and expanding my wings as far as they would go inside my tiny trailer. Josephine's words ran over and over in my mind, and I found myself smiling. I curled a pillow under my head and sighed. I wouldn't sleep. That much, I knew. But for the first time, I didn't mind at all.

11. Melted Stone

Sunrise broke softly over the oaks and stately pines, illuminating the silhouette of Copper Mountain whose green form rose above the forest like the back of an enormous sleeping dragon. A breeze ruffled the canvas tents and pavilions. It was a peaceful sound, like the continuous splash of white-capped waves against a sun-bleached beach.

I uncurled from my crouch, rolling my shoulders as I welcomed the morning. My trailer had been too stifling for my elated feelings, and at some point – while the moon was still high and the stars still bright – I had climbed atop the roof to enjoy the fresh night air.

Though I hadn't seen Quentin and his party leave, I knew they were gone. My stomach felt more settled, and the icy cold had dulled to a mere occasional shiver. It felt amazing. I tucked the copy of *Much Ado About Nothing* I'd been reading under my arm and rolled my shoulders again, this time stretching my wings to their full length.

I allowed myself a sideways glance. The wings still disgusted and terrified me most of the time, but the gentle warmth of the rising sun felt so irresistibly good against the leathery membranes that I tilted them into the morning light and enjoyed the moment. I knew the sunlight would become brutal soon enough.

Movement caught my eye from below, and I snapped my wings against my back. The traveling Gypsies were early risers – and busy ones. My alone time was over for the morning. I wasn't keen on the thought of being seen crouched on the top of my trailer like some wild animal, so I leapt from the roof, letting my wings unfurl just enough to aid my landing.

My stomach alerted me to the need for breakfast, and I ducked inside my trailer to get ready for the day. I picked up my phone and peered at the screen. There was a message from Hugo.

How's it going?

I rolled my eyes and smirked, then pressed the button for his number. He picked up immediately.

'Hey.'

'Hey,' I replied, 'You know I can't really text back, what with the claws and all.'

I could hear him chuckle on the other end. 'Right. Sorry about that. So, how are things going? Has Karl been helping you out?'

I pulled out some fresh clothes as I talked. 'Yeah, he has. As much as he can, anyway. He's been busy the last few days, going through some old books that belonged to his grandfather.'

'What books?' Hugo asked.

I shrugged, even though my brother couldn't see it. 'I'm not really sure.' I switched the phone to speaker and started the daunting task of zipping and buttoning up my shirt.

'Karl just said the books are important to shadowen history, whatever that means.'

Hugo made a muttering noise on the other end of the line, which told me he was mulling over his next line of questioning. 'So, how are things with the rest of the Circe?'

'Everything's good, Hugo. I think everyone's slowly warming up to me.'

'*Everyone*?'

I felt heat on my face, and I was glad Hugo wasn't actually there. 'Oh, definitely. Quentin and I are going out for a round of mini-golf later today.' I waited for another appreciative laugh, but Hugo was silent. I took a deep breath and lifted my gaze to the mirror, studying my reflection. 'Look, I've got to get to breakfast before all the food's gone, but I'll fill you in on the details later. Everything's fine, honest. It's taking a little getting used to, but I think I'm going to fit in here.'

'Okay,' Hugo replied, sounding a little reluctant. 'Well, everyone here says to tell you hello, and to say they are appreciating actually having food in the refrigerator for once.'

I couldn't help grinning. 'I'll talk to you later, Hugo.'

We hung up, and I finished zipping up the back of my shirt around my wings. As I stood in front of the mirror, I debated retrieving my nylon straps from the trash. But I resisted. I'd made my decision last night, and I was sticking to it. No more jackets, hoods, or pent-up wings. I wasn't going to hide anymore.

I yanked opened the door and stepped outside.

I sniffed the air, detecting smoked meat and coffee. I sighed in contentment and strolled confidently to the pavilion, but as I passed under the canvas roof, my good mood vanished. People gawked openly at me; their expressions wary and even scared. One woman pulled her curious child protectively to her side and hurried to the opposite side of the pavilion. I may have been one of their fabled guardians, but that didn't seem to matter. I was still different. And I was still alone.

Francis and his group weren't at breakfast. I didn't see Karl, either. But since I was salivating at the sizzle of bacon and the scent of meat, I headed for the food line. Before I got too far, I felt – rather than saw – a Marksman approaching. It was Jacque, the one assigned to Francis.

'Your presence is requested at the home of the Romanys,' he said formally, but with a biting tone that was unmistakable. I wondered if Quentin taught classes in the art of sarcastic conversation. Jacque's close-set eyes narrowed. 'Immediately.'

I looked longingly at the Gypsies enjoying breakfast. 'Sure,' I replied. 'I'll be right there.' Jacque sized me up with an expert eye, his broad chest bowing with defiance as he walked away. My upper lip curled back from my teeth. 'What is it with those guys?'

Nicolas met me at the door, seeming more relaxed as he ushered me inside. 'Sebastian, thank you for coming. You'll excuse us, but my family's just finishing breakfast.'

My stomach groaned.

Sabina cleared dishes from the kitchen table while Francis downed a huge glass of what smelled to me like some kind of protein shake. Josephine leaned against the counter with a coffee mug between her hands.

I paused just inside the entryway, knowing I'd never get both my body and my wings into the small kitchen area without doing serious damage to dishware or wall decor. I dipped my head and smiled as politely as I could. 'Good morning.'

Sabina looked up from the sink. 'Good morning, Sebastian. It's going to be a beautiful day. Don't you think?' Though her expression was genuine, I got the feeling that she was trying hard to make me feel normal. 'Did you sleep well last night?'

'I don't really sleep much.'

Francis dumped his cup into the sink. 'You know, Mom, it's that whole creature-of-the-night thing.' Sabina shot him a warning look that only made him laugh. 'What? I'm just saying.'

My lips twitched into a grin. Francis seemed the most comfortable having a guy with gray skin and dragon wings interrupting the family breakfast. Sabina nodded apologetically as her son helped himself to a glass of orange juice.

Everyone fell silent. A nervous feeling skittered up my spine. Had Nicolas rethought his decision? It wasn't like I'd been taking courses in guardianship or shadowen fighting techniques. Unlike the Marksmen, I wasn't trained. I clenched my hands behind my back, just underneath my wings. 'Jacque said you wanted to speak to me?'

Nicolas settled into a chair, and he was suddenly all business. 'I wanted to let you know that we're shifting the caravan to the back of the lot today in order to make room for the carnival and tents to go up. I've left instructions for your trailer to be located directly behind ours. It will make your job easier.'

I breathed a sigh of relief. 'That would be great. Thank you.'

'I've also given strict instructions to the remaining Marksmen, including Phillipe and Stephan, regarding your activities. You have free rein of the camp and the Fairgrounds, and are allowed anywhere Josephine goes. The time has come for you to fulfill your guardian duties, Sebastian Grey, without restrictions or hindrances.' Nicolas' eyes grew hard – an expression I'd seen before. It made him seem ancient and dangerous. 'You will do whatever it takes to keep your charge safe. That's been the way of our old stories, and that is what I expect of you now. Your duty is your life.'

'Father,' said Josephine, glancing at me with a sort of guilty sympathy. 'Sebastian's not our servant.'

'Yes he is,' said Nicolas, keeping me pinned in his sight. 'His kind is bound by our laws. He's been branded, and he'll do as we command.' The glint in his eyes changed, and I could see a flash of fear – but only for an instant. I understood why. He was allowing a shadow creature freedom inside his camp and in close proximity to his daughter. If Nicolas didn't believe that he controlled me, then he was putting his people in danger.

I didn't know how much truth was in the *bandoleer's* declaration, but if I wanted this chance, then Nicolas needed to be convinced that he was ultimately in charge of my actions. 'Of course,' I said quickly. I pulled up my sleeve, exposing the dandelion tattoo on my wrist. 'I'll look after Josephine. I've been sealed, and I know what I'm supposed to do.'

The harshness in Nicolas' countenance instantly faded. He relaxed and took up his fork. 'Good,' he said, taking a large bite of scrambled eggs. My mouth watered as I watched him eat, and I had to stifle a hungry whimper. Nicolas finished his food before speaking again. 'Now that everything's settled, I've got things to take care of.' He pushed his plate away and stood. 'Josephine, I suggest you go over your daily routine with the gargoyle so he knows when he's needed.'

I didn't feel things were really *settled* at all. 'Routine?'

'She won't require your immediate presence during all parts of the day, of course. But I think it only fair you have an idea of when you'll be expected to accompany my daughter.' The edge in his voice returned. 'I don't want to make this arrangement obvious to the rest of the clan. There's no need to stir up more insecurities among the troupe, especially this close to the opening of the Circe.'

I nodded. 'Understood.'

'No one knows about the chimera in our camp last night, except the Marksmen. As far as the clan is concerned, we're merely on alert. Everything will continue according to schedule. Francis,' the Romany leader continued, 'your mother and I are heading into town to purchase supplies, so I'm leaving the overseeing of the setups to you.'

'Yeah, no problem, dad,' his son replied. 'I'm on it.'

Francis barreled out of the trailer. Sabina wiped her hands with a dishtowel and brushed by her husband on her way out the door.

'We'll be back this afternoon, Josie,' said Nicolas, kissing her forehead.

I stood straighter, trying to look as professional as I thought a teenage gargoyle could. Nicolas' gaze lingered on my tattoo, as if assuring himself of my branding, and then he hurried out the door.

'He's scared of you,' Josephine mused softly, watching him through the window.

'You think so?'

She seemed surprised by my answer. 'Of course, Sebastian. Who wouldn't be?'

I pondered this, trying to view myself through Nicolas' eyes. I thought of myself as a hideous freak, maybe, but not as someone who was actually dangerous. Josephine, like her brother, seemed oblivious to the other Gypsies' fears, but I noticed her conflict each time she observed my unusual features. 'I guess I just don't really see myself that way.'

Josephine regarded me steadily, regretful concern radiating from her eyes. 'I'm sorry for the way my father treats you sometimes,' she said. 'He's got a lot on him right now.'

'You don't need to apologize, Josephine.' I grasped the table with one hand. I was starting to feel the effects of not eating breakfast. My teeth throbbed against my gums as I inhaled a trace scent of eggs and cheese. 'I *am* marked, after all. Apparently it's pretty standard procedure.'

My last comment was rewarded with one of my favorite smiles – the one that was crooked and caused her lips to pucker. 'Yeah, I know,' she replied. 'You've got your duty.' There was something in her tone that sounded unsure.

I watched Josephine place her mug in the sink. 'I'd protect you, tattoo or not,' I answered. 'Duty has nothing to do with it.'

Something in the set of Josephine's shoulders changed, and I felt relieved at having spoken my thoughts out loud. She turned from the sink. She was dressed in casual workout clothes that hugged her body. My heart played racketball between my ribs.

'Did Quentin and the others get away last night?' I asked.

Josephine brushed back a strand of hair that had pulled loose from her ponytail. 'Yeah, they did.' She sighed, and I sensed her sadness like cold rain on my skin. Then Josephine looked me up and down. Her expression changed. 'Sebastian, are you all right?'

I stepped back defensively, afraid that I'd suddenly grown fur or something else horrific. 'Why do you ask?'

'You don't look . . . I mean, you look like you don't feel well.'

Josephine barely referenced my gargoyle appearance – just the comment about my wings and that I still looked like me. I should've been grateful, but instead, it made me feel worse. I wished Josephine would just come right out and tell me I was a repulsive monster.

'It's nothing.' I leaned against the edge of the kitchen table. 'Just feeling a little weak. I haven't eaten in a while. Really eaten, I mean.'

Josephine flushed. 'I'm so sorry, Sebastian. I assumed you'd already had breakfast. Let me fix you something.'

I was too hungry to protest. I spun one of the chairs around and straddled it as Josephine pulled out some bacon and set about cooking the slabs in a pan. My mouth watered uncontrollably at the smell, and I groaned softly, propping my head in my hands and closing my eyes. My teeth ached, pulsing with insatiable demand for food. Within minutes, the Gypsy girl set a plate of food in front of me.

I was ravenous.

'Thanks,' I barely managed to say before I lit into the bacon. It was maddeningly good, and I didn't stop until my plate was completely clean. Josephine watched me closely. Heat seeped into my face. 'I'm a fan of bacon.'

'Yeah,' she grinned. 'I can see that.'

'I have a weird appetite,' I said, feeling a little embarrassed at my carnivorous display. I noticed she'd brought me a mug of coffee. I took a long drink, enjoying the sting of heat against my throat.

Josephine seemed to be either pondering my explanation

of my eating habits, or she was thinking of something else altogether. I couldn't quite read her expression, and I was having difficulty processing the influx of emotions. I wasn't even sure if they were hers, or mine. I raised my brows, hoping she would say something to clue me in.

'Are you okay with this?' she finally asked. At first, I thought she meant my appetite, and I was ready to explain that I'd always been this way – except for my developing preference for meat. 'I mean, with all the guardian stuff,' she clarified. 'I dumped a lot on you last night, I know, maybe too much. And no matter what my father says, I don't want you to do something you don't want to do.'

'Don't *want* to do? Josephine, how could being around you be something I wouldn't want to do?' I bit the inside of my cheek. I hadn't meant to say that much. Telling her I loved her all those months ago had been awkward enough. I refused to go down that path again. 'I want to help you and your family, Josephine, no matter what that means. Believe me when I tell you that I'm all right with it, okay?'

I felt Josephine striving to sift through my feelings. Currents buzzed around me, and I let myself sink into the depths of her gaze. God, I loved looking at her. At some point – and I hadn't entirely realized when it had happened – Josephine's face settled into a soft expression, and she was no longer searching me, but looking *at* me — right into my silver eyes the way I was looking into her green ones.

A small smile slid over her lips, and I struggled with the sudden depletion of oxygen in the room. Then, just as suddenly, I broke the gaze and cleared my throat. Josephine took my empty plate and deposited it in the sink. When she whirled around to face me, her mood seemed lighter.

'Well, are you ready to go?' she asked.

'Where?'

'To the rehearsal tent. I've got practice.'

My brow furrowed. 'But your knee—'

'Is fine,' Josephine finished. 'Andre and I are behind on our routines, and if we want to be ready by opening night, I can't miss a rehearsal.' She caught my look and beamed in a way that reminded me of her brother. 'Don't worry. I won't endanger myself.'

Her last sentence took me by surprise, and I actually laughed. 'I'm going to hold you to that.'

'Well, come on then,' she said, gliding past me to the door. 'And I'll show you where I work.'

'I go where you go, Josephine.'

12. A Perfect Mistake

It was an overcast Monday morning – the start of my second week as an inhabitant of the Circe de Romany. I sat alone under the pavilion, which had been relocated near the back of the lot, just beyond our living quarters. With the opening of the Circe getting close, no one had time to gather for breakfast anymore.

I nibbled absently on my tenth piece of smoked ham as I surveyed the Fairgrounds. It was rapidly transforming into the bright carnival circus atmosphere I'd remembered from the Circe's last visit. Large tents consumed the sky, along with the massive Ferris wheel that still made me shudder when I looked at it.

I reached for another piece of meat, my thoughts revolving around that fateful ride with Josephine the night of her birthday party. I saw myself seated in the bright yellow car as clearly as if I was there. Vaguely, I became aware that something was happening. My body tingled with cold as the image seemed to freeze itself in my brain.

Then something wafted past my face.

I blinked it into focus. A tendril of mist – black in color and with an oily consistency – curled around me like a snake. For a split second I thought it came from the cooking area, but as I sat back, a sickening realization gripped me. The mist was coming from . . .

Me.

It seeped from my hands, right through the skin and into the air. Mist like I'd seen around Ezzie before she simply vanished. I sucked in a breath and waved my arms, panicked. Instantly, the mist disappeared. I stared, slack jawed and gaping at my hands, seeing nothing out of the ordinary – apart from the gray skin and wicked claws I was only now coming to grips with.

I puffed out a breath of relief. I didn't need anything else happening to me right now. The wing growth spurt and my new set of horns were almost more than I could handle at the moment. Not to mention my new duties as Josephine's—

My gargoyle radar went off – a flood of scents and sensations all at once – and a familiar tingle raced over my skin. I sniffed the air in anticipation, determined to forget the mist for the time being. A few seconds later, Josephine appeared. Like clockwork, my heart jerked beneath my ribs. I brushed my hands against my jeans as I rose to greet her.

'Good morning.'

'Hey, there,' she replied, her tone light. She glanced at my empty plate. 'How was breakfast? Is Alcie going to have to replenish the meat supply again?'

'She's not too happy with me,' I confessed, giving Josephine a wide, but close-lipped smile. 'I've put a serious cramp in her menu plans.'

Josephine laughed, and I went warm all over. 'I've never seen anyone put food away like you, Sebastian.'

'Hey,' I replied, coming around the table to join her. 'Karl told me I needed to work on developing my shadowen skills.'

'So you're training to be a competitive eater, then?'

'Everyone needs a hobby.'

Josephine laughed again and slipped an elastic band from her wrist. I watched as she wound her hair into a loose braid. Against the backdrop of gray clouds, Josephine was as bright as the dandelion flowers on the Circe's logo. 'Well,' she said, flipping the braid over her shoulder. 'Are you ready to go?'

She glanced towards the front gates, as she'd done every morning for the last few days. Quentin hadn't returned from his trip – which was a highlight of my life. I didn't know what was keeping him in North Carolina so long, but I'd memorized enough expressions on Josephine's face to know that his task was having an effect on her.

I gestured for the Gypsy girl to take the lead. 'I'm following you.'

Since being officially assigned to Josephine, a routine had developed between us. Without any protocol to follow, I'd made the decision to trail behind Josephine wherever she went inside the camp. I'd seen how Phillip, Stephan, and Jacque kept their eye on the other Romanys, and I tried to copy them.

They reminded me of bodyguards in the movies: always alert while not seeming to be doing anything at all. The remaining Marksmen patrolled the fence like security guards, taking shifts in pairs. And they were good. Like Secret Service good. Only my gargoyle senses told me they were there.

I kept to the shadows of the pavilions as we walked through the Fairgrounds. Josephine was busier than I'd ever imagined possible. I marveled at how she'd tackled public high school while working at the Circe. Josephine was also rarely alone and this limited any conversation between us to a few sentences each day.

But we both settled into our roles. Josephine worked and rehearsed. I practiced my guardian techniques. Being near Josephine was everything I'd wanted since the day she'd walked into my life and flipped my world on its end.

Squelching those feelings was the hardest thing I've ever done, but it also became part of my daily routine, just like learning how to sculpt a perfectly stoical exterior, no matter what emotional battle was eating me up inside.

We neared the large rehearsal tent. Its red and gold striped body fluttered in the summer breeze. I passed a small group of Marksmen, and I heard one of them spit. My gargoyle hearing easily picked up their whispered conversation.

'I'd like to clip those wings,' muttered one under his breath.

'Wonder how far I could drive my knife into his stony guts,' said another.

My pace slowed unconsciously. Heat began to churn inside my stomach, and I breathed hard through my nose. The Marksmen had been ordered to leave me alone, but they made it perfectly clear that they neither accepted me nor trusted me inside their territory.

'Give it time, boys,' said a third. 'One wrong move on that demon's part, and he becomes target practice.'

I'd stopped moving completely. My rational mind recognized the signs: the slipping control. Warning shots fired in my brain. I felt my eyes burning, and I turned my claws into my palms. The edges of my vision blurred into red.

'Sebastian?'

Josephine's voice snapped me to attention. She paused in

the opening of the rehearsal tent, looking back at me. The rising fire immediately cooled, followed by a wave of irritated shame at the power Quentin's men had over me. I quickly added another task to my mental list: quit letting Marksmen get under my skin.

'Sorry about that,' I said, hurrying to catch up. 'I didn't mean to keep you waiting.'

We passed through the opening of the tent.

Josephine studied me. 'Is everything okay?'

'Yes.' I pried my claws out of my skin. 'Totally fine.'

She regarded me with a strange expression. I knew how the Marksmen felt about me. I knew how the other Gypsies felt. But I couldn't read Josephine Romany the same way. I recognized her moods and emotions – they'd become as familiar as my own. And I'd learned to pinpoint her location using my senses. This was – I had to admit – one of my favorite pastimes. But as to how she felt when it came to *me*, I was completely in the dark.

'Okay,' she finally replied. 'Well, I guess I need to find Andre.'

'Break a leg,' I said with a smile.

She nodded and jogged across the floor. Dozens of performers crowded the practice tent, eager to nail down their acts before the opening night of the Circe, just days away. Several heads turned in my direction. With my wings fully visible and my appearance no longer disguised with jackets and hoods, I was difficult to miss. My only consolation was my ability to blend into the shadows when I wanted. I located an empty section of bleachers in an unlit corner and settled in to watch.

I didn't know how to be a guardian. The only gargoyles I'd known had it out for me – with the exception of

Esmeralda. But the last time I'd spoken to Hugo on the phone, he said he hadn't seen or heard from my former teacher. And while Karl could tell me the effects of sunlight and diamonds, and he helped my understanding of how shadowen functioned, there was nothing in his books to guide me in this weird role.

It was something I had to figure out on my own.

As I watched the groups of performers, I grew increasingly curious about the Outcast Gypsies and their past. Had they always lived with the threat of shadow creatures? Did other clans function the same way? There were so many questions I would've loved to ask Karl, but I'd been too busy with my new duties – like watching Josephine rehearse. It had become the best part of my day.

She maneuvered through the cluster of performers, and I perched on the top bleacher, letting my gaze run over the room; training myself to take in my surroundings, to focus on what my instincts and senses told me. The more I listened, the more I discovered about the world around me.

I knew that Andre – Josephine's partner in her routines – waited for her on the other side of the tent. Though I'd encountered him once before when I'd burst into Karl's trailer, my real knowledge of him came from our official introduction to each other. The first day I'd followed Josephine into the rehearsal tent, the large man had crossed his arms over his chest, muscles bulging, and glared at me.

'Andre,' Josephine had said with a smile, 'this is Sebastian.'

The man's eyes bored into mine. 'Yeah, the gargoyle. I know who he is.'

'His name's Sebastian,' Josephine repeated, but in a tone that made my heart swell inside my chest. 'And he's with me.'

Andre surveyed me hard for a moment, and I simply let him. I knew there was something in my face that made people back down – maybe the inhuman silver color of my eyes or the flash of my jagged teeth as I spoke. The barrel-chested performer gave a surrendering grunt and extended his hand for me to shake.

My brain automatically registered his unique scent. The spicy aroma of the Gypsies differed between individuals. Most scents were pleasant – exotic or otherworldly. Others, like the Marksmen's, made my nose burn. After two minutes with Andre, he was cataloged in my inner Gypsy registry like a piece of badly burnt garlic toast.

'Pleased to meet you,' I'd replied.

That had been it. Since that first day, Andre tolerated my presence during their rehearsals with a kind of controlled exasperation. And I tolerated his smell.

I'd only seen Josephine perform two routines since I'd come to the Circe. She was good at traditional Roma dance, and she also excelled with the aerial silk ribbons: an act I'd joined unintentionally when I was trying to save her from Augustine's gargoyles.

Her routines with Andre were completely different. They consisted of a series of balancing acts. Andre was the base and support – using poles, ladders, and chairs – for Josephine to balance on over his head. She had extraordinary strength and control, and I was amazed at how steady she could be. Andre was a perfectionist when it came to performance. I appreciated that particular quality, especially when it came to Josephine's safety.

Today appeared to be another balancing routine. Andre was doing some warm ups with a ladder as Josephine approached. People bustled around them; everyone scurrying to get their own practices in. Trapeze artists claimed the lofty spaces above, and other performers were divided among the three circular performance spaces on the floor.

Andre gave Josephine a lecture about her knee that she promptly dismissed. She was stubborn, and I liked that about her; though I worried about her injury as much as her partner did. Finally, Andre relented and they practiced their first stunt. Josephine handled everything fine, but I caught her wincing occasionally.

After an hour, they took a short break. Josephine walked to a water cooler near the bleachers. She took a long drink and filled her cup again. Her face glowed with physical exertion, and a few strands of hair clung damply to her neck.

'So how's it looking so far?' she asked, glancing up at me.

I wasn't used to being addressed during practice, and it took me a moment to reply. 'You're amazing, as usual. I don't know how you do it.'

She stopped mid-sip, her glistening skin taking on an even more amazing shine. 'Thanks.'

'You're welcome.'

The sound of revving engines filled the tent. Five men on motorbikes sped out from behind the partition, followed by crew members towing a spherical metal cage. I'd seen an act like this before. The motorcyclists raced around the inside of the cage at high speeds, narrowly avoiding each other in the process. I recognized Brishen among the performers waiting to rehearse the stunt.

The crew locked the circular cage into place. Someone flipped down the ramp, and the first two bikers raced inside. The scene was so impressive that I almost didn't notice

Andre's return. He was riding a motorcycle, and two men walked behind him carrying an oddly shaped bar, which resembled the swing in a birdcage, only much larger – large enough for a person to sit on.

'Looks like I'm up,' said Josephine.

She trotted to Andre and the motorcycle. A long cable ran from a platform on the floor to the high scaffolding on the opposite side of the tent. Crew members lifted Andre's bike, positioning it on the cable and attaching a third wheel. They fastened a large swing beneath the contraption so that it hung beneath the motorcycle, just under its back wheel.

My heart catapulted up my throat as the crew set up for the stunt – one I'd never seen Josephine and Andre attempt. A man placed a stepladder on the platform, and Andre mounted the bike. The cable bowed under the weight as the crew held the swing in place. Josephine sat on the bar of the swing, her legs dangling.

Sweat trickled down my back as I tried to manage my rising panic. Josephine was a professional. This was her job. Neither of those thoughts prevented my nerves crackling like severed electrical cables.

Andre gave the crew a thumbs-up signal. Josephine mirrored the gesture. The crew backed away. Andre revved the engine, and the motorcycle roared across the cable, climbing higher and higher as it crossed the tent. Josephine sat perfectly still, her expression serene yet focused.

They reached the scaffolding, nearly in the rafters. Andre stopped the bike and it drifted backwards down the wire. He put on the brakes, and they hung there, perfectly suspended and balanced over the floor of the rehearsal tent. Several agonizing seconds passed. Josephine locked her knees over the bar and let go of the sides. Then, slowly, she leaned back until she was hanging upside down. I stopped breathing. Andre raised himself from his seat, extending his arms, and the two balanced in that position for what felt like hours.

Finally, Josephine pulled herself up, and Andre returned to his seat. The bike drifted toward the lower end of the cable. But before I could inhale, Andre revved it once more and started up at a speed I wouldn't have thought possible on such a thin wire. They reached the top and slid down to the middle again. Josephine executed another move – this one more precarious, as she dangled by only one foot and one arm. The bike wobbled as Andre stood.

My shoulders cramped so hard the pain radiated down my spine. Josephine slid out of her posture and returned to the swing. I rubbed my neck, eager for the stunt to end. Andre leaned over the bike, speaking to Josephine. I saw her nod, and she gripped the sides of the swing as the motorcycle sped up the wire once more.

Josephine stood on the bar, and Andre leaned heavily to one side. The swing angled in the opposite direction. Josephine pushed her weight against the outside corner of the swing just as her partner leaned to the other side. The entire contraption began to rock back and forth like a giant pendulum. Josephine provided the counterweight to Andre's momentum. And then, suddenly, they were spinning completely around the cable in a giant circle.

Over and over they went – first Josephine was under the cable, and then she was over it. They moved so quickly that it was difficult to see just how hard they were working. The motion looked effortless and weightless. I watched in awe.

That's when it happened. It was so sudden that I could've missed it. But I was so fixated on Josephine that I saw every detail as though time screeched to a halt. As she came around the underside of the cable and pushed against the bar, her injured knee gave out. Her foot slipped, and she lost her balance. The perfect rhythm was disrupted. Andre lurched in his seat. The hard shift jolted the contraption, and I knew.

I knew she was going to fall.

There was no time. No thought. No hesitation. My feet pounded over the stretch of bleachers. My shoulders went taut, my back muscles flexed. Every pledge I'd made never to fly melted under the fire of adrenaline as I picked up speed.

Josephine clung to the metal bar. Something primal exploded inside me. My wings snapped out. I was airborne and streaking across the tent like a rocket. Wind smacked my face as my wings pumped, carrying me to her. Josephine's fingers slipped. I dove for her plummeting body.

Oh God! I wasn't going to make it! I snarled and pushed forward, stretching with all my might, intercepting her fall. My arms wrapped around her. Josephine's body pressed against mine.

I had to pull up! I had to pull up!

I pumped my wings. It was like pulling an oar through water. The air wouldn't relent. I gritted my teeth and forced my wings to move. My ears reverberated with the sound of flapping leather. The floor grew closer. Then, suddenly, my body changed direction, and we were climbing through air.

Fresh adrenaline coursed through me. I snarled and banked hard to the right, avoiding the network of scaffolding and platforms as I flew around the high ceiling of the tent. The feeling was incredible; the sensation unlike anything I'd ever known. I threw my head back, almost laughing, until I felt trembling against my chest. Josephine wept into my shirt, clinging to me with iron fingers.

Elation turned to horror. What if I hadn't made it in time? She'd be—

I banked again, gliding beneath the scaffolding. Everyone in the tent had stopped what they were doing and gathered at the center, pointing up at us. Andre hung from the motorcycle. The momentum had flung him upside down, and he was gripping the bike to keep from falling. I pumped my wings in his direction.

There was no way I could pick him up, and I didn't have a lot of control. I aimed for the swing that hovered above the cable. Holding Josephine tightly with one hand, I gripped the metal bar with the other as I flew by. I pulled in my wings slightly and dropped down, bringing the entire swing with me until the contraption righted.

Andre settled himself expertly into the seat as I let go, and he drove the bike back down the cable. The crew was on him as soon as he was low enough. As I passed over, I could see his face. He was shaken, but seemed okay.

I tipped my left wing to change direction, and I circled. My speed decreased as I closed in on the tent floor. The crew members and performers backed out of the way as I descended.

I pressed my lips to Josephine's ear. 'Hold on, I'm going to land.'

I'd only experienced a crash landing the first time I'd flown, and I wasn't sure how this would work. I circled one more time, slowing as much as possible. And then I folded my wings. I hit the ground jogging, but that didn't stop the jarring pain that shot up my spine as I made contact.

I came to a stop several lengths from where my feet first touched. Quickly collapsing my wings against my back, I dropped to my knees and eased Josephine to the ground.

She held to my shirt, still unwilling to let go, and I kept my arms around her.

'I'm here, Josephine,' I breathed softly. Her tears soaked through my shirt, and their warmth seeped through my skin. 'You're all right, Josephine.' My eyes closed as I heard the rush of people coming our way. 'You're all right.'

13. *Closely Separated*

People pressed in all around us, talking frantically, but my attention remained on Josephine. Her shoulders quaked as she fought against tears, fingers wrapped so tightly in my shirt that I could feel the strain of the fabric against the back of my neck. Overwhelming sensations of terror and relief washed over me. I drew her closer, and stroked her hair. It was softer than I'd even imagined.

'Josephine, please,' I said, trying to catch my breath and calm her down all at once – and finding it impossible to do both. My voice was thick, heavy with a growl. I swallowed and tried again. 'Josephine, it's okay. You're safe.'

'Get out of the way, people!' yelled a voice from the crowd. Karl pushed his way through the performers. 'Let me through!' The old trainer knelt beside me. His eyes met mine, and understanding flashed quickly over his face. 'Josie,' he said in a soothing, yet forceful tone. 'Josie, look at me. I need to know where it hurts.'

He reached for her knee, fingers pressing into muscles. Josephine cried out. The sound ignited fire inside me. I pulled her closer; my body shifted around hers in a protective crouch. I glared at Karl, the edges of my vision blurring into red.

'Easy, Sebastian,' he said softly, staring me right in the eyes.

My lip curled back, and I bared my teeth.

Karl raised his hands. 'I'm not going to hurt her.' He turned his palms out and slowly spread his arms. 'I just need to examine her, all right?'

He was talking me down. My low growls echoed in the sudden silence of the tent. Gypsy faces surrounded me – everyone watching, wary and unsure. *Of me.* I squeezed my eyes shut. Adrenaline pumped hotly through my blood, and I felt it banging like a hammer in my brain. I gritted my teeth and took deep breaths through my nose, forcing the protective instincts to let me go.

I nodded slowly at Karl and released my grip on Josephine. He rubbed her shoulder and called her name again. Josephine's trembling body gradually stilled. Her hand slid from my shirt, her fingers lingering on my chest for one brief moment. She turned her face to Karl, and he smiled.

'May I?'

'Yeah,' Josephine replied, wiping her face.

Karl's fingers probed around her knee, and I saw the Gypsy girl wince. She was pale, but her expression was solid, almost defiant.

'Josie, what were you thinking?' Karl sighed. He glanced up at the long high wire cable. 'Your knee may have been feeling better, but doing stunts like this won't help it heal.'

Josephine brushed the last streak of tear away, and a hard glint came into her green eyes. It seemed to be a Romany family trait. 'I had to, Karl. The Circe opens in a few days, and we've barely had time to review that stunt. I'm not about to let it get axed!'

'Josephine Romany, you're impossible,' he grumbled. 'No practices for the rest of the week.' She gasped and tried to get up, but the trainer put his hand on her shoulder. 'I mean it. If you want to perform in the show, you have to give it a rest.' Karl looked over his shoulder at Andre. 'Can I trust you on this?'

Andre's face was lined with concern. 'Yeah, no practice, Karl. I'll make sure she doesn't.'

'Karl,' she pleaded. 'I'm fine.'

Josephine pushed up to standing this time, and I stood along with her. She took a step forward and gasped in pain, catching my shoulder. I put my arm around her waist.

Karl rose. 'Sebastian, take her home.'

His face was set on Josephine, and the tone of his voice was firm enough to quell whatever protest may have been on her lips. I felt Josephine's frustration keenly, and I hated acting on Karl's instructions, even if it was for the best. But with a guilty nod I slid my other arm under her legs and lifted her easily, cradling her against me.

To my surprise, Josephine didn't protest. Her body relaxed, and she slid her arms around my neck. I was acutely aware of the tense silence that had fallen over the crowd as I stood there with Josephine Romany in my arms. When I moved forward, the Gypsies immediately parted for me. I walked through the crowd and out of the tent, holding the most important thing in my life protectively against me.

I expected Josephine to stiffen at any moment and insist I put her down, but she never did. Instead, she curled into me wearily, her head bobbing gently against my chest. She didn't say anything. Neither did I.

I crossed the center of the caravan, walking as smoothly as I could, soaking up the moment and feeling guilty while I did it. We reached the Romany's trailer quicker than I wanted to, and I pushed open the door, nearly bowling Francis over in the process. His eyes widened as he moved aside to let me pass.

'Whoa, what happened?' he asked.

Josephine sighed. 'It's my own stupid fault, France. Andre and I were working on the bike stunt, and my knee gave out.'

With great care – and a good bit of reluctance – I eased Josephine onto the living room couch. Her arms left my neck, and she gingerly stretched out her leg. Francis shook his head disapprovingly at her.

'Didn't Karl—'

Josephine cut him off. 'Yeah, I know. But I couldn't skip another practice on that stunt. We're too far behind as it is.'

'Well, now it looks like you're even more behind,' Francis replied, crossing his arms. She shot him an angry look and then tenderly prodded her knee, wincing again. Francis glanced at me. 'So what happened?'

'She . . . fell.'

Francis sucked air through his teeth.

'But Sebastian caught me,' Josephine added quickly.

'Caught you?' Francis repeated. His gaze drifted to my enormous wings. Then his tone changed. 'Oh, wait.' His brows lifted. 'Do you mean, like, *caught* you?'

'I slipped from the swing, and I was falling. And then, he was just . . . there, somehow. And we were . . . we were flying.'

I studied the patterns in the carpet as the twins discussed my feat. My nerves weren't completely settled, and I clenched my fists behind my back, just under my folded wings. I could feel Francis' eyes on me.

'Huh,' he mused, sounding impressed.

'I did what I had to do,' I said.

'You should've seen it, France,' said Josephine. 'It was like something right out of the show. Talk about an act that would have people on their feet!'

'Except that nobody would ever see it,' Francis replied, clapping me on the shoulder. 'Can't have the whole world knowing about our resident gargoyle, right Sebastian?'

I tried not to flinch at his words. What it took to make me fly was exactly what I hated. It made me a freak. But that other part of me – the part that clawed deep at my guts on quiet nights when I was alone – had not only enjoyed the sensation, but *craved* it.

'Yeah, we can't have that,' I replied, my voice tinged with a growl.

'Well, I've . . . uh . . . got some work to do with dad,' said Francis, taking a step back. He looked at Josephine and cleared his throat. 'I'm glad you're okay.'

'Please tell Father that I'm fine,' she said quickly. 'I'm sure the whole troupe has heard about this by now.' She hesitated for a moment before continuing. 'And tell him that Sebastian's with me, and I'm going to rest my knee for a while.'

I looked at Francis, and he looked back at me. He made a face I couldn't entirely interpret, a smirk tugging at one corner of his mouth. He shrugged. 'Okay, whatever you say, Josie. I'll see you two later.'

He shot me another look, and then he was out the door.

I bit my lip, my head already tingling. Anytime I was alone with Josephine, every sense in my body went into heightened overload. I was used to concealing it, but my hands trembled behind my back.

'Could you bring me some ice, Sebastian?'

Josephine rolled her pants up to her thigh to examine her swollen knee, and I could see faint tinges of pink along her cheekbones. Something about her coloring made my heart rate accelerate.

'Yes, of course,' I replied, hurrying out of the room. When I returned, I found Josephine attempting to arrange several pillows under her leg to prop it up. 'Here, let me,' I said, kneeling beside her. I adjusted the pillows and then held out the ice pack. 'Do you mind if I put this on your knee?'

She nodded. I gently placed the ice on her skin. Josephine gasped, but she made no move to hold it in place, so I kept my hand on the pack. She closed her eyes, pressing her lips together. The tingling in my body grew worse. The scents in my nose were distracting, and I had to breathe out of my mouth and look away –to focus on something else in the room.

'That's really, really cold,' Josephine whispered.

'I'm sorry.' I lifted the pack off her knee. 'Should I get a towel?'

Josephine put her hand over mine and warmth radiated up my arm. 'No, it's fine,' she replied, guiding the pack – and my hand – back to her knee. 'It's just not exactly a good feeling,' she finished.

Maybe the ice wasn't, but the feeling of her hand on mine definitely was. 'Okay.'

'Thank you . . . for saving my life today.'

I swallowed hard, not looking at her. 'You're welcome.'

Josephine laughed, and I couldn't resist lifting my eyes to meet hers. 'You've been saying that a lot to me lately, haven't you?' she asked, smiling. She shook her head. 'Then again, I've been thanking you a lot lately.'

I returned her smile with one of my close-lipped ones. A silence fell between us that only heightened the current of electricity humming through me. For the hundredth time, I wished on everything sacred and precious that I could read Josephine's mind. I felt the emotions swirling around her, and I was sure I could decipher them, if I concentrated hard enough – not that I could concentrate on anything right then.

She brushed a strand of hair from her neck. 'You know, back there in the tent, you lifted me like I weighed nothing.'

The corner of my mouth tugged up. 'That's because you don't.'

'Something every girl wants to hear but, believe me, I weigh a lot more than *nothing*.' Her gaze left mine and traveled down my shoulders. 'You're really strong. I mean, I could feel it, when you picked me up.'

My half-smile dropped. I wasn't sure how to answer. Josephine touched my arm, and my bicep tightened reflexively under her touch. 'Like I said, you don't weigh much.'

'Have you always been that strong?' she asked.

'I guess.' A memory of Avery pinning me down in a mock wrestling match not long after I'd started attending school surfaced in my brain. I'd thrown him off easily – too easily. I'd shied away from physical altercations after that. But knowledge about my strength – just like everything else about my life before I'd awakened – was just a void. 'I never really thought about it before.'

Josephine's gaze drifted along my shoulders. Warmth

spread across my face. My wardrobe had always included a jacket over whatever I was wearing. But now, after deciding not to hide my wings, I was suddenly very conscious of the lack of protective disguise.

'What else can you do?' Josephine's voice was quiet, intensely curious. 'Besides saving stubborn girls who don't listen to their doctors, I mean. I remember that day in the cave under the bridge; you could see in the dark.'

Out of the corner of my eye, I caught sight of her fingers trailing under the collar of her shirt, searching for her dandelion pendant. I remembered that day in the cave so well; the day I'd been changed. The day I'd pledged to protect Josephine, no matter what.

The day I'd told her that I loved her.

'Yeah, I can,' I said, pushing the thought from my mind. 'But it's different than how I see in the daylight. There's no color, exactly. Things look more like a black-and-white photograph, just really, really clear.'

'That's gotta be cool,' she said.

'Well, it keeps me from stubbing my toe on the way to the bathroom.'

Josephine's nose wrinkled in a laugh. 'And what else?'

'My senses are pretty good . . . smell, hearing . . .' I saw Josephine's gaze flick to my pointed ears, and I ran my hand self-consciously through my hair. 'And I suppose I've got a pretty thick skin – at least, according to Karl.'

'I remember what he said,' Josephine said. 'Diamonds are harder than stone.'

'Apparently,' I replied, studying my arm. 'And I thought werewolves had it bad with the whole silver bullet thing.'

'Well, at least diamonds are more difficult to come by, right?'

'Unless you're a Marksman.' Instantly, I regretted my comment. We sat there for several moments, not moving. My hand still held the ice pack on her knee. 'Have you heard from him today?' I asked.

Josephine looked at me, surprised by my question. 'No, I haven't. Quentin doesn't usually communicate with me when he's out on assignment, but I honestly didn't expect him to be gone this long, either.'

'I'm sure you'll hear from him soon, Josephine.'

The smile that spread across her features made the turn of conversation worth it. I couldn't help staring at the way her lips framed her teeth so perfectly. The smile worked its way over her entire countenance, making it shine.

'Thanks, Sebastian.'

'For what?'

The Gypsy girl took the ice pack from my fingers and set it on the floor. 'For being my friend.'

She grabbed my hand. Despite her fingers – which were cold from the ice – intense heat seeped into my skin. My clawed fingers curled tentatively around hers.

'Of course,' I whispered.

Josephine took a deep breath, and her bright eyes clouded over. 'I've never really had many, you know. Friends, I mean.'

Her confession floored me. How could someone like Josephine *not* have people beating down the door to be her friend? I remembered how easily she got along with everyone at school and how much Katie gushed over her. And I remembered the huge crowd at her birthday party. Josephine read my expression. She smiled, but this smile was not the one that lit up her face and made my heart flutter.

'You don't believe me?' she asked.

'Is it that obvious?'

'Well, it's true,' she continued. 'I'm not like Francis.' She gave a tiny laugh. 'He could make friends with anyone, and he does. He's just got that kind of personality.'

'But so do you, Josephine. Everyone adores you.'

One of her brows arched delicately. 'That's not the same thing as having a real friend, Sebastian.'

Slowly, her meaning dawned on me. She and her brother had the same charisma and charm, but their relationships were different. Francis had real friends. Josephine had doting acquaintances. So it seemed that – in our own ways – she and I were both alone.

'You'll always have my friendship, Josephine,' I said softly. 'No matter what.'

She squeezed my hand for a moment and then – almost as if she remembered herself – she let it go. Josephine studied her fingernails. 'You know all that stuff I said to you before, about how I've never told anyone about my fears?'

'Yes.'

She curled her fingers into her palm. 'Well, it's true, Sebastian. You're the only one who knows about that. I've never trusted anyone enough before to let them inside that way.' She let out a breath, nearly laughing. 'Crazy, isn't it?'

My gaze fell on her pendant. 'Perhaps not.'

She looked up suddenly, and her pained expression was replaced with amusement. 'Has anyone ever told you that you sometimes talk like—'

'Like I'm in a novel?' I finished for her. 'I've been accused of that a time or two.'

'I've noticed it more since you came here. Almost formal.'

I pulled a face. 'Formal?'

'Not all the time,' she said. 'Just little things, here and there.'

'Old people talk?' I replied, quoting Avery.

Josephine laughed – a rich, genuine laugh – and it filled my ears with pleasant humming. 'And why is that exactly, my good sir?'

'I'm not really sure, to tell you the truth. Chalk it up to my former life, I suppose.'

My former life. What *had* I been doing before Hugo's parents brought me to him? What lay beyond the black void of my memory? Did I even exist before then? Cold chills prickled along my arms.

'Sebastian?' Josephine's voice brought me back.

'I'm sorry. I was just thinking.'

'About what?' she persisted.

'About my life . . . or lack thereof.'

The clouds returned to her eyes. 'So it really is true, then. You don't remember anything before coming to Sixes, like you told me last year? It's because of the car accident, right? With your biological parents?'

'The accident was a lie,' I said, my jaw tightening. 'My parents, the foster care, all of it. Everything I thought I knew about my life was made up, planted inside me somehow by Hugo's parents. It's like I told you the first night I came here. The *sclav* and brand didn't do this to me. Hugo said I've always been a gargoyle.'

'But . . .'

'I don't know,' I said before she could finish the thought. My wings fluttered in my peripheral vision. 'I don't know why I looked normal before I was branded and why I'm this way now. My past is like one big piece of Swiss cheese.'

'But I thought Karl was helping you figure all that out.'

I shifted my body into a crouch and rested my arms across my thighs. I looked at the arrangement of cushions under

Josephine's leg. 'Well, things aren't working out quite like I'd hoped. It seems like everything I need to know is some part of shadowen knowledge that's been lost. He's helped me in a lot of ways. I just wish . . .' I let my thought trail off. I didn't want to tell Josephine about my battles with my emotions and instincts, or about my inability to control them. I was repulsive enough as it was. 'But enough about me,' I said, looking up at her. 'What about you? How are you dealing with your fears?'

Josephine's gaze drifted across the room. The painting of the cathedral on the living room wall had captured her attention. 'It's the weirdest thing, really. I used to have nightmares all the time.'

'Nightmares?'

She nodded. 'The really bad ones. The kind that feels so real that you wake up thinking you're still right in the middle of it.' Josephine's eyes fixated on the painting. 'In my dreams, I was always dancing, but it wasn't at the circus. It was autumn, and I was somewhere else. There was something watching me. I couldn't see it. I could just hear it snarling at me through the mist.' Josephine closed her eyes. 'It would reach for me, and then I would wake up.'

I struggled to take a breath. She'd seen the image, as well – the one I'd been plagued with for months before the Romanys came to Sixes. I stood quickly and backed away. If Josephine was the woman in the vision, then I was . . . the *monster*.

'What is it, Sebastian?'

'It's nothing.' I stared at the gargoyles in the painting. 'It's just that I've had a similar experience, only it wasn't a dream. More like a picture in my head.'

'Really?' Her fingers wrapped around her necklace. 'I've

had the dream all my life, Sebastian,' she said quietly. 'But it stopped, right after you came to live here.'

Josephine pushed herself to her feet and limped towards me. I quickly closed the distance and caught her as she stumbled forward. Electricity buzzed between us, and I could tell that Josephine felt the same sensation.

'This whole thing is just so confusing,' she said.

'I know.'

Her brow furrowed. 'So what about you, Sebastian? Do you still see the picture?'

'No,' I replied. 'It stopped after I met you.'

The connection between us was more than obvious, and her dream only seemed to solidify that fact even more. It was hard enough being assigned as her bodyguard, but feeling linked to Josephine like two crossed wires was torture. For Josephine, I could only imagine the connection felt like interference in her relationship with Quentin.

'Sebastian?'

A look crossed Josephine's face – an expression that I'd come to recognize. She wanted to say something more. My heart started beating faster for some unknown reason, and the current kicked up a notch.

'Yes?'

Suddenly, the buzzing of a cell phone broke the electricity, and Josephine reached over to the end table, picking it up. She glanced at the screen.

'It's Quentin,' she breathed, sounding relieved.

'I'll let myself out,' I replied.

I wanted to make my exit as quickly as possible before my stoical expression cracked. But Josephine was right behind me, the phone still ringing in her hand.

'Sebastian.'

It took all my strength to glance back at her. The phone went off again. Josephine pursed her lips and then smiled. 'I'll see you later.'

'Until then, my lady,' I said, bowing slightly.

Josephine's eyes sparkled appreciatively. 'Indeed, my good sir.'

14. Certain Perplexity

That evening, after dinner, the Circe held a test run for their carnival rides. Francis dragged me along. One thing I'd learned about the Romany twin: he was difficult to ignore. Josephine was spending the evening at home with Sabina, with Marksmen posted around their trailer. She insisted that I go with her brother, so I was left with no excuse.

As we approached, Phoebe flagged us down excitedly. 'Are you guys ready for some fun? I've been waiting for this all week!'

Francis spun her around in a circle. 'I swear, Feebs, you act like you're four years old sometimes.'

'Oh yeah, look who's talking!'

'Hey, guys!' called Claire, joining us. 'I so needed this break! Aaron's running the trapeze like a drill sergeant, and it's getting ridiculous!' She tossed her red hair out of her eyes. 'I mean, we could perform those routines in our sleep.'

Zara sauntered over, her bright lips turned up in a sly smile. 'Oh, I'm sure you do, Claire.' The acrobat glared, but Zara only laughed and winked at me. 'Hey there, gray boy.'

'Hey back.'

Brishen, who was standing close to Claire, scrutinized me with narrowed eyes. 'We haven't seen you in a while.'

His greeting, while not cold, was not exactly welcoming either. Zara tugged at his sleeve, a reprimanding look in her blue eyes.

'Nicolas has kept me pretty busy,' I replied.

Francis, who had either missed the interaction or chose to ignore it, rubbed his hands together briskly. 'Well, are we going to do this or what?'

'You know it,' replied Zara, maneuvering herself next to me. 'I vote for the teacups first.'

There was a general groan from the rest of the group.

I raised an eyebrow. 'Teacups?'

Phoebe laughed and grabbed Francis' arm. 'You'll see.' She yanked him along with her. 'Come on!'

The rest of us – all neatly paired off – followed them to the carnival rides, all crammed into the front section of the Fairgrounds and positioned to attract the attention of the town. All the lights were on – flashing in their multicolored patterns – and the motors and engines hummed steadily with life.

'So how did we swing this job, exactly?' I asked Francis, staring dubiously at the rickety contraptions.

'No one else wants to do it.'

'Yeah, I can see why. No offense, but carnival rides always seem a bit on the sketchy side to me. I mean, can you really trust something that's constantly being assembled, taken apart, shipped to another town, and assembled again?'

Francis grinned. 'Chicken.'

The teacup ride Zara had suggested was a metal platform shaped and painted to look like an enormous serving tray. Nine giant teacups, with room for two passengers in each one, were bolted to the floor.

Zara tugged at my arm. Perfect teeth flashed against her red lipstick in the evening light. 'So, are you ready?' she asked, and something about the tone of her voice made the back of my neck tingle.

'I feel as though I should be very afraid,' I replied.

She laughed, and while it wasn't the same pleasant sound that Josephine was capable of, it was still nice. I really looked at Zara for the first time that evening. She was dressed like something out of an old movie. Her long skirt and top clung to every curve. Gold jewelry sparkled everywhere, all the way down to her sandaled feet.

I remembered what she said about her role in the carnival: playing the stereotypical Gypsy fortune teller. She laughed again, and I realized I was staring. I averted my gaze, focusing on the ride instead. Francis and Phoebe had already picked out a teacup and were pulling down the safety bar. Brishen was inside another car with Claire.

Which left only the two of us.

'Well?' she said, offering me her hand. 'They're waiting.'

Her skin was soft, her fingers long and thin. She stepped onto the platform, choosing a teacup on the outside of the circle. She gathered her skirt and slid in, making room for me on the bench. I pushed through the narrow opening and frowned. Even folded tightly against my back, my wings were pretty bulky.

'Ah, this may not work,' I said.

Zara glanced over my shoulder, touching my arm in the process. But when her fingers slid along the edge of the framework of one wing, my stomach did an odd flip. The sensation filled me with guilty pleasure, and I shifted my body quickly around to face her.

She tilted her head towards me. 'What is it?'

'Nothing,' I replied quickly. 'It's just that, with all the space my wings take up, I don't think I can sit far enough back in the seat to lower the safety bar.' A low-pitched warning horn blared three times. Apparently test runs didn't include adhering to safety rules – like having the bar in place *before* the ride started. I plopped in the seat. 'What should we do?'

Zara tucked her arms around my waist, under my wings, and around the upper edge of my belt. 'Well, it looks like you're just going to have to keep me safe, gargoyle-boy!'

The huge platform gave a protesting creak, and then it began to move – slowly at first, but then it picked up speed, rotating in a circular pattern. The engine chugged, the metal groaned, and then the teacups began spinning all on their own. I forgot about the Gypsy girl wrapped around my waist as the world rocked and spun out of control.

Now *this* was a ride!

The wind whipped through my hair, and I laughed, clinging to the side of the teacup. As we whirled, I caught glimpses of the rest of the group, their own teacups wildly out of control. I heard Phoebe squealing with each pass.

When the ride began to slow, I remembered Zara. She held me tightly; her head snuggled against my chest. Once again, I felt a wave of guilty pleasure at the contact. She was a beautiful girl, and for some reason she seemed intent on flirting with me.

'That wasn't what I was expecting,' I said as the teacup stopped spinning.

Zara lifted her head from my chest, her face just under mine. Her brilliant eyes searched my face as a smile spread over her red lips. 'I hope it was better,' she said lowly.

I was at a loss for words, and all I could do was blink back at her. Thankfully, Francis appeared around the teacup and pounded loudly on the metal frame.

'What's the holdup, guys?' he said, pointing over his shoulder. 'We've got six more rides to test!'

I jumped out of the teacup and helped Zara off the platform, careful not to brush my claws against her hand. The others took off for the next ride as soon as we hit the ground. Zara's eyes were on me as we walked towards a brightly lit metal track.

I glanced over, feeling self-conscious. 'What is it?'

She looped her arm through mine. 'Oh, I'm just trying to figure you out.'

'There's not that much to figure out, really.'

Her arched brows lifted. 'Are you serious?' Her fingers tightened around my bicep. 'You are quite the enigma, Sebastian Grey. And I like a good mystery.'

Subtle was one thing Zara was not. Her blue eyes danced, and I found myself smiling back at her. 'I take it that you don't have a lot of gargoyles come through here.'

'Not any as interesting as you.'

I was taking the bait, but I couldn't help myself. 'What do you mean, exactly?'

Zara took my shirt in her hands and pulled me directly in front of her. The rest of the group continued on ahead of us. As I stood there, wondering what Zara was up to, she reached up with one hand. I thought she was going to run her fingers through my hair – something I wouldn't have entirely minded – but instead, her fingers curled around something just above my temple.

'These are a nice addition to your look, by the way,' she said as she gave a little tug.

My head responded immediately to the pull, dipping slightly. I flinched.

Zara tilted her head curiously. 'What's wrong?'

'Sometimes I forget,' I said with some reluctance, 'that I have them.'

I'd grown used to the stares and wary glances – so much so that I barely noticed anymore – but people rarely commented on my appearance, especially since I'd made the decision not to disguise myself. I was the gray elephant in the room, or in this case, the camp. Even Josephine – *especially* Josephine – avoided the topic. Sometimes, I almost forgot how I looked.

Almost.

Zara rubbed her finger along the grooved spiral of one horn, and I gulped suddenly. Something about this felt very good . . . and very wrong. I quickly reached up and took her hand. Zara smiled, almost knowingly, and I cleared my throat, embarrassed.

'I think horns are very . . . fierce,' she replied.

Her hand pressed mine, and I let go, but my movement only caused her smirk to widen. She looked at me through thick lashes, and I stepped back, unsure of exactly what I was feeling towards the beautiful Gypsy girl.

'I'm flattered, believe me,' I said. 'But why are you so interested in me?'

'I like analysing people who intrigue me, Sebastian,' she said with a coy laugh. 'It's part of my profession around here, you know.'

Zara walked a slow circle around me – her skirt swishing around her ankles – and her gaze swept over me. 'Let's see,' she mused, putting a finger against her lips. 'Firm body, strong arms. I bet you're more than a match for the guys around here.' She completed her circle and lifted her gaze to study my face with the same thoughtful expression. 'Mesmerizing eyes, to be sure, and a face that's very difficult to read. It's deeply brooding, in a mysterious, quiet-type sort of way.' Zara placed her hands on her hips, smiling in satisfaction. 'And the whole gray thing is definitely . . . dark.'

The way she said 'dark' sent a burst of heat along my spine, and I swallowed hard, trying to keep my head clear of the barrage of sudden thoughts and impulses that flashed through my brain.

'I think you've got the wrong person, Zara. I'm not . . . that's not me.'

She walked her fingers shamelessly up my arm. 'You should look in a mirror sometime, gargoyle-boy.'

As I looked at Zara, I had – for the first time – a twinge of doubt about my feelings for Josephine. What if I really *had* confused my guardian connection to her with what I thought was my love for her? Hugo said we shouldn't feel love, only duty. Augustine claimed that gargoyles weren't even capable of love.

Josephine was with Quentin. She may have felt the same confusion I did, but it was clear how she felt about the Marksman. My own mixed-up emotions had only made things harder, and I'd sworn I wouldn't let them get in the way of my duty. But what about someone who wasn't my charge?

Zara's scent – heavy with exotic spices – lingered between

us, and her face moved closer to mine. My nose wrinkled pleasurably, and I couldn't stop myself from taking another whiff. Her blue eyes searched mine, and the curve of her painted lips was inviting.

Maybe I wasn't capable of love, but I was capable of feeling *something*. And even if I could love, Josephine didn't love me in return. So why was I torturing myself this way? A gorgeous girl was practically in my arms, and she'd done nothing all evening but express interest in me.

What was wrong with returning that interest?

Zara was so close that I could feel her breath on my face. It was warm and sweet. My gaze settled on her lips. My breathing had slowed, and my eyelids were heavy. I leaned down. Everything felt comfortable. Nice. I could do this. I *should* do this. Her lips brushed against mine, and my eyes drifted shut.

I can't.

My lips froze, barely touching hers, and my body went tight.

'I can't.'

Zara's lips swept over mine again, and she murmured softly. 'Yes, you can.'

Her hand stroked the outer edge of my wing, and the sensation snapped me back to reality. I lifted my head and pulled back. Zara's eyes fluttered open, and she looked at me in surprise.

'You want to, don't you?' she asked, blinking slowly.

The warmth of her lips – tinged with the taste and smell of sugared cherries – still lingered on mine, and I had to look away. 'It's not that,' I replied, reining in my senses and taking a cleansing breath. 'You're very beautiful, Zara.'

She smiled, but I could see the slight narrowing of her

eyes as she tried to ascertain the meaning behind my words. Then her expression shifted to one of understanding. 'So who is it, then?' she asked, looking at me with a steady gaze. 'Who is she?'

My carefully crafted expression nearly crumbled. Karl knew how I felt about Josephine, and Francis suspected. I couldn't afford any more than that. If I was ever going to put my feelings in their proper place, then I had to make sure that no one else ever found out.

'Guardians can't have relationships, Zara,' I replied slowly.

She crossed her arms over her chest. 'That sounds like something Karl would say.' The Gypsy girl rolled her eyes. 'God, he used to bore us to tears around the campfire with all his stories from the old country and those fairy tales from his books.' Her voice had taken on a sarcastic lilt. 'But what does he know? After all, we are taught that guardians don't exist anymore. But here you are. So, why don't you just lighten up a bit, Sebastian?' Her hand found its way to my chest. 'I'm not looking for anything serious, if that's what you're afraid of.'

Zara was quite convincing – in her own way. And her scent was very inviting. I studied her hand as it rested on my chest. 'That's not what I'm afraid of.' I looked up, feeling completely conflicted and yet absolutely certain that – no matter what – I couldn't allow anyone else into my life. 'It just wouldn't be right. I'm sorry.'

Zara looked stunned. Her icy blue eyes widened for a moment. Then her hand slid from my chest, her fingers rippling across the contours of my shirt. She fumbled with one of the gold bracelets at her wrist – the first awkward gesture I'd seen from her. 'Well, I suppose I should thank you for being honest with me,' she replied in a tone that was more awed than upset. 'Even if I do think you're missing out on something good.' Her sly smile was back in place. 'But if you change your mind . . .'

I smiled back. 'You'll be the first to know.'

I couldn't be certain if she was convinced or not, but it no longer mattered. The moment had passed. She took my arm and spun me towards the small roller coaster. 'Well, come on, gray boy,' she smiled. 'We're missing all the fun!'

'Now that's one ride I never get tired of,' Francis remarked as he plopped down on the metal bench next to me. 'I mean, it's no five-star coaster or anything, but it's got some serious kick. You could lose your lunch on that.'

I watched the cars whiz by on the track in front of us, all trimmed with red and yellow flashing lights. 'It looks pretty impressive,' I said. 'Too bad I couldn't fit in the seat.'

Francis chuckled. 'Yeah, sorry about that.'

'They just don't design shoulder restraints for people with wings. I may have to report this carnival to the Gargoyle Bureau of Investigations.'

The Romany twin glanced sideways at me. 'Sounds pretty serious.'

'Oh yeah. They could shut this whole place down. It's discrimination, you know.'

In truth, I hadn't minded opting out of the ride. After what happened with Zara, I needed a little breathing room. My heart picked up speed when I thought about the brief kiss – and the guilt stabbing me in the middle of the chest when I'd touched her lips. Thankfully, Zara didn't seem to hold anything against me. I liked Francis and his group, and I didn't want anything ruining the few friendships I had in the camp.

Francis leaned back, spreading his arms across the top of the bench. 'Man, I can't believe we're about to open the Circe. It feels like we were just in Sixes. Time flies, right?'

'If you say so.'

It felt as if I'd been here for months, moving through my routine like a ghost – one who saw the world around him, but couldn't take part in it. Not that I was complaining. I'd definitely take an uneventful day over one with rogue chimeras or bullying Marksmen. But the more time I had on my hands, the more I questioned things.

Doubted things.

'So what went on with Zara tonight?' asked Francis.

'Nothing,' I replied automatically.

'Didn't sound like nothing to me. Zara said you turned her down.'

A muscle jumped in my jaw. 'That's not exactly what happened.'

'Oh yeah?' Francis leaned forward with a curious twinkle in his green eyes. 'So enlighten me. Not many men turn down Zara Stoakas.'

I sighed. 'It just wasn't going to work.'

'Well, probably just as well,' Francis continued. 'I love Zara, but she's a piece of work. None of the guys around here interest her. We're all old news. Every time we hit a new town, it's sort of a long-standing bet to see how long it takes Zara to pick up some poor soul and then drop him like a bad habit the moment we pack up to leave.'

'Thank you, Francis,' I said, looking sideways at him. 'That does wonders for my self-esteem.'

He laughed, shaking his head. 'No, I don't mean it that way, man. I just meant that she's a woman who likes a challenge.'

'A challenge.'

'Uh huh.' Francis pointed at me. 'Like you.'

I rolled my eyes. 'Sure.'

'Come on, Sebastian,' Francis reprimanded. 'You're the most interesting thing around the Circe these days, in case you haven't noticed. You can't really blame her for trying. But for a guy like you to turn her down, well.' Francis regarded me for a moment. 'That's got to be a new one for her.'

'She's great,' I replied, feeling yet another stab of guilt. 'I liked hanging out with her.' I shifted in my seat, suddenly uncomfortable. 'I just can't get involved with anyone right now.'

'Yeah, I guess not.'

I examined Francis' expression. 'What does that mean?'

He shrugged. 'I can see you're leaving your options open, that's all. You know, in case someone else comes around.'

'Well, she's not going to,' I said before I caught myself.

I could see in his eyes that he was enjoying unearthing my little secret. 'You never know.'

I gritted my teeth. There was no hiding anything from Francis Romany. 'It's like you said before, my . . . *kind* . . . doesn't get feelings like that, remember? I'm her guardian, and I'm concerned about her well-being. We share a connection to each other, that's all.'

Francis pondered my words for a moment. I clenched my fists, pricking my skin with my claws. I suddenly wanted to go back to my trailer and curl up in the dark. Maybe I could convince Karl to shoot me up with some more of his vitamin D sedative.

'I've seen the way my sister looks at you, Sebastian,' Francis said in a quiet tone. 'You look at her the same way.

I don't know anything about this connection stuff, but I *know* that look. You can deny it all you want, but that doesn't change the truth.'

I struggled to keep my face carefully composed, succeeding only in tightening my jaw and looking away. 'Well, Josephine and Quentin—'

'Screw Quentin!' Francis snapped. 'I could care less about Marks. But I *do* care about my sister, and she's been unhappy for a really long time.' Suddenly, Francis' expression changed, and I saw a hint of the same burden I'd seen in Josephine. 'She won't talk to me about it, but I'm her twin, and I know her too well. We have our own connection, you know?' He ran his hand over his eyes. 'There's something dark inside her. Some pain she hides, but I can see it. Quentin eased that pain for a while, and I thought she was finally happy. But she's not. She's not, Sebastian, and it hurts me, as her brother, to see her like that.'

I looked hard at the ground, trying to still my quivering wings. My head pounded, and I pinched the bridge of my nose between my fingers. I saw Josephine's face in my mind. I saw the pain Francis spoke about in her eyes. I'd sworn I'd protect her, and I'd give my last breath, if it ever came to that, but that's as far as our relationship could go.

'I'll keep her safe, Francis.'

The park bench creaked as Francis stood. I slowly lifted my head. He put his hand on my shoulder. 'Josephine doesn't need to be kept *safe*, Sebastian. She needs to be *saved*.'

'How?'

Francis smiled. 'Only you can answer that.'

15. Ebbing Sway

It was late by the time we'd finished testing the rides. I wasn't sleepy, but I was mentally wiped. Lanterns and the occasional modern work light illuminated the paths between RVs and tents as I made my way back to my own trailer. I heard the sounds of a late-night rehearsal in the Big Tent, and the faint strumming of a guitar in another part of the camp.

I paused a few yards away from the Romany home and glanced in the window. Sabina strolled through the living room space, a phone in her hand. Josephine sat nearby; a small laptop resting across her legs; her hair pulled up in a ponytail. The sight of her made my head tingle, and for a split second I considered stopping by. But the idea vanished as quickly as it came.

Just outside the front door, two Marksmen stood guard; arrows strapped across their backs and their bows propped up against the RV steps.

Ice churned in my stomach, and I breathed out of my mouth automatically. Smelling Marksmen wasn't one of my favorite hobbies. I hadn't realized how close I'd edged to the Romany trailer until I saw their bodies tense, hands drifting towards weapons. I felt the flicker of adrenaline and promptly backed away before it could become a flame.

I had my freedom, but it simply wasn't worth the confrontation.

Suddenly, I felt someone behind me, and I turned fast on my heel. My right wing slammed into Karl and sent him stumbling a few paces. He made a grunting sound and several objects tumbled out of his hands to the ground.

'I'm sorry, Karl,' I said, reaching out to steady him. 'I didn't know you were there.'

The old trainer chuckled. 'Distracted, were you?'

I refused to look back towards the window and concentrated on the ground instead. I wrapped my clawed fingers around a thick book bound with dark green leather. Two other similar books lay nearby. I gathered them up. 'I don't remember seeing these before.'

'They're from my private collection,' he answered, taking the books.

'You have a private collection?'

'Not very extensive, I'll admit,' he said. 'Just these three. I don't normally keep them in my trailer with my other books, but I wanted to get some research done tonight.'

'On what, exactly?'

At that moment, my stomach rumbled.

Karl's wrinkled face cracked a smile. 'Hungry?'

My appetite was downright embarrassing sometimes.

'That's another thing I wanted to check on,' he continued, not really needing an answer from me. 'Shadowen appetites I know a bit about, but yours is a tad unusual, even by shadowen standards. If you don't mind me asking, how do you feel when you don't eat?'

'Weak and grumpy,' I said.

'Anything else?'

I swallowed and my throat felt suddenly dry. 'It gets hard to think.'

'You mean concentrate?'

'No, I mean think altogether,' I replied, reaching up to brush my hair out of my eyes. The air felt suffocating around me. 'About anything. Except eating.' My hand strayed to my chin, and I pressed my fingers firmly against my jaw. 'My teeth ache . . . like they're starting to right now, and it doesn't get better until I'm chewing.'

Karl frowned so deeply I could barely see his eyes. 'I know there were several methods used by our ancestors to manage a shadowen's behavior. Food was, perhaps, a conditioning technique of some kind.'

'Karl,' I said slowly, 'if you're about to compare me to Pavlov's dog, I may seriously consider altering my dinner menu to include circus trainers.'

His frown quirked upward. 'Threatening an old man, are you?'

I rolled my shoulders, folding my wings in tighter against my back. 'Trust me, you have nothing to worry about. The most challenging thing I ever intend to eat is one of Alcie's overcooked cubed steaks.'

'Forgive me for all the questions,' said Karl, patting me on the shoulder. 'It's just fascinating what I've uncovered so far about the Outcast clans and their system for controlling the creatures they created.' He caught my expression and quickly added. 'Not that we intend to do any of that to you. But it's useful information.'

I felt the eyes of the Marksmen watching like vultures from their nearby post, daring me to make one wrong move. I jerked my chin in the direction of a small storage trailer several paces away. Karl immediately fell into step beside me until we'd rounded the corner.

'What's so different about this private collection of yours?' I asked.

'Well,' said Karl, shifting the books into the crook of his arm, 'as I've mentioned, most of my library contains volumes on Roma and shadowen history, full of stories and tales from our past. But these . . .' Karl's eyes grew distant. 'A few days after my grandfather's funeral, I received a parcel in the mail containing these three books. With them was a note in his handwriting. He told me I was to keep them absolutely secret from anyone in the clans. He said I would need them one day.' Karl paused to look at me. 'And he said I'd know when that time came.'

'How long ago was that?'

Karl pursed his lips in thought. 'About thirty years ago.'

It felt like someone had released a swarm of bats inside my stomach. 'So you pulled out these books because of me.'

'Not entirely,' he replied, his eyes shining in the lamplight with unveiled excitement. 'But between your continuing symptoms and the increased shadowen activity lately, I can only assume this is the time my grandfather was referring to.'

I sighed heavily. 'Now I really need a snack.'

Karl nodded. 'Probably a good idea from what you've told me. And I need to get home. I'm going to burn the midnight oil tonight going over these pages. Most of the writing isn't in English, and it's going to take time figuring out the text. Why don't you stop by tomorrow after dinner while the night rehearsals are in session? We'll go over them together.'

'Sounds like a plan,' I said, clutching my jaw. 'I'll see you then.'

I sprawled across my bed and shut my eyes, hoping I could sleep my way out of hunger. But all I managed was a brief catnap: nothing remotely resembling actual sleep and definitely not enough to take mind off the emptiness in my stomach. Finally, my grating insides couldn't take it anymore. I had to get some food.

I checked my phone before stepping outside. It was just after midnight, and I decided to check the food tent first. I mentally kicked myself for not bringing food back to my trailer each day after meals. I was going to have to start hoarding after this.

I kept close to the perimeter, walking a good pace. The scent of Marksmen was everywhere – so much so that I couldn't separate them out. My nose wrinkled. Between the regularly scheduled night patrols and the increased guard Quentin had placed on watch before he'd left, I could barely go fifty feet without running into one of them, no matter how much I kept to the shadows.

The sound of chickens rattling around in the nearby cage reached my ears, and I was disgusted at how quickly my body responded. My stomach tightened and cramped, and my mouth watered so hard I had to brush it away with the back of my hand.

'That's fantastic,' I grumbled as I neared the food tent. 'But just so you know,' I said to the empty sky, 'I don't care how hungry I get. I'm not raiding the chicken coop.'

'That's a shame. 'Cause I'd really like to see that.'

My shoulders tensed as I turned to find Phillipe smirking at me from underneath his leather Marksmen hood. Six Gypsies clad in black stood in a line, weapons in hand. Bales of hay, stacked three high, were set up along the length of the fence, each with paper bullseyes fastened to them.

Stephan crossed his arms and leaned against one of the bales. 'What are you doing out this late, gargoyle?'

I eased back several steps, very slowly, hands outstretched, as though trying to escape a pack of rapid wolves. 'Just looking for something to eat.'

He smirked. 'Aren't your kind supposed to stay away from food after midnight?'

'I think that's gremlins.'

'Same difference,' said Phillipe, closing the distance between us with deliberate steps. 'And equally as ugly.' His hands rested on his belt, near his knife. 'Of course, if you're looking for a snack, I'm sure you can find a rat or two around the garbage bins.'

I remembered the similar remark I'd made to Thaddeus and felt suddenly nauseous, despite the hunger pangs. I summoned enough energy to craft a grim smile across my face. 'Thanks for the suggestion. But I think I'll stick to leftovers.'

Phillip moved around me, rejoining the group. As if on cue, each Marksman notched an arrow to his bow and posed like a member of a firing squad, aiming in my direction. 'How about a little late-night target practice, then?'

'Listen, guys . . .' I began.

An arrow zipped by, the point catching the edge of my sleeve before it drove into the bullseye beside me. The sound it made rang in my ears.

'Whoops,' said a Marksman who looked several years younger than me. 'My bad.'

I felt my eyes flash. 'Don't do that again.'

Heat licked the inside of my skin, and my spine prickled in warning. It was the worst possible time to be this hungry. And exhausted. I'd gotten used to Josephine's presence acting as a calming influence the last few days. But she wasn't here.

It was just me.

I surveyed the line of armed men. Lamplight glinted off the diamond-encrusted arrows like sparks. Phillipe drew his knife – a long, vicious-looking dagger that seemed to shine with a gleam of its own. He made a show of cleaning its jagged edge with the sleeve of his jacket.

'Scared, freak?' said Stephan.

Some part of me wanted to fight – to jump into the middle of the group and let the terrible thing inside me loose. The rest of me wanted to run away screaming; to hide from everything, especially from myself. My brain and body were two locomotives, coupled together and firing in opposite directions.

'Answer me,' Stephan demanded.

His arrow left the string, aimed at the bullseye to my right. In that split second, I visualized my hand catching it. There was a wisp of black smoke and, suddenly, I was there, fingers clamped around the arrow shaft.

I stared at it, eyes wide. The black mist swirled and vanished. I wasn't exactly sure what had happened, but my anger suddenly faded, just like the weird smoke. I snapped the arrow between my fingers and let the pieces fall to the ground.

'If you really want to shoot me,' I said, looking up. 'Then shoot me. But I'm not wasting another minute of my time.

Now, if you'll excuse me, I'm sure there's a leftover cubed steak somewhere with my name on it.'

I walked away, daring any of them to make a move. I was done stooping to their level. I felt their hatred churning like storm clouds behind me, but no one said a word. I shoved open the tent flaps and pushed through.

As soon as I was inside, I collapsed to my knees and took several big gulps of air. My gums screamed at me. I found myself baring my teeth and felt them slice into my bottom lip, completely out of my control. I clutched my stomach, trying to remember why I was in the tent. What was I doing here?

Food.

I pushed myself to my feet. Everything felt hazy, surreal, and quiet, like being underwater. My blood rushed to my ears.

At that moment, an old woman walked out from behind one of the long shelves. Her eyes lit on me, and she stifled a scream. I jerked away from her as quickly as possible. I could only imagine what I looked like.

'Alcie,' I said, through clenched teeth. 'I'm sorry. I didn't think anyone would be here.'

'I couldn't sleep,' the old woman replied. 'So I decided to get an early start on breakfast.'

I groaned, imaginary bacon floating in my head. My knees wobbled, and I held onto one of the tables. It was definitely the worse I'd felt so far from not eating. Dealing with Phillipe and his buddies had taken more out of me than I'd thought. I straightened my shoulders and turned around. Alcie's wrinkled face drew tight.

'Are you all right, boy?' she asked.

'Fine,' I answered. 'Well, no. Not fine. I need something to eat.'

I breathed in through my nose and out through my mouth. All I could think about was meat.

'Of course,' Alcie said. 'There's always plenty here.'

I immediately felt guilty for my earlier comment about her cooking, even if she hadn't been there to hear it. 'Thank you.'

'Come with me,' she said. 'Let's see what I've got in the fridge.'

I followed her across the tent. She flashed a friendly smile as she began pulling out various containers that smelled – thankfully – like chicken and gravy. As I watched the old Gypsy woman begin to plate the food, I made a decision right then and there to stop letting the Marksmen get to me. It was clear that Quentin's men would never be on my side. But finally, and at long last, it seemed that the opinions of the rest of the troupe were beginning to tip in my favor.

And that thought was more satisfying than the cold chicken Alcie set in front of me.

Well, almost.

16. *Gentle Thunder*

The next morning, I had just returned to my trailer from the crew showers – having decided to use their facilities after the incident in the Romany trailer – and I was scrubbing my hair dry when there was a knock at my door. I jerked at the sound and snagged the towel on one of my horns, ripping a large hole in the fabric.

'Just a second,' I called out, growling to myself as I tossed the mutilated towel in the sink.

I grabbed a dark gray T-shirt and hastily zipped it up the back around my wings – too concerned with getting dressed to focus on the pleasant current buzzing across my skin. I opened the door, and my mouth dropped open.

'Morning,' said Josephine brightly. 'I was hoping you'd be awake.'

I tugged down my shirt, smoothing out the fabric with nervous strokes. 'Ah, yes . . . well, I've been up for quite a while, actually.'

'Oh, right,' Josephine laughed. 'I keep forgetting you don't sleep much.'

A sudden wave of panic hit me. 'Have I missed something?'

Our routine consisted of breakfast separately, followed by Josephine's scheduled rehearsals and other business around the Circe. It was just after 7:30 – a bit later than I usually went to eat, but still well before our normal day began.

'No, not at all. Just a change of plans.'

I noticed she wasn't wearing her typical rehearsal attire. Instead, she had on jeans and a crimson top that complemented absolutely everything about her. Mismatched jewelry sparkled against her skin, and her hair fell loose around her shoulders.

'What's on the agenda?' I asked.

'I got the day off,' she announced, sounding happier than I'd heard her in a while. 'I guess being stubborn, going to practice on an injured knee, and then nearly getting killed in the process pays off sometimes. It took some convincing on my part with Father, but he finally agreed to let me go – as long as you were with me, of course.'

'Go where?'

'Away from here,' she replied, glancing over her shoulder. When she looked back at me, her face held an odd expression – almost embarrassed. 'So, anyway, I stopped by to ask if you would mind going with me today.'

My heart shifted up a gear. 'You know you don't have to ask me, Josephine. I go where you go.'

'I know,' she said softly. 'But I wanted to.'

We shared a moment of awkward silence.

I smiled. 'Do I get breakfast first?'

'Yeah, you get breakfast first. In fact, I'll meet you at the pavilion in an hour, okay? I've got a couple of things to take care of.'

'All right, I'll see you there.' I couldn't believe how calm I sounded.

As soon as she disappeared around the corner of my trailer, I closed the door and leaned against it. The room spun, and I pressed my head against my forehead, trying to squelch the crazy tingling in my brain as I reprimanded myself.

'You're just her guardian, Sebastian,' I said out loud. 'Don't forget that.'

As I devoured my plate of sausage links and turkey bacon, I tried to figure out what Josephine had in mind for her day off. She'd been pretty confined since the Circe arrived in Sixes, whether by her choice or her father's. Maybe she wanted to get a coffee or even catch a movie – but neither were activities where I could accompany her. I was at a loss, but no sooner had I finished off my coffee than her scent tickled my nose.

'Are you finished?' Josephine asked.

I quickly dumped my empty plate. 'Ready when you are.'

I felt eyes on me, and glanced up to see Francis. His expression was one of carefully concealed curiosity as he passed by. Thankfully, Josephine didn't notice her brother's look. She was swinging a small basket in one hand.

'What's that?' I asked, pointing to it.

'It's a nice day,' she answered, looking at the sky. 'I thought a picnic would be fun – if you don't mind, that is.'

'A picnic?'

'Yeah,' she replied. 'Just the two of us.'

'Works for me.' My reply sounded casual enough, and I prayed she couldn't hear the drumline beating under my sternum. 'But is your knee up to it?'

'Sebastian . . .'

I caught the warning tone and couldn't help smirking. 'Right. Won't mention it again.'

We left the pavilion together and crossed the center of the caravan. Josephine walked with a slight limp, but I kept my word and didn't comment on it. She was tougher than half the players on the high school football team. When we got to my trailer, I paused. 'Hang on just a sec,' I said, reaching for the door.

'What is it?' Josephine transferred the basket to her other arm.

I scanned the sky. The mid-morning clouds were thick, but summer weather in the South was unpredictable. I entered the trailer and rummaged through my things. I didn't have another long jacket like the one Hugo gave me, but I found one with a deep hood. I tucked it under my arm and closed the door behind me. 'Just in case,' I said, patting the jacket.

Josephine studied me carefully. 'Does the sun . . . hurt you?'

'Just gives me a killer headache. And a desire for a nap.'

We reached the front gate of the Fairgrounds. A Marksman leaned against the iron bars. My nose wrinkled automatically at the nasty smell and the cold chill. He gave me a customary look of disdain as he produced a key and pushed it into the lock. Josephine thanked him, and we passed through. The gate shut with a clang behind us.

The forest was thick with summer foliage, and the smell of earthy things was strong. We walked in silence, heading towards the river. Though the gravel road was wide, I found myself falling behind Josephine, as I did when I followed her around the Circe.

'You can walk *with* me, you know,' she said, smiling softly over her shoulder at me. 'Consider yourself off-duty.'

'I don't think I'm supposed to really ever be off-duty.'

She sighed. 'Okay, then, can you at least pretend to be more friend and less guardian for a while?'

I quickened my pace to join her. 'Josephine, I *am* your friend.'

'I know you are,' she replied. 'I just want to get away from the troupe for a while, and I don't want to think about opening night or Quentin being gone, or our clan being in danger. I don't want to think about any of it.'

'I'm sorry, Josephine.' I studied her face, seeing the lines of worry along her forehead and the edge of her mouth. 'I can't imagine what it's like to have all that hanging over you. I never realized how complicated your life was before I came to the Circe.'

Josephine froze in the middle of the road, her eyes searching mine. 'God, Sebastian,' she breathed, 'you really are unbelievable.'

My chest tightened. 'I wasn't implying you couldn't handle it. I was just—'

'No, that's not what I meant.' Josephine pressed her fingers to her lips and exhaled through her fingers. 'You're unbelievable because you're always so concerned about me, all the time. I don't know how you do it, especially after everything you've gone through.' Her gaze swept over my body. 'I mean, *look* at you.'

She'd brought up my appearance at last, but I'd been wrong about how I thought it would make me feel. Avoiding the subject *had* been easier. 'What's done is done,' I said, pulling my shoulders back, keeping my gaze level. 'And it's been worth it. If it takes being a monster to protect you from monsters, I'm okay with that.'

'You're not a monster,' she replied in a voice as firm as her look. 'Not even close. Remember what I told you before my family left Sixes? You're a different kind of guardian angel. Just because your wings aren't made of feathers and you have horns instead of a halo . . .' Josephine's hand pressed against my chest. Right over my heart. 'The way you look doesn't change this.'

The ground felt like melted butter. My lips tugged up as I watched the determined glow I loved dance across her face. 'I guess sometimes I just need the reminder.'

'Well, consider it done,' she replied. Her other hand cupped my cheek. 'And you're not as terrible as you think you are, okay? You were handsome before you looked like this, Sebastian. Being a gargoyle hasn't taken that away. If anything, it's added to it.'

My breath took a detour on its way from my lungs. I stared hard at Josephine, afraid I was reading too much into her words. 'Why are you telling me this?'

'Because I'm your friend, and you deserve to know,' she replied. 'I hear how people talk about you around the Circe. But you can't believe them. I don't care what anyone else says or thinks. You're not a freak, Sebastian. I wish you could see that.'

How was it possible for my heart to soar and sink at the same time?

'Thanks.'

She moved away from me, then took a few steps down the deserted road. I watched her, my guts torn with emotional knives. But the look on Josephine's face was like a bandage, reminding me that – even with the pain – I'd still live.

'Well,' she said, 'are you coming?'

We continued our walk, side by side. The silence that fell between us was more comfortable now. *Friendly*. I knew the time had come to release the painful feelings and nurture the good ones. She and I were friends, and that made Josephine happy. And because she was happy, I would be, too.

Josephine talked, and I listened. It was satisfying to hear her so unguarded, so free. She scooped up a handful of rocks as we crossed the Sutallee Bridge. She tossed a pebble into the water and offered me one. I took aim and sent the rock skittering across the ripples. It was as if each pebble was some wounded piece of my heart, and with each toss, I felt more whole.

I was going to be okay.

This was going to be okay.

We passed over the bridge to the other side. Josephine dropped her basket and leapt acrobatically down the bank, testing her knee and her weight as she hopped from one large rock to another. I followed behind. The roar of the water was so loud that we stopped talking and simply watched the river as it rushed by.

Josephine's bright eyes were riveted on the water. A ray of sun slipped from behind a thick cloud, turning the river into a current of diamonds. I shrugged on my jacket and pulled the hood low. Then I crouched on a large, jagged rock, and watched her. In the light of the sun and with the burdens gone from her eyes, Josephine looked like an angel.

Her eyes fell on me, and her smile faltered. 'How are you feeling?'

'Perfect. Although, I am getting a bit hungry.'

'But it's only ten o'clock,' she replied. Then a beautifully sheepish look crossed Josephine's face. 'Oh, right!' She picked up the basket and slung it over her arm. 'That's like an eternity for you when it comes to food, right?'

'Close,' I said with a shrug. For sure, I didn't want Josephine to see me the way I'd been last night before Alcie came to my rescue. I squinted into the trees. The sun was out fully now, and the canopy of leaves provided little cover. I felt my muscles stiffening and the beginnings of a headache at the base of my skull. 'So, any thoughts on where to have your picnic? Besides here, I hope?'

'Shade would be good, wouldn't it?' Josephine crossed her arms over the basket. 'I mean, I don't want to spend the afternoon talking to myself while you take a nap.'

'No napping, I promise. But I might shut my eyes for a bit, every now and then. If I start to snore, though, maybe you'd better kick me or something.'

'Well, I'll try my best not to be boring,' said Josephine.

I rose from my crouch and headed for a clump of trees near the bank. 'Unless you're intending to teach a class on advanced trigonometry, I don't think that's really possible. And maybe not even then. Of course, maybe that's just the sun talking.'

The corners of Josephine's eyes crinkled. 'So it makes you delusional now, is that it?'

'Nah,' I said. 'That's only when I don't eat. And let me tell you, breakfast sausage doesn't go far in a gargoyle stomach.' I peered at the sky, studying the puffy clouds, their bellies fat and gray. Gradually they overtook the sun, obscuring its hazy form. 'Now, that's more like it,' I said. 'I was pretty sure the weather report said mostly cloudy, so I'm good for wherever you want to set up picnic camp.'

Josephine swung the basket behind her. 'Well, I have a confession to make.'

'And what's that?'

'I've always wanted to go up to Copper Mountain.'

I brushed my hands across my jeans, wiping off bits of dirt. Copper Mountain was a historical site from the Civil War, and it was Sixes' most impressive landmark. 'It's too far to walk, I'm afraid,' I replied. The mountain and surrounding park areas were on the opposite side of town.

Josephine glanced over her shoulder. 'I was hoping we could fly there.'

My good mood disappeared as quickly as the sun. I clamped down on my bottom lip for a moment, tasting blood as I looked away. 'I don't fly.'

'Yes, you do.'

'Okay,' I admitted. 'But not as a general rule.'

'Why not?'

The question hung heavily between us. Suddenly, I became conscious of my wings once more. It'd become easy to ignore them, so long as I kept them tightly folded and pressed against my back. I'd only flown out of necessity to save Josephine from danger. Never just for the sake of flying.

Never for the pleasure of flying.

'Because,' I said. 'It's easier to . . . forget . . . when I don't.'

Josephine moved closer to me. 'But they're a part of you, Sebastian. You have them for a reason.'

'You sound like Karl.'

He'd told me that I needed to improve my abilities. And I agreed with him. But when it came to flying, I'd completely blocked out his instructions. It was the stuff of horror movies.

People who flew weren't human.

I jolted when Josephine's hand touched my arm. 'I'm

sorry, Sebastian,' she said. 'I'm not trying to force you to fly. I just thought you'd want to. I've barely seen you use your wings since you came here, but the day you caught me when I fell, I remember your face. You looked so complete, like you were doing something you were meant to do.'

I still felt it keenly – the sensation of being utterly free – as I'd shot through the air. Josephine was right. I was meant to fly, and it scared me so badly that my hands trembled. I shoved them into my pockets, struggling to keep my face calm.

'All right,' I breathed.

Josephine's eyes widened. 'What?'

'All right,' I repeated, closing my eyes. 'I'll do it.'

17. *Healing Wounds*

Saying I was going to fly was one thing. Actually doing it was another.

With only two flights under my belt, I knew I needed some running room for my take off. I didn't feel particularly comfortable around so many large trees, so Josephine and I hurried along the path, peering through the foliage until we spotted a field just past the river, large enough to use as a runway.

I shivered in my skin with anticipation. We strolled through the wild grass, talking about the logistics of flying as if it was the most normal thing in the world. It was crazy. It was *insane*. Yet, for some reason, I was totally okay with it. I was about to come to terms with something that had terrified me from the moment I'd become a gargoyle.

'So what does it feel like?' Josephine asked.

I pushed my hood from my head, avoiding the grooved horns at my temples. 'It's . . . well, I guess it's sort of like running. Pumping my wings is work, and making them move where I want isn't easy. But the energy is pretty awesome.'

I glanced at Josephine, feeling weirdly shy. 'It feels . . . good.'

Josephine smiled at me. 'I'm glad.'

The sky had turned completely gray, without a hint of the sun's earlier rays, and the clouds loomed with the possibility of an afternoon shower later. The weather was perfect, and the overcast day was like a breath of fresh air. I let out a grateful sigh. We were far from the road, and the thick forest hid the town from view. We were completely alone.

'This looks like a good spot,' I said.

Josephine was a bundle of scarcely contained curiosity. 'So, what do you do first?'

I couldn't help laughing as I shrugged off my jacket and Josephine tucked it inside the picnic basket. 'I don't really know. The other two times I flew, I was just moving on instinct, really. I didn't think about the details.'

'Creature of instinct,' she murmured to herself. Her brow knitted in thought. I pulled my gaze away to keep from staring at her. 'Okay,' she continued in a louder voice. 'Then I guess you should do the same thing now, right?'

'Right,' I repeated, my nerves kicking in. 'Instinct.'

I took a deep breath and flexed my back. The movement flowed into the muscles and bones of my wings – which still felt foreign in so many ways. They were a part of me and I controlled them, but it was like moving my arms after they'd fallen asleep – a weird, tingly sensation. My wings expanded with a heavy flapping noise. I glanced to my left and right.

God, they really *were* huge.

'Wow,' said Josephine, clearly thinking the same thing. 'That's got to be, like, twenty feet across.'

'Eighteen and a half,' I replied, feeling uncomfortable but

also strangely excited. 'They've grown a bit since I came to the Circe. Karl measured my wingspan a few days ago.'

'How did you ever hide these in your jacket?'

I folded them in and out like an accordion to demonstrate. 'I guess it's because I don't have to worry about all the feathers, right?'

The way Josephine smiled made my head spin. 'Ready for lift-off?' she asked, backing away.

'Here we go,' I said with more confidence than I felt. I stroked my wings like big leather oars. Only my wings weren't stiff. The bone framework curled and uncurled like giant fingers; the leathery membranes rippling with each flap. Against the gray clouds and yellowish grass, the skin of my wings held an incandescent sheen.

Josephine watched me with a silent kind of contemplation that I couldn't quite read. I fluttered them several more times, and allowed myself to enjoy the stretch. Then I folded them tight against my back in preparation. I lifted my eyes to the grassy clearing and planted my feet against the ground, ready to push off like a sprinter on the blocks.

'On your mark,' said Josephine, her eyes bright.

'Get set,' I added, bracing myself.

Josephine spread her arms. 'Go!'

I bolted forward in a dead run. I gained speed quickly – quicker than I'd imagined I could. And then, I just *felt* what to do next. I leapt and – at the same moment – unfurled my wings. They caught the air, and I pumped them with all my strength. The movement shot me up and forward like a bullet, and I pumped again.

And again. And again. And again.

When I looked down, I was shocked to see how far I was above the ground. The wind whipped against my face, ruffled my shirt, and tore through my hair. Thinking back to my rescue of Josephine, I leaned to one side and tipped my opposite wing towards the clouds. I turned with the air current and changed direction. Josephine stared up at me, looking awed and thrilled, like she was watching one of the Circe's performances.

As I rapidly approached the takeoff area, I wondered if I could stop. I knew how to make a running landing, what about when I was actually *in* the air? Images from a cheesy fantasy movie Hugo and I'd seen last year popped into my head. The dragon in the film had hovered in midair by angling its body and tilting its wings. It was a bad film, but not a bad idea.

Just as I passed over Josephine's head, I arched my back, forcing my shoulder blades together, and thrust my legs toward the ground. It was as if my wings knew exactly what to do. They angled, and I flapped them at a slower pace. The tactic worked.

I hovered above Josephine, my body moving like I was treading water in a swimming pool, only with wings instead of legs. 'How was that?'

'That was awesome,' Josephine called up to me, clapping her hands. 'You look great.'

'Thanks,' I grinned back at her, forgetting for a moment about my appearance and reveling in the freedom I felt. 'Maybe I'm getting the hang of it.'

'Well, I hope so,' Josephine answered quickly. 'Because it's my turn.'

'And what exactly did you have in mind?' I asked, feeling my stomach jumping to the beat of my wings.

She held up her right arm. She said, 'Wrap your fingers just above my wrist.'

I angled my body downward, wobbling slightly as I adjusted the tilt and flap of my wings. I grabbed her arm, and she grabbed mine. Our linked arms felt strong – the grip I'd seen her use in her routines with Andre. 'Okay, now what?'

She winked. 'Just lift and fly. Straight shot across the field.'

I pumped my wings and took off. She swung beneath me – several feet above the grass – testing the sensation. It was like watching her on the silk ribbons of the Circe act again. There was no fear in her expression, only exhilaration. I saw the flex of muscle in her arms; the taut tendons in her neck. It was as if a routine had been specially crafted for us – a blend of gargoyle and Gypsy, like an ancient bond between us.

I kept low to the ground, flying at a leisurely speed and growing quickly accustomed to how my gargoyle body functioned in the air. Josephine called instructions up to me, and we switched arms as she dangled below. We reached the other end of the field, and I slowed as much as I was able without adjusting the nearly horizontal position I'd been flying in. She nodded at me, and I lowered her down and released my grip.

Josephine touched the grass with a circus performer's skill. I flapped once, tucked my wings, and dropped beside her. My own landing was softer this time. I bent my knees to cushion the impact, and my body settled comfortably into a crouch. My adrenaline was pumping, but in a very different way.

'We may have to rethink that idea of you joining the troupe,' said Josephine, sounding both pleased and amused. 'We'd make one really spectacular act.'

I laughed. 'In case you've forgotten, the last time I tried performing in front of an audience, I made Shakespeare roll over in his grave. I think I'll just stick to the behind-the-scenes guardian stuff.' My stomach rumbled, and I pressed my hand against my torso. 'And speaking of which, I'm going to need some lunch if I want to keep up with my duties.'

Josephine looked over my shoulder. 'Oh, I left the picnic basket on the other side of the field. Guess we're going to have to fly back over and pick it up.' She glanced at me. 'On our way up to Copper Mountain, of course.'

The mountain loomed behind her, taunting me. It was isolated enough, but that wasn't what made me nervous. 'I've never gone that high before, Josephine. Are you sure you want to do this?'

There was no hesitation in her voice. 'Definitely.'

My already racing pulse went into overdrive as Josephine moved in front of me. With slow determination, I scooped her up into my arms. It was impossible to get Josephine's scent out of my head or ignore the heat of her arms around my neck as she held onto me.

I dug my heels in preparation. 'Copper Mountain, here we come.'

Josephine's eyes met mine, and the look on her face was so open, so trusting. I promised myself I'd never do anything that would change that. I broke into a run, pressing Josephine against my body to ease the jolts. This time, it only took half the distance before I knew I was ready to take flight.

I pushed off hard and beat my wings. My balance was slightly off with the Gypsy girl in my arms, but I immediately compensated. We streaked across the field, slowing only enough for Josephine to catch the handle of the picnic basket as we flew by. I pumped my wings, and soon we were easily twenty feet off the ground.

Energy drove through my veins; I flapped harder, sending us higher into the air. We soared over the tree line. To my left, the town fell away and then disappeared altogether. Up ahead, the secluded mountain's green form grew larger. I angled my body in that direction, and we cut through the sky like a rocket.

'This is amazing, Sebastian!' Her arms tightened around my neck. 'I feel like I'm dreaming!'

Copper Mountain rose before us, a mixture of green hardwoods and dark pines. Jagged cliffs of granite peeked out among the clearings of trees. I caught sight of the one narrow road that led up the mountain, and banked quickly, turning us in the opposite direction – away from any possible civilization. Though the mountain was a historic site and no one lived there, tourists and locals occasionally visited the spot.

I aimed for a deserted clearing, and we whisked through a grouping of oak trees. At the last moment, I righted my body hard and jerked to a stop in midair. I spread my wings wide and set us down on a flat chunk of rock.

Josephine glanced around the clearing. 'Nice landing.'

I placed her on her feet. 'I hope this spot works.'

There were a few stone picnic tables, but it appeared as though no one had used them in some time. It was off the beaten path. An old wooden sign stuck out of the ground with the number of the picnic area scrawled onto it, and just underneath, another sign read:

Hiking Trail – Lover's Leap – 0.2 miles

'It's perfect,' said Josephine.

We located one table situated near the edge, which

provided a clear, unhindered view. Josephine pulled out a blanket and arranged it, smoothing out the wrinkles. She sat atop the table, feet on the bench. I mirrored her posture. My wings draped behind me and over the side of the table. Josephine set the basket between us, opened the lid, and we both peered inside.

'Were you planning on having company?' I asked, studying the piles of Tupperware.

'Nope. Just you.' She retrieved a plastic container and pried off the lid. It was full of lunch meats. The smell hit me hard. 'I haven't forgotten how you eat.'

'You know me so well,' I replied, wiping my mouth.

'Well, I've watched you enough.'

My hand froze across my jaw. I didn't look at Josephine, afraid she would see my expression, and then everything I'd been working for all afternoon would crumble. 'Well, my appetite has a bit of a reputation.'

There was the sound of crinkling plastic wrap. 'There's that,' Josephine replied, 'but I've also noticed *what* you eat. Mostly meat, right?'

I stared at the roast beef, turkey, and ham she'd unfolded in front of me. 'Actually, pretty much all meat.' My stomach growled, irritated at the delay.

'Any particular reason?' Josephine's mouth sounded full. The sound was cute, and I stole a glance in her direction. She was chewing on a tomato sandwich and wiping juice from her lips. 'For the change, I mean,' she continued. 'I don't remember you always eating that way. Just eating *a lot*.'

'I can't really eat too much other stuff.'

Josephine set her sandwich down. 'Can't?'

I picked up a piece of turkey between my claws and

studied it. My teeth ached for the meat, straining just below my gums. 'Most foods don't agree with me too well anymore. I'm all about the protein. Karl says it's a gargoyle thing,' I continued with some reluctance. 'Eggs and cheese aren't too bad, but apparently meat's about the only thing on the shadow creature food pyramid.' I didn't tell her how many evenings I'd spent retching over the sink in my trailer before I'd finally figured that out.

'That's really weird,' she said finally.

'A pretty accurate description for most things pertaining to me.'

Josephine laughed, and I took the opportunity to tear into the sandwich meat, whimpering softly. The pressure in my jaw lessened instantly. The sensation unnerved me, especially after my conversation with the circus trainer the night before.

As if reading my mind, Josephine spoke up again. 'So how does Karl know what you can and can't eat?'

I gnawed on a hunk of sliced turkey before swallowing it down. 'He's got some old books he's going through.' I suddenly paused, wondering if I'd said too much. I didn't want to keep anything from Josephine, but I didn't want to betray Karl either. Josephine took another bite of her sandwich, and I chose my next words carefully. 'Just a bunch of old stories, really. Nothing concrete.'

Josephine nodded, chewing thoughtfully. 'So, what about liquids?' she asked after a few moments. 'Are you limited to protein shakes, or what?' She smiled, but the look in her eyes was serious.

'Water mostly. And coffee. Maybe because it's so thick. I don't know. But thankfully, I can still drink that.'

'Remind me to brew a large pot when we get home.'

'Will do,' I replied.

She handed me a bottled water. We ate in comfortable quiet, with only my occasional involuntary growls breaking the silence as I devoured the meal. Josephine pretended not to notice. She'd packed a few hamburger patties as well, and I munched on them like a true carnivore, while she finished her sandwich and a bag of chips. After we'd eaten, she stared into the basket.

'Well, I brought along a couple of pieces of my mom's chocolate cake for dessert,' she said. 'But I don't guess that's really on your menu.'

'I could try it,' I offered automatically, seeing the disappointment on her face.

Josephine smiled hopefully, and she pulled out a plate covered with clear wrap, piled high with the most delicious looking cake I'd ever seen.

'You're sure?' she asked as she pulled back the plastic.

The smell of chocolate filled my nose, but it wasn't as appealing as I'd hoped. I shook it off. A few bites wouldn't hurt anything. 'I think it would be rude to let your mother's hard work go to waste.'

Josephine produced a couple of forks. 'That's true.'

She took a bite, and I watched her chew. Her face took on that glow that could only come from a rush of sugared bliss. I licked my lips, remembering the way it used to feel. 'Your mom must be a good cook.'

'Try some,' she said as she went for another bite.

I stabbed into the cake with my fork and brought it to my lips. Layers of icing hung thick over the sides. The cake should've tasted amazing. But the smell was all wrong, and as soon as I'd placed the bite in my mouth and began to chew, I knew I'd made a mistake.

Reflexes kicked in, and I gagged. I jerked my head in the opposite direction and spit the chunk out of my mouth. I gulped water until the horrible taste was finally off my tongue. I leaned forward, grimaced, and wiped my lips with the back of my hand. 'Okay, bad idea.'

Josephine was completely quiet. Then I heard the crinkling of paper once more. When I glanced up, the cake was gone. 'I'm sorry, Sebastian.'

The look on her face made my heart hurt. Impulsively, I reached out and touched her shoulder. As I did so, it was like placing my fingers in a socket. I pulled back, taking a deep breath as tingles of electricity sizzled down my spine.

'Don't worry about it,' I replied with only a trace of a quiver in my voice that I prayed Josephine would overlook. 'With my appetite, I'd have finished off the entire cake and left you empty-handed.'

'Well, you saved me from an extra workout. Mom's cake is pretty heavy.'

'I do what I can to help,' I replied. At that moment, a soft flow of understanding and mutual connection passed between us. My senses were awake and alive, but everything outside our small world was nonexistent.

'Do you miss it?' she asked after a while.

I glanced sideways at her. The breeze whispered through the trees, wafting through her hair. I could smell her scent even more clearly in the mountain air. 'The food? Yeah, sometimes. I have – *had* – a weakness for pizza. And salt and vinegar potato chips.' Josephine made a face, and I shrugged. 'It's an acquired taste.'

I leaned back, propping myself on my arms. I wasn't sure how long we sat there enjoying the mountain scenery, but I would've gone on forever. I'd never felt so relaxed around

Josephine before, not like this. As if I could finally – almost – be myself. But then Josephine shifted, and the buzzing current between us was gone.

She packed the remaining containers and gathered the basket. Our picnic had come to an end. I leapt from the table and folded the blanket. The clouds were heavier, and the sun was invisible. It would make for an easy flight back to the clearing.

'Are you up for a hike?' she asked suddenly.

'I'd love to, but are you sure you have time?' My gaze darted to the sky. 'It's getting late.'

She crossed her arms, eyes narrowed. 'That remark bordered more on guardian and less on friend, just so you know.' She pulled her cell phone from her pocket. 'It's only three o'clock, Sebastian. We'll make it home for dinner.'

'Then I guess it's time for a friendly hike.' A grin tugged at my lips. 'How was that remark? Better?'

'Much better.'

I slipped my jacket on. We left the rest of our things on the picnic table and followed the arrow on the old wooden sign, the narrow trail, forcing us to walk single file. I allowed Josephine to take the lead, but I stayed right behind her.

The woods were cool and shady, mostly free of undergrowth and carpeted with thick moss. Josephine chatted over her shoulder back at me, and I allowed my senses to focus on her voice – low and rich, flavored with whatever emotional undercurrent accompanied her topic of conversation.

The more I listened to Josephine, the more I understood her. Our connection as guardian and charge had deepened since being together, but this was a different level entirely. The conversation opened doors to our lives we'd both kept closed before, and it gave me a sense of something more definable than just an invisible bond. It was sharing life – the good and the bad, the beautiful and the ugly.

Josephine told circus stories, and I added a few of my own about Hugo and the *Gypsy Ink*. Talking about my foster brother made me miss him more than I had in a while. I thought about the Corsi clan. I thought about Esmeralda. And I wondered when I'd see them again. I hadn't realized I'd drifted out of the conversation until Josephine's face flitted in front of mine. There was a panicked look in her eyes.

'Put your hood up,' she ordered. I blinked at her, not understanding. Josephine tugged on my jacket urgently. 'Hurry, Sebastian. There are people coming down the trail.'

18. *Close Distance*

I saw the group approaching – seven teenagers – laughing as they chucked empty beer cans down the side of the mountain. It was Drew Garrett and other members of the football team. A group I'd never cared for. They felt the same about me. I yanked my hood low over my forehead, concealing my horns.

Panic raced up my spine. No one outside of the Roma had seen me since I'd changed. I stared at Josephine in frantic desperation as it all hit me at once. I wasn't normal. People couldn't see me like this. The Gypsies accepted me, even if they didn't like me. But these guys were part of the real world.

My old world.

The world I'd never be a part of again.

'Sebastian,' whispered Josephine, her voice mirroring my thoughts.

Muscles tautened across my back, and I felt the familiar, dark stirrings creep up the base of my skull – my instincts taking over. I breathed hard through my nose, my vision going hazy. I tried to blink it away. The logical part of my brain screamed at me to run. Grab Josephine and book it down the path.

'Sebastian . . .'

Josephine's voice was urgent. I felt her hands on the edges of my jacket.

My eyes narrowed to slits as I honed in on the rapidly approaching group: the bright clothing flitting between the trees; the alcohol-scented breath; the harsh voices. People. Outsiders. *Humans*. My brain was slamming shut like gates on a castle. My vision tunneled. A snarl rippled along my lips.

I felt my body moving forward.

Then, without warning, Josephine shoved me against the trunk of an elm tree. Her arms wrapped around my head, pulled me down to her, blocking my face from view. Her cheek brushed against mine, our lips inches apart. I squeezed my eyes shut as emotions clawed up my throat like wild animals.

I heard the voices of the football players. I heard every footstep and felt every lewd glance tossed in our direction. Josephine pulled me closer, holding me against her shoulder. I heard snide comments and the crunch of aluminum between fingers. I felt the rush of air as they passed by.

As they passed by.

They didn't stop. They didn't see me. My wings were crushed against the tree, obscured by my jacket. Josephine's slender arms enveloped my head. I was hidden within the shadows she'd created. The footsteps grew fainter, and the voices dropped away. Their scent faded. But Josephine didn't move. A new awareness of her embrace overwhelmed me.

I couldn't imagine anything more intense. Her soft, erratic

breathing warmed my skin. I felt the tension in her arms, smelled her fear. Her lashes fluttered against my cheek like tiny butterflies. My arms slipped around the Gypsy girl, near but not touching; my fingers hovering just above her back. Josephine's lips were so close. I wanted to kiss her with an insane, crippling desperation. I was suffocating, and she was the air I needed.

My hands clenched into fists. I was doing it again. Being utterly selfish. I squeezed harder, and the pain of cut flesh in my palms steadied me. I pressed my arms defiantly against my sides. When I opened my eyes, Josephine was looking at me. God, the way she was looking at me.

I blinked at her, but the haze around her face wouldn't clear; the red edges remained around my peripheral. I shook my head fiercely. I needed space, a chance to breathe. I curled my hands tighter and forced my feet to move, to break free from the torture. I spun away from Josephine. My foot landed sideways on a crumpled beer can, and I stumbled forward.

'Sebastian, are you okay?'

The sight of the can, combined with the smell, stirred the fire inside me again. I dropped into a crouch, and yanked the hood from my matted hair. I focused on a bright clump of moss, fighting to regain my control. 'Yeah.'

'They're gone,' she said.

The calm sound of Josephine's voice eased the pounding in my head. I mentally pushed back against the haze and it subsided. I stood up, straightened my shoulders, and slowly opened my fists. 'Good.'

'I'm so sorry,' Josephine brushed her hair out of her eyes. 'I couldn't think of anything else to do. If those guys saw you—'

'I know,' I replied, leaning against the tree, trying to regulate my breathing and speak around the thickness in my voice. 'It was quick thinking on your part.'

'Sebastian, what'd you do to your hands?'

Drops of inhumanly purple-black blood pooled in my palms, and a trickle ran along the edge of my skin, disappearing into the cuffs of my jacket.

'It's nothing.' I brushed them off against my jeans. 'And I'm the one who should be apologizing. I never got along with those guys in high school, and I guess seeing them sort of set me off. I've not been that great at controlling my . . . um . . . instincts . . . lately.'

Josephine's suspicious look turned to open curiosity. 'You scared me for a minute there. You had that wild look you sometimes get in your eyes, all fierce and flashing. I thought you were going after them.'

I exhaled, and it came out like a growling sigh. 'Yeah, I think I would've, too, if you hadn't stopped me. It's ridiculous. I don't know what happens to me, sometimes. It's like a rush of impulses in my head, and everything gets hazy.'

'Instincts,' repeated Josephine.

I grimaced. 'It's kind of hard to explain.'

She took a step closer to me. 'Can you try?'

I took off my jacket and pressed the fabric into my palms, concentrating on blotting away the blood so I wouldn't have to look at her. I felt suddenly raw, like she'd ripped off my skin and was staring right into my soul. 'It's like there's two parts inside me. There's *me*. And there's . . . something else. Most of the time, I feel like I'm in charge. But lately, it seems like the other part has gotten a lot stronger. It just takes over.'

'And this other part,' said Josephine slowly. 'You mean—'

'I don't know how to reconcile the two.' I wrung the jacket in my hands. 'I don't know how they're supposed to work together, or even if that's possible. I keep trying *not* to feel like a gargoyle, but what if that's exactly what I'm supposed to do? I want to embrace what I am, like Karl says, but it scares me.'

Josephine was silent. Finally, I glanced up. She was looking past me, off into the woods. Her expression held the burden I'd witnessed before. 'I'm not going to pretend I get what you're going through, Sebastian. But I do understand what that feels like to be scared of something you can't control.' Her eyes flicked back to me. 'But you don't have to be afraid. You've got me, now. We'll look out for each other, okay?'

Warmth burst inside my chest, and I couldn't help the smile that worked its way across my lips. 'Well, If I read the handbook right, I'm supposed to be the one protecting you.'

Josephine pushed up her sleeves and ran her fingers through her hair, combing out the tangles. 'Technically. But friends have each other's backs. So you're going to just have to deal with that, Sebastian Grey.'

The way she said my name sent the heat in my chest straight to my head. 'Looks like you're not giving me much choice.'

'Nope,' she replied.

'I guess I'll deal with it, then.' I wadded up my jacket and tucked it under my arm, feeling steady. My crackling emotions were dormant once again. 'Although you may live to regret it. I'm very high maintenance.'

'I can't imagine you being worse than Katie.'

Our smiles dropped at the same time.

'Have you heard from her?' I asked hesitantly.

'I wasn't allowed to make contact this time. Father never liked the amount of interaction Francis and I had with the *gadje*, but he tolerated it.' Josephine shrugged. 'Besides, she's still in New York, right?'

My brows rose. 'How did you—'

'We may have exchanged a few texts,' she added with another lift of her shoulders. 'What about you?'

'I went to her graduation party,' I replied. It was Josephine's turn to look surprised, and I felt my face twitch. 'Actually, I just stalked it. In disguise. A really bad disguise. But it wasn't my best idea. She nearly saw the . . . new me.'

'Have you considered telling her the truth?'

'I can't. She's not a Gypsy. And I couldn't do that to her.' A tremor went through my wings from the base of my shoulders continuing all the way out to the tips. 'Besides, she freaks out over zombie movies. And bats. This would probably be a bit much.' I managed to keep my voice light, but a cold lump settled in my chest, and I sighed. 'I miss her.'

'I miss her, too,' Josephine said, reaching out to touch my arm.

We stared at each other, and I felt our strange connection pass between us. It stitched me up and sliced me open at the same time. I broke the gaze and studied my palms. The bleeding from my claw wounds had stopped, and the eight small cuts had already scabbed over.

'Well, you're just Mr Supernatural, aren't you?' she said, clearly impressed.

'Just scratches, Josephine, nothing out of the ordinary.'

'So says the guy with wings.' Before I could reply, she looped her arm in mine and started up the trail. 'Well, now that we've had our fun little detour, we'd better get going. It's still a way to the top.'

The current between us swirled into a comfortable hum as she led the way. Only the faint stinging in my palms reminded me of just how close we'd been to each other. We rounded a bend and the trail suddenly forked. The right side was a continuation of the path we'd been taking. The left side turned into a set of steps carved out of granite. A wooden rail flanked the staircase and, at its base, a sign indicated the way led to Lover's Leap.

'So where to?' I asked.

Josephine ran her fingers over the carved arrow in the sign. 'I've got to admit, I'm curious about any place with a name like that,' she replied. 'I say we take the stairs.'

The stone steps were wider than the trail, and we were able to walk side by side. I'd frequented Copper Mountain over the last couple of years, and I'd seen most of the points of interest. I couldn't blame Josephine for being curious about this one.

Our conversation lulled as we climbed. By the time we had reached the top, there was only amicable silence between us. The last step opened up into a flat expanse of granite. The wind gusted stronger, hinting at our near proximity to the edge of the mountain. The overcast sky peeked through the thinning trees.

And then, we were in the open. The landscape spread below us in rich detail. The colors sharpened by the darkening sky. Ribbons of roads, splotches of developments, and patches of concrete displayed the visible evidence of humanity's encroachment on Mother Nature. Miles of forests and meadow stretched before us, disappearing into the misty peaks of the Appalachian Mountains on the distant horizon.

'It's beautiful,' breathed Josephine.

'Yeah,' I answered, totally unconcerned with the scenery.

Josephine, thankfully, was too busy looking around to notice. Her lips pursed in thought. 'I don't really understand why it's called Lover's Leap, though.'

'This isn't Lover's Leap, Josephine.' I lifted my hand and pointed. 'That is.'

19. *Sweet Agony*

Twenty yards above where we stood, an enormous chunk of granite jutted from the side of Copper Mountain, its jagged form prominent against the backdrop of clouds stretching across the sky. The plateau of rock extended several yards over a sharp ravine.

'Oh,' Josephine said near my ear. 'Now I get it.'

The lump of rock was impressive – dark and foreboding, like an awe-inspiring testament to nature. A thin footpath ran in the direction of the granite cliff, disappearing just inside the tree line. I looked at Josephine, questioning, and she nodded enthusiastically.

We made for the rock, weaving through the trees along the narrow trail. Another flight of stone steps greeted us, with another sign. Josephine blew right past it, and I followed close behind, taking two steps at a time.

Suddenly we were on the rock, and the world opened up before us. The view was more breathtaking than before. A safety rail guarded the perimeter, keeping enthusiastic hikers from walking too close to the edge. Josephine leaned over the metal bar, her eyes bright.

'This is incredible,' she said, breathless. 'I wonder what the story is behind it.'

I looked over the side of the plateau with the fierce drop-off and the rushing stream below. 'It's an old Native American legend.'

Her curious eyes darted to my face. 'Really?'

I'd heard the tale in history class once, and for some reason, it had stayed with me. Josephine waited in expectation for her lesson, and I wasn't about to refuse.

'A long time ago, two Indian tribes lived on this mountain, and they were enemies. The chief of one tribe had a daughter, and she secretly fell in love with a brave from the opposing tribe.'

'A story of forbidden love,' Josephine surmised with a knowing smile. 'Now you're really going to have to tell me the whole thing.'

'Well, the girl was promised to a prominent warrior in her own tribe,' I continued, 'but she didn't love him. Her father, the chief, demanded that she marry him. But the girl was stubborn.' I grinned sideways at Josephine. 'Instead, she began meeting the young brave every night in secret at this rock, under the cover of darkness. But one evening, fate was not on their side.'

'Go on,' said Josephine, nudging me playfully in the ribs.

'The girl was followed by the warrior, who'd grown suspicious. When he reached the rock, he saw the lovers together. Furious, the warrior returned to the village and told the chief. A small band of men hurried to the rock. They captured the brave and tied him up. The chief ordered him thrown over the side of the cliff. But the girl – when she saw the brave fall to his death – broke free and leapt from the rock, choosing to die with her love rather than live without him.'

My eyes drifted to the gorge below as I finished. Something warm touched my hand. Josephine's fingers pressed over mine.

'That's some story,' she said, her voice more serious. 'I wonder if it's true.'

'Either way, it's how the rock got its name.'

We stood there looking over the precipice as the wind sifted through our hair and clothes. I closed my eyes, enjoying the breeze, until Josephine's soft laughter brought me back. I glanced over, confused.

'What is it?' I asked.

'I guess we should probably find a place to hang that's not on the path. You're a little conspicuous.'

She pulled her hand from mine, and her gaze went from my face to my wings. They'd unfurled in the few moments I'd allowed myself to relax, splayed out on the mossy granite around my feet.

I snapped them back into place. 'Yeah, definitely not in the mood for any more close calls today. Besides, it looks like it may rain soon. Maybe we should think about returning to the Fairgrounds.'

'Not yet, Sebastian, please,' she said. I felt curls of emotion inside the pit of my stomach, which I knew were coming from Josephine, but I didn't understand them. She took a deep breath. 'I'm just not ready to return to real life yet.'

'Okay.' I surveyed the height of the railing for a moment before leaping over it. I offered her my hand. 'Then allow me to take you on the unofficial tour of Lover's Leap. But we'll just keep this between you and me. Park rangers aren't real keen on this sort of thing.'

'I'll keep that in mind,' she said as she took my hand and swung herself over the railing with a performer's grace. On the other side was a groove in the rock just large enough to sit in without impeding the view. Josephine settled in and patted a place next to her. 'This spot's perfect.'

I sat and shifted my body until my wings were sufficiently out of the way. 'And totally out of sight,' I added. 'If I'm still enough, I might even blend in with the scenery.' I slid my hands along the smooth granite. 'There is a certain resemblance.'

She hid her laugh with the back of her hand. Then we were quiet again. I tried not to look at her too much, afraid she'd see too many of my thoughts, but it was hard to keep my gaze averted.

'So, how do you like living with us at the Circe?' she asked. 'When you're not fending off groties or narrow-minded carnies, that is.' She leaned forward, wrapping her arms around her knees. 'Do you miss your clan?'

I watched a hawk flying low over the tree line. 'Sometimes. Especially my brother. He's the only family I've known. But the Corsis aren't really my clan.' I made a sound somewhere between a laugh and a huff. 'In some weird way, I wish I *did* have a clan. A group I belonged to.' I pushed up my sleeve and studied the dandelion tattoo. 'And not because I'm some possession; the way your clan views me.'

'I don't think you're a possession, Sebastian.'

'I know.' I shoved my sleeve back down and glanced at her. 'Josephine,' I began with some uncertainty, 'what did you mean when you said you understood what it's like to be scared of something you can't control?'

I felt her body stiffen beside me. 'I'm not allowed to say.'

'Hey, I told you about the whole Jekyll and Hyde thing

I've got going on.' I'd meant it as a joke, but the deeply serious, conflicted look in Josephine's eyes staunched the humor I'd been going for. 'I'm sorry, Josephine. I didn't mean to pry. Just forget abou—'

'I'm next in line,' she said.

'What?'

'To be Queen,' she finished in a strained voice. She crossed her legs and clasped her hands in her lap. 'My aunt is the Queen of the Outcast clans. The Romanys are more than just a head family. We're Gypsy royalty.'

I leaned back so I could look at her better. 'But your father—'

'Gave up his rights to the throne a long time ago,' she continued. 'I don't know why. But since my aunt never had kids, she's permitted to name her successor. Francis could challenge me for it, but he has no desire for a life outside of our troupe. Father intends to leave the Circe to him someday, and it's always been my brother's dream to head it up.'

'What about you?' I asked. 'Don't you have a choice in the matter?'

The look in her eyes was soft, understanding. 'About as much as you have in being a gargoyle.'

'So that's why I'm your guardian.'

Josephine shrugged. 'That's why Father thinks you were sealed to me, yeah. The Queen bears the responsibility of maintaining order within our *kumpania*. All *bandoleers* are under her authority. She's also the only Outcast allowed communication with the Old Clans in Europe. We've maintained a pretty uneasy truce with them, which basically means we stay out of their business, and they stay out of ours.'

I stared at my shoes, turning the new information over in my head. 'I heard that someone from the Boswell clan claimed to be the King of the Gypsies a while back.'

Josephine tilted her head to the side. 'You've been talking to Francis.'

'Maybe.'

The look that crossed her features was somewhere between amused and reprimanding. 'My brother never could keep things to himself.' Josephine shifted, and our shoulders brushed. 'But it's true. Lots of *bandoleers* and even members of the High Council are hungry for the throne. No one knows who the Queen intends to name, and many are vying for their chance. My aunt believed keeping her decision secret was the best way to keep me safe. Our *kumpania* meets twice a year in Savannah, our primary Haven. The next meeting is soon, and there are rumors that the Queen is supposed to make a public announcement.'

'Will she?'

'No.' Josephine plucked a strand of moss from one of the cracks in the stone. She began picking it apart with her fingers. 'Even though I'm eighteen, I'm not quite an adult by Outcast Gypsy standards yet.' Josephine tossed the greenery aside, irritated. 'There's still one requirement I have to fulfill.'

I opened my mouth to ask, but quickly changed my mind. It was clear by her expression that she wasn't fond of the subject, and I wasn't about to push. One step at a time, I reminded myself. I waited a few moments before cautiously venturing ahead.

'So why are you telling me now, if your father ordered you to be silent about it?'

Josephine held my gaze with a strength that made the

hair on the back of my neck rise. 'He wanted to test you to see how far you would go to protect me, to reassure himself of your loyalty to our clan. But I don't feel the same way he does. I trust you, Sebastian. I always have. I don't need a test for that.'

A distant rumble of thunder caused us both to look up. The skies had grown steadily darker while we'd talked, and now it seemed that rain was inevitable. The breeze felt cool against my face as it wafted up the side of the mountain and rustled the trees.

'Can you fly in the rain?' Josephine asked.

I ran a hand through my hair, scanning the gray sky. 'I don't know, actually.' A heavy mist was developing, hiding the landscape below. 'I don't exactly have a radar system, well, for flying, I mean.'

Josephine smiled broadly and covered her mouth again. My brows rose in confusion. She put her hand on my knee. 'I don't mean to laugh,' she apologized. 'It just seems funny that you don't know your own abilities.'

'I'm actively living in denial.'

'You sound like an episode from *Oprah*,' she said. '"Coming up next: The Art of Being a Shadow Creature. Learning How To Overcome Your Weaknesses and Tap Into Your Hidden Strengths".'

I laughed then. I mean, really laughed – good and long – for the first time in months. Josephine sympathized with me, but she didn't pity me. I hadn't realized just how much I needed that.

'Hello,' I said. 'My name is Sebastian Grey. And I'm a gargoyle.'

'Hello, Sebastian,' she replied. 'Welcome to the show.'

Thunder rumbled again, but it didn't bother me. We laughed

again, and everything inside me felt at peace. Things were as they should be. As a few stray droplets fell on my face, I tilted my head to the sky, welcoming the cool water on my face.

'You have a great smile,' she said suddenly.

I frowned reflexively. I'd forgotten myself for one moment. I gave a half shrug and smiled, this time with my lips closed. Then I looked away. 'Thanks.'

'No, I mean it.' The sincerity in Josephine's voice turned my head, and I regarded her with wary curiosity. Her hand rose to my face, and I couldn't take my eyes from her fingers. 'And it's not just your smile. Your teeth . . . they're just . . .'

I couldn't swallow, much less speak. My blood roared in my ears. Josephine's hand drifted closer. Drops of rain slid down the bridge of my nose, but I didn't move. She stared at my mouth, and her emerald eyes were deep.

I felt her fingertips warm and soft on my cheek. Her palm rested against the curve of my jaw, holding me in place. Josephine's gaze was still on my mouth, and I had to look away. My brain felt like it was short-circuiting. Her thumb moved to my bottom lip, pausing there for what seemed like forever. And then, she gently slid her thumb across my skin. My mouth went slack, and my eyelids fluttered closed. She lingered at the corner of my mouth. My breath caught in my throat.

The edge of her thumb grazed the sharp points of my teeth – hesitantly at first, and then with a more confident touch. I felt lightheaded. I tried to speak, to move, but my body wouldn't obey. Gradually, her fingers left my mouth and slid up along my jaw; her fluid gesture continuing to the very tip of my pointed ear. It took every ounce of strength to hold myself together.

Josephine's voice was a whisper. 'Why do you make me feel like this?'

'Like what?' My voice was thick.

Our eyes met. She caressed my cheek.

'Like I'm alive.'

The skies opened up with rain.

Josephine gasped and dropped her hand. Instinctively, I hugged her to my side and snapped my wings open, positioning them over our heads like a giant umbrella. She stared at the wide expanse of leather and bone above her. And then she grinned.

Thunder rumbled in the distance as the rain fell, but we stayed dry under the shelter of the rock crevice and my gigantic wings. For a long time, neither of us said anything. Josephine shivered and pressed closer to me. She rested her head against my shoulder. I didn't know what was happening, and I didn't care. I just didn't want it to end.

The rain continued – not a downpour, but a soft summer shower – and soon trees were glowing with a watery sheen. I lost track of time. The peaceful rustle of rain and the soft wind along the side of the mountain lulled me into a peaceful state. But the feeling of Josephine's body next to mine kept me alert. My wings ached, but I refused to allow her to get wet. I felt her contentment, and my desire to do anything for Josephine welled up so strongly that my eyes stung with the force of it.

Her head felt heavier against my arm, and I sensed a shift in her being. My ears picked up on her breathing: slow and deep. I smiled to myself.

She'd fallen asleep.

I sat in perfect stillness. My heart slowed to a manageable trot, and I studied the sleeping girl at my side. Her skin was dotted with a few freckles along her cheeks and there was a tiny scar below her left temple I hadn't noticed before. Her lips parted as she breathed. The top lip was smaller than the bottom, coming to a delicate point under her nose. Lashes hid her green irises from view, but not the shadowy circles under her eyes.

A gust of wind fluttered a strand of hair across her cheek, and I reached up to brush it away. The sight of my gray hand and dark claws against her skin filled me with sudden disgust. Why couldn't I be someone else?

Why couldn't I be some*thing* else?

There was no answer to my unspoken questions but the soft pelting of the rain.

20. *Dawning Night*

Time passed, and the rain tapered to a drizzle, then stopped altogether. Josephine slept against me. My body had long since gone rigid, my brain sluggish. I wondered if this was what it felt like to be stone – to be nothing more than a statue, suspended in time and space – a frozen slumber. Would it be freedom or a cage?

The evening sun peeked through the clouds, bathing everything in shimmering gold. It was like heaven opened in front of me. Josephine's head rested in the crook of my arm. One hand was tucked under her chin; the fingers curled into the fabric of my sleeve.

I gently shook my wings free of water. Then I tentatively curled the edge of one wing around Josephine's shoulder, hugging her to me. She stirred in her sleep and tightened her grip on my sleeve. For a split second, I pictured myself leaning in to kiss her. The internal reprimand came quicker this time, and I turned my head. A painful smile pinched my lips as I stared out over the horizon, content with thoughts of holding her tight, shielding us both from the world below.

Until everything went cold.

Sebastian . . .

My entire body snapped to attention. Josephine sighed and turned her face into my shoulder, still asleep.

Sebastian . . .

The voice in my head felt oily, dark, and taunting. It was also familiar. My lip pulled away from my teeth as I sniffed the air and smelled rotting fish. I curled my wing closer around Josephine and studied the sky, then the trees, but I couldn't see anything. I shot back a mental reply.

Anya. I hadn't seen her since we'd fought on the bridge. Though it seemed a lifetime ago, her scent and voice were imprinted on my psyche like an inky stain. *What do you want?*

Laughter reverberated in my brain.

You killed one of your own, little brother.

I growled in my head.

I'm not your brother.

Matthias' thick voice broke into the mental conversation, squeezing itself uncomfortably into my head. *You murdered Thaddeus.*

The image of the chimera ricocheted through my head, making me feel sick.

He attacked me. He was threatening the clan. I did what I had to do.

I searched the trees as I relayed my thoughts, but I couldn't see the gargoyles. I kept my body perfectly still. Josephine continued to sleep, oblivious to the internal conversation.

No, little brother. Anya's voice slithered against my cranium. *You did what the Gypsies ordered you to do. They've manipulated you. Brainwashed you. Made you their pet. We offered you freedom once, but you refused. You've chosen the wrong side, Sebastian, and you're going to pay for that.*

I forced steadiness into my inner voice. *So one minute, you're calling me your brother like we're one big happy family, and the next, you're threatening to kill me? That's a little dysfunctional, don't you think?*

Anya answered. *You turned on your own kind.*

He wasn't a gargoyle. The sight of his hideous form flashed before me again. The darkness inside him that surpassed anything I'd ever felt from the gargoyles – a viscous, primal evil that froze my blood. *He'd changed.*

We're more closely linked than you want to believe, Sebastian. Her laughter felt like shocks of static. *You can deny it all you want. But, deep down, you know that it's true.*

I ground my claws into the granite. *What happened to Thaddeus?*

Silence flowed through my brain like a river of sludge. A slight movement in the trees caught my eye. I sensed the shadow creatures' invisible stares penetrating the cover of leaves, but they were no longer fixed on me. Josephine's body was still warm and heavy against my arm. Every muscle in my body constricted as Anya's biting voice returned.

I see your guardian abilities haven't improved since last we met. You're a long way from the Circe. There are no Marksmen on the mountain – no one to protect your little Gypsy charge, except you. Tell me, Sebastian, do you still believe you love her?

Something unpleasant wormed its way through my stomach.

What's it matter to you? I demanded.

It's so pathetic, this delusional state you continue to live in, believing yourself capable of such a weak human emotion. Although – Anya's voice turned sickly sweet – *she* is *very pretty. And she smells better than dinner. I wonder what it would be like to rip off her flesh and suck her bones clean.*

And then – like a light switching on in a darkened room – I became aware of what my senses had been screaming at me for the last several minutes. The intense cold in my blood, the primal slithering inside my head.

'No . . .'

Josephine jerked against me as I spoke aloud. I eased my arm from her waist and rose slowly to a crouch – my eyes never leaving the trees. Laughter rang out, and this time, it was not in my head.

'The Gypsies thought they could enslave us,' said Anya, her real voice every bit as frightening as her telepathic one. 'But with each marking, with each seal they forced upon their creations in their quest for dominance, they unleashed an evil they couldn't control.'

Tree branches creaked under a sudden gust of wind. Beside me, Josephine snapped awake. I pulled her up with me, wrapping my wing more securely around her.

'What happened to Thaddeus?' I yelled into the swirling current.

Anya materialized from the trees with Matthias at her side. Josephine gasped.

My own appearance had a certain demon-like resemblance, but compared to them I could've passed as one of Michelangelo's cherubs. Like Thaddeus, their bodies retained a vaguely human form, but there was no humanity in their expressions. Crackled skin covered their bodies; their bare feet were misshapen and as hideously clawed as their hands.

Solid silver eyes narrowed and wicked grins drew tight lips back from terrible teeth.

Josephine gripped my arm. 'Sebastian . . .'

Her voice sent every defensive mechanism flaring to life. I felt her fear inside my gut, and my instincts shifted into overdrive. Adrenaline streaked through my veins. I backed slowly along the rock, herding Josephine behind me.

'It's going to be all right.' I tried to speak gently, but my voice was already thickening, and my words rumbled with growls. Josephine's eyes fixed on my mouth as my lip curled, exposing my teeth. 'Just be ready to run.' I reached for her hand, which she took, but I felt her flinch against my touch. I glared at Anya. 'You're chimeras.'

'Close enough, little brother,' she replied. I felt her bitterness like soured milk on my tongue. 'And you're as good as dead.'

The trees around us exploded with wind. It hit with the force of a tornado, sending thousands of wooden shards into the air like shrapnel. My wings snapped out like giant shields for Josephine as I ducked.

Debris rammed into me, and I leaned into the storm, my wings taking the brunt of the explosion. It was like smashing against a wall of needles. The wooden splinters pinged off my body without breaking the skin, but it hurt like mad. When it finally stopped, I whirled around with a snarl. But Anya and Matthias were gone.

An inhuman shriek pierced my ears. Before I could react, they were on me. I lost my hold on Josephine as they grabbed me. My arms snapped outward; my shoulders popped. I kicked furiously, but I was being carried, my feet dragging against the rock plateau. I fought desperately for a foothold, but they were moving too fast. My body slammed into the safety rail, which gave way under the force, but it didn't slow me down.

We plunged over the edge of the cliff.

My wings wouldn't work. There was a heavy weight against my back. My arms were on fire. Laughter echoed in my ears as we sped towards a mass of granite boulders at the bottom of the ravine. They were going to crush me against the rocks – stone against stone.

Matthias suddenly wailed and convulsed. Josephine straddled his back, clinging to him for dear life. Something bright flashed in her hand as she drove her fist repeatedly into the joints of his wings. Blood gushed. He writhed and released me from his clutches.

I wrenched out of Anya's grip and dove for him. His right wing hung limp as he flipped with Josephine hanging on. Matthias lashed at me. His teeth plunged into my shoulder. I grabbed his neck and ripped him out of his downward spiral.

We lurched to a stop in midair – a split second – but all I needed. I plucked Josephine from his back and slammed my feet into his chest. He dropped from the sky, but Anya was on us in a rush of wings and claws.

Suddenly, I was falling out of the air, careening end over end and out of control. Josephine clung to me and screamed. Visions of crashing jet planes flashed before my eyes. I strained my wings, frantic to stop our fierce rotation. I could see Matthias' crumpled body on the boulders below.

I shoved my body in the opposite direction of our tailspin, gasping as my wings finally caught air. I dodged tree branches as I rapidly brought us down among the rocks. I stuck my landing, but no sooner had I released Josephine than Anya surged at us in a mist of smoke. But I was faster this time.

I caught her by the wing and flung her like a giant discus into a boulder. She screeched as her body hit the granite with a sickening thud.

Matthias tackled me from behind. The world went upside down and my face scraped stone as he rammed his knee into my back. The pain coursed like rocket fuel through my body, eating me away. I grabbed my head with a wild snarl. The dark instincts clawed and fought and tore at me. My control burned away like dead leaves on a fire. Everything went red.

I threw Matthias off me, sprang to my feet, and dove at him with a vicious roar. Our bodies slammed together. Pain was nothing to me now. We were a tangle of arms and wings, claws and teeth. Then I had him on the ground. My claws slashed his chest, penetrating shadowen flesh. Inky blood. I threw my head back and roared. Hand poised to strike the final blow.

'Sebastian, don't!'

The words cut through the haze. My hand froze. Adrenaline pumped hard inside me, fighting against my brain.

Josephine's voice was calm. 'Please, Sebastian.'

My stomach lurched. For an agonizing moment, I was suspended between two courses of action. Fierce emotion burst through my throat, strangling me. Choking me. I leapt up, gasping for air, and stumbled back, tripping over my own feet and rolling into a crouch. Instincts and logic warred for dominance.

'Do it!' Anya sneered and pushed herself painfully to her knees. Fiery hatred burned in her silver orbs. She clawed her way across the boulder. 'Kill us, little brother. You know you want to. Give in to the urge.'

The muscles in my back went taut as the red film around my eyes narrowed my vision once more. My breaths turned shallow as I rose to my feet, body hunched forward. I felt my fingers splay wide. Then, a touch on my shoulder.

I jolted, a snarl escaping my lips. Josephine moved into my line of vision. I saw the fear in her eyes, smelled it in her emotions. But she didn't move away. Her fingers wrapped gently around my arm. Her touch soothed my inward battle, and I closed my eyes, biting hard on my lip, tasting my own blood. Josephine simply held onto me, waiting patiently.

Waiting for me to come back.

I stood shaking with instincts; the pressure inside me slowly releasing like steam from a boiler. As the adrenaline ebbed away, my face grew hot with shame. I felt disgusted – completely and utterly disgusted with myself.

'Josephine . . .'

She closed the distance between us, her emerald eyes intensely searching mine. 'No,' she said firmly. 'No apologies this time.' She placed her hand on my shoulder. 'Just take us home, Sebastian.'

Without hesitation, I lifted her into my arms, cradling her body against my chest. What was left of the darkness inside me evaporated, and I took a breath of cleansing air. I stared at Anya's inhuman form, this time without the red haze over my eyes. She coughed, and trail of black liquid spurted from her mouth.

'You're such a waste, fledgling,' she spat. The venom in her voice oozed like blood. 'Augustine was convinced you were the one. But you won't even allow yourself to be a gargoyle. Why did he think you could be anything else?'

I hesitated. If I left, they'd only come after us again. My lips quivered against another snarl. I should finish them off while I had the opportunity. Anya's molten eyes burned with challenge. I felt a spark of fire reheating inside me.

Josephine's whisper brushed against my chest. 'Please, let's go.'

I wanted to protect Josephine so badly that my blood sang. I was capable of ending Anya's life, if I just gave in to my instincts. But if I killed her in cold blood, then what kind of gargoyle – what kind of person – would I be? Conflict swirled like nausea, but the feeling of the Gypsy girl in my arms kept me focused.

'Augustine doesn't control me,' I growled. 'And neither do you. Sorry to disappoint, but I'm not going to kill you.' My eyes narrowed. 'At least, not today.' I turned away from the chimeras' hideous forms.

Matthias hissed. 'You can't leave us here like this.'

'Don't worry,' said Josephine, her voice colder than I'd ever heard it, 'you won't be alone for long. As soon as we get back to the Circe, I'm sending the Marksmen after you.'

I flashed my teeth over my shoulder in a grim smile. 'I suggest you run.'

I spread my wings wide and leapt into the air. There was no running start, no takeoff. I didn't need them anymore. We gained height quickly, bursting through the green canopy of Copper Mountain and heading home.

Josephine was quiet for some time. I couldn't blame her. The half-gargoyle, half-chimera creatures were something straight out of a nightmare. And it had only been Josephine's pleading voice that kept me from killing both of them. I shuddered at the memory, and then I noticed something in Josephine's hand – the object she'd used on Matthias. She clung to it tightly, hugging it against her chest.

'What's that?' I asked.

Josephine's fingers opened, exposing the object to my view. It was a knife, thin and compact – its blade glinting in the evening light with hundreds of tiny diamond specks. I understood then how she'd wounded Matthias.

The Gypsy girl shrugged against me. 'Quentin gave it to me before he left. He wanted me to have some protection.' She turned her face towards me, and a smirk danced across her lips. 'From you.'

'Remind me not to get on your bad side,' I replied.

I worked to return her smile, but an uneasy feeling settled in my gut. Did Josephine really trust me, as she claimed? I turned my attention to the ground speeding by below us. I could learn to live without her love, but if she didn't trust me, what future was there between us?

I felt warm fingers on my jaw.

Josephine met my look with serious eyes. 'Bringing the knife was just for show,' she said. 'For the sake of the Marksmen only. I know you'd never do anything to put me in danger. And I promise the same thing to you.' She searched my face. 'Okay?'

My anxiety released itself inside of me. Josephine was right. Trust had to work both ways. She needed mine as much as I needed hers. At that very moment, I decided I'd never doubt it again.

'Okay,' I replied, feeling my smile relax. 'But could you maybe put it away, you know, just to be on the safe side? You're pretty scary with a weapon.'

She laughed and tucked the knife into her belt. 'I'll take that as a compliment.'

I beat my wings against the evening sky, speeding our course towards the Fairgrounds. A few stars peered down at me through the thick indigo clouds. I opened my mouth to speak, then closed it again. Josephine glanced at me, and her forehead creased.

'What is it, Sebastian?'

'You came after me when they dragged me off the cliff.' My mind replayed the image of her body wrapped around Matthias' back as we plummeted towards the ground. My throat went dry. 'You jumped.'

Josephine's hand found my cheek, and she smiled. 'No, Sebastian,' she replied. 'I leapt after you.'

21. *Waking Slumber*

Josephine snuggled into my chest as I descended slowly through the twilight; the breeze in my wings and the damp of the evening air on my face. But I couldn't be selfish for long. Danger signals flared in my brain, and my volatile instincts still lurked just beneath the surface of my logical thoughts. Josephine needed to be home, safe behind the iron fences of the Fairgrounds.

We needed to tell the Marksmen about the shadow creatures we'd left on the mountainside. And I needed to talk to Karl. Somehow, Augustine's gargoyles had changed into hideous chimeras. But how, and for what purpose?

And where *was* the renegade Gypsy?

I didn't want to risk being seen by anyone who might be on the road, so I drifted down to the field where we'd first taken off. My landing was sure-footed this time. The act of flying had transformed from something I feared to something that felt natural now – an innate part of me that had been dormant too long. I snapped my wings, flinging off the excess moisture, and folded them to my back.

'We need to hurry,' I said, setting Josephine down and taking her hand. Shadows formed in the trees, creeping around the thick foliage. The gates to the Fairgrounds were uncomfortably far. 'I don't want to be caught out here in the middle of the woods when those two decide to take another swipe at us.'

'I don't think they'll be following us anytime soon,' said Josephine.

I flinched. Though she didn't say it out loud, I knew what she meant. I could've killed them. In fact, I'd come dangerously close. My head pounded with guilt and loathing. 'That doesn't mean we're safe. I need to get you back to the Circe, and we have to tell your father what happened.' I bypassed the road and led us into the forest. 'Their injuries will heal eventually, and I can't imagine those two will just quietly return to wherever they came from.'

'I don't understand how Augustine is connected to all this. He's *marimé*. I hadn't heard his name even mentioned until I met you.' Josephine slowed down and blinked up at me. 'All this has something to do with you, doesn't it?'

I matched her pace reluctantly. The need to get Josephine safely into Romany territory was snapping at my heels. 'I don't see how it could. I refused to join him, and I was sealed to you. End of story. There's no reason for him to care about me now.' I glanced sideways at her. 'I'm not the kind of gargoyle he wants.'

'But those chimeras,' said Josephine, 'they said Augustine thought you were the one. They said you weren't letting yourself be a gargoyle – that you weren't giving in. What does that mean?'

I snarled under my breath and shoved a clump of leafy branches aside. 'Come on. We need to move faster.'

'Sebastian,' said Josephine, pulling against me. 'What you did back there—'

'I don't want to talk about it.'

'But—'

'Please, Josephine.' I let go of her hand and continued moving, twisting my wing-laden body to squeeze through the narrow trees. 'When I told you I was scared of the stuff I couldn't control that's exactly what I meant. What happened back there – what I did – it wasn't me.' I wiped the back of my sleeve across my eyes. 'It's not . . . it can't be me.'

Josephine hurried to catch up. 'For a moment, maybe it was. But you were still in there, Sebastian. It was still you inside. And when I called your name, you came back.'

We were deep in the woods, far from the road. I sniffed the air, but the scents were too mingled to sort out. 'I know.'

Conflict darkened Josephine's face, and she picked absently at her fingernails. She was preparing to say something, and I found it suddenly hard to look her in the eyes. 'Sebastian,' she began, 'what I said to you . . . when we were sitting near Lover's Leap . . . on the mountain . . .'

I kept my attention on the trail I was forging, waiting for the words I knew were coming – the regret she felt and the explanation to follow. I braced myself for the blow. 'Yes?'

'What do you feel when you're around me, Sebastian?'

I stopped in my tracks. A fresh current of electricity spiraled up my spine and buzzed through my head. It made me want to jump out of my skin. I looked past Josephine, staring deep into the forest. All sorts of lies crept to my lips, full of denials and dismissive excuses. But the truth fought past them all. 'I feel everything.'

For a moment, she was silent, and I put a foot forward to keep moving before I vomited out more stupidity. Her hand on my elbow stopped me.

'That's how I feel, too,' Josephine replied.

My eyes lifted to hers. 'Really?'

She laughed. 'Well, maybe it's more accurate to say it feels like stepping on a live wire.' Her face turned serious. 'But, at the same time, it's as if all my chaos goes away. I can take a real breath and I know everything's going to be okay.'

'Same here,' I said, keeping my voice carefully even.

It was Josephine's turn to look away. Her laughter was gone, her eyes distant. 'When I say I feel alive around you, what I mean is, it was as if I was just going through the motions before you came along.' She shook her head. 'So how does all this fit into the whole Gypsy-guardian bond we're supposed to share?'

I pressed my lips together. It was like asking how my crazy, undeniable love for her fit into our weird relationship. I opted for the attempt at humor. 'Yeah, these *sclavs* and brands seriously need to come with instructions. I mean, if they can manage a booklet for Lego sets, you'd think we'd at least get a—'

Josephine touched the dandelion on my wrist, effectively cutting off my words. Her fingers drifted tentatively across my claws – examining their roughly curved shapes and thick tips with hesitant strokes – and then her hand closed around mine. She squeezed with determined, comforting pressure. It felt so perfect, as though my hand had been fashioned for hers, just like this.

The world felt complete.

I wanted to hold her, to confess my feelings for her. My

chest was so tight I couldn't breathe. Before I realized what I was doing, my other hand was on her cheek, the claw of my thumb sliding hesitantly across her skin. The sensation was like an electric shock.

'Why are you doing this to me?' I whispered desperately.

Josephine's eyes glistened. 'I could ask you the same question.'

It was then that I saw the tortured look behind her eyes – the same torture I'd grown accustomed to living with for so long. I steeled myself, summoning every bit of courage I possessed. 'Josephine, could you ever—'

'I don't know, Sebastian,' she said, her words cutting me off in a soft, painful breath. There was an agonizing beat of silence, and the Gypsy girl closed her eyes, hiding her soul from my view. 'I don't know.'

A long moment passed. There was something reverential in the air, and my hurt and longing mingled together until nothing made sense. Josephine leaned into my hand. There was neither acceptance nor denial in her expression – just raw emotion.

I stroked her cheek with painstaking tenderness, like caressing fine porcelain, and every minute touch resonated deep in my soul. Our eyes locked, and the electric air enveloped us in a sheltering canopy.

Until something crashed through the trees.

I pulled Josephine behind me as I squared off to meet the thing head on. A snarl rose to my throat. I cursed myself for letting my guard down and not using my senses.

Esmeralda Lucian burst from the underbrush and stumbled, pitching forward into the leaves and dirt. Her red-tipped hair was disheveled, her clothes were torn and dirty, and blood oozed from a gash over her right eye.

'Ezzie!' I cried, gripping her arms. 'What happened?'

She coughed twice, wiped a bit of blood from her lower lip, and shrugged me off. 'I'm fine,' she said through clenched teeth, though she looked like she'd just been beaten up in an alley. 'Mangy dogs. I should have realized they'd catch my scent.'

My former teacher tried to stand, but gasped and went back down. She muttered something unintelligible and yanked up the hem of her ripped jeans. A nasty bite mark extended across her shin, and her leg was covered in blood.

'The Marksmen's dogs,' I said, remembering Caliban. The guard dog's sharp teeth couldn't penetrate my skin, but Esmeralda Lucian wasn't a full gargoyle. She no longer shared my durable shadowen hide.

'I've been human for so long,' Ezzie said grimly. 'Sometimes I forget that I still retain remnants of my old self. Like my scent.'

'Ms Lucian,' sputtered Josephine, kneeling beside us, 'we need to get you help.'

Her eyes were wide, and it dawned on me that the Gypsy girl didn't know what to think. The last time she'd seen Esmeralda Lucian was as a high school teacher directing plays, not crashing through the woods, running from shadowen hunting dogs.

'It's just Esmeralda,' she replied, shaking her head at Josephine. 'And I'll be fine. I need to get home.'

'Can you stand?' I asked, offering my hand. She nodded and I helped her up. She felt remarkably strong, and favored her wounded leg only slightly. 'So where's home?'

The gargoyle woman met my gaze. 'Under the bridge.'

The sound of dogs baying resounded through the forest. I pressed my palm over my icy torso. I sniffed and smelled

Marksmen on the wind. 'What's going on, Ezzie? What are you doing out here, and why are they after you?'

'They weren't, initially.' Esmeralda grunted in pain and limped towards the trees. I came beside her, putting my arm around her waist. Josephine moved to her other side and did the same. Ezzie forged ahead as she talked. 'I was tracking Anya and Matthias. I sensed them this morning, and I've been on their trail. Unfortunately, they have certain advantages over me, and it took a while to pinpoint their location. By the time I arrived here, the Marksmen were out in full force. No doubt also in pursuit.'

Ezzie directed us around a clump of trees and down a small embankment with a speed that belied her injured state. I sniffed the air, checking to see how close the patrols were. Their unpleasant scent was growing stronger. 'Anya and Matthias are the threat, not you.'

'If a Marksman sees an opportunity to take out a shadow creature – even a banished one like me – they'll seize it.' She looked around quickly. 'Shoot first, ask questions later. You know that's how they function, Sebastian.'

Josephine gasped. 'Wait. You mean, you're *the* Esmeralda?'

I jerked around in surprise. 'You know about her?'

'Well, yeah,' she said, staring at Ezzie like she was an artefact in a museum. 'I heard a lot of stories about the original guardians of the Old Clans when I was a kid. Esmeralda is kind of famous.'

Ezzie snorted impatiently. 'Ridiculous Gypsy folklore.'

'So we'll explain everything to the Marksman,' continued Josephine. 'She's like you, Sebastian. She's not the enemy.'

Esmeralda's eyes sparked silver. 'Are you sure about that?'

I slowed my pace. 'Original guardians?'

She snarled in frustration. 'Look, I'm about to choke on the smell of those Gypsy mutts, so if you don't mind, let's save our talk for *after* we get out of the open, all right?'

The barking of the dogs was frantic now, and we hurried through the woods to the Sutallee Bridge. Despite my changed status among the Romany clan, I had no doubt that the Marksmen would jump at a chance to corner two gargoyles – guardians or not.

The rippling waters of the Sutallee River materialized into view. Esmeralda made straight for the abandoned mine shaft under the bridge – the one Josephine and I had taken cover inside last autumn.

Darkness surrounded us as soon as we passed through the opening. Nothing had changed inside the small room with its dirt walls and wooden beams – except for a few additional beer cans and wads of trash. Just down the shaft was a door, hanging precariously from its hinges, its wooden slats ready to disintegrate at any moment.

'Come on,' Ezzie said, breaking out of our hold. 'They're getting closer.'

She limped ahead; obviously still able to see well enough in the dark, but Josephine wasn't so lucky. I took her arm and we followed. Ezzie grasped the rusty handle of the door and pulled. The hinges creaked as it opened, and a blast of chilly air filled the room.

We crept along a narrow passageway with a low ceiling. The air was stale and heavy with the smell of earth and rock. I could see the evidence of human activity. This place certainly wasn't a secret. And if drunken vandals could find their way in here, then the Marksmen could too.

Appearances can be deceiving, Sebastian.

I jolted with the buzz of Ezzie's voice in my head. She

was eerily perceptive. I glanced at Josephine, who was staring blindly ahead, and I answered back in my mind.

Where are you taking us?

I told you, returned Ezzie's soothing voice. *To my home.*

We came to a fork in the tunnel. Two tunnels led off to the right and left, their entrances blocked with rotting boards and rusty signs warning us to keep out. Directly in front of us was a pile of rubble, barricading what had obviously been a third tunnel before it had caved in.

It was a dead end.

'So what now?' I asked.

Esmeralda Lucian turned around. In the darkness, her eyes burned silver. I supposed mine did, too. A faint smile crossed her lips. 'It's time to enter the shadows.'

'Say that again?'

'You have to use your shadows in order to pass through the wall.' She gestured to the large pile of debris in front of us. 'It's the only way to get inside.'

'Inside what?' Josephine asked in a wary tone.

Her fingers tightened on my arm as she stared in the direction of Ezzie's faintly glowing eyes. The tunnel was too dark for her to see anything else. I opened my wing and curled the bony, talon-tipped edge reassuringly around Josephine's shoulder.

'There are three tunnels,' I answered. 'The middle one has caved in, and there's pile of rocks blocking the entrance. How do shadows help us get through that, Ezzie?'

'It's one of your abilities,' she replied, and I sensed she was trying very hard to be patient with me. 'And I'm going to assume that Karl hasn't shared this with you, since you're looking at me like I've gone mad.'

'We've been kind of busy,' I said.

Her face tightened with disapproval. 'Too busy . . .'

'But not anymore,' I said with a low growl. 'Tell me about this shadow thing.'

'*Shadowing*. That's what we call it.' Ezzie's eyes glinted. 'You've realized by now that you have a way of blending into dark spaces.'

I felt strangely uncomfortable. 'Yes, but I just thought it was, you know, because of my . . . my coloring.'

'It's because of what you are, Sebastian. Roma legends say that stone formed our bodies, but shadows formed our souls. We can manipulate those shadows – bring them to the surface from within.'

Slowly, things began making sense. 'You're referring to the mist.'

'Yes,' she replied. 'That's how I'm able to live here, right under the Marksmen's noses. The shadows allow us to travel short distances, like passing through a door, even walls as thick and impenetrable as this.'

I'd seen the other gargoyles disappear within the thick, oily mist. A nervous prickle went down my spine. The idea that I might be able to do the same thing was terrifying.

'It's almost happened to me before,' I said. 'But nothing like what you can do, Ezzie.' My blood drummed a cadence in my ears. 'I didn't have any control. The mist just appeared, and then it was gone again.'

I heard the barking of the Marksmen's dogs growing closer. It would only be a matter of time before they caught our scent again. Adrenaline pumped through my veins, demanding I get us to safety. I felt my lip curl away from my teeth.

'You can do this,' said Esmeralda.

I studied the pile of rocks. 'What about Josephine?'

'She can travel with you,' the gargoyle woman answered. 'It's not going to be easy on either of you, unfortunately. Carrying a passenger is difficult, especially when you haven't done it before. But this is the only way.'

'Wouldn't it be safer for you to take her?'

'I can't.' Esmeralda wiped at the blood trailing from the gash on her forehead. 'Though I retain a few shadowen abilities, I no longer have your strength. This human body needs to recover, and I can't be out of commission while those traitor gargoyles remain a threat.'

'They aren't a threat,' I said, the statement ringing through the cavern like a confession. 'At least, not right now.'

Esmeralda limped to me and studied my expression in the tunnel's darkness. Understanding flashed in her silvery eyes. 'Then you've been honing your guardian skills. Well done, Sebastian.'

'I don't want to be congratulated.' My rising frustration burned like indigestion under my ribs. 'I killed Thaddeus in the Romany camp. *Killed him, Ezzie.* With my bare hands. From what I remember of it, anyway.' I bit back a snarl. 'And I almost did the same thing to Anya and Matthias. If Josephine hadn't stopped me—'

'Then you would've done what you were created to do,' finished Esmeralda. 'Protect the Roma. Those gargoyles have been hell-bent on revenge, even before joining Augustine. They made a choice to abandon their calling a long time ago.'

'It's more than that,' I said. 'They're chimeras now, like Thaddeus . . . or something really close. But I don't understand how that's possible. We're different, right?' I pressed my hands against the spiraled horns protruding from my forehead. Everything in me wanted to scream. 'I thought we're supposed to fight them, not become them. Just when I think this shadow world stuff makes sense, it suddenly doesn't. What's going on Ezzie?'

For the first time, Esmeralda looked genuinely disturbed. Her eyes dimmed to normal hazel, and seemed suddenly far away. She crossed the tunnel and ran her fingers along the wall of rubble and stone. 'We need to hurry, before the dogs sniff us out.'

I set my jaw. 'What do I have to do?'

'Focus on one thought,' she answered. 'Think only of exactly where you want to be. In this case, right on the other side of this rock wall. Then let your body do the rest.'

'That's it?'

'That, and one other thing.' Mist curled around Esmeralda Lucian, swirling with a life of its own through the dead air of the mineshaft. It thickened and changed in color and hue from oily black to heavy smoke. She smiled at me through the inky haze. 'Trust yourself.'

The mist engulfed her body, and Esmeralda was gone. I stared at the crumbled rock, as her words hit me between the eyes like a hammer. She was right. It was time to stop fearing what I was capable of. If I could fly, I could do this.

'Wow,' said Josephine straining to peer into the darkness. 'She just vanished.'

'Yeah,' I said, letting out a deep breath. 'And now, it's our turn. That is, if you're okay with trying this.'

'Let's do this.' Josephine's confidence in me swelled my heart. She slipped her arms around my waist and rested her head against my chest. Shockwaves rushed through me. 'Good luck, Sebastian.'

My nerves melted into a tremor of anticipation. I relaxed and concentrated on what I was about to do. I replayed

Esmeralda's exit in my mind. I slowed my breathing. I closed my eyes, visualizing the wall in front of me. Then I imagined myself passing through it, straight to the other side. But something was holding me back. Air was being sucked from my lungs. I couldn't do this . . . I couldn't . . .

Esmeralda's voice buzzed in my head.

Stop resisting it, Sebastian.

I squeezed my eyes so hard my head ached. I saw myself going through the rock. I wanted to be on the other side of the rock. I needed to be on the other side of the rock.

Please, let me make it to the other side.

Cold shattered my body like I'd just plunged into a frozen lake. My fingers and toes went numb. My breath lodged in my lungs. I felt like I was drowning in a current of frozen ice. I fought to move, but it only made things feel worse – like my chest was being crushed under an iceberg.

Relax, my mind screamed. I struggled to obey. The pressure released, and I felt myself moving through the frigid current. My lungs burned with the need for oxygen, but there was nothing to breathe. My eyes snapped open. Light flashed around me, and I resurfaced from the freezing depths. I was standing in a cavernous room. Josephine was in my arms.

Esmeralda greeted us, a smile on her pale face. 'Welcome to my home.'

22. *Frozen Fire*

The world tilted.

My knees buckled, but I managed to release Josephine before crumpling to the ground. I panted through clenched teeth, choking back a nauseous dry heave.

'What's happening to him?' I heard Josephine ask, but the roar in my ears nearly drowned out her voice. She knelt beside me, looking worried.

'Have him sit until it passes,' said Esmeralda. She leaned against the rocky wall, breathing heavily, her eyes closed. 'It only lasts a few moments.'

To my right was a long wooden pew. With Josephine's help I pushed myself up and sank onto the bright red cushions, and prayed I wouldn't vomit on the furniture. Josephine sat next to me. Her breaths sounded shaky.

'Are you okay?' I asked.

'A little dizzy,' she replied. Her emerald eyes searched my face in such a way that made me feel both excited and uncomfortable. 'That was incredible! Sebastian, how . . . how did you *do* that?'

'I don't know, but I don't think I want to do it again.'

'You're just full of surprises, aren't you?'

She smiled at me: the crooked, full-lipped smile I loved. The nausea lessened, but in its place, butterflies skittered. This was ridiculous. How could I smother my feelings for Josephine when one smile rocked my world?

'I like to keep you guessing,' I replied, the corners of my mouth twitching into a grin.

The walls of the cavern sparkled with flecks of granite and pyrite. Heavy fabrics hung throughout the cavern, and oil paintings lined the walls, framed with curtains to give the semblance of windows. The ceiling was higher than I expected and vaulted like a cathedral dome. It seemed impossible that something so elaborate existed in the ground below the Sutallee Bridge.

The cavern was sparsely furnished: a small desk and chair, two long pews, and a round table. Worn rugs covered the floors; candles and papers competed for space on the desk, and books were stacked into the nooks and crannies of the room.

'Now you know what it feels like to use your shadows,' said Ezzie. She pushed aside a heavy curtain and disappeared behind it. She reappeared, holding a small bowl and a cloth. 'It's a lot more intense when carrying a passenger.'

'The other gargoyles didn't seem to have problems with it.'

'They've been around a lot longer than you.' She leaned against the desk and ripped the leg of her jeans up to her knees. 'You're technically still a fledgling. In the past, each time a gargoyle was awakened, he was given time to acclimate to the world and develop his abilities before he was branded into Gypsy service. You were left to learn most things on your own.'

I watched Esmeralda wipe the blood from the bite wound. 'I had you.'

'I wasn't able to help you as much as I would have liked.' She set the cloth aside and glanced at me. 'Surely you know that.'

'I figured Hugo ordered you not to talk about shadowen stuff with me.'

'Hugo Corsi is not my master,' Ezzie snapped. Her eyes flashed dangerously. 'No one is.' She scooped something out of the bowl and rubbed it into the wound, forming a paste. 'A little Roma trick,' she said, calm once more. 'Herbs to speed the healing process.' Esmeralda dried her hands then ran her fingers through her matted hair, smoothing the black and red strands into place. 'But back to your shadowing abilities, Sebastian. You'll soon learn to manage the side effects.'

'You mean like the desire to lose my lunch?'

She smiled faintly. 'Nausea is the worst, isn't it? That's why I prefer to use shadowing only in emergencies. My human body especially doesn't handle it well.'

Josephine shifted closer to me, but her eyes were on Esmeralda. 'You really live here, Ms Lucian?'

The gargoyle woman's smile froze into place. 'Just call me Ezzie, Josephine. I'm hardly your teacher anymore. And yes, I do. Just through that tapestry is a smaller cavern I use as my sleeping quarters, but with no indoor plumbing, I've appreciated the convenience of working at the school.'

I couldn't resist a smile. 'So the rumors about teachers really living at school—'

'Have some merit in my case,' finished Ezzie. 'Although, Hugo has given me the use of his apartment, since you left.'

My brows shot up. 'You're living with my brother now?'

'To keep an eye on the clan,' she replied levelly.

'Tell me how you're really connected to Hugo and the others,' I said. 'It's not about being old friends or trading favors back and forth.' I rose slowly, gingerly from the pew and met her gaze. 'So what is it?'

Esmeralda pushed herself from the desk, her posture rigid, even defiant, but when I didn't back down, she looked almost pleased. Her steely expression softened as she moved to face me head on. 'Markus was a Corsi.'

'Your charge,' I said, mostly for Josephine's benefit, but the words affected Ezzie more than I'd expected. I saw the pain flare behind her eyes. *The Gypsy you fell in love with*, I added telepathically.

Her gaze moved briefly to Josephine then returned to me. The stoical expression that set Esmeralda's face could've been my own. 'Yes. I was assigned to him a long time ago, before the Sundering of the Old Clans. It was my duty to protect him, and I failed. Because of that, I feel I owe it to him to watch over his clan, in what little ways I'm able.'

'But why Sixes?' I pressed. 'They aren't the only Corsis.'

'I followed Hugo's parents here from Savannah. I stayed because Zindelo appointed Hugo the head of the clan when they left.' She studied me carefully. 'And I stayed because they'd brought with them a young gargoyle who looked like a boy.'

My wings cramped. I flexed my shoulders, allowing them to expand for a few seconds, then I snapped them in place and shrugged. 'Well, I don't anymore. I'm just your average, teenage, run-of-the-mill shadow creature now.'

Ezzie's smile returned, less frozen this time. 'No, you're different, Sebastian, and Hugo's clan went to great lengths to hide you. Of course, your presence isn't a secret anymore.

I've no doubt that word of the Romany's gargoyle is spreading among the *kumpania*.'

Josephine's scent permeated my senses as she moved to stand beside me, giving Ezzie a bewildered look. 'So what if it does? I'd think hearing that a guardian is protecting our camp would be a deterrent to whoever's behind all this. Like posting security system signs, or one of those "beware of dog" stickers. Only . . . well, you know.'

I glanced sideways at her, and she shrugged apologetically, making me grin. Esmeralda stepped past us, her limp already gone. Whatever Gypsy herbs she'd gotten a hold of they certainly were effective. She knelt beside a stack of worn books in the corner. I turned my thoughts to a question.

Why do you think I'm different, Ezzie?

Her hand paused – the only indication she'd heard my telepathic voice. *I haven't figured that out yet. Hugo's parents told me nothing, nor do I think they wished my involvement, so I've had to be very careful. You aren't the only gargoyle in hiding, Sebastian. No one outside of the Corsi clan . . . and a few of the Romanys . . . know who I really am.'*

When she didn't continue, I spoke out loud. 'Why won't you tell me your whole story, Esmeralda?'

Her face hardened like a sheet of ice. 'Because I can't.'

Why do you tell me things, only to push me out again when I want to know more?

Ezzie's eyes fixed on me, and their hazel depths were flecked with silver. *Our kind exists for one purpose which is to guard the Roma.*

That's not an answer, Esmeralda.

She sighed in my mind. *There are Roma out there who are more powerful than you can imagine. They could rip the very memories of my life from me, if they choose. It's part of my curse as a banished guardian. One wrong move on my part, and my human existence could be taken away.*

I was only half-conscious of switching to normal speech. 'But I thought you hated being human.'

She responded in turn. 'I do. But it's better than death. While I'm alive, there is always the hope that I might redeem myself. That I might, somehow, receive a second chance.'

'Is that why you keep trying to help me?'

'Yes, I must confess that is partly the reason,' Ezzie replied. Then her voice tingled inside my brain. *But also because you remind me so much of myself, Sebastian.*

She glanced at Josephine – my charge – with a pointed expression. She didn't say anything more, but she didn't have to. I understood. Ezzie pried a book loose from the bottom of the pile. It was bound in thick green leather and small enough to rest in the palm of her hand as she held it out to me.

The leather felt warm against my skin. Something about it also felt familiar. It reminded me of the books Karl had been taking to his trailer to study, but anything that might have been engraved on its cover had faded away long ago. I opened it carefully, the pages crackling between my claws.

There was nothing written inside.

'What is this?' I asked.

Josephine leaned over my arm. 'I've seen books like this before,' she said, studying the pages. 'My uncle Adolár used to have some in his study when I was a little girl. I recognize the script.'

I stared at the empty pages, confused. 'There's nothing inside, Josephine.'

Now it was the Gypsy girl's turn to look confused. 'Yes there is, Sebastian. It's covered with words.'

'You're both right,' said Esmeralda simply. 'It is an ancient Roma book. Only those of Gypsy blood may read it.'

I flipped through the remaining pages gently. Each one was blank like the first. Josephine stopped me at one particular page, and I felt a burst of heat as her fingers touched mine. I searched her face.

'Can you read it?'

The Gypsy girl shook her head. 'Not really. I understand a few words, but that's it. A lot of the writing is strange.'

'What about your uncle?' I asked. 'Would he know what it says?'

'Probably, but he moved to Paris when I was five.' Josephine traced the flowing script at the top of the page, her brows knitted together in memory. 'I don't remember much about him, just his library.'

I looked at Esmeralda. 'So why are you giving it to me?'

'Actually, it's meant for your charge,' she replied, glancing away. Her fingers played absently along her neck, and I could see a hint of the faded tattoo on her skin – what remained of her brand. She took a long breath, deep and filled with unnamed memories. 'The book belonged to Markus. He was a member of the *Sobrasi* – a group established by the High Council to oversee the shadow world.'

Josephine took the book from my hands. 'I've never heard of them.'

'Of course not.' Esmeralda looked at us again. Her expression was as smooth as glass. Whatever emotions she'd been wrangling with were tucked neatly away. 'The society was cloaked in deepest secrecy. Each member was imparted with a book containing vital shadowen information. After the Sundering, the *Sobrasi* hid them away to ensure that no one clan would have access to such power again. Before he died, Markus entrusted this one to me.'

'But the Sundering happened over two centuries ago,' said Josephine.

A weird, jittery feeling passed over me. I knew Esmeralda had been around a long time, but I hadn't really, *really* considered what that meant – for her . . . or for me. I blew out a sudden breath and shoved the thought aside. 'You've had the book for that long?' I asked.

'I made a promise,' Ezzie replied, looking older and more tired than I'd ever seen her. 'And I've kept it faithfully. But things are not the same. I feel ties from the past rising up again like increasing waves before a hurricane. I don't know what information the book contains, but I believe it may serve some purpose in the future, and it would be better off in your hands than mine.' Her eyes hardened. 'Don't let anyone know you have it, Josephine.'

Josephine closed the book with gentle reverence and slipped in into the back pocket of her jeans. 'I'll take care of it, Esmeralda.'

'Is there anything more you can tell us?' I asked. 'What about the chimeras?'

'I don't know, Sebastian,' she replied. 'I've felt something stirring within the shadow world for months, something dangerous. I don't know what part Augustine may have in it or who else may be involved.' Her hazel-silver gaze switched to Josephine. 'But I fear this is much larger than your Gypsy family knows. I advise both of you to use caution in your dealings, even among your own kin, Josephine.'

'I'm going to find Karl as soon as we get back,' I said. 'Maybe he's been able to find out something from his grandfather's books.'

Esmeralda nodded and sank into a cushioned chair near her desk. 'Yes, I think that's wise. And you should be going. It's late, and you need to get your charge back to the Fairgrounds. I'm sure the Marksmen have picked over the entire forest by now.'

'You're right,' I said. 'But, are you going to be okay, Ezzie?'

'I need rest,' she replied. 'But I'm fine. Now, I trust you know the way out?'

'Unfortunately.'

Josephine placed her hand on Ezzie's arm. 'It was an honor to meet you, Esmeralda. Properly meet the *real* you, I mean. If I'd known—'

'That your teacher was a former creature of the shadow world? Perhaps you would've worked harder on your theater projects.'

Esmeralda gave us both a faint smile then rose slowly from the chair and, with some effort, walked across the room and disappeared behind the heavy tapestry. I felt strangely sad as I watched her go – like there was something final in that moment.

'We'll see you again, won't we Ezzie?'

'I'm not that easy to get rid of,' she replied. 'Now, get out of here. Both of you.'

'Are you ready?' asked Josephine, turning to me.

'Yeah, let's go home.'

Josephine wrapped her arms around my waist. I stifled a longing sigh, resisting the urge to curl the Gypsy girl into my chest. I had to concentrate. I conjured up the image of the tunnel on the other side of the rock wall – using every ounce of willpower I could muster. I felt my body growing cold, but just before I closed my eyes, Josephine's face came into view. She looked positively angelic with her bright smile and her eyes shining with trust.

'You're amazing, Sebastian Grey,' she said.

And then the icy current of mist swept us away.

Ten minutes later, we were back on the gravel road. The second shadowing hadn't been as bad, though I'd been forced to lean against the underground passage clutching my stomach until the nausea passed. I was also beginning to feel the weakness of hunger pangs. It had been several hours since we'd had our picnic.

Josephine separated herself from me as we walked. I studied the moonlight on the road, trying to coax my stomach into submission, until I felt her gaze on me. I looked up, seeing a question forming behind her eyes.

'What went on between you and Esmeralda back there?' she asked, searching my face. 'It's like you guys went in and out of conversation, and then, you'd just stand there, staring at each other.'

'Sorry about that,' I said, scratching my head self-consciously. 'I didn't realize it was that obvious. We can speak to each other inside our heads. It freaked me out the first time it happened, but I'm getting used to it.'

Josephine's eyes looked like saucers. 'You read minds?'

'No, nothing like that,' I replied quickly. 'It's just like talking, only without using your voice. That's all.'

'And can you do this with *anyone*?'

'Just shadow creatures, so far as I know.'

I could have sworn I saw a look of relief pass over Josephine's features. I stuffed my hands in my pockets as we neared the front gates of the Fairgrounds. An occasional breeze wafted traces of her scent in my direction, and it took everything in me not to sniff at the air for more. The Gypsy girl felt like a part of me – I was as aware of her as I was of myself.

'Josephine?'

Her eyes were bright against the darkness. 'Yes?'

The way she held my gaze made my heart beat quicker. 'Do you think—'

Shards of ice prickled my stomach. An ominous clang rang out into the night. A large group of Marksmen stood in front of the gate. Some held torches and kerosene lanterns, and the eerie glow reflected off their diamond-encrusted weapons. I pulled up quickly, shielding Josephine with my arm.

The black-clad Gypsies parted, and a cloaked figure moved to the front of the group. I didn't have to see his face to know who it was. Even in the shadows of the Marksman's hood, I saw the piercing black eyes and the sharp features. His inky voice filled the night.

'We've been looking for you.'

23. *Immovable Currents*

Josephine moved from behind me.

'Quentin!'

She rushed forward, and he met her, flinging off his hood. I dug my heels into the ground as Josephine wrapped her arms around him. Quentin embraced the Gypsy girl with one arm and positioned his body in front of her.

'Restrain the creature,' he said.

Instantly, four Marksmen were at my sides. Two grabbed my arms, and the others pinned my wings. Someone produced a set of thick straps and harnessed them around my torso. My wings crushed painfully against my back. Josephine pushed away from Quentin in shock.

'What are you doing?' she demanded.

'I'm sorry Josie, but I have no choice.'

Metal cuffs clamped on my wrists. I jerked my arms against them, and instantly, sharp pain knifed through my skin. I sucked in a breath and looked down. Tiny spikes composed of glittering diamonds coated the inside of the metal. My purple-black blood trickled from underneath the cuffs into my palms.

'I wouldn't try that again, if I were you,' snapped the Marksman at my left. 'The more you struggle, the tighter they get.'

I closed my eyes, intending to shadow through the bonds, but nothing happened. I tried again. No cold. No void. My eyes popped open in surprise. I couldn't summon the mist. It was like there was an invisible wall preventing me.

'Diamonds,' said the Marksman on my right with a proud sneer. 'We're not oblivious to shadowen trickery.'

The men yanked my arms behind my back, but my wings were too bulky for my wrists to meet behind me. I heard the clank of a chain as the bonds were connected like a pair of handcuffs and locked into place. My strained shoulder blades lit up with fire.

I gritted my teeth. 'What's going on?'

Quentin ignored me, but Josephine grabbed the tunic of one of the Marksmen who'd just spoken.

'Let him go, Lucas,' she commanded. 'You have no right to do this. My father—'

'Your father gave the order,' said Quentin.

His words dropped like weights. Josephine seemed to freeze for a moment, then she looked from me to Lucas, and finally to Quentin. 'I don't understand.' She stepped back, shaking her head slowly, disbelieving. 'Why would he—?'

'There's no time to talk, Josie,' he continued, his smooth voice stretched thin with impatience, 'we have to get inside. Bruno, take the dogs out again. I don't want any of these creatures left alive, do you hear me?'

The man named Bruno whistled to three Marksmen who were holding the leashes of three vicious looking mongrels. The animals were muzzled, but their eyes fixed murderously on me, and rough patches of hair stood up along their backs. The men and their dogs melted into the night. Esmeralda wouldn't be leaving her cave home for a while.

'This is wrong, Quentin,' said Josephine. 'Father gave me permission to leave the camp. Sebastian's my guardian, and he's been instructed to stay by my side. I don't understand why you're doing this.'

Quentin steered Josephine towards the gate. 'I told you, I'm following orders.'

She planted her feet. 'Look, if Father wants to see him, then we'll go. But take the handcuffs off him. He's not our prisoner.'

Quentin paused. His face was dark against the shadows of the night. 'Are you asking me to defy the *bandoleer*, Josephine?'

Her shoulders rose, then dropped. 'No, of course not.'

'Then we need to get moving.'

Josephine glanced at me, her face wrenched with conflict.

'It's okay,' I said, straightening up casually, though my shoulders hated me for it. 'We'll get this worked out.'

When we got to Nicolas, we'd explain everything to him. I'd tell him about Anya and Matthias. Then we'd talk to Karl. Josephine continued to hesitate, and I nodded at her, trying my best to convey my thoughts. A slow, silent resignation passed over Josephine's countenance. She didn't resist when Quentin clasped her hand and led her through the gate.

The Marksmen shoved me along after them. I didn't put up a fight. I plodded between the four men, only protesting when their diamond weapons cut my skin or their grip on my wing straps grew too tight. My wrists throbbed, but there was nothing I could do about it. I'd just have to wait until we reached Nicolas.

Watching Josephine walk beside Quentin was the real torture. I'd taken for granted the days I'd spent around her without his interference. Now, I doubted things would ever be the same again. They talked in hushed voices, their heads dipped low and tilted together, but my pointy gargoyle ears picked up their conversation easily.

'When did you get back?' Josephine asked. 'Why didn't you let me know?'

'I tried, but you never answered your phone.' Quentin's voice was smooth, as always, but I could detect a hint of something darker underneath the manicured tone. 'We arrived an hour ago.' There was a pause. 'Reception must be bad on the mountain,' he said.

Another brief moment of silence, this one more awkward.

'Quentin, talk to me.' There was desperation in Josephine's voice. 'Why all this secrecy? Why won't you tell me what's going on?'

'It's not my place, Josie. You'll have to ask Nicolas.'

'I intend to.'

Though Quentin still held her in the crook of his arm, I saw the stiff set of her shoulders – a display of the fierce obstinacy in her that I loved.

'Josie,' said Quentin, his tone soft and disarming. 'I've missed you.'

She glanced up at him. 'I missed you, too.'

I forced my attention away from the couple and stared straight ahead. We were well inside the grounds, but the Circe looked different. The carnival rides, which had been routinely lit for the past week, weren't on. Everything was dark, the lampposts, the trailers, even the security lights along the fence.

An arrow jabbed against my back, and I realized I'd

unconsciously slowed. I glared at the Marksman and bared my teeth. I may have been going quietly, but that didn't mean I had to be happy about it.

We took a wide arc around the Big Tent and headed for the smaller tent just behind it. The gold and red stripes of the canvas were dulled to shades of gray against the violet sky. Quentin stepped through the opening with Josephine, and the rest of us followed behind.

An array of lanterns hung from beams inside the Holding Tent, casting eerie shadows on the canvas. A circle of bleachers encompassed the center of the room, crammed with people. Those that couldn't fit in the seats spilled out along the sides and against the walls. It looked like every Gypsy in the troupe was present. Warning tingles raced down my spine as my eyes swept over the crowd.

The standing Gypsies parted for Quentin and Josephine. People murmured as they passed through and disappeared from view. My escorts stopped outside the circle. I turned to the Marksman on my right.

'Where's Nicolas?'

For an answer, I received a thin-lipped smile. The sound of something banging against wood reverberated through the tent. The noise reminded me of a judge's gavel. The crowd quieted, and a sharp voice replaced their murmurings.

'Bring it in.'

Amber light illuminated the circus ring and spread across a sea of eclectic Gypsy faces as the Marksmen herded me through the crowd. Rough hands forced me to my knees in the center of the open space. I found myself peering up at a long, rectangular table located on the far end of the circle.

Several prominent members of the clan hovered behind the chairs. Nicolas sat at the center of the table, his head bent towards a gray-headed man on his right. Andre – Josephine's circus partner – was at the far end, with Brishen next to him. Quentin sat on Nicolas' left, and his black eyes were fixed on me. Ominous realization pricked my skin like a thousand needles.

I was in the Romany clan's secret court – the *kris*.

Francis stood beside his mother, just behind the table. His face was uncharacteristically blank, and his jaw was stiff. Josephine had joined him, taking up position on his opposite side. Seeing them together like this they looked like children of the *bandoleer* – calm and emotionless in the presence of the court. Neither spoke nor reacted to the chaos around them.

Josephine's face was carefully poised, chin defiantly set, but as our eyes met, I not only saw the fear behind them, I felt it inside my chest. Her face glistened in the lamplight as she reached for her twin brother's hand. He slipped his fingers around hers, but his gaze remained resolutely focused on a point in the canvas wall.

I pushed myself to my feet. 'Nicolas, I don't—'

'Chain the creature,' said Quentin.

The Marksmen dragged me to a gigantic support pole directly in the middle of the tent. Metal chains were flung across my chest and yanked taut. The wrist cuffs pierced my skin as the Marksmen clamped my arms to the pole. Heat built inside my lungs, churning into a growl.

I glared at Quentin. 'What's going on?'

Nicolas shook his head. 'It's not your time to speak, Sebastian Grey.'

A Marksman raised his fist, ready to emphasize Nicolas' words with a punch to my face, but Quentin's sharp command prevented the blow. The *bandoleer* pushed back his chair and rose with a solemn air. Everyone fell silent as his gaze traveled around the circle.

'We've called this *kris* because what happened tonight affects the entire clan – and not just us, but everyone in our *kumpania*.'

I looked around the tent. Had there been another chimera attack while I was gone? Sweat prickled my scalp and forged a trail past my eye. I wanted to brush it away, but my hands were bound so tight that my fingers were numb.

Nicolas nodded to the gray-haired man to his right. 'Leo, as you are the appointed head of the court, I turn the proceedings over to you.'

The old man stood with a wrinkled frown; his lips as stiff as the thin ponytail at the nape of his neck. 'As *kris-nitori*, it is my duty to remind you all that the purpose of this *kris* is to determine the guilt or innocence of the accused. Anyone may step forward to give an account of either of the events that have occurred or to provide other information that is relevant to this trial.'

Trial?

'Nicolas,' I called out. I saw a Marksmen's fist in my peripheral. I ducked with a snarl. 'I demand to know why I'm here.'

Leo's head snapped around with a speed belying his age. 'You will speak only when directed to, *gargoyle*!'

'I have the right to—'

'You have no rights in this court,' Andre said coldly from his end of the table.

There was a shift of emotion in the crowd, followed by a round of murmurs.

Quentin leaned over, shifting his gaze to the old man and then back to me. 'Leo,' he said in a voice like an oil slick.

'For the benefit of the court . . . and the accused, of course . . . why don't you state the accusation?'

'Very well,' said Leo with narrowed eyes. 'Sebastian Grey, you are on trial for the murder of Karl Corsi.'

It was like being punched in the stomach. The air whooshed from my lungs, and I slumped against the chains. The crowd clamored and yelled, but the blood pounding in my ears was so loud I barely heard them.

Karl was dead? Why? How? I struggled to right myself, to focus. He'd been the first to show kindness to me, to help me. He'd been my friend.

How could someone take his life?

'No,' said Josephine. I looked up through blurry eyes as she escaped from her brother's grasp and approached the table. 'That's not possible. Sebastian was with me all day.'

Quentin's jaw set like steel, and he went rigid in his chair.

Nicolas turned to his daughter, his face collected, steady. 'We'll cover the details in time, Josephine. Go back to your place.'

She seemed caught between speaking in my defense and obeying her father's instructions. I could feel the smothering authority of the council as much as she did. Josephine nodded stiffly and allowed Francis to guide her back.

'Well?' said Leo, his attention back to me. 'What's your plea?'

'I didn't kill him.'

The crowd shouted around me as though they wanted to drive a diamond pitchfork into my heart.

'Silence!' thundered Leo. The noise dulled to a low mutter. 'The court needs to know exactly what happened,' he continued. 'Who found the body?'

'I did,' said a voice from the far end.

Alcie stepped from the crowd, her large earrings jangling against her neck and her too-bright make-up caked in her leathery face. She avoided my stare.

Leo returned to his seat and propped his elbows on the table. 'Tell the court how you made the discovery.'

The old woman wrapped her sweater around her thin frame and shuddered. 'Karl wasn't at dinner tonight, so I made him a plate, like I do sometimes, and I went to his trailer. He didn't answer when I knocked, but the door was unlocked.' She paused, flicking her eyes in my direction, and she made a sign with her hands that I didn't understand. 'He was . . . lying there . . . on the floor, and his body was . . .' She broke off, putting a hand to her mouth.

The tense atmosphere of the circle crackled with negative energy.

'Go on, Alcie,' said Leo in a softer voice. 'Tell us what you saw.'

The old woman gathered herself. 'His trailer was destroyed – furniture overturned; all his belongings strewn about, his medical supplies ripped up. And Karl . . . Karl's body was . . .' she faltered, shaking her head back and forth, and when she spoke again, her voice was barely above a whisper. 'He was torn apart.'

The Gypsies erupted in chaos. I slumped against the pole, sick to my stomach. Leo banged on the table, bringing order back to the proceedings.

'Is there anyone else who can attest to the condition of the body?' Leo demanded.

Stephan and Phillipe – who'd been hovering near the Romany family like a couple of guard dogs – came forward

'I can,' Phillipe said gruffly. 'When Alcie reported what she'd seen, Nicolas sent Stephan and me to investigate. It was just like she said – debris everywhere, like there'd been a struggle. Karl's body had sustained several deep, jagged wounds on the neck, and his chest and arms were slashed open.'

The room reacted again, but even among all the noise, I distinctly heard Josephine's horrified gasp. Leo banged on the table again.

'And what do you think was the cause of this violent death?' he asked.

'He wasn't killed with a weapon,' said Stephan boldly. 'His body was too ripped up, as if he'd been attacked by a pack of rabid dogs.' The Marksman turned slowly, his eyes fixing on me like dagger points. 'Or some other creature.'

The outburst among the Gypsies rose to a frantic level. Quentin sat calmly, a pleased glint in his eyes.

Nicolas leapt from his chair. 'We will not jump to conclusions here! This doesn't prove the boy is guilty of the crime!'

Andre glared. 'He's not a *boy*, Nicolas; he's a beast! Look at him! Who else could've done such a thing to Karl?'

'But what would be the motive?' questioned Brishen.

It was the first time he'd spoken, and I looked his way. Claire, Zara, and Phoebe were in the crowd behind him, all staring at me. Francis kept close to his sister, his expression eerily blank. Josephine's eyes bored into mine – pleading, questioning.

Doubting?

I strained against the chains, fighting to control my rising anger. I couldn't freak out. Not here, of all places. I drew in a deep, calming breath. 'There wasn't a motive because I didn't kill him. I could never do something like that.'

A gloved fist smashed into my jaw, sending a shower of stars across my vision. The force was enough make my knees wobble.

'You lie!' yelled Phillipe. 'I saw you take out that chimera behind Karl's trailer.'

'Yes, he did,' Nicolas interjected. 'Because he was protecting our camp. What does that have to do with this trial?'

'It shows what that creature is capable of, Nicolas.' The Marksman advanced with confident strides. 'You saw him that night. You saw what he *did*.'

The room had gone strangely still.

'He defended us,' said Francis suddenly.

'Maybe he did,' said Stephan with a sharp glance. 'But that's not the point. What this gargoyle did to the chimera; the wounds he inflicted . . . Karl's body had the same marks. The cause of death was identical.'

The Gypsies burst into heated arguments.

'But I wasn't in the camp today,' I shouted over them.

'Karl was dead long before Alcie found him,' snapped Phillipe. 'Whoever murdered him did it last night.'

Last night.

I'd been in my trailer alone.

All night.

Oh, God.

I was being framed.

'It wasn't me!' I cried out, struggling against my bonds. I looked desperately at the Gypsies I'd befriended during the last few weeks. 'I didn't kill Karl! You know me. You know I would never do anything like this!' No one moved. 'Nicolas,' I pleaded, 'I had no reason to kill Karl. He helped me. He was my friend.'

The murmuring tapered off while I spoke, and every eye fixated on me. My nerves felt like they'd been strung across a gorge. Karl was dead, and I was being blamed for it. And Josephine hadn't looked at me – not since Phillipe had compared the circus trainer's brutal death to the chimera I'd killed with my bare hands.

'I think I can shed some light on a possible motive for this crime,' said Quentin smoothly. The Marksman's chiseled face was a mask of professionalism.

Leo nodded. 'Please, share it with the court.'

'It's not my place to accuse Sebastian Grey of Karl's murder.' His gaze traveled around the circle. 'But as leader of the Marksmen, I've sworn to protect this clan. It's my responsibility to present any information that might serve to explain this tragedy.'

'What information?' Francis demanded in a venomous voice.

Nicolas silenced his son with a hard look.

'When I returned home tonight and heard the reports,' Quentin continued, 'I went to examine Karl's trailer for myself. You've already heard that his home was torn apart. And that's true. But the destruction wasn't random.' Quentin brought his piercing gaze back to the table. 'Karl's books were missing.'

Leo frowned. 'What would someone want with those?'

Quentin looked at the *bandoleer* pointedly. 'Karl Corsi had the most extensive collection of the Roma's written histories and lore,' Nicolas replied. 'And, since our people write down so little of our ways, he was a valuable resource.'

'And isn't that why you had him join our clan?' Quentin asked.

'Yes,' Nicolas admitted.

Quentin rose and walked towards me, but his dark eyes remained focused on the *bandoleer*. 'Karl also had books about the shadow world, didn't he?' The Marksman gestured to me. 'He knew what these beasts were capable of.'

'Karl and I have discussed the research he was doing on the Old Clans and the origins of the shadowen,' said Nicolas, his eyes glittering dangerously. 'But I can't say I know the extent of his knowledge.'

'That's the problem,' Quentin replied. 'No one did. But it appears his research had been quite fruitful as of late. In fact, the Marksmen I assigned to watch your home last night overheard bits of a conversation between Karl and the gargoyle, just after nine o'clock.' Quentin leaned against the back of his chair. 'Isn't this true, Henrik?'

A short, thick-shouldered man stepped from the contingent of Marksmen surrounding me: one of the two guards I'd seen posted outside the Romany trailer. He nodded at Quentin. 'Yeah, it's true.'

'And what did you hear?' questioned Leo.

'Karl was talking about some books he had about shadow creatures,' Henrik answered with a smug look on his bearded face. 'Something about knowing how to control the beasts. I didn't hear more than that, because they moved away, but I can tell you one thing,' Henrik's cold eyes shifted to me, 'the demon didn't look too happy.'

Quentin's voice slid through the room like heated mercury. 'No Roma would attack another of Gypsy blood without just cause. That's our strictest law. But shadowen are not Roma, nor are they human. They have been our enemies since their creation. We've witnessed their bloodthirsty nature. And yet, we've allowed one into the heart of our camp. Now the one man with the most knowledge of shadowen lore – their abilities and powers, but most importantly, their weaknesses – that man is dead, and his personal effects are gone.' Quentin turned on his heel and pointed at me. 'What have you to say to that, gargoyle?'

A growl burst from my throat. 'I didn't do it!'

Quentin smiled at my reaction. Shouts for justice pinged across the tent like machine gun fire. It didn't matter what I said. The crowd had made up their mind long before I'd been dragged in front of the *kris*.

The men at the table bent their heads together in deep discussion among the chaos. The tension in the room was suffocating, and the crowd felt like an angry mob, ready to riot. I stared into the faces of the Gypsies – some had accepted me, others tolerated my presence, and some had expressed nothing but disgust from the beginning. Now, it seemed my list of friends had dwindled.

My visual circuit of the room ended with the Romany family. Sabina and Francis barely moved. The resolute set of their shoulders was nearly identical. Fierce anger blazed in Francis' eyes. Josephine clenched her hands in front of her, the knuckles white. Her tanned face was unusually strained, and her eyes were downcast, as if she couldn't look at me anymore. And after what she'd witnessed from me earlier tonight, I couldn't blame her.

She'd seen me lose control.

She knew *exactly* what I could do.

At last, the leaders came apart. Leo took up a large black stone that had been sitting on the middle of the table. All eyes turned to him, and the room went very still. The *krisnitori* held the stone in the palm of his hand.

'Sebastian Grey,' he began slowly, 'you've been charged with the murder of Karl Corsi. You will now listen to the verdict of this court.'

Andre leaned over, placing his hand atop the stone. 'I've seen the power of this creature in action, and I have no doubt that he's capable of this crime. Therefore, I announce his guilt and call for justice.'

A mumble went through the crowd, and I stared in shock at the man whose life I'd saved. If he was so quick to convict me, what could I hope from the others? A dark, terrible despair slithered through my chest.

Brishen rose as he set his hand atop Andre's. 'Let's not confuse the capacity to commit a crime with the execution of the crime.' His solemn gaze roamed the tent. 'When this gargoyle first arrived, I felt like many of you. I didn't trust him. I even feared him. It's how we've been taught to regard shadowen. But we're not talking about grotesques or chimeras or the shadow world. We're talking about Sebastian. And I don't believe this boy, no matter what he is, would intentionally kill a Roma for his own gain. Therefore, I announce his innocence and call for acquittal.'

It was the most I'd ever heard Brishen speak, and he defended me with the eloquence of an orator. Francis nodded in fierce agreement behind him, though the others continued to avoid making eye contact with me.

Nicolas Romany took his turn next. I knew that as *bandoleer* Nicolas' words held greater weight than anyone. He drew his shoulders back and placed his hand over the others, and he spoke out with a voice that was calm and authoritative.

'It was my decision to bring Sebastian Grey into our clan, and I stand by that decision. Things are changing among the Outcasts. The feuds and divisions we sought to escape so many years ago have seeped into our clans. We must be prepared for whatever lurks on the horizon. This gargoyle was given to us for a reason, and I'm not willing to throw away something that may prove to be beneficial to the clan.'

His eyes settled on me. 'Therefore, I announce his innocence and call for acquittal.'

I let out the breath I hadn't realized I'd been holding. Maybe Nicolas still thought of me as a servile creature, but I was important to him.

Leo placed his hand over Nicolas. His wrinkled face hardened. 'I don't know this creature as well as others. But that makes no difference. I have listened to the reports and I find the evidence and the witness accounts too compelling to dismiss. Since there are no other suspects in this case, I therefore announce his guilt and call for justice.'

Two innocent verdicts. Two guilty.

One judge remained.

Quentin Marks.

All eyes turned to the Marksman. A wave of anticipation rippled through the tent. The heat burning in my chest was nearly unbearable. So it came down to this. The man who hated me most was in charge of my fate. He placed his hand over the others.

'I've fought my share of shadow creatures,' he said, 'and I'm familiar with their methods of killing. This gargoyle was aware of Karl's knowledge of the shadow world, and I believe there's something he doesn't want us to know about his kind. The question is, would he be willing to kill Karl to keep that information from us?' The Gypsies in the circle whispered among themselves. Quentin let his question hang in the air for several moments before continuing. 'I can't prove that this creature committed the crime. But I can't disprove it, either. Therefore, I'm withdrawing my verdict. I refuse to vote, one way or the other.'

The other men at the table turned stunned eyes to Quentin. He sat back in his chair, his face devoid of all emotion, but

I caught the corner of his mouth turn up, ever so slightly, as he met my gaze.

'You have to render a verdict,' said Leo.

Quentin didn't take his eyes from me. 'No, I don't.'

'Well,' said the *krisnitori*. 'Then it seems the council is divided.'

24. *Veiled Revelations*

For one brief instant, no one breathed. Then the room exploded. The Gypsies' fierce anger slapped me in the face. Everything I'd done, the efforts I'd made – crushed under the weight of their fury. Marksmen surrounded me, their weapons drawn. Leo banged on the table with the stone, trying to regain order.

'You've heard the decision of the council,' Leo shouted over the crowd.

'Where's justice for Karl?' yelled a voice.

Others took up the cry, demanding something be done with me. A hung jury wasn't enough for them. I was the enemy now. I lowered my head, emotionally numb. Whatever protests I had left fizzled on my lips.

Nicolas' booming voice cut through the tumult. 'Everyone knows the law. If a decision can't be made by the *kris*, then it must be taken up in a higher court.'

Heavy solemnity descended on the group, and several members made strange signs with their fingers. Nicolas flicked his eyes to Leo, and the old man nodded.

'The *kris* is concluded,' said Leo.

Phillipe stomped forward. 'How dare you put this off on the High Council, Nicolas!' the Marksman spat viscously. 'They'll think we can't handle our own problems! You'll make us look weak before—'

Quentin cut him off. 'That's enough, Phillipe.'

'But this gargoyle,' protested Phillipe, gesturing at me with the point of his long diamond-encrusted knife. 'He can't be set free!'

'I agree,' replied Quentin. His eyes were like shards of black ice. 'We can't allow the creature to roam free in our camp. His guilt hasn't been determined, but neither has his innocence.'

Gypsies all around the tent shouted their support.

Nicolas turned to the crowd and raised his voice. 'I understand your concerns, but we have to treat this situation logically. If the gargoyle isn't responsible for this murder, then we're dealing with something that has eluded an entire regiment of Marksmen.' Nicolas' face darkened. 'I'm ordering everyone to confine themselves to their quarters for the rest of the night.'

'And the demon?' Phillip pressed, glaring at me.

'Will be contained.' Nicolas met my gaze for a brief moment, but it was impossible to read the expression on his face. 'I'm placing the gargoyle directly under the supervision of Quentin Marks until I can contact the High Council for instructions. Does this satisfy both the *krisnitori* and the *kris*?'

Agreement was unanimous.

'I want all council members and family representatives in my trailer immediately,' continued Nicolas. 'We have matters to discuss concerning our next course of action. As for the rest of the troupe, we'll meet in the morning to inform you of our plans.'

And with that, the *kris* was over.

Quentin barked out orders, instructing his Marksmen to double the perimeter sweeps and camp security. The dark clad Gypsies shouldered their weapons and scurried out of the tent. The rest of the troupe was slower to leave, and their sharp glances felt like rocks being hurled in my direction as they passed.

I lifted my head and saw Phoebe walking out with Claire and Zara, on the outskirts of the departing group. Our eyes met.

'I didn't do this.' My throat felt like cracked leather as I spoke. 'Please believe me.'

Zara turned away, pulling Claire with her. I swallowed hard, feeling the hot sting of moisture in the corners of my eyes. But Phoebe hesitated. Her normally smiling expression was gone. Her gaze snapped briefly to the Marksmen around me. Her clan. When she looked at me again, I noted the slightest nod of her head in my direction.

'Thank you,' I whispered, more to myself than to her. I nodded back, wanting to feel grateful that not everyone had totally turned on me, but my chest felt painfully hollow.

Francis stood next to Nicolas, exchanging tense words as the tent emptied. Nearby, Quentin had joined Josephine behind the table. I could sense the argument between them in emotional waves, though I couldn't hear anything over the crowd and their flinging insults.

My back tightened as I watched Quentin touch Josephine's arm. She shrugged him off. He leaned in, speaking close to her ear. At first, Josephine's chin lifted, but I felt her emotions shift as he continued to talk. Finally, she nodded reluctantly.

Quentin wrapped his arm around her shoulder, guiding her towards the back exit. Josephine didn't look at me as they left.

Suddenly, it wasn't the chains pressing on my chest, suffocating me. It was the dark, oppressive feeling of utter hopelessness. I closed my eyes, praying for some kind of release from the sensation.

I wasn't expecting my prayers to be answered so soon.

'Hey, freak!'

My head jerked up. Phillipe scowled at me, his arms crossed over his chest. Gathered around him were seven Marksmen – Stephan and Jacque among them.

I really didn't like these guys.

'We're talking to you, beast!' Stephan spat.

'Yeah, I gathered that, what with the clever insults and all.'

Jacque's thin face came close to mine. 'Funny, gargoyle.'

Each man was large and imposing in his own way, but I singled Phillipe out of the crowd. 'Aren't you supposed to be guarding the camp or something?'

'Oh, we are,' he replied menacingly. 'From you.'

The Marksmen formed a half circle around me. My shoulders cramped painfully. I felt weak from lack of food, and the diamond wrist cuffs not only prevented my attempts at shadowing, they seemed to drain my energy as well.

'Defying Quentin's orders, are we?' I said through clenched teeth. 'I never pegged you guys as the independent types. That involves a higher level of thinking that requires, you know, a brain.'

The smile stretched thin on Stephan's face. 'We are following orders, beast. We were told to watch over you until suitable . . . housing . . . is arranged for your worthless carcass. But that doesn't mean we can't have a little fun while we wait.'

Phillipe reached for his belt. An imposing looking whip hung in coils from his hip. He unfastened it and gripped the thick leather handle. The cord fell to the floor like a long black snake. The whip sparkled in the torchlight, and I saw shards of diamonds embedded in the leather.

Oh, great.

My lip curled away from my teeth, and I strained against the heavy links of chain around my arms and torso. The other Marksmen laughed in eager anticipation – like hyenas closing in on a kill.

'It's been a long time since I've properly tortured a shadow demon,' Phillipe said. 'I'm really going to enjoy the refresher.'

'Go ahead, then,' I growled, anger flooding my senses. 'I wouldn't want to interfere with your job satisfaction.'

I heard the whip before I saw it – cracking in the air like a firework on the Fourth of July. When it struck, the air went out of my lungs, temporarily obliterating any other sensation in my body.

And then the pain hit.

My head exploded with it, and I clamped down as hard as I could, grinding my teeth so I wouldn't cry out. My leg gave way beneath me. My haze-filled vision caught sight of a deep slash along the top of my thigh. Phillip yanked the whip back with a sneer.

'Cuts through gargoyle flesh like a hot knife through butter,' he said. 'An expensive weapon, but well worth it.'

The air shifted, followed by another crack that pierced my eardrums. When the pain hit, everything went red. My other leg caved in, and the chains dug into my ribs. This time, though, there was no banter from the Marksmen – no chance for me to recover.

The whip struck again and again; each blow ripping through my clothes and splitting my skin. In the back of my brain, I knew he was taunting me; the whip could do more damage than this. I was just part of the Marksmen's playtime.

After the twelfth blow, everything around me started to spin. But I flexed my shoulders, raised my chin, and stared defiantly at Phillipe. My eyes flashed hot, and a snarl erupted from my throat.

'Is that all you've got, Gypsy?'

The Marksman's wicked grin disintegrated into a furious line across his lips. He flicked the whip behind him, and his fingers tightened around the handle until his knuckles bulged.

'You're going to beg for death!' he thundered.

I readied myself for the blow.

Suddenly the tent flap burst open and Bruno tore through, his bow in one hand and an arrow in the other.

'Come quick,' he shouted, 'we're under attack in the woods – can't spare any more men – need to keep a guard on the camp!' He gestured with his bow, already moving towards the exit. 'Hurry!'

The group shouldered their weapons and made for the opening in the canvas with trained efficiency. My brain fought against the pain. Under attack? I had to get to Josephine! I yanked with all my strength at the chains. A black shadow crossed my face. Phillipe's large form towered over mine, and there was hatred in his eyes.

'I'm going to take care of your demon spawn friends,' he said darkly. 'And then, I'm coming back for you.'

His body moved like lightning, and the whip was nothing

but a blur. The skin of my chest split open as the diamond shards ripped my flesh. My agonized roar pierced my ears. White bolts of pain blinded me. I slumped forward.

And all went black.

When I came to, the tent was empty. It hurt to move, so several minutes passed before I lifted my head. My frayed nerves registered pain in so many places at once that my head pounded with it.

Purple-black blood coated the thighs of my jeans. The same was true of my arms. My wrists ached and my ribs were sore. My flesh felt like it had been flayed alive. Blood seeped through my shirt along a nasty gash that stretched across my chest in a diagonal line. I groaned, feeling weak all over.

I sniffed the air. The Marksmen were long gone and their burning scent had faded, but my body felt chilled and feverish at the same time. What was happening in the woods? I shifted my body uncomfortably against the chains and manacles. At least Josephine was with her family, and Quentin would make sure she was safe.

Something changed in the air. I jerked upright and sniffed. Josephine's scent flooded my nostrils. She was supposed to be with Quentin, not here. Adrenaline fanned my instincts. She needed to be with someone who could keep her safe. I desperately searched the empty tent. She was lingering just inside the opening, her eyes searching as well.

Until they met mine.

She closed the distance between us so quickly that I didn't have time to catch my breath.

'Sebastian!'

'Josephine!' My throat felt like sandpaper. 'What are you doing here?'

Her gaze swept over my body in horror. 'Oh God, what have they done?'

'I'm fine,' I replied, forcing a smile.

She gave a choked laugh, which sounded like she was on the verge of actually crying. 'You suck at lying, you know.' She glanced around the tent. 'Are they still here?'

'They're in the woods,' I said, repositioning my body to alleviate the pressure of the chains. 'Bruno said they were under attack and needed more men. Are you okay? What's going on?'

'A handful of grotesques near the back gates,' she replied, and I heard reluctance in her voice as she looked away. 'And two chimeras.'

I growled, low in my throat. 'I should've—'

Josephine's fingers pressed against my mouth, stopping my words. 'Don't go there,' she said firmly. 'I'm the one who told you to leave them. The Marksmen will deal with the shadowen. Even if you had killed those chimeras on the mountain, it wouldn't have prevented all this from happening.'

I swallowed down another growl. Josephine was right. But the truth didn't help the pain. And it wouldn't bring Karl back from the dead. Her hand left my mouth and settled against my neck, pressing against my collarbone. Our eyes locked, and emotions passed silently between us; the kind of unspoken conversation that I'd grown to treasure.

A wave of pain flashed across my back, and my wings cramped. I shifted my body against the chains to ease the pressure, trying my best not to grimace. 'You should get back, Josephine. If your father knew—'

'I refused to sit there listening to them argue about what to do next, not when I knew you were still here, tied up like an—' She stopped short of finishing the thought. 'Quentin won't listen to me. And my father can't usurp the will of the *kris*.' Josephine's gaze drifted down my body, and her face contorted. 'I had no idea they were doing this to you!' A tear escaped and trailed slowly down her cheek.

'Josephine, I'm fine, really. Supernatural creature, remember?'

The wound across my chest had closed, but I knew it would take some time to fully heal. I flinched at the sight of my dirty clothes, caked with dried, inhumanly colored blood, and the hideous lacerations criss-crossing my skin.

There was a glimmer of hope in her expression – a desperate look. 'Are you sure?'

'Absolutely,' I said. 'Believe me, I've had worse.'

Josephine stared at me with a sort of incredulous wonder that made me warm and cold all over. 'They're wrong about you. I should have challenged my father and the *kris*. I should have forced Quentin to change his decision.'

'There's nothing you could've done. You just said that not even your father can go against the ruling. I don't know much about your people's laws, but I saw the power of the council tonight. They'd already made up their minds.'

Josephine's shoulders slumped; her face a mixture of relief and guilt. 'I know my words wouldn't have changed anything but, believe me, I'm not done trying. There has to be another way.'

A strange, charged quiet fell between us as we stood looking at each other inside the empty tent. I leaned forward as much as I could against the chains, searching her face. 'Thank you,' I said. 'For believing me.'

'I've always believed you, Sebastian.' Her hand left my neck and traveled gently to my cheek. 'You're the only one I can believe.'

My wings shuddered beneath their straps as she stroked my face with the backs of her fingers. I wanted to run my hands through Josephine's hair, to touch her face, to hold her hand in mine. But I couldn't. I was trapped.

By more than just metal chains and diamond spikes.

My gaze drifted to the floor, and the pain returned – but this time, it was on the inside.

'You need to get back to your family,' I said. 'And Quentin.'

Then Josephine's body shifted, and suddenly she was right against my chest; her head dipped underneath mine. Her mouth opened in a quiet gasp, and her breath bathed my skin with electricity.

'Josephine . . .'

I was pleading, protesting, my body caving in on itself – and then our lips touched.

Sunlight met shadows.

All the times I'd imagined kissing Josephine Romany – none of them compared. It was soft, chaste – yet sweet and spiced, like tangy cinnamon and warm caramel on an autumn evening. I forgot about my wounds and my pain as my world melted away. I didn't feel the biting chains. Nothing mattered but her and the purity of that moment. It was more than I could've ever dreamed.

And it ended too soon.

I felt the hesitant tightening of her lips, and I pulled from the kiss at the same time. Her eyes slowly opened, lashes fluttering like butterflies. There was uncertainty in her look – an uncertainty I could feel – because it mirrored my own. But there was something else, something that warmed me almost as much as her kiss.

Hope.

Josephine's fingers left my face and traced a delicate line down a muscle in my neck. Her touch felt cautious, even wary, but something seemed to compel her actions. I wondered if she felt the same draw; that need to make some kind of contact – something to offset the intense connection between us.

'What can I do?' she asked quietly.

'I need to know you're somewhere safe,' I said, forcing the words to leave my mouth. I yanked once more at the chains – a uselessly frustrating gesture that made a snarl burn through my chest. 'Please.'

'Okay,' said Josephine stepping back. Her fingers left my chest, leaving me chilled. 'I'll get you out of here, Sebastian.'

It was a hollow promise, and we both knew it. We stared silently at each other for a moment. Then she turned and darted for the exit. As she passed under the canvas flap, she spun to face me. Her mouth opened, but she seemed to change her mind. She shook her head and ran out.

My body trembled. Soon I was shaking all over, and my heart threatened to crack my sternum with its fierce beating. Thoughts swirled in my head so fast that I couldn't make sense of anything – and I didn't want to.

I leaned against the tent support and tried to recover, though I knew it was impossible. Josephine's warmth lingered around me. I wanted to live in it as long as possible. I didn't know what the future held, but that one brief kiss had given me new life. I would find a way out of this mess. Everything was going to be okay.

Then I felt the cold.

A snarl rippled my lips as I searched the darkness of the tent. It didn't take long to pick him out of the shadows. His tall form strode slowly towards me – a collected, confident gait. He reeked of burnt spices and pungent arrogance. He circled me casually, taking in the series of slash marks across my body.

'My boys have been taking care of you, I see.'

I followed his movements carefully. 'Not really. Actually, I'm thinking about filing a complaint.'

Quentin stopped, his perfect lips pressed into a firm smile. 'Not a bad idea. Their job performance is obviously in question, since they left you not only coherent, but with the ability to run your mouth.'

'Why are you here?' I demanded. 'The best Marksman in the camp should be protecting the Romanys right now. Unless, maybe you don't qualify anymore.'

He backhanded me so hard across the jaw that my teeth rattled. I grunted and my knees wobbled, but I pushed myself up determinedly. I spat black blood onto the floor.

'I see where your buddies get their substandard job training.'

Only the sparking glint of fire in the Marksman's black eyes conveyed his emotions. 'I assure you, the roughing up you received this evening will be nothing compared to what I do to you. I've been content to bide my time, follow all the rules, and wait for the right moment to kill you. But that was before I saw your little Romeo act a moment ago.'

The cold spread from my stomach to my heart like an infection. How long had he been hiding in the shadows of the tent while my senses had been occupied with Josephine?

'I don't know what you're talking about.'

As thanks for my reply, I received a hard fist in the stomach. I doubled over as far as the chain would allow and came up snarling.

Quentin grabbed my shirt, slamming my head against the pole. 'You think you've won Josephine over?' he said fiercely. 'You believe she'd ever give a demonic abomination like you a chance? You're deluding yourself, gargoyle.' His hand moved to my throat, and a knife I hadn't noticed before was suddenly slicing into the outer layers of my skin. 'This connection you share has grown irritating. I'm through with you fawning over my fiancée like a pathetic little puppy.'

I tried to force a stoic face, but Quentin caught my reaction. A sly smirk twisted his features. The diamond knife dug into my skin as his brows rose in feigned surprise.

'I'm sure Josephine's told you how our traditions work,' he continued. 'You see, she and I have always been intended for each other. The Romany family maintains close blood ties with the Marks'. It's been that way for centuries.'

My jaw clenched. 'You don't love her.'

'Of course I do. What's not to love?' He leaned closer, twisting the knife. 'She's beautiful, and charming when she wants to be . . . a little too stubborn, but it's a trait all Queens should possess.'

I couldn't hide my shock. 'But I thought—'

'That her right to the throne was a secret?' The Marksman laughed, low and mocking. 'Nicolas hasn't done as good a job of hiding things as he thinks. You ask me if I love Josephine Romany. Let's just say, I love the possibilities she represents.' His knife burned hot on my throat. 'But all in good time. We'll be married first. Seal the union, so to speak.'

I snarled, lunging at the Marksman. The chains rattled and the wooden beam crackled in protest.

Quentin gouged the knife deeper. 'I don't know what's more amusing,' he sneered. 'The idea that you think you're capable of real human emotions or the delusional belief that you actually had some chance with my future wife.'

I forced my lips back over my teeth and stared the Marksman down with all the heat in my gaze. Anger poured through me like molten lava, but so did pain – deep, biting pain that came from the truth of his words.

'So you're going to kill me now, is that it?'

'Of course not,' Quentin replied coolly. 'As much as I'd love to break my knife off in your stony guts, I'm not above the law. But once you're found guilty of Karl's death, I'll watch fate take revenge for me.'

'That's why you didn't vote at the *kris*,' I said bitingly around my teeth. 'So they'd be forced to send me away.'

'There is some intelligence in that thick gray skull after all.'

'You're so sure this High Court will find me guilty?'

Quentin's smile curled like a snake. 'Oh, they will, once they see what kind of creature you really are.'

Something in his words froze my blood. I swallowed hard past the blade of his knife. 'What do you mean?'

The Marksman released the blade from my skin. He wiped my blood on the side of his pants and sheathed the weapon at his hip. 'Karl's books have been very helpful. Everything you would want to know about subduing shadowen was in those pages.' He studied my surprised look. 'You mean Karl never told you? He was always such a firm believer in the old tales. He thought he was protecting your kind by keeping his secrets. Unfortunately, he's no longer around.'

'You had something to do with his death,' I said, my voice thickening. Quentin adjusted his bow across his back. I could see the tips of his feathered arrows over his shoulder as he simply stared at me, neither admitting nor denying my accusation. Anger and dread stabbed at me. I growled, feeling my chest rumble against the chains. 'Did you just come to gloat, Marks, or is there something else?'

Quentin reached into a small pouch hanging from his belt. He pulled out a syringe – one that looked ominously familiar – like the one Hugo had used on me after I'd transformed. The Marksman rolled it casually between his fingers.

'You know, if I had my way, your blood would be decorating the floor right now. But at least I can have the satisfaction of seeing the High Council convict you of Karl's death. And once that happens, it's all over for you, gargoyle.' He stepped closer to me, his eyes cold. 'Because after we're finished with you, Josephine will be sickened at the thought of ever touching you again.'

I fought against the chains as the needle sank into my neck. The pain was brief. Almost instantly, my body felt heavy. I tried to speak, but the words slurred over my tongue. The Marksman capped the syringe and returned it to his pouch.

'Good work, Quentin,' said a low voice from the corner of the tent.

I rolled my head, trying to see through my swirling vision.

Quentin huffed. 'Well, personally, I'd have preferred something more painful.'

A man stepped out of the shadows. I blinked up at him. He tucked a loose strand of black hair behind his ear, revealing a long white scar on his cheek.

'This is just the beginning,' the man replied. 'After all, we've much work to do.' He turned to me. 'Hello, Sebastian. It's been a while.'

I stared into Augustine's smiling face.

Then my head slumped uselessly against my chest.

25. Controlling Destiny

The chains squeezed mercilessly against my rib cage as vitamin D coursed through my veins. No matter how hard I tried, I couldn't muster enough strength to lift my eyelids, let alone move. I was helpless, and worst of all, Quentin knew my weaknesses. Anger ran hot inside me even as my body went cold.

'So what now?' Quentin asked. 'I'm sure it won't be long before someone comes to check on the creature.'

'And why is that?' Augustine enquired.

There was a slight pause.

'Josephine was here earlier and, she . . . saw him.' Quentin's tone turned harsh. 'I can only assume she went to her father. Somehow, this beast has managed to invoke Nicolas' sympathies, and I highly doubt he'll approve of his current condition.'

'Why should that concern you? Didn't you tell me you'd been put in charge of the gargoyle's confinement?' Smooth mockery laced Augustine's voice. 'I thought you were second in command around here.'

'Nicolas' word remains law.'

'In most matters, yes,' Augustine mused. 'But the council holds the power within the *kris*, and opinions were divided, despite Nicolas' efforts on the gargoyle's behalf.'

'It was easy to take advantage of the clan's unrest.'

Augustine laughed ominously. 'Taking advantage of vulnerable situations is a tactic that works rather well, don't you think?'

'I'd rather be carving this demon's stone heart from his chest,' he replied. 'I've done as you've asked, Augustine, but I don't see the point of getting him before the High Council. He's a shadow creature. He needs to be destroyed. It's as simple as that.'

Boots crunched over the floor as Augustine moved closer to me. The stench of burnt incense was strong, but I couldn't cough. 'Now you see, that's your problem, Quentin,' he said. 'You always fail to see the bigger picture. You Marks have let your overzealous commitment to clan protection taint your vision of the future. Shadowen were created to serve our purposes, but you've never acknowledged their potential – how they can work to our advantage.'

The Marksman made a scoffing noise. 'How can these demons be worth anything to us? Look at your own pets, Augustine. They're being hunted down in the woods by my men as we speak.'

'Yes, they are,' Augustine replied. 'And providing an adequate diversion while you and I stand here, having our little talk. There is some worth in that, don't you think?'

'I assure you,' said Quentin. 'Their deaths will be painful ones.'

Augustine chuckled. 'Well, truth be told, I'll be glad to

be rid of them. They were a gift, you see,' he continued, and I heard something change in his voice – a mixture of displeasure and pride. 'Part of my bargain with the High Council long ago. Those shadow creatures served their purpose for a time, but when something outlives its usefulness, it's time to move on to other things.'

I felt him studying me, though my eyelids were still too heavy to lift. Goosebumps skittered up my frozen arms.

'Then move on with it,' Quentin snapped. 'I kept the Marksmen from killing your creatures for months. I've allowed you freedom to do as you please, going so far as to protect you from the Corsi clan when you tried to take this gargoyle the first time. I even agreed to keep your presence in Sixes hidden from Nicolas. But I've grown tired of waiting, and my patience wears thin.'

'*Your* patience!' Augustine's voice turned malicious. 'How dare you talk to me that way, Marksman. You forget who I am.'

'Nicolas is *still* the *bandoleer*.'

The air crackled with black emotion.

'For now,' Augustine said gratingly. 'But that injustice will soon be rectified. When that happens, you will have the chance to reap the benefits. Isn't it why we're working together in the first place?'

Quentin's scent singed my nostrils. I felt his hand grab my shirt, and he yanked me forward.

'But why keep this one alive?' he demanded, rattling my unresponsive body against the chains until I could hardly breathe. 'What's so different about him?'

'My gargoyles provided useful subjects,' Augustine replied. 'But we'd reached the limits of our experiments. Now, with Karl's books, the missing pieces are falling into place.' I felt his cold eyes on me. 'As for Sebastian Grey's importance, that's my own business.'

Quentin jerked me once then released me. 'Fine. We'll play things your way. So what happens now?'

'Tensions are heated already,' Augustine said. 'We need only fuel the flames.'

'And just how do you propose to do that?'

Metal clanked, and there was pressure against my wrists. The manacles fell to the floor with a heavy thump. Fingers curled around my wrist, and Augustine lifted my arm, pulling it across my chest. He ground his thumb into my palm, and I felt my frozen fingers splay reflexively.

'Like this,' Augustine replied.

My arm was slung forcibly through the air, and I felt my claws connect with skin. Quentin cursed in fury. I heard him stumble back.

'What did you do!' he bellowed.

My arm dropped limply to my side.

'Just making things look convincing, Quentin,' said Augustine.

'You slashed my face!' the Marksman spat.

'It had to look real,' Augustine replied smugly. 'And I'll admit, the amount of blood running down your cheek is quite impressive.'

Quentin spat again. 'You'll pay for that.'

'I'm doing you a favor, Marks. As you said, Nicolas wouldn't approve of your treatment of the shadow creature. That is, unless the gargoyle viscously attacked the head of his Marksmen and therefore needed to be locked away from the rest of the camp. From *everyone* in the camp.'

I knew exactly what Augustine meant.

And so did Quentin.

The Marksman paused for a moment – probably wiping his face. 'So how does this benefit *you*, Augustine?'

'Actually, it all works out beautifully,' he replied. 'Not only will this situation aid to usher in my return, but it also provides me with the perfect opportunity to put my newfound shadowen knowledge to work.' Augustine's breath was hot against my ear. 'You see, Sebastian, I knew you would serve me eventually, in one way . . . or the other.' His words hung in the air, and I felt a dread – far deeper and colder than my paralysis – seep into my bones. 'Because by the time I'm finished with you, Mr Grey, you'll be all the proof I need to sway the High Council to my side.'

'And after that?' Quentin demanded.

'Then the Marks can deal with the shadowen in whatever way they see fit.'

A silence of mutual agreement fell between the two men as I hung lifelessly between them. After a few moments, Augustine clapped his hands.

'Now, I believe you have an appointment with the Romany family, Quentin. Those gashes will stop bleeding eventually. And do make sure to give a convincing performance. In the meantime, with your permission, I'll escort the gargoyle to his new confinement.'

'Very well,' Quentin replied. He gave a sharp whistle and the tent flap snapped back. I heard two men hurrying in our direction. 'Thomas and Ian will assist you.'

'Give me an hour,' Augustine said. 'Then you can bring the family. You know where we'll be.'

'Understood.'

Quentin's scent grew fainter until it disappeared completely.

'Unchain him,' ordered Augustine. The Marksmen yanked my arms until they threatened to snap. Then I was falling, unable to do anything about it. I hit the ground with a thud. Augustine knelt beside me. He grabbed me roughly across the neck and I felt his cruel smile like the heat of the midday sun. 'After all this time, it seems it's finally come to this. You no longer have to concern yourself with a charge, Sebastian Grey. Now, you're going to have a master.'

'God, this kid's heavier than he looks,' muttered one of the Marksmen.

'He's a freaking gargoyle, Thomas,' the other huffed. 'What'd you think he'd weigh?'

I was aware that I was being carried through the tent by Quentin's men, but it felt like I was in a coma. I heard the canvas flap being shoved aside, and then we were outside. The scents of the night were heavy in my nose and helped clear my head.

My journey abruptly ended when I was unceremoniously lobbed through the air, and I landed in a pile of something stiff and prickly. It was hay – but not the fresh, sweet-smelling kind. It was old and reeked of damp and mildew. Hinges squeaked; a heavy door clanged closed, and I was left alone.

For a long time, I lay unmoving in the stench, trying to get my bearings. I was still outside, but far away from any activity I could hear or smell. The two Marksmen who'd carried me to my new location were nearby – guarding me, I assumed. The rotting hay made my nose burn, and the occasional breeze wasn't enough to provide any relief.

My mind drifted to Josephine. My lips still burned from her kiss, and it seeped through my skin like a dull ache. My heart beat her name inside my cold motionless prison until a fire smoldered in my chest. It burned through me like hot coals. Then, with a burst of strength, I opened my eyes.

Hay was piled in clumps over a slatted wooden floor. Rusty iron bars surrounded me. I rolled my eyes upward. A metal ceiling stretched overhead – so low that I wouldn't be able to stand upright. The heat inside me boiled into anger. I was in a cage – a disgusting, smelly animal cage in the back lot of the Fairgrounds.

I groaned and rolled over, forcing my body to work through the lingering vitamin D in my blood. I shook my head groggily until my vision cleared. The chains were gone, but the metal bands with their diamond spikes remained in place, digging into my skin. My wings were still pinned behind my back. I took a deep breath of night air and pushed myself onto all fours.

'Finally,' said a voice outside the cage. Augustine leaned against the bars. He smirked when our eyes met. 'I was beginning to think I'd given Quentin too high a dosage in that syringe. I'm still learning, so I pray you'll forgive any errors that I make during our time together.'

'If you wanted . . . a date with me . . . you should have just asked.' My throat was scratchy and raw. 'No need for all the . . . ceremony.'

Augustine's black eyes glinted with malicious amusement. 'I like your resilience, Sebastian. You're much stronger than the others.'

A growl rumbled my vocal chords. 'Guess that means I'll be that much more annoying when I fight back.'

Augustine narrowed his eyes, and the white scar on his face bulged. He studied me closely, measuring me up. I shifted into a crouch, steadying myself by grinding my claws into the rotting wooden slats. The Gypsy adjusted something along his shoulder: the strap to a leather satchel hanging at his hip. He saw my look and patted the bag.

'Karl's books,' he remarked. 'I'm so glad he finally brought them out of hiding. They make excellent reading while one is waiting to make his first appearance before the Romany family.'

'How did you—?'

'Easy enough,' he said, cutting me off. 'When you work with the right people.'

'You didn't have to kill him. He was a good man.'

'Yes, he was. But he was also a necessary casualty. Many who have attempted to keep secret the books of the *Sobrasi* have met the same fate, including his own grandfather. You must admit, though, Karl was a perfect victim. After all, Sebastian, if you'd kill someone like Karl, then you'd kill anyone to get what you want.'

I crawled to the edge of the enclosure. 'And what is it that I want?'

'You want what all shadowen want,' he answered. 'The death of the Roma.'

'You know that's not true.'

'We all change, Sebastian. Given the right circumstances.'

Chills ran down my spine, but I kept my face expressionless. 'Then, for the sake of argument, suppose I do. You're a Gypsy. If the shadowen want your people dead, that includes you.'

Augustine tilted his head. 'Not if I'm the one in control.'

'In control of what?

'Not what, Sebastian. *Who*.' He rummaged through the satchel and took out a small velvet pouch. 'I'm your new master now.'

'We've played this game before. It didn't work last time. You think throwing me in a cage is going make things different?'

'Consider this a new game, only the rules have changed.' Augustine smiled – a slow, slithering smile. 'Tell me, Sebastian. Did Karl ever tell you the legend of *La Gargouille*?' His brows lifted. 'I can see by your face that he didn't. I'm sure that it would've come up eventually, but since you two won't be having any more conversations, I'll fill in the blanks.' He juggled the velvet pouch between his hands, caressing the fabric like it was priceless. 'It's the creation story of your kind, Sebastian – an old tale of a French priest whose homeland was plagued by a terrible winged monster who breathed fire and water. The priest defeated *La Gargouille*, and its head was mounted on the village cathedral to ward off future evil spirits.'

I gripped the iron bars and glared between them. 'I don't see the point of this.'

'Ah, the impatience of youth,' said Augustine, untying the pouch. 'To the *gadje*, this was just a story; an explanation for the statues that have adorned medieval cathedrals since the twelfth century. But we know the truth. We know that a young Gypsy convict named Keveco Romany assisted the priest in the killing of *La Gargouille*. We know the priest took pity on Keveco because he'd been persecuted for his Roma heritage. And we know the priest ground the body of the monster into ash and presented it to Keveco as a gift to help his people.'

An uncomfortable feeling churned in my stomach. 'A gift?'

Augustine poured a small amount of the pouch's contents into his palm. I pressed against the bars, eager and wary to see it for myself. It was a fine powder – silver in color and speckled with purple and black. 'Yes, Sebastian,' he said. 'A gift. With this dust, Keveco was able to fashion the first shadowen.'

'It's *prah.*' I stared, transfixed, at the powder. 'Like what Hugo used in the ink for my tattoo.'

'It comes from the same source,' he replied. 'But branding dust is a diluted concoction, mixed with Gypsy herbs, used only in the process of sealing guardians to their charges. What I have here is the concentrated form. Very rare. Very valuable.' Augustine tilted his palm, and the powder glittered under the light of the stars. 'I've searched for years for the original *prah* from the urn of Keveco Romany.'

I let go of the bars in shock. Hugo's parents – according to their letter – had been looking for the same thing.

Augustine moved closer, studying me with amusement. 'You know about the urn,' he said. 'I'm sure Hugo Corsi told you that his parents went on their own quest for it. Unfortunately, they didn't have all the details as to its location. But, thanks to some clever connections on my part with the Old Clans, I was able to secure it.' Augustine rubbed the dust between his fingers. 'You see, Sebastian, this particular *prah* is very special. For with it, shadow creatures can not only be awakened, but modified.'

I saw the contorted bodies of Anya, Matthias, and Thaddeus in my memory – their wicked faces devoid of humanity and consumed with hate. My heart sank. Somewhere, in my subconscious thoughts, I had known the truth. I just hadn't been willing to confront it before now.

'You turned your gargoyles into chimeras.' I clutched the bars until my knuckles bulged. 'But why?'

Augustine poured most of the dust into the pouch, but a trace amount remained in his palm. 'My ancestors created your kind. I believe we have the right to alter your design as we see fit.'

'As *you* see fit, you mean.'

He smiled pleasantly. 'There isn't much difference between gargoyles and other shadowen, really. It's simply a matter of finding the right combination of elements. Anya and the others came up lacking.' Augustine pulled the pouch string tight with his teeth and dropped it into his satchel. 'But I have far better plans for you, Sebastian.'

I snarled. 'Like what?'

'First, I'm going to create an army of shadowen. And then I'm going to fashion a general to lead them.'

Dread crept up my throat like bile. 'How?'

'Patience, fledgling,' he replied with a glint in his eyes. 'I can't give away all my plans now, can I? Otherwise, you'd have nothing to look forward to. But don't worry yourself too much. I promised I was going to set you free. And I intend to keep that promise, beginning with your liberation from the Romany camp.'

'You're *marimé*,' I said, forcing my lips back in a smug smile. 'You're banished from Gypsy society. Even with Quentin helping you, there's no way Nicolas is going to hand me over to you.'

'We'll see about that.' Augustine whistled sharply. One of the Marksmen that had dumped me into the cage appeared, a quiver of arrows strapped to his back. Augustine slid one of the arrows free and held it to the light. 'To maintain the upper hand in a game, you find ways to keep the deck stacked in your favor.' He handed the arrow to the Marksman. 'I'm a very patient player, Sebastian, and you're the card hidden up my sleeve.'

I retreated slowly, my eyes fixed on the arrow. 'So my dead body's supposed to be the game changer?'

'I was under the assumption those pointed ears enhanced your hearing,' he replied in a mocking tone that reminded me of Quentin. 'Haven't you been listening? If killing you was my intention, I'd have done it long before you fully awakened.'

My lip curled. 'Remind me to send you a thank you card.'

Augustine regarded me, serene and confident. 'Keveco Romany brought stone to life with *prah*. But it was only when mixed with human blood that a guardian was created. Burn away the humanity and you're no different from your other shadowen brethren.' The arrow's diamond-encrusted tip glittered dangerously. Augustine brushed his hand over it, coating it with *prah*. 'Here, let me demonstrate.'

The Marksman notched the arrow to his bow.

I recoiled against the bars at the far side of the cage. Trapped. 'I'm a guardian. That's not going to change.'

'Say what you like, Sebastian Grey.' Augustine sauntered along the front of the cage until he was in my line of sight. His black eyes and his white scar glared from the depths of his tanned face. 'Consider how long you've fought against what you are: those dark impulses and instincts. You struggle to keep them at bay but deep down, in the very marrow of your bones, you know there's more to you than this.'

His words sent a tremor through my wings. 'You don't know anything about me.'

'I wouldn't be so sure of that,' he replied. He studied me through the bars. I felt like a rat in a laboratory cage, but I couldn't look away from Augustine's piercing stare. He tapped his fingernail against the metal. 'I have many questions yet unanswered concerning you. But thanks to my newfound knowledge, I do know this: where I have failed with other shadowen, I will succeed with you.'

'I'll fight you,' I said, snarling fiercely. 'No matter what I am.'

'Oh, there'll be fight in you, to be sure, but the fight won't be with me.'

My body screamed a warning. I dove across the cage, but I wasn't fast enough. The arrow whizzed through the bars and sank into my shoulder. My pierced flesh burned like fire, and I clawed at it desperately. The diamond tip ripped loose, pulling skin with it. The wound bubbled as I flung the arrow away.

Suddenly, every dark emotion I'd ever experienced rammed into me at once. Red haze blinded my vision. Liquid flames loosened my muscles. I leapt for the bars of the cage, blazing with fury, and slammed into them so hard that the entire wagon rattled. I threw myself against the cage, over and over, until my head threatened to burst. I shook off the pain, panting wildly, and glared into Augustine's face.

He was laughing.

'A more impressive display than even my own gargoyles,' he said. 'This may prove to be easier than I thought.'

My head was drowning in a sea of lava, and I struggled to think rationally. My shoulder throbbed. I wiped at it with my hand, smearing purplish-black blood across the remains of my ripped shirt.

'W . . . what . . . did you do,' I gasped.

'Just a little experiment. The first of many I have planned.' Augustine brushed the remaining *prah* off his fingers and into the pouch. 'As you've just experienced, when the *prah* enters your veins, it runs through like poison, eating away the human blood you have within you. I've found a small amount produces a temporary reaction . . .'

'And a large amount?' I asked, grinding my teeth together.

'You might have asked Thaddeus,' he replied, 'before you killed him.'

Augustine turned to the Marksman, and the black-clad Gypsy notched another arrow. I coiled into a crouch, ready to spring.

'Not to worry,' he continued. 'There's no need to shoot you again. Unless, of course, you disobey my orders.'

My eyes narrowed. 'What orders?'

Augustine wrapped his long fingers around the bars. 'Quentin will be arriving shortly with the Romanys. They must be convinced that you are a serious danger to the camp and must be removed immediately. In order to do that, I'll need your assistance.'

'I don't think so.'

'Then you will be responsible for ending your precious Josephine's illustrious circus career. How dreadful it will be for her to sustain a life-crippling injury the night before the Circe opens – and all while you are stuck in this cage, helpless to protect her.' A snakelike smile twisted his features. 'I may even give the task to Quentin. I'm sure he wouldn't mind the—'

'Don't touch her!'

I thrust my arm through the cage. My fingers were around his throat before he could duck. His eyes bulged. But an arrow was at my neck almost as quickly. Thomas held it like a spear, ready to run me through. I hissed and released my hold. Augustine stumbled back, gasping for air.

'You're in no position to make threats, demon,' he panted. 'Not when you're behind bars and I'm out here.' His eyes glittered. 'Play your part, Sebastian, and she'll be left alone. Cross me in any way, and I promise you, she'll never perform again. Are you prepared to have that on your conscience for the rest of your life?'

I clung to the bars as raging emotions burned inside me.

I was caged like an animal, while Josephine was on the outside, unaware and vulnerable. I had to buy some time, give myself a chance to think clearly. I met Augustine's gaze steadily.

'What do I have to do?'

'You're a gargoyle,' Augustine answered smoothly. 'It won't be that difficult for you to convince them you're dangerous.' He smiled. 'Rest assured, though. You're doing the right thing. After all, Josephine *is* my niece, and I would hate to see her suffer. I have such a tender place in my heart for family.'

The haze and the pain vanished at his words. Augustine nodded in satisfaction.

'Yes, Sebastian,' he continued, 'I'm her uncle. Though I doubt she's ever mentioned me. You see, Josephine was quite young when I was banished, and when I lived among the Romanys I went by another name.'

'Adolár,' I said with a growl.

He chuckled. The sound made me want to throw myself against the bars. 'So she has mentioned me,' he said. 'Then you understand why I was so adamant about keeping you from this clan when you and I first met. But so much has changed in my favor.' The renegade Gypsy clasped his hands and sighed in triumphant pleasure. 'Now that I've acquired the *prah*, Karl's books, and most importantly . . . you.'

I swallowed hard past the lump of fury in my throat. 'If I do this, if I get myself removed from the Romany camp, you're saying you're just going to leave Josephine alone?'

'Of course,' he replied. 'I don't like harming innocent people, really.'

'How can you expect me to believe you?' My lip curled, exposing my teeth. 'I heard you and Quentin talking. I heard your plans. She's in more danger now than ever.'

'Only if I allow it,' he replied. 'Quentin is a powerful man, but even the most powerful can be bought with the right price. He has sworn allegiance to me, and the Marksman will do nothing without my express command.' Augustine's lips flatted into a narrow line, and for once, the sneering look in his eyes was gone. 'I give you my word, Sebastian. Josephine will be safe with her family, and you'll be—'

'Standing trial in front of the High Council.'

'Yes, you will,' he said. 'But I have no intention of leaving you there. Going before the Council is just the beginning of our journey together. Under my control, your potential will finally be realized.'

I turned away, my gaze wandering over the rotting hay and metal chains of the cage. So what if the Corsis and Esmeralda thought I was different? I was still just one person. I shook my head fiercely. No. One *gargoyle*. A single creature. No matter what Augustine thought he could do to me, it didn't change that fact. The Outcasts had dealt with my kind for centuries.

They'd kill me eventually.

But before they did, I'd make sure Augustine went down. And with us both gone, everything could go back to the way it was. My wings snapped against my back, and my shoulders tightened in resolution.

This was it. All the fighting against what I was, my desperate attempts to embrace it – the hope of a life with Josephine – it had all come to nothing. But for these last few moments, I was *still* her guardian, and I would keep her safe. Like I'd promised. Bittersweet emotion swept through me, and then, it was gone. I turned hardened eyes to Augustine.

'I'll do it,' I replied coldly. 'I'll do it.'

26. *Unending Finality*

'A reasonable decision,' said Augustine. 'And really, the only one you could make. The clan doesn't trust you. The *kris* put too many doubts in their minds, even those who were on your side. As the chimera attacks increase – and believe me, they will – it will be only a matter of time before they rip you from your charge permanently.'

'It's your game, then.' I pressed my face against the bars. 'For now.'

Augustine motioned to Thomas, and the two Gypsies began untying the heavy ropes knotted at the front corners of the cage, releasing a molded tarp from the roof. They pulled it over the bars, leaving only a narrow opening in front of the cage door. My hay-filled prison went instantly dark.

'Quentin should be along any minute now with my loving family,' said Augustine, smoothing down the fabric. 'I'd better not hear one word, not one snarl, from you. Not until I'm ready to showcase you for what you really are.'

He started to turn, and I pushed forward.

'Wait.'

Augustine glanced back at me over his shoulder, one brow raised. I positioned my head between the bars so I could look him right in the eyes. 'If you want a show, you'll get one,' I said through clenched teeth. 'But you have to do something for me.'

Augustine sighed. 'And what is that?'

'Quentin goes, too.' My eyes flashed with heat. 'You'll need an escort to the High Council, won't you? Make sure Quentin Marks is the one heading it up.'

'I don't think you're under—'

My acid snarl cut him off. 'If you're really holding the upper hand, then prove it. Make it happen. Besides, if I'm as big a threat as you claim, I don't think it will be that difficult for you to convince Nicolas to send his head Marksman along.'

Augustine smiled with thinly drawn lips. 'Honestly, Sebastian. Does it really make any difference? Once we arrive in Savannah, Quentin will merely return here to the Circe . . . and to Josephine. You have no control over that.'

'Do we have a deal or not?'

'Very well,' he replied.

I leaned against one corner of the cage, breathing hard. A fierce wave of hunger crashed over me. It made me feel thickheaded and hazy, almost as much as Augustine's *prah*. I stifled a groan.

Augustine observed me from the outside of the cage. 'Ah, you haven't eaten in a while, have you?'

I clutched my stomach. It was futile to pretend otherwise. Not only did Augustine have possession of whatever information was written in Karl's books, it seemed apparent he'd acquired more than just those. And I was certain he was behind the murders in the Boswell clan, whether he said it directly or not.

'Well, I'm sorry about that,' Augustine continued, with an expression that showed the complete opposite. 'But I'm afraid you'll have to remain hungry. There's far too much to do, and I believe things will go far better for me if you don't eat.'

Karl had said food was a technique. Did it mean his ancestors starved shadowen into submission, or was there something more to it? Something I hadn't experienced yet? What would happen to me?

Something changed on the breeze. My head jerked up, and I caught a whiff of air. The scents of all the Romany family – as well as Quentin, Phillipe, and several other Marksmen – filled my nostrils. My stomach turned sour. I'd already been painted as a bloodthirsty monster. Now, Josephine's last memory of me would be like this. 'They're here,' I said quietly.

'Right on time,' said Augustine.

He laughed softly and tugged the tarp closed, blocking my view. I smelled Thomas taking up his guard position near the door, and I heard Augustine's feet as he slipped around the outside of the cage, hiding himself from sight. I squeezed my eyes shut and prayed it would all be over quickly.

'This is where you're holding him?'

The voice belonged to Nicolas, but I couldn't see anything beyond the canvas wall. I pressed my face against the cold bars and kept my eyes closed.

'I wanted to keep him as far away from everyone as possible,' said Quentin.

'In a cage?' Josephine's voice. Demanding. Beautifully

angry. 'You could've held him anywhere but here. He's not an animal, Quentin.'

'No,' the Marksman replied. 'He's worse.'

'Sebastian isn't some stupid grotie,' said Francis. 'He's one of us. And, in case you've forgotten, he wasn't found guilty. The *kris* was divided, remember?'

'Yes, thanks to me,' Quentin replied. 'And, trust me, I would've preferred to remain impartial. But this creature has become uncontrollable. I had no choice but to restrain him like this. I told you what he did to my men. And he attacked me as well. He nearly clawed out my eyes.'

'Yeah, and how did that happen, exactly?' The Romany twin huffed. 'When I left the *kris*, he was chained to a tent pole.'

'He's a gargoyle,' said Quentin dangerously.

'Enough, both of you.' Nicolas took a deep breath. 'This is not the time to fight among ourselves.'

The wind wafted through the bars of my cage, carrying Josephine's scent. I tried my best to wrinkle my nose against it, but it was impossible. I clenched my hands into fists, concentrating on the pain as my claws pierced my skin.

'Nicolas,' said Quentin. 'My men are exhausted from patrols and hunting shadow creatures. The troupe is on edge. The Circe opens tomorrow. We have to remove this gargoyle from our camp now. Having him here has done more harm than good. Let the High Council deal with him. We have to take care of ourselves.'

'He's sealed to the Romanys,' said Josephine. I could feel her heated emotions like shockwaves through my chest. 'Sebastian deserves the same care and respect as anyone here.'

'Josie,' said Quentin in his sickeningly calm voice. 'I know you're sympathetic towards the gargoyle, and I wish there were a better solution, but we have to think of our clan. If the demon – if *Sebastian* – is truly innocent, the High Council will make that determination, and then the matter will be settled. Despite how it looks, the truth is, Savannah is the safest place for him right now.'

A silent pause followed.

'That may be true, Quentin,' said Nicolas after a moment. 'But we have no way of getting him there. You don't have men to spare, and we need everyone else tending to Circe duties.'

Augustine's scent intensified as he rounded the corner of the wagon. I bit back a growl. He'd been waiting for just the right moment to appear, and Quentin had played the family expertly into his hands.

'I'll take him,' he said in a pleasant voice.

I felt the Romanys' shocked reaction as they saw him.

'How dare you set foot in our camp,' Nicolas said furiously.

Augustine made a reprimanding sound. 'Now, is that any way to greet your long-lost brother, Nicolas? I'm hurt by your lack of hospitality.'

'You're not welcome here,' replied Sabina, her voice bitter.

'Thank you for the reminder, dearest sister-in-law, and trust me, I have no intentions of hanging around.' Augustine sighed. 'I was simply passing through Sixes. But news travels fast, and I heard about the murder. I knew Karl well, and I wanted to express my condolences. I've been made aware of your situation and it just so happens that I'm traveling to Savannah tonight. I could take the gargoyle to the High Council for you.'

'That's absurd,' said Nicolas. 'You're no more welcome there than you are here.'

'Normally, I would agree with you,' he replied. 'But I have a feeling my reception will be different this time. Of course, I would prefer a little hospitality when I arrive. Delivering something to the High Council would put me in good standing with them.'

'You mean with *her*,' Nicolas answered.

Sabina snorted. 'You think it's that easy to overcome *marimé* status, Adolár?'

I heard Josephine gasp. 'What do you mean?'

'Since when has uncle Adolár been banished?' demanded Francis.

'Since he broke the law of the High Council almost fifteen years ago,' said Nicolas, his voice cold as steel. 'When he lost his Gypsy blood and his Roma name was changed to Augustine to mark him as *marimé*.'

'You're Augustine?' I heard Josephine whisper in disbelief.

'Surprised, children?' said Augustine. 'Then again, it's been a long time, and your parents felt you were too young to understand what really happened to your uncle when I left the Circe. My moving out of the country was a much easier explanation. Keeping secrets is a difficult thing. One can only hold onto them for so long.' His tone turned mocking. 'Does it bother you that someone this traitorous is related to you by blood?'

'*Was* related,' snapped Sabina. 'Not anymore.'

'One day, perhaps, that will change,' he replied. 'And speaking of change, Nicolas, I know you feel it coming. When it does, I just want to make sure I'm on the right side.'

'How,' demanded Francis. 'By killing members of the head families?'

'I'm hurt, nephew,' said Augustine. 'I may have my grievances with the current leadership, but I would never stoop so low as to take the life of a fellow Roma. But someone is, and it won't be long before everyone is involved. It would be a shame if they discovered the Romany clan was keeping a gargoyle suspected of murder hidden in their camp.'

Another pause filled the air, this one heavy with indecision.

'The Queen won't see you,' said Nicolas harshly.

'Oh, I think she will,' Augustine replied. 'When I inform them that the Romany clan has violated the terms of my *marimé* by killing my three noble gargoyles who, as you may recall, fall under the same protection as I do. How do you think that news will sit with the Council, Nicolas?'

'They weren't gargoyles,' he replied. 'And they invaded our camp.'

'Minor details,' said Augustine, glancing at his fingernails. 'But it doesn't change the terms of my agreement. Now, unless you want me to address these issues directly with the Queen, I propose you hand the shadowen over to me. The creature will be my invitation through the front door.' Augustine stopped talking, and I could feel the heavy weight of his words. When he continued, his voice was softer. 'All I require is the chance to gain an audience with our sister. Allow me that, and there will be no mention of any of this to anyone.'

Another silence. But this time, I felt a shift in the air.

'I've already contacted the Council and apprised them of the situation,' said Nicolas. 'If you fail to arrive without the gargoyle—'

'Then they'll have my head,' Augustine finished with a condescending voice. 'Believe me, I know better than most the power of the Council. No, brother, I intend to deliver your package. In fact, why don't you tell our sister that I'll be leaving immediately?'

'No!' cried Josephine. 'You're not taking him anywhere!'

Augustine laughed: an ominous sound. 'Ah, my dear, headstrong niece. I'm not giving your father a choice.'

'Nicolas,' said Quentin, 'as much as I hate to admit it, this is the best way to carry out the wishes of the *kris*.'

'You're the *bandoleer*, Father,' continued Josephine, ignoring him. 'There has to be some way you can overrule the *kris's* decision. Sebastian is supposed to stay with us. You know he didn't murder Karl. He'd never do something like that. He's my guardian.'

'You still refuse to believe this creature is dangerous,' said Augustine with unnerving calm.

'I never said he wasn't dangerous,' she replied coldly. 'But he won't hurt us.'

I smelled Augustine draw close to my cage. I crawled reluctantly towards the door, digging my claws into the wood to hold myself in place. I couldn't turn back, especially now. Another growl welled in my throat, and this time, I didn't try to choke it down.

'You have much faith in this shadowen,' said Augustine. He drew back the flap just enough for me to see his face. Thomas's arrow was in his hand with a fresh coat of *prah* sparkling at its tip. Hair prickled along the nape of my neck. He leaned closer, his voice so low only I could hear. 'Just in case you were thinking of changing your mind.'

Before I could even draw a breath, he gouged the arrowhead into my wounded shoulder. I winced as a sharp, stinging pain flowed down my arm. I shook my head, trying to focus, but fury was already churning in my stomach.

'What are you doing?' I heard Francis say.

The flap opened wider, revealing the rest of me. Augustine pulled something from his pocket. I squinted through the rapidly forming haze in my vision. It was a key. I felt the Marksmen around me tense. My chest heaved. My wings strained against their bindings.

Augustine glared at the Romany family. 'I'm showing you the truth.'

Nicolas stepped forward. 'Adolár . . .'

The strange Roma dust surged through my veins, turning the world around me into a blob of dizzying red. I snarled in the back of my throat. Augustine's eyes met mine.

'Make it convincing,' he whispered as he shoved the key in the lock.

I heard it click.

And I was free.

I burst through the door and landed on all fours in the middle of the Gypsies. The Marksmen surrounded me, weapons drawn. I whirled on them in blazing rage, and my wings snapped free from their restraints.

I heard Nicolas yell my name. But I didn't listen. I whipped the air into frenzy with my wings. Debris spewed. The *prah* shut down my brain, filling what was left with dark instincts, and I let them take me. I grinned – baring all my wicked teeth – eager for a fight like I'd never been before.

The Marksmen were on me at once. I felt sharp knives in my flesh. I slammed one Marksman against the bars of the cage as another leapt onto my back. I ripped him loose with my claws. I was bleeding, and I didn't care. Someone shouted for reinforcements. They came, weapons glittering. I attacked, throwing them in every direction. I fought until their numbers overwhelmed me.

It took nine Marksmen – including Quentin – to finally bring me down.

I was on my stomach, a thick boot crushing my neck from behind. The Marksmen used their weight and weapons to secure me, but I jerked and writhed, causing more damage than they were inflicting. The *prah's* power worked like anesthesia, numbing me to pain. I felt nothing.

Until Josephine's pale face appeared in front of mine.

I froze, overwhelmed by her proximity. I felt her warm breath on my skin as she gasped. She was on her hands and knees, staring at me with so much emotion that it pierced through the red haze, cracking me open, deep inside. Regret and doubt seeped through my resolve.

'Sebastian!' she cried. 'No! This isn't you. Please, stop this. You need to come back. Show them you're not dangerous, Sebastian. Please. Show them who you really are!'

Black despair swept over me.

Play your part, Sebastian, and she'll be left alone.

My heart quit beating.

Cross me in any way and, I promise you, she'll never perform again.

I choked on the fury that Augustine's powder unleashed in my blood. Josephine's hands cupped my face, caressing my jaw, holding onto me with desperation. I needed her warmth like I needed air. Every moment I'd spent with her flashed before me – every detail sealing itself inside my heart. The depths of her eyes. The sound of her laughter. Her scent on the breeze. The way I felt when she touched me.

Her kiss.

'Sebastian . . .'

Hot tears pricked my eyes, stinging me to the core.

I'll always love you, Josephine.

No matter what I am.

I closed my eyes, but the tears escaped, rolling down my cheeks, soaking her fingers. I made a horrible, painful sound in the back of my throat. I forced the sound into words – thick and gravelly, barely above a whisper – and for her ears alone.

'Josephine . . . please . . . forgive . . . me . . .'

I summoned my strength and fixed blazing eyes on Josephine. My lips pulled away from my teeth, revealing every jagged edge. I let loose a viscous snarl. She jerked back in shock; her eyes wide with a horrible fear that I'd never forget.

Then I hurled myself at her.

The Marksmen barely caught me. I thrashed in their clutches, roaring like an animal – teeth and claws and madness. Josephine screamed. She fell back into the dirt and scrambled away. Francis caught her and dragged her to her feet. His arms wrapped around her. Her terrified expression was like a spear through my chest.

'Please, no . . . no,' she cried. 'How could you . . .'

She broke off and buried her face in her brother's shoulder. Quentin flashed between us, brandishing a long knife pointed at my heart. After that, everything felt like it was underwater. Sounds were muffled, images were slow and indistinct. I heard voices. Shouts and orders. My body was slammed into the ground. I turned my face into the dirt, choking on sobs that racked my body worse than the rage ever had. I'd done what I had to do. I'd found the strength to protect her one last time – from Augustine. And from myself.

Now, it was over.

So I didn't care when the needle full of vitamin D was

jammed into my neck. I didn't care when I was flung mercilessly into the cage. And I didn't care when the heavy tarp was lowered over the bars, shutting out the night.

I didn't care about anything.

Not anymore.

Epilogue: Awakening Dreams

It was dark outside – and raining. My slippers were soaked and muddy, and I pulled the flimsy silk robe around my shoulders to protect my costume from the damp. It was pointless, and Yvette was going to kill me for ruining one of her well-designed masterpieces, but I didn't care. I ran faster, splashing water as I plowed through puddles.

Behind me, cheers and applause from the audience filtered through the canvas of the Big Tent. It wouldn't be long before they discovered I was missing – most likely when they gave the warning call for my next act. But they'd just have to survive without me.

I had to see him.

I was lost among the abandoned vehicles and I stumbled aimlessly, out of breath and frantic. And then my heart jumped as I spotted one lone wagon, set apart from the rest and covered with a large, moldy tarp. I rushed forward, untying the corner with shaking fingers. I pulled it free of the cage and looked inside.

I gasped.

He was huddled in the far corner of the cage, his body shaking with small spasms, and his cheek pressed hard against the cold bars. He breathed shallowly through gritted teeth, and his eyes were closed.

The sight scared me. I'd never seen him look like this before – so animalistic. Granted, there were moments since I'd known him when something dark and wild would pass across those strange silver eyes of his – veiling them like the moon behind a cloud – and then it would be gone. But this was different. He seemed almost . . . savage.

I breathed his name softly.

'Sebastian?'

His eyes slit open to silvery half-moons.

'Josephine.'

He said it without seeing me. But he'd already known it was me. He'd always been able to feel my presence that way.

Just like I could feel his.

His shirt was torn, clinging to his body by only a few shreds. His gray chest, trim and broad, reflected the glow of the torchlight behind me. His rounded, muscular shoulders heaved as he breathed, and I had to look away for a moment. I'd always thought Sebastian Grey was attractive, even back in school. Then, his look had been cute and mysterious. Now, it was dark and alluring. My heart jittered. I shook off the feeling quickly.

'Sebastian,' I said again, louder this time.

'You shouldn't be here,' he said softly. His dark lips parted as he spoke, revealing glimmers of his sharp rows of teeth. 'You must go back.'

The resonant tone of his voice drifted over my soul, giving rise to those same unexplainable feelings I always got around him, and I blinked to clear my thoughts.

'I had to see you,' I replied.

'Why?'

Sebastian's silver eyes flicked in my direction, and I froze at both the primal power and the gentle spirit in their eerie depths. I searched his face, lingering on the spiral horns above his temples, half hidden by locks of gorgeously thick pewter hair. His enormous wings quivered around his body, shimmering in the starlight. I'd learned to read his emotions in their movements, and I knew he was confused.

'Because I had to tell you,' I said.

His gray brows furrowed. 'Tell me what?'

I reached through the bars. Sebastian hesitated, his expression full of self-loathing. But that didn't stop me. I found his hand and wrapped my fingers around his, feeling his thick claws smoothly grazing my skin. I stared into his silver eyes and took the deepest breath I'd ever taken.

'I love you.'

'Josie!'

I flailed in my chair, sending a nearby vase of flowers crashing to the floor. Glass and water shattered everywhere. I jumped up, trying to focus my blurry eyes. Andre stood in the opening of my dressing room, his arms crossed.

'They just called the warning cue,' he said brusquely. 'Didn't you hear it?'

'I — no,' I muttered, kneeling down to clean up some of the water with a towel. 'Fell asleep.'

My less-than-compassionate partner shook his head. 'Well, hurry up. We've got a full house coming tonight, and we've got less than three hours to finish this run-through before they arrive.'

'I know.'

'Listen, Josie, I know you had a rough night. We all did. But you've got to get your head back in these routines. We need a good opening night.'

I forced a smile. 'Of course we do. And I'm good. Don't worry about me.'

Andre plodded out of the room, grumbling to himself. I studied the flowers strewn over the floor. Broken glass sparkled on the red petals like diamonds.

Diamonds.

My mind snapped to the daydream. I could see his tortured silvery eyes burning into mine. I jerked in pain as I caught the tip of a rose thorn in my finger. I flung the flower angrily across the room and sat back on my heels.

My skin went icy when I thought of how he'd lunged at me. He'd never been viscous like that – not with me. Something happened to him – in that horrible moment when he'd looked at me, bleeding and desperate – when he'd begged me to forgive him. One instant, I was staring into his soul, and the next, there was nothing there. Like someone had yanked a television plug out of its socket and the screen flicked to black.

Quentin said he'd become an animal, but I didn't believe it. I *wouldn't* believe it. Not Sebastian. But I'd been helpless to do one freaking thing about it as my father ordered Augustine to take him away. I'd yelled and cried and pounded on Quentin's chest, but it made no difference. I wasn't the one in charge. I was just the daughter of the *bandoleer*.

Seventeen hours. That's how long he'd been gone. And they'd been the longest hours of my life. I hadn't slept. I'd barely eaten. My insides felt gutted out. I knew I was sabotaging my own performance with my reckless behavior. I covered my mouth with my hands so I wouldn't scream. I couldn't let my troupe down. We depended on the Circe to survive. It was our life. My life.

But I felt anything but alive. Every time I blinked, Sebastian's shadowed face haunted me. I kept listening for his gentle voice, reassuring me that this was all just a bad dream and I'd wake up. But it wasn't.

They'd carted him off in the middle of the night, his cage rolled into one of our unused horse trailers and hitched to my father's truck. All while Augustine . . . while my Uncle Adolár . . . looked on in smug satisfaction. And then I watched as Quentin climbed in the driver's seat and drove them away.

Quentin.

I picked up another rose – carefully this time. He'd had them sent to my dressing room, just like he did every night before I performed. I felt a pang in my heart. How could he have changed so much? What had happened to the man I'd always loved – the guy who used to make me laugh when we were children? We were destined to be married. My little fairy tale ending.

There was six years' difference in our ages – which seemed strange to outsiders when I was younger – but among the Roma our betrothal was natural. It was expected. And I'd always been okay with it, though I'd begged to wait for marriage until after I'd graduated. There was no hurry, not with my aunt reigning comfortably as the Queen of the Outcast clans, and my succession to the throne a secret.

When Quentin pressured me for an official engagement, my father wasn't opposed. A few months ago, I wouldn't have minded. I'd always thought he was a good man. His sculpted looks made me the envy of every girl in our clan. I'd caught the biggest fish without even trying.

But there'd always been something about him that bothered me – an underlying darkness behind his eyes; a part of him that he kept closed off from me. Each time it surfaced, one of his gorgeous smiles or a fiery kiss would melt my doubts away and I could pretend it wasn't there. Our lives had been entwined together so long that I'd never imagined things could be different – that I could *feel* different.

As I crouched on the floor of my dressing room, holding his wilting rose in my hands, I realized that it wasn't Quentin who had changed these last few months. It was me. The awareness had taken too long to grow, the process painfully slow. But now, I knew what really bothered me most about Quentin Marks.

He wasn't Sebastian Grey.

And suddenly, I knew what I had to do. I only hoped I wasn't too late. Throwing what clothes I had nearby into my bag, I rushed out of the dressing room. Behind me, I could hear Andre yelling my name, but I didn't look back – not until I was gazing at the diminishing outline of the Circe de Romany from the rearview mirror of Quentin's SUV.

I tore across town, praying for green lights and no traffic. My heart pounded so hard I could barely breathe. I pressed my hand against the dandelion pendant at my neck. But for the first time since Sebastian had gone before the *kris*, I felt a sense of peace.

I'd lived in a world carefully planned – my future in the clan, my career, even my relationships – neatly aligned, perfectly balanced. Then my life collided with his – the strange boy with the shy smile and soulful eyes — and suddenly everything changed. I'd wasted months trying to right myself; trying to figure out how Sebastian fit into my ordered life.

But he didn't fit. He was more than my friend, more than even my guardian. He filled in parts of me I hadn't known were missing. But I'd been too concerned with upsetting the balance to allow myself to see it. I'd been teetering like an acrobat on a tightrope, scared to move – knowing there wasn't a safety net to catch me if I fell.

My balancing act was over. It was time to take a deep breath.

And jump.

I pulled into the parking lot, threw the SUV into park, and leapt out. The neon sign in the window cast a weird light over the black door as I grabbed the handle. I burst into the waiting room of the *Gypsy Ink*.

A group of heavily tattooed men turned to face me. I swallowed hard, feeling my resolve waver as I yanked my robe tighter around my Circe costume. My gaze roamed over the men until I recognized a large brown-eyed man behind the counter.

Hugo Corsi.

I stood there shaking with nerves and trying to find my voice between breathless gasps. He stepped around the counter, intent and suspicious.

'Josephine?'

My stomach clenched as I remembered the way Sebastian used to say my name and the way it always made me feel. Like I'd been searching for home and finally found it. And I was safe. Warm. Complete.

Loved.

I squared my shoulders. 'We need to talk.'

Hugo tossed his cleaning towel aside. 'What's happened?'

'A lot,' I replied, keeping my voice steady despite my trembling body. 'With Karl, and with our council . . . and with Augustine.'

His brows came down heavily over his eyes. 'Where's Sebastian?'

'I need you to take me to Savannah.'

'Why?' he demanded.

The others pressed closer, but I kept my gaze focused on Hugo.

'It's where he took Sebastian,' I answered firmly. 'And I'm going to find him.'

Acknowledgements

Thank you God, for giving me this amazing opportunity. I am humbled and grateful. Proverbs 16:3.

Once again, I send out many thanks to my critique group Trail Mix. Your support has kept me afloat. Thank you for all the pep talks, wonderful critiques, and for cheering out loud every time you see a copy of my book.

Thank you to my agent Jill Corcoran for your steady support and dedication.

Thank you to the fantastic team at HarperCollins/HarperVoyager: Janette Currie for your keen eyes, Cherie Chapman for your fantastic covers, and Natasha Bardon for stepping in and being awesome.

So many thanks to my editor Rachel Winterbottom. I cannot express just how much I appreciate everything you've done for this project . . . and for me. Thank you for all the encouragement and advice. Thank you for believing in this series. Thank you for all the lovely geek chats – I will miss them terribly. And thank you, most of all, for loving Sebastian.

Thanks to my family – who've been so enthusiastic about this series and talked it up to everyone they've met. To my parents, my in-laws, my husband Doug, and my kids. I love you!

Once again, I say thank you to all my students past and present. You mean the world to me, and this series is so much about you.

And finally, thank you to all my readers. I couldn't do this without you. You are all fabulous. Thank you so very much!